NOT MY GRANDFATHER'S WALL STREET

DIARIES OF A DERIVATIVES TRADER

DAVID von LEIB

America Star Books
Frederick, Maryland

Softcover 9781682298145

PUBLISHED BY AMERICA STAR BOOKS, LLLP

www.americastarbooks.pub

Frederick, Maryland

TABLE OF CONTENTS

AUTHOR'S PREFACE

Michael Lewis wrote his now famous book about the world of finance and trading, *Liar's Poker,* at the beginning of his career. I am writing my book on the same basic topic towards the end of mine. Michael got famous sooner rather than later; maybe I will do so later rather than sooner.

As I start typing here, I am onboard the 6:08 p.m. *Midtown Direct* commuter train from New York City back home to Morristown, New Jersey, and I can only hope that I will have the perseverance of another commuter author of some fame, Scott Turow, who wrote his first novel, *Presumed Innocent*, while commuting to downtown Chicago.

This is not the first time that I have started a book. At age 14, during a somewhat slow-moving summer where I was at loose ends in between a volunteer job to help take care of elderly shut-ins (not recommended as a soul-expanding exercise, albeit an experience that has lingered in my psyche ever since), I took out an old Royal typewriter owned by my mother, and started banging out my view of the world at that tender age. One of those chapters has been resurrected and included within these pages.

I wrote exactly seven short chapters at the time—mostly revolving around my somewhat eclectic and often alcoholic-infused dad who taught me how to gamble on football, bet on the horses, and above all else, how to play backgammon, gin rummy, and other card games.

It had been an odd youth.

Mine was not an allowance won for mowing a lawn or taking out the trash. Instead, at age seven, I had stared up at my dad one Friday evening and enquired: "What are all those slips of paper on the dining room table?"

"Football bets," came the answer.

"But why are there so many slips? And who are you rooting for?" I continued.

"I don't know who I am rooting for," my father answered. "People bet with me, and I just put the slips in my pocket. I was particularly busy with one stock today, and I didn't really have the time to look at which teams people were choosing."

My dad was a specialist on the Floor of the New York Stock Exchange, and even at age seven, I vaguely understood that this meant he stood—much like a doorman—by an assigned post each day and dealt with incoming buy and sell orders in things called stocks. In an age pre-computers, slips of papers abounded—with stock orders often fed to the floor on these slips by clanky pneumatic tubes.

And I knew that he loved sports, and betting, and football betting in particular. But the fact that he did not even know who he was rooting for bothered my already innate Virgo sense of organization.

"But then how will you enjoy watching the games? Would you like me to help add up the amount people have bet on each team?" I asked.

"That would be a lot of work," my father responded, 'But if you feel up to it, go ahead. Here is my odds sheet with all the games listed on it. If you write down the name of each team you see on a pad of paper, and then mark a "1" next to that name for each $10 you see bet on that team, that would be great. Maybe you can even help me correct some of the betting slips on Sunday after the games are over, and figure out who owes me money, and who I owe money to."

So began my career with numbers, odds, betting, and probabilities. It was a bonding father-son partnership, and watching football games suddenly took on a great deal of meaning for me with my Dad's money on the line. Indeed, soon it became *my* money on the line when he offered to give me a seven-percent partnership interest in his little bookmaking business. Seven percent was chosen mostly because I had started at age seven years old.

And money we made. On an average weekend he might have $10,000 of different bets—maybe $15,000 on a New Year's Bowl Game weekend. And when all the tallying up was done on Sunday afternoons (long before the advent of Monday Night Football), it seemed to me that on about ten out of twelve weekends, "the book" was a winner. Often the total take was a few thousand dollars, so as a seven percent partner, I might be handed a few hundred dollars. I opened a Citibank passbook savings account and set a goal to get it beyond four digits—in other words, above $9,999. That goal transpired by the time I was about 13, and the account was above $20,000 by the time I was 15 and went off to boarding school. At that point, seven- percent partnership ended because I was "not available to do any work anymore."

Along the way, I became quickly cognizant of the bookmaker's edge. Mathematically, in the sense of a "win parlay" where if you bet all of your money on one team, and won, and then placed all of your new capital on a second team, and won, and then placed all of these funds on a third team, and won, an initial $10 wager would be worth consecutively $20, $40, and finally $80, so a $70 profit to the original $10 risked, or 7-1 odds. In our book, we offered 6-1. Moreover, it was hard to win because there were point spreads involved, and if a point spread happened to result in a net tie, betters on both sides of that game lost to the book. Just like a casino where a Roulette ball landing on "0" or "00" was a win for the house, we had a statistical edge. And although we never "laid off" any bets, and had tons of idiosyncratic game risk on any given weekend, this edge prevailed nicely over time.

As I said, it was an odd youth. When my mother cooked artichoke for dinner, my Dad particularly loved the heart of the artichoke. From down the dining room table, I would hear a shout: "Would anyone like to make a quick dollar?—Just sell me your artichoke heart." After his initial bid of $1, I would typically hold out for $2, and when I got bold, maybe $3. Upon occasion, I would arrange with my older brother to feign a bidding war to push up the price.

I learned psychology and tactics at an early age.

Life was not without angst, however. My dad drank too much, and his tolerance for liquor was poor. The good news was that In general, he was a happy funny drunk. As he got lubricated at the cocktail hour, we'd often be throwing a football around the house until it might inevitably hit a light fixture or sideboard. My father would get scolded, and the football retired for the evening. But we'd start afresh the next evening.

But at times, in a drunken stupor, he would become dismissive or feign anger. We often ate dinner in the library on small table-tops watching television. I can remember one night when my father— angered by some small reprimand—said to my mother: "Ya know what I think of this dinner? This gruel?" and proceeded to purposefully tip over his tray table. Peas were on that nightly menu, and then at age five or six, I remember us all trying to pick the peas up off the floor, my mother in tears. In his own way, my father was trying to be funny, not bitter—but he often went too far. He caused scarring and pain.

Divorce followed. When my Dad moved out, I used to call him every night at almost exactly 6 pm. His sense of humor was such that he once told a guest to answer the phone, and say in a strange Chinese-accented voice: "You looking for whom?" He wanted to see what I would do. Of course, I just hung up quickly—thinking initially that I had dialed the wrong number. But then I quickly realized that I had been tricked. I stopped calling as much or as regularly after that. The joke had turned a bit hurtful. That was the way it was with my dad—fun until it wasn't.

But hold on a second. What exactly am I writing here? I am not famous, and as such, who really cares about such detailed childhood memories. I don't know of anyone who would purposefully want to read an autobiography of me.

What I am going to write about is a history of Wall Street as I have known it from about 1980 to about 2015—three-and-a-half decades of change starting with the ebullience of markets during the Ronald Regan era, only to be followed by a more difficult chop-chop period of the past fifteen years.

In telling this story, I do not want to chastise anyone or even pass judgment on this period as having been good or bad, better or worse, than the Wall Street era that preceded it. I simply want people to understand the market environment as I have known it and lived it—the stories that I have persevered through, the mistakes that I have seen made, and the mysteries of markets that I have uncovered.

Along the way, a young kid at a venerable white-shoe bank will go from rising star to almost being led off in handcuffs, resurrect himself to be market guru, and then ultimately become unemployed. A hedge fund manager will go to jail. A former banker will be killed. All of these things actually happened. If other fine details of this story did not happen exactly the way this book depicts them, these events certainly could have happened in the manner described. Markets will ebb and boil, mature and change. The span of this era could easily be called from the birth of derivatives to the first serious Congressional questioning of derivatives circa 2008-2012. It is a story of loss of innocence in multiple ways.

For the sake of quality story-telling, the balance of this book is written in the third person within a technically fictional narrative. But most of my main character's experiences are certainly based on my own actual life. The spirit of the text wants to be non-fiction, but the reality of the situation is that I have no need for a lawsuit at age 56 from one of my former employers claiming that I broke some sort of past confidentiality agreement. Thus, characters in this book have been somewhat adjusted in terms of their names and described backgrounds. I also write using a pen name. I'd hate to have the IRS come after me for all those early bookmaking days, and in a way, this lets me tell a better and more enjoyable story. People who know me personally may be able to recognize the reality of the people and circumstances that I discuss. If so, this is fine and acceptable in my mind. But on an official basis, consider this book a piece of fiction. Yeah, right.

But before I begin my tale across the world of derivatives and capital markets, let me dedicate this book to my grandfather who I will refer to simply as George. The Wall Street that I describe would have been oh-so foreign to his more gentile memory of it. Understanding his story may give one a better relative appreciation of mine.

My grandfather George hailed originally from a German meatpacking family that had settled in Louisville, KY in the early 1860's. The family's main pork-packing factory was located at Louisville's 3rd Street near the intersection of Kentucky Street.[1] This was at least until this pork-packing factory burned down one day, and the insurance company covering the building claimed no responsibility because there had been no night watchman on duty—as required in the fine print of the insurance contract.

Our family became natural cynics of the insurance industry after that. Maybe this also helps make me a good natural cynic of the modern-day derivatives market today.

George was good at math, good at speaking, good with people, and good at business. He was a charming and suave young man who was a natural salesman, but also someone with an honest streak a

---

1 http://www.oldlouisville.com/streetscapes/thirdavenue/3rdE-1000.htm

mile wide. When George was trying to sell something to someone, it was only because he really believed in his product.

But Louisville was not a place in the first decade of the twentieth century for a young man with a penchant for business and finance. All the action was either in New York or increasingly on the West Coast in California. George saved his money and went west to visit his mother's brother who had become a large landowner in a place called Marin County, California. He arrived just a few years after the Great San Francisco Earthquake of 1906.

The timing was not all bad for young George. Bankers in San Francisco had been besieged with reconstruction loan requests. Municipal bonds also needed to be sold to rebuild the city. After a short period working as a teller for the Crocker National Bank in San Francisco, 23-year-old George found a job as a municipal bond salesman for a family holding company called Louis Sloss & Co. In addition to helping rebuild San Francisco, Louis Sloss & Co. was active underwriting the development of the Sacramento Valley. Elsewhere in the office other young men were also brought onboard, among them a young fellow named Dean Witter, and a slightly more senior chap named Charley Blyth. [2]

The three young amigos soon became fast friends. During the day, they canvassed the city of San Francisco to find new clients and potential purchasers of the bonds that Louis Sloss & Co. was underwriting. By night, they often retired to the small apartment of Charley Blyth, and over cards and beer, spoke about their dreams for the future. None of them were married yet, and none of them had a tremendous amount of money, but they all had jobs they liked, and a passion to succeed.

But then one day in early April 1914, the proverbial roof fell in on the three compatriots. The more senior members of Louis Sloss & Co. decided that they wanted to shut down the business. With the passage of the Federal Reserve Act in December 1913, fears had swept over the banking community about the exercise of government control over the nation's banking and monetary policies. Credit policies had naturally started to tighten, and there was a noted reduction of loan commitments, with some existing loans also getting called. This was all too much for the conservative managers of Louis Sloss & Co.

2 The Blyth Story 1914-1964, page 1, published by Blyth & Co., 1964.

"You boys are welcome to the office furniture if you want it," a senior manager at the firm, E.R. Lilianthal, told Blyth. "But if you do carry on in this line of work, you will have to find yourselves another company to work for, and another office to work from."[3]

George, the most financially strapped of the three young friends, was initially despondent at this development. But the somewhat more affluent Dean Witter and more elderly Charley Blyth spied an opportunity.

"Let's just build our own firm. How tough can it be?" suggested Blyth.

Witter then proffered that they might be able to get a loan from his well-to-do family for the bulk of their working capital needs.

Only George seemed less enthusiastic. "Don't investment firms need a *great deal* of capital?" George asked, "And as far as I am personally concerned, capital is something that I sorely lack."

"But how about that fur coat on your back?" Blyth shot back. "It's a mighty fine coat, George, but this is San Francisco, and you hardly ever need an overcoat here most of the year. And yet, I'm sure that many a gentleman would love to own that coat, and pay a fare sum for it. That could be your stake in our firm, George!"

And so it was that Blyth, Witter & Co. was formed on April 28, 1914 with Charley Blyth and Dean Witter each contributing $200 dollars apiece to paid-in capital; two other salesmen chipping in approximately $100 apiece, and George hawking his overcoat for an even more modest 10% stake in the firm. In total it was about $650 of paid-in capital. Thankfully, the family of Dean Witter did come through with a $10,000 loan, and $9,400 more came to Blyth, Witter & Co. via a promissory note from the brother-in-law of the new firm's attorney. This was a business truly started on a shoestring.

---

3 Ibid, page 4

Based out of offices in San Francisco's Merchants Exchange Building, the young salesmen friends went straight to work placing various utility, railroad, municipal and corporate bonds. Eleven days after it opened for business, Blyth Witter reported security sales of $132,531 and a net profit of $2,262, and ongoing success for the firm seemed likely. [4]

But when war was declared on July 28, 1914; all exchange trading ceased; and certain banks reneged on funding commitments to Blyth in support of their bond underwriting business. It was a first test of the three amigos to find alternative financing, and thankfully an old friend at the Bank of California came through in the clutch to fund the firm.[5]

A key merger transaction involving Mt. Whitney Power & Electric Company soon followed. Firm profits soon grew to $176,154 by 1916, and a Los Angeles office was opened. Offices in New York, Seattle, Oakland, and Pasadena followed by 1919. JP Morgan soon took a fond eye on the honorable young men from San Francisco and included them in Morgan bond underwriting syndicates.[6]

While George shipped off to Europe in late 1914, and served honorably as a U.S. infantry officer in France, he returned to Blyth

---

4 Ibid, page 10
5 Ibid, page 12
6 Ibid, page 13

Witter & Co. immediately after the war's conclusion, only to face another immediate problem.

Blyth had underwritten an issue of China Mail Steamship Corporation 7% bonds in August 1918, with these bonds secured by mortgages on the steamers *Nanking* and *China* and capital stock of the China Pacific Steamship Co., Ltd.

When global commodities started to collapse in price after the end of World War I, the China Mail Steamship Corporation defaulted on its first bond interest payment. The trustee legally seized the ship assets, and technically placed the bondholders in the position of owning the assets until the bonds could be repaid.

Per the 1964 book, "The Blyth Story:"

"The *Nanking* arrived in San Francisco bay on a wintry Saturday morning and George...received a telephone call at his home from the United States marshal who told him that there were 330 hungry Chinese crewmen aboard who were threatening to jump ship unless they were fed.

"But it was the weekend, and the ship and its passengers were not legally allowed to clear customs and come onshore until the customs office reopened on Monday."

The marshal advised that the U.S Government would levy a $1,000 fine on the steamship company for each alien crewman who entered the United States illegally. A potential $330,000 lien could theoretically have been placed ahead of the bonds. As the underwriting agent, Blyth, Witter & Co. itself might have ended up on the hook for some portion of this fine— potentially wiping out the nascent growth in their firm's capital.

George asked the marshal to try to guard the ship while he went into motion on a Saturday afternoon shopping for 330 hungry Chinese. Racing from one retail market to another, he got enough rice, flour, milk, and vegetables to feed the crew until Monday when the crew was transferred to the U.S. Immigration Service on nearby Angel Island.

The *Nanking,* which was later rechristened the *Emma Alexander*, was sold to the Pacific Steamship Company and the bonds of the China Mail Steamship Corporation were eventually paid off at par.[7]

---

7 Ibid, page 19

George would later state: "We cannot guarantee the securities we sell, nor can we ever say that the companies we finance will not get into trouble. We do say that if a company that we finance does get into trouble, we will work to our utmost to see that it is reorganized or sold in order to protect our clients. So far, we have been most fortunate in this endeavor."[8]

TRAVEL BY WATER—FIND OUT FOR YOURSELF JUST HOW GOOD IT IS!

S.S. "EMMA ALEXANDER" OF THE PACIFIC STEAMSHIP COMPANY.
A TRANS-PACIFIC LINER IN COASTWISE SERVICE. SEATTLE—SAN FRANCISCO—LOS ANGELES—SAN DIEGO

A Portland office followed for Blyth, Witter in 1920, and then Spokane, Sacramento, and Chicago offices were opened in 1922. Boston followed in 1924, and Louisville in 1925. Then it was Philadelphia and Indianapolis in 1928 and Minneapolis in 1929. Within the post-World War era, capital was in demand to finance European reconstruction at the same time that American industry needed capital for expansion. It was a heyday for a bond underwriting firm. When commodity prices weakened in 1921 during an inventory panic, bonds were particularly sought after.

Streetcars in San Francisco started carrying advertising placards that read: "Thousands Safely Invest Millions Through Blyth, Witter & Co.—Bonds."[9]

But alas, George soon had another bond crisis with which to contend. Blyth, Witter underwrote the bonds of Portland Flouring Mills Company in 1921, and the owner of this company, Max Houser,

8 Ibid, page 19
9 Ibid, page 27

promptly invested the proceeds of the bond sale in a million bushels of wheat at $2.50 a bushel. Houser thought that the price of wheat might double, but instead it promptly dropped to a dollar, and once again George faced a situation where Portland Flouring Mills was unable to pay its first interest coupon when due. George traveled to Portland for the better part of a year and slowly negotiated the successful sale of Portland Flouring Mills to Sperry Flour Company, and once again investors eventually got repaid their money effectively at par together with all interest that was due.[10]

After a year in Portland, and perhaps as a reward for a job well done, George was offered the chance to travel to Europe in mid-1922 to open up a Paris office for Blyth, and as things turned out, this is when he would find the love of his life.

While George had not been back to Louisville for over 10-years, his family was still known there, and news of George's growing success, and posting to Paris, had trickled back through the mails. Two young Louisville sisters—Isabelle Haldeman and Bessie Haldeman—daughters of Walter Haldeman, the prominent publisher of the Louisville *Courier Journal*—were traveling to Paris for the summer, and had been instructed by their mother to be sure to look up George when they got there.

As the story goes, Isabelle dialed George's number shortly after they arrived at Paris's Hotel Bristol, but he was away on business. The girls went about their site-seeing for multiple days, but by about the fourth day, Isabelle fell quite ill with a stomach bug—as is sometimes the fate of American tourists on their first trip to France. Isabelle was lying flat on her back, feeling horrific, when the phone rang at their hotel on the fifth day.

"Yes, well hello, George," Bessie had answered. "I so wish that we had gotten in touch with you several days ago. Isabelle is not..."

"If that is George, I am *not* sick!" Isabelle was heard shouting from her bed. "When does he want to get together?"

It was almost as if Isabelle had a sixth sense about this Parisian blind date with this successful ex-Louisville man. When they did eventually meet, it was a powerful mixture of his general optimism, good nature, and gentlemanly ways instantly melding with Isabelle

10 Ibid, page 29

Haldeman's forceful Louisville enthusiasm for life. Isabelle was a 5' 5" pistol of girl compared to George's 6' 5" tall stately and soft-spoken self, but somehow they complemented each other in a perfect way. Sister Bessie was flabbergasted as Isabelle fell deeply in love with George ever so quickly, and within three short weeks, George and Isabelle were standing at the American Cathedral in Paris getting married. Bessie, a chatty but less self-assured young lady than her older sister, was the Maid of Honor.

Within a reasonably short time after their Parisian marriage, George was called back to California, and Isabelle began a lovely life in suburban Burlingame, California. Three sons—Gordon, Jack, and Bruce—were born between 1923 and 1928. Business was booming across the 1920's for George, and life was grand. It would only be later in 1933 that George would drag the family eastward to the skyscrapers of New York.

In 1924 Dean Witter left Blyth—partly because of a dispute over the desirability of continuing eastern offices, and partly because of a plethora of Witter children for whom Charley Blyth was not always disposed to find jobs for at the firm. But despite such frictions, the original $650 of 1914 paid-in capital by this point was worth $1,286,656.[11]

In 1925 and 1926 increased international bond underwritings followed in Argentina, Austria, Germany, and Peru. By 1928, the firm decided to purchase a seat on the New York Stock Exchange and allow its well-developed sales force to handle stock business in addition to its traditional bond business. As it did so, the firm's official name got changed to simply Blyth & Co. By the middle of 1929, the $650 of initial 1914 paid-in capital had ballooned to be worth approximately $12,000,000! George's 10% stake in the firm technically made him a millionaire—when that term still meant something.

But across 1929, as underwritings and stock business boomed, so too did left-over inventories of securities at each office, and despite a valiant and important effort to trim back these inventories across the summer of 1929, Blyth & Co. still entered the tumultuous Crash of '29 period with a modest book of medium- to low-grade securities on the firm's books, as well as margin debt exposure to individual clients.[12]

---

11 Ibid, page 31
12 Ibid, page 39

Within fourteen months of joining the New York Stock Exchange, the senior team at Blyth & Co. then made a difficult but important decision to their eventual survival. Moving into the equity business at the height of the 1928-1929 market frothiness had been a mistake. They needed to reverse course, and leave the equity brokerage business. They decided to resell the recently purchased NYSE seat in mid-1930. Charley Blyth also quietly negotiated an added injection of six million dollars of capital into the firm by selling a 49% stake of Blyth to the Blue Ridge Corporation—one of the larger investment trusts at the time.

During the spring and summer of 1930, all of the Blyth sales force then united in attempting a massive liquidation of various issues of inventory such that by the latter part of the depression, Blyth & Co. was finally able to operate without borrowed money. Notwithstanding, across 1931 and 1932 there were still two consecutive 10% salary cuts applied to everyone at the company, and many people were simply let go. Several branch offices stayed open only because their local partners agreed to work with no salary until the firm turned profitable once again.[13]

But for the longest time, business simply stagnated, and spirits remained low. When FDR enacted an originally punitive Securities Act of 1933, all public offerings of securities effectively came to a halt for two years, and by the end of 1933, the $12,000,000 value of Blyth & Co. back in 1929 had declined to only being worth approximately $1,900,000. 1152 employees in 1929 had similarly shrunk to only about 250 employees nationwide.[14] It was a depressing moment that saw a number of other securities firms simply close their doors.

But the attitude at Blyth as espoused by George was: "If the new Securities Act interferes with the distribution of securities, then the new Securities Act will have to be changed." Meanwhile, Charley Blyth quietly approached the Blue Ridge Corporation and negotiated the repurchase of its 49% stake in Blythe for just $1,100,000. This was a bold move of optimism in an otherwise dour moment of time when investment banking was effectively dead.[15] Indeed, to even make this

13 Ibid, page 42
14 Ibid, page 53
15 Ibid, page 47.

re-purchase offer, Blyth was sorely squeezed elsewhere. At one point, Blyth & Co. actually experienced cash flow issues to meet its payroll, and did so only at the good graces of JP Morgan who trusted that the boys from California would remain "money good."

George then became the most vocal advocate within the firm that Blyth should re-emphasize its historic roots in municipal bond underwriting. One chance to do had started to take shape in late 1932 when the construction of the Golden Gate Bridge was proposed.

There was widespread opposition to the Golden Gate Bridge at the time. Some land developers feared that by opening up access to a relatively large undeveloped block of land in Marin County, other areas of San Francisco real estate would be hurt. Others doubted that the huge undertaking could be financed; and that if it could be financed, then they wondered if the bridge could actually be built; and even if the bridge got built, most believed that the revenue that the bridge could generate would never be self-supporting when compared to the massive construction costs.

Despite the public doubt and opposition regarding the project, Blyth & Co. and three other San Francisco-based investment firms agreed to provide construction funds to the project in October 1932. Then, between July 1933 and April 1937, the firm launched nine consecutive bond offerings to the public, and was able to successfully place all of the bonds. The bridge opened on May 27, 1937, and was a huge success. [16]

After the first of the Golden Gate offerings was placed, George moved to New York. His sad task was to downsize that office further, and nurse the firm slowly back to better health. Thankfully, the Securities Act of 1933 was indeed amended in 1934—per George's earlier prediction of such—and securities offerings started to be launched once again. Blyth & Co.—which had effectively had made no money since 1928—was able to finally limp back to a small annual profit by 1934.

The outbreak of World War II soon brought the expansion of American industry, and with this expansion, a plethora of new corporate and utility offerings. While there were constant rumblings that the government might impose required competitive bidding

---

16 Ibid, page 51

for utility bond issuances, the nation's attention was soon directed abroad and not at Wall Street. By 1945 for the capital of Blyth was once again worth $8,653,000—a level last seen seventeen years earlier in 1928.

Despite a slightly scary market break in late 1946, capital markets generally started to head northward, and in an early taste of the tech boom years to come, Blyth started underwriting equity issuances for a number of West Coast tech companies, one of which, in 1953 was Ampex Corporation. Ampex was an early pioneer of memory products based on the use of magnetic tapes, and out of which television programs could be put on tapes and then re-run. Ampex would later go on to introduce slow motion technology to television and fingerprint recording devices to Scotland Yard. It was a huge success.[17]

So George had had a hand in bringing not only the Golden Gate Bridge to San Francisco but television video and slow motion replay technology to every home. In January 1956, Blyth & Co. also led the underwriting of the Ford Motor Co. with George acting as Blyth's point person for the underwriting. At the time, the $742 million equity offering was the largest ever made in American history.[18] Soon, by the mid-1960's common stock underwriting had once again eclipsed Blyth's historic bond underwriting roots, with stocks not bonds resulting in the bulk of firm revenues.

George succeeded Charley Blyth as Chairman of Blyth & Co. in 1959, and led the firm to further success for the following 14 years. In 1970, he negotiated the firm's eventual sale for $55 million to the Insurance Corporation of North America, and then was instrumental arranging a further merger in 1972 with merchant banking firm Eastman Dillon & Co to form Blyth, Eastman, Dillion & Co. Seven years later, Blyth, Eastman, Dillon then became part of PaineWebber Inc. PaineWebber Inc. in turn eventually got swallowed by UBS.

George—the boy of humble Louisville roots—eventually made his home at 740 Park Avenue—one of the most grand duplex apartment buildings in Manhattan. At age 80, as Chairman Emeritus of Blyth, he was often known to get up early and walk from 71st Street and Park

17 Ibid, page 77
18 Ibid, page 84

Avenue all the way to his 14 Wall Street offices—a distance of well over five miles.

This man became known to me not as "granddad," but as "the Viking" for his unbounded optimism and strength of resolve. If—on any given weekend—we might visit a Long Island beach and the ocean waters were a tad cold or on the rough side, "the Viking" was always the first in the water and never worried about the height of the waves. He was tough like his German Hessian roots, and he tried to instill that toughness in his family as well.

So why'd I just tell that entire story? Because by the time I graduated from Princeton, this was this type of man that I looked up to, and this was the type of impact on the world that I wanted to emulate. Here was one man who had not needed to go to Princeton to achieve access to this world; someone who had done it all from scratch; the son of a German meat-packer who had a varied hand in actually building things; someone who had had enough vision and enthusiasm to persevere through all the different economic and geopolitical trials of the 1930's and 1940's, and live to reap the benefits of this perseverance in the 1950's, 1960's, and 1970's. Indeed, more amazing to me than anything else, "the Viking" had stayed at the same firm for almost 60 years!

I still have a picture of "the Viking" and myself that I am quite fond of—with me at about age five plopped on his lap early one morning when he must have been ill and I had been brought by his apartment to cheer him up. The kindness emanating from his eyes in that picture remains radiant today.

I just wonder what "the Viking" might think of me now sitting in suburban New Jersey another fifty years later so thankful for the roots that he set down for me, but at the same time so upset with the path my own Wall Street derivatives career eventually took.

In my instance, there would be no sixty-year stay at one firm, but instead the incessant bounce, shuffle, and repeated change that have come to be almost normal within the financial job market today. In my generation, financial executives regularly seem to have eight to nine stops to their career, and I listen to news reports that the average college graduate today may have up to twelve different jobs before they are done. The world is moving faster, but it doesn't seem quite as pleasant as the world that George conquered from Louisville to New York, by way of California and Paris—all effectively at one firm.

So now that you have heard George's story, let me tell you another far different one.

CHAPTER 1

THE SWISS CARTEL AND A SUBWAY RIDE HOME
Zug, Switzerland

Bruno Geisler was an energetic little man. Born towards the end of World War II of Swiss parents in a small village near Zug, Switzerland, he had from childhood been exceedingly ambitious. He had worked for a time in the local pharmacy and had always proved particularly adept at managing the cash register. Under his careful watch, not a centime of change would ever go missing or be unaccounted for.

Bruno's family had not been particularly patrician or aristocratic, but he had grown up well—wanting for little. From birth to age 10, a small house at the far end of Bahnhoffestrasse had sufficed as his home while his father, Herman, commuted each day to Zurich by train. Bruno had loved his father: admired him for his good humor, good stories, and good heart. During the summer when the European light lasted so beautifully late into the evening, Bruno would often peddle his bike down to the Zug train station and wait for the train whistle that would mark his father's return from a long day at Bank Leu. Had his father had a good day? What new loans was he working on? Now that World War II was over, was Bank Leu losing some of its foreign clientele, or was money still pouring into the Swiss banking system?

Bruno had been ever so inquisitive even at the young age of 10 as to how a bank worked. He had been particularly impressed when on a special occasion for his school class, his father had arranged for a visit to the bank's vault.

"The floors need to be triple reinforced, eight feet thick laid concrete," his father had proudly explained. "Anything less than that would risk the foundation cracking or collapsing under the weight of the stacked bars of gold."

And the stacks were everywhere—resting on small wooden pallets with small bar numbers and names marked on little signs near each stack. It was like a miniature city, Bruno had thought. All that was missing between the various piles that passed for building were the cars.

"Most of this gold is 'allocated gold," his father had explained. Clients had purchased and delivered specific bars, each with its own unique serial number, for investment and safekeeping. "Allocated" meant that Bank Leu's clients were entitled to the exact bars back should they ever arrive at the bank and demand delivery. In actuality of course, each 400-ounce bar was so heavy and cumbersome to move, few clients ever actually took delivery outside the bank's vault. Instead, the little stacks of bars remained relatively constant and untouched year after year, a bar here or there simply being moved from time to time to reflect a sale by the client to the bank's account, or occasionally an additional purchase by a client.

Bank Leu itself was one of the small preeminent private banks that had emerged in the late 19th century, and which had truly begun to flourish in the mid 1910's as the Russian Republic had begun to crumble and the safe-haven no-questions-asked mentality of Swiss banking had first become internationally appreciated. Bruno's father was a private banker in the middle levels of the 220 bank employees. Most of his clients dealt in stocks and bonds, and in simple bank loans and deposits, but Herman had always found that gold—not paper— was intellectually more sexy and appealing to bank visitors than anything else. When new clients were given a tour of the bank's head office, it was always the gold vault that marked the highlight of their visit. School children were little different. The ability to feel and touch and try to lift a 400 ounce bar was special. For Herman, touching a gold bar was second only to the one time when Herman had visited South Africa and been able to participate in a molten "gold pour" at a gold mine.

The client had been a struggling gold mine owned by the Rand family, and in the throes of negotiating a new loan for their venture, they had allowed Herman to dawn special protective gloves and goggles and actually share with a trained professional the slow pouring of molten gold into a pre-cast bar-shaped mold. The experience had electrified Herman, and it was in turn, one of Bruno's favorite stories from his father. The photograph snapped during the occasion still sat atop their family's living room mantle. "Papa at work," Bruno always thought. How fun it would be to become a banker himself one day.

Fast forward. The year is 1985 and Bruno is sitting atop the 8th floor of the venerable Pierrepont Bank in the downtown bowels of Wall Street's financial district. His office is a standard one for a Pierrepont Senior Vice President replete with a mahogany desk, a few chairs and a small leather couch. The walls are decorated by two prints of downtown Manhattan during the late 1800's. Bruno is sitting at his desk waiting for the phone to ring—nervous, agitated, restlessly fiddling with his pencil—staring at three small luminescent green screens sitting atop his desk. The Reuters system flashes the latest update to the price of the U.S. dollar against the Deutsche mark. Ronald Reagan is in the White House, and Jim Bacon has just taken over the helm of Treasury Secretary. The U.S. dollar has recently done nothing but go up.

The phone rings.

"Ya," Bruno answers quickly, "Geissler here."

"Bruno," the voice answers, "This dollar, it is going up." The voice on the other end of the phone speaks English, but it is a Swiss voice and accent. Bruno and his friend from Zurich have both worked in western capital markets long enough that they float between English and their more traditional Swiss-German language almost interchangeably over the next few minutes. Then Bruno comes racing out of his office, hands pointed upward, face flustered, heading straight for the trading desk.

"We buy dollar-mark," he shouts, "Get quotes." The fifteen or so dealers on the desk quickly put aside their own activities and positions. They call out over direct lines—to Chase, to Chemical, to Citibank, to others. The telex operators scurry as well, madly punching in the appropriate codes for Barclays, and Lloyds, and Bank of America.

"30-40" a well-groomed young dealer, Richard, shouts out. Bruno pulls his hand towards his chest with a flick, the sign to buy—to pay the offer.

"35-45"

"40-50," the quotes start being shouted out faster.

"We buy! We buy!" Bruno shouts, blood vessels pumping on his forehead.

"70-80"

"Take!" he shouts back, "Everything up to the figure."

Then, a few moments later, he holds up his hands and says, "OK, stop!" His eyes canvas the room. "What have we done?"

Anyone who has only bought $5 million U.S. dollars holds up one hand; $10 million they hold up two; $20 million they stand up; $30 million, they stand up and raise both hands as well.

"90-figure" a late quote gets shouted from the telex operator.

"95-05," someone else shouts. "Off. Figure-10."

"No," Bruno shouts disdainfully, "We're OK." He runs back to his office. He has just bought $350 million dollars on behalf of the bank as a speculation, and he intends to keep this position for at least several days. His earlier phone call with his Swiss colleague had revealed that there was huge European buying of American assets developing, and the two friends had quietly agreed to front-run the inevitable purchase of dollars that this investment—primarily into U.S. equities—would require. His friend in Europe did not have any specific customer orders already in hand, but he had told Bruno that by 10:00 a.m. New York time, these orders would most certainly arrive. European equity fund clients were all so predictable, never actually purchasing the dollars that they needed until after they had already purchased the actual stocks that they wanted to buy. An early conference call between the Swiss bank's equity desk and the foreign exchange desk each morning served very much as a valuable crystal ball as to how the dollar would fare after New York stocks opened.

Bruno was a rainmaker for the Pierrepont Bank. In crude terms, he had big balls in terms of his general proclivity to take large positions, and serious connections to friends at other banks. In a good year, he would make the bank $70 to $120 million dollars, and while at some New York investment banks such performance would have translated into a 10% bonus for Bruno's personal pocket, he was happy with the $1 to $3 million bonus that the Pierrepont Bank usually offered him. After all, this was the Pierrepont Bank, the preeminent place to work on Wall Street.

Bruno had come to this position after five years working in Switzerland for the Union de Banques Suisse, and had subsequently worked his way up from a lowly Swiss franc dealer to the head of

Pierrepont's Foreign Exchange Department. His panache and keen sense of self-confidence were legendary. He could often smell the jugular vein in markets, and also was not afraid to countermand instructions that he was given that he considered dumb.

One story that circulated about Bruno on the Pierrepont trading floor was that he had specifically ignored his department head at UBS who in a morning team meeting had instructed each of his dealers to sell dollars: the Deutsche mark dealer was to sell $200 million; the Swiss franc dealer another $200 million; the British pound dealer was to buy 75 million pounds against the dollar; and Bruno—then trading the U.S. dollar against Canadian dollars—was to sell $100 million dollars. Fifteen minutes after the meeting, when each of the other dealers had faithfully executed their instructions, Bruno had secretly ignored getting short U.S. dollar-Canada. In fact, he was actually a bit long dollars, and the dollar was rising on all fronts despite the selling initiated by his Swiss boss. By lunch time, the bank's computer system—which showed positions and profit-and-loss by trader to the dealing chief—revealed Bruno as not only NOT short dollars, but as the only profitable dealer on the day. Bruno had been beckoned into the chief dealer's office.

"I thought I told you to sell $100 million U.S. against the Canadian," the chief dealer had snapped.

"I will by the end of the day, when the time is right," Bruno had answered with some impertinence.

"So you specifically disobeyed my instructions?"

"No. I just delayed executing them. I've made good money for the bank today..." Bruno had tried to explain.

"You're fired," the response had come back. "If I can't trust you to do what I tell you to do, then find yourself a job elsewhere. You are a smart little guy, Bruno—too smart for your own good, I'm afraid."

Bruno had been thunderstruck. Here he was—one of the few dealers consistently making the bank good money in a currency pairing USD/CAD that they knew nothing about, and had no significant order flow or competitive advantage—and he was being fired? The Prussian-Swiss-German way of doing things—the hierarchy—was just a joke in Bruno's mind, and that night he had decided to pack his bags and head for New York.

It was now seven years after that occurrence, and Bruno had further refined his calling. He was brilliant and yet devious in his work, turning every scrap of information that came his way to his advantage, and fearing little. At the time, most foreign exchange dealing was done by phone, and Bruno had a wonderful ability to hear the inflection in a counterparty's voice which was indicative of either dealing from strength or weakness.

A dealer from Bankers Trust would call: "I need dollar-mark in $100 million."

"He's short and caught," Bruno would shout, "Get quotes!"

Before he had even made the Bankers' dealer a price, he was already buying dollars. "If he doesn't pay me, he'll pay someone else," Bruno would mutter, and then shout to his underlings: "Just buy!"

Finally, he would make the Bankers Trust caller a price. The last quote on the screen for USD/DEM would be 2.4000-2.4010, and Bruno would quote 2.4010-2.4040, bidding flat to the market's offer, but knowing that the 2.4010 offer was only for small size. The Bankers' guy would mutter and perhaps curse, and finally say "Nothing there" as he quickly tried to get the dollars elsewhere. Now Bruno would listen to the squawk boxes like a vulture swirling above its prey.

"20-30, 25-35, 30-40...40-50!" multiple voices would fill the air from brokerage firms like Cantors and Bierbaums.

Bruno would stand quietly for a moment, often stroking his chin.

"OK, we sell," he would suddenly shout. This trade was not of the three-week variety. It was going to be a quick flip instead. The bank would pocket a few hundred thousand dollars all because Bruno could read the inflection in his friend's voice—the difference between confidence and fear—and it was fear in this instance that he had heard. At that juncture, his friendship with this Bankers' trader had not mattered. Squeezing some juice from him had.

But while Bruno had a keen sense of markets, of strategy, of the value of a given piece of news, and the split-second willingness to act upon his instincts, he had not developed a keen sense of being a good manager. Indeed, he tended to treat the people who worked for him as if they were as important as bathroom toilet paper. If they talked back to him, they were fired. If they disagreed with him, they were ignored. If they questioned him, they were berated. His dealing staff lived in day-to-day fear and loathing of his moods, his rantings, and his temper. It was truly ironic that the young Swiss boy who had himself not kowtowed to the Swiss banking system now demanded that others kowtow to him. Bruno was admired, feared, and despised all in the same breath.

The young head of Bruno's FX option desk, Thornton Lurie—a somewhat soft-spoken Princeton graduate and a reputed rocket-scientist type—approached Bruno late one afternoon. The FX options business had been a growing profit center for the bank since about 1981 when the bank had trepidatiously started to quote clients over-the-counter currency option prices based on a then new-fangled model called Black-Scholes. The business had grown so fast however, that operational glitches abounded.

"Bruno, I know it is not my responsibility to get involved in back-office matters, but we have a problem. I have asked our operations people to do three things for me: first, to prove all of our positions—to make sure that the book of positions that we are trading is what we really have; second, to confirm our trades with outside counterparts; and third, to provide us with a valid profit and loss statement as often as possible."

"Ya, ya..." Bruno had said indifferently and in a distracted, impatient way.

"As it stands at present, the position proof is coming an average of 24-hours late, confirmations are going out an average of three days after a trade, and we are getting a P&L about once a week. This is not a way to run a good business. It is dangerous, and because of it, we are risking having a real trade problem someday soon."

"So vhat do you want me to do?" Bruno had retorted.

"We need to stabilize our back office systems off of PCs, and onto something more stable, faster—two Univax systems perhaps."

The processing speed of early IBM-AT computers circa 1985 was still ever so slow, and when the Black-Scholes pricing software was being applied to a book of options that was growing more extensive by the day, the machines would just crawl. The back office had taken to splitting the book of over-the-counter options on three different PC's—one PC for Deutsche mark and Swiss franc options, another one for yen options, and yet another for British pound and Canadian options—just to crank out reports with some semblance of timeliness. Even in this manner, all three machines would often be left running and crunching numbers overnight.

"Trust me," Bruno scoffed, "In a few years you will be able to talk to your PC."

"I don't want to talk to my PC. I just want a correct position and P&L," Thornton pushed on.

"So how much would your two Univax systems cost?"

"Maybe $300,000 total including the software upgrade," Thornton dropped the bad news as softly as possible. "It's a small investment really given the growth potential of this business."

"300,000? No. Absolutely not. For that I would have to go to the Management Committee for approval. No—you will just have to make do. This is not a top priority for me. You will just have to make do. Be patient. You trade, and let others worry about the back office."

Thornton was disappointed. It had taken all of his nerve simply to approach Bruno on this subject, and he was now just supposed to slink off with nothing to show for the effort.

His business was thriving, but his business was also complicated. As an option dealer he was like a master chess player involved in a battle of strategy on a multidimensional board. He had to worry not only about the price of different foreign currencies moving up and down, but he also had to worry about interest rates moving which would affect currency forward prices upon which option prices were based; he had to worry about movements of option volatility levels—so-called "vega" exposure—that affected the replacement value of the positions that the Pierrepont Bank was carrying; and he had to worry about a little beast called "theta"—the Greek word that represents the change in an option's value given the passage of a day in time, otherwise known as time decay. There were so many different ways to make or lose money—often unwittingly if one wasn't careful. The last thing that he wanted to also worry about was back-office stuff.

Thornton's ability to slice and dice his various market exposures was not what he wanted it to be. He was very much running his group and his positions on instinct and common sense as much as anything else. But as such, he needed a formal P&L to keep his instincts at least somewhat close to reality. Without it, the margin of error to miss something important—a mis-booked deal, a forgotten premium receipt, and improperly exercised option—markedly increased.

"Imagine telling me that I would be able to talk to my computer someday soon," Thornton thought to himself. "Bruno knows about as much about computers as I do, and is just enough of an asshole to really muck up my whole business."

As Thornton grabbed his overcoat and trudged off to the subway for his fifteen-minute ride across the East River to the quiet pleasantness of his Brooklyn Heights apartment, he was inwardly fuming.

It was already 7 pm, but at the subway platform, he only saw a mass of people waiting. It was like a bad dream of faces as Thornton navigated his way toward the end of the platform. There appeared to have been earlier train delays. When the graffiti-laden number 5 train did eventually screech into the Wall Street station, Thornton had to squeeze his way onto the first car, and stand. The clattering, albeit short, decent under the river was going to do little to enhance his mood.

The sweat of the train's passengers was ever-present and demoralizing. Thornton had been taking the New York subway system for over five years now, and despite certain improvements to it— such as functional air conditioning instead of noisy and ineffectual overhead fans—he still hated the time he spent here.

The girl next to him had a ring piercing through her noise, her hand draped suggestively down her boyfriend's thigh, and a skimpy shoulder-strapped dress molding her figure in a cheap suggestive manner. Her boyfriend at the same time looked like a hulk—a hulk who worked with his hands, which were huge, rough, and dry. His hair was close-cropped and neat, but he had a three-day growth of stubble on his beard, and he emanated body odor as he leaned over to kiss miss nose-pierce behind her left ear.

Thornton wondered how she could stand his touch, let alone smell. Thornton certainly felt too close to this brewing intimacy to be entirely comfortable. He decided to try to move—spying a small area of space in the middle of the subway car, away from the doors. The trick was to get there.

"Excuse me, excuse me," Thornton croaked meekly as he started to push his way through the closely-packed bodies toward the small oasis of space. "Excuse…"

"Hey…man…what do you think you're doing?" a large burly black man suddenly shot back at Thornton. "You just shoved me, man. Who do you think you are?"

"Sorry, I'm just trying to get over to that space in the middle of the train," Thornton responded firmly but nicely. "I'm sorry if I bumped you."

"Well fuck you man. Who do you think you are?" He gave Thornton a stiff shove on the shoulder.

All of the angst and anger Thornton had been feeling towards Bruno in his earlier conversation suddenly welled up in Thornton.

"Well fuck you too," Thornton found himself answering back, "You're making a big deal about nothing."

"What you say to me man? Did I hear you right man?" Another small shove. Thornton glared back in return. His week had been too long, his conversation with Bruno too irritating—he was in no mood now to get harangued on the subway by a street tough. He should not have let his temper rise to his initial nasty retort, but he was tired and already feeling pissed-off.

"You're making a big deal about nothing," Thornton continued more calmly. "Now if you'll just let me scoot over there…"

A sharp punch suddenly caught Thornton's left eye. Shock, surprise—an involuntary tear started to roll out of Thornton's aggrieved eye socket. He did not know what to do. He did not know how to respond. The subway car, though packed, was almost dead quiet. There was only the noisy clatter of the tracks now deep under the East River. People stared. Thornton felt suddenly claustrophobic. There was a second involuntary feeling of wetness dribbling down his left cheek. Was that blood or more tears? Thornton wasn't sure, and scared—maybe unable—to lift his hand within the crowded conditions, he refrained from checking. Instead he just stared back at his assailant. He glowered at him in silence. If he had had a gun, he would have surely used it right then and there to rid the world of this ass-hole—Clint Eastwood "Dirty Harry" style. But Thornton had never owned a gun—and probably never would. Thornton was a trader working for a conservative bank, not a vigilante. He hated the way New York City made him feel just at that moment: weak, trodden-upon, and defenseless except for his ability to glare.

"Who you staring at? Who you staring at?" the black guy, now in a noticeable sweat, started to shout at Thornton. Thornton averted his glare to the floor, bracing himself mentally perhaps for another attack. The crowd around him remained silent. Not a word. Thornton wondered who exactly they were rooting for—the beleaguered banker with his suit and tie and briefcase, or the young street thug who had just put this preppy-looking WASP in his place. Thornton did not feel entirely among friends. Packed as he was between people, all hurling at 60 miles-per-hour under the depths of the East River, he somehow had never felt quite as alone. Thornton stared at the floor intently. He was too afraid to raise his head and face his tormentor.

When the lights of Henry Street station finally appeared, Thornton felt a wave of relief—he had made it; he was going to survive. The train jerked to a stop and the doors opened. Thornton bolted for the platform, not looking back—not looking for the police or a trainman or a helper amidst the crowd—but eager simply for air, for freedom. Quite a number of people got off with him, but his assailant did not—clearly bound further into the bowels of Brooklyn.

The train doors closed, and as they did, Thornton turned around to glare one last time into the eyes of this hostile stranger. They were two souls of such different backgrounds passing for a moment in a busy city, and probably destined never to meet again. Still feeling a sense of anger, but increasing safety as the train slowly started to move down the tracks, Thornton flipped the assailant the bird. It was his meek way to try to have the last dig. Did the assailants' glaring eyes within the train car even see the gesture?

Thornton was not sure whether he had won or lost his sudden confrontation on the way home that Friday night, but he did know that his eye hurt. It was tearing, throbbing, slowly closing a bit as it puffed and turned a mottled shade of blue. Thornton caught a reflected glimpse of himself in a storefront window, and was shocked.

Kim, his wife, was going to have a good laugh at this one.

Thornton quickly walked down Henry Street. He would normally have continued on the subway one more stop to Borough Hall—a four-block walk from his top-floor two bedroom apartment on the tree-lined Hicks Street—but his friend on the subway had left him with a ten-block walk instead. It was November—not Thornton's favorite: too late to enjoy the leaves and the freshness of fall; too early to enjoy the crisp feeling of winter. November was also a month too late in the year to have one's profit and loss dramatically impact one's Pierrepont bonus, but still damn far away from that day in March when bonuses would actually be paid. November sucked, and Thornton's eye stung and teared further as a cold wind whipped at him as he turned down Clinton Street, then westward along the shop-lined main drag of Brooklyn Heights, Montague Street, before he finally turning left once again down Hicks.

At the door to his apartment building, he ducked his head a bit to miss saying hello to a passing neighbor, and was grateful when the elevator arrived empty to lift him to the third floor without any other neighborly encounters.

Thornton unlocked the door, inserting the four-edged double-lock key into the special upper lock that so many city apartments seemed to have. The serenity of his recently refinished gleaming oak floors, his peaceful view of New York harbor from the Statue of Liberty to the downtown skyline, his twelve-foot high ceilings all awaited him. When he stepped into his apartment, a last glimpse of the sunset over New Jersey was still visible. It was peaceful. He was safe. It was the weekend.

But then he noticed—the apartment was also cold, no heat emanating from the radiators as he walked over to touch one.

"Shit," he thought to himself. The hot-water based pipes that served as his co-op building's heating system seemed to have a nasty habit of developing air locks early in the heating season when the actual need for heat fluctuated with the vagaries of the late fall New York weather.

Thornton took off his coat and tie, deposited his briefcase in the spare bedroom, and set to work "bleeding" the first of the apartment's radiators—pumping a small lever up and down to allow air to escape, together with small spurts of warm water, which slowly dribbled onto the floor. Kim wasn't home yet, working late at her law office, he was sure. With six radiators to tend to, he was also sure his mood would spiral further southward by the time she finally arrived.

Thornton decided at that moment that he simply hated New York: he hated that dickwad Bruno to whom he had to report, and he hated that guy on the subway having besieged him. He hated heating systems that did not work, and hated the fact that his eye hurt. He hadn't even fully looked at himself in the mirror yet—nor did he really want to.

As the first gurgling of truly hot water made it up through the pipes, Thornton inwardly celebrated at least one battle that day that he had a chance of winning. But in his heart he cried.

CHAPTER 2

AN AQUEDUCT EXPERIENCE
Queens, NY
November 1971

"11 on top in a $2 Trifecta Wheel, with 1, 7, and 13 swung underneath," Thornton had told the old teller without making eye contact. He fanned out his racing forms like a poker hand, studying, tabulating. Plenty of losers, so far. A rough day by any measure. "Give me a $2 Trifecta Box 1-11-13, too."

Almost a decade before arriving at the Pierrepont Bank, Thornton had already developed a love of gambling and a weird ability to spot patterns where others saw nothing—mixed with a bit of luck.

His father Gordon would accept or make a bet on anything—and was particularly fond of football betting. Gin rummy, backgammon, bridge, and chess matches with Thornton constantly abounded, and everything involved a wager. Each weekend was like a running scorecard of who owed whom—and how much—across a wide variety of activities.

But more than anything else, as a kid, Thornton specifically loved studying the *Racing Form*—it was just like another game to him—a game that required one to pare down and eliminate horses, carefully consider past performances, pedigrees, speed statistics, and workout times, and then weigh these factors versus Jockey standings and trainer reputations. Thornton at the age of 13 already knew more about which trainers were good and which were not than his father Gordon did. He even had come to recognize that the game was not always rigged fairly, and he suspected that some trainers were crooks.

As his Dad often passed the hours reading through his newspapers, watching football, and—toward evening time—filling up his glass with Scotch, Thornton was quite regularly planted in an overstuffed arm-chair studying the records of the horses that were scheduled to run the following day. Then, when he had dutifully made his way through the entire Belmont or Aqueduct card to the last race, scribbling his selections on a second piece of paper as he progressed, he would simply bet directly with his Dad, Gordon.

Once, after having cashed in a number of long shots bets, Thornton had sheepishly explained to his father with some pride and amazement a pattern that he had found.

"You see, Dad, this trainer Gil Peters, I've noticed that he loves to claim horses," meaning that this trainer would purchase horses for a claiming price out of races where one is permitted to do so.

"By racing regulations, he then has to move any claimed horse up in class into a higher claiming race or an allowance race if that horse races again within 30 days. The next time out, racing against this higher class of competition, the horse usually does horribly—comes in maybe 10th or 12th—often dead last.

"After that, for the following start, Peters can legally drop the horse back down in class, but then he purposefully puts the horse in a race at the wrong distance—maybe a mile if the horse is a sprinter and can only make it six furlongs. The horse does horribly again.

"But then the third time out—now back at the right class level and also now back to a shorter distance that suits—but looking horrible to the public on paper in his last two races—presto, the horse is flying and often comes in first at odds of, like, 35-1.

"I figure Peters wants to make back the money that he pays out to buy the horse pretty quickly. Setting up a betting coup like this at long odds makes this possible. I guess it's all legal," Thornton had finished.

"Although not very ethical—if that is what he's doing," Gordon added.

Gordon was amazed by his son sometimes, and Thornton's ability to spot this "pattern" of a given trainer amongst a whole universe of past performances was among those achievements of Thornton's that made him special—different, and which made Gordon quite proud of his son. This little thirteen-year-old not only knew how to play chess and backgammon, but he could analyze the *Racing Form*— and do it damn well.

And so it was that Gordon and Thornton had headed off to Aqueduct one dreary November Saturday morning, and Thornton had come to stand in front of that ticket seller's window.

Always considered the more blue-colored and downbeat of New York's two tracks, and plopped not far from Kennedy Airport, but within a Queens neighborhood otherwise densely packed with small single-family houses, Aqueduct in 1971 already had the feeling of a left-over behemoth of past American expansionism. While the track could formally seat 17,000 people and could accommodate standing crowds up to 40,000 milling about, on that cold November Saturday, only about two thousand people were there. It was like walking into a giant ghost facility—a ghost ship to an earlier era.

Brazen assumptions punctuated Thornton. Neither Gordon nor Thorn really knew any owners, but when they visited the track, Thornton had picked up the habit of bluffing their way into preferred seating. "We're friends of Ogden Mills," Thornton would simply tell the white-capped track attendant guarding the owners' box area— knowledgeable that Ogden Mills was an elderly owner who hardly ever used his box. And if they looked and acted the part, they would generally just glide their way to a prime finish line box seat. The attendant would then simply come by a bit later to give them some official ticket tags to affix to their lapels. Sometimes Thornton's dad offered this man a small tip to help seal this deal, and keep everyone happy. This place was—after all—pretty empty.

Even though he was only 13, and the legal wagering age was 18 at the track, Thornton had also long since discovered that when you arrived at a betting window with cash in hand, no teller had ever turned him away. It was *not* like sneaking into a casino at age 13 where a pit boss or security guard of some sort would seemingly arrive within seconds to usher a kid away from playing the slot machines nearest the casino door. Children were allowed within the track. They just weren't supposed to be doing any betting.

Thornton knew that this rule wasn't enforced, and when he didn't bet directly against his Dad, he regularly went to the window to place his own bets. He preferred to bet against the track. Otherwise the wealth creation of winning was too circular and less satisfying. Winning against his Dad did not send both of them home happy.

"Are you going to take my bet?" Thornton had asked anxiously to the teller that day.

"Like I said, I want the 11 on top in a $2 Trifecta Wheel, with 1, 7, and 13 swung underneath. Thanks. Also give me a $2 Trifecta Box 1-11-13."

Thornton, as always, had done his handicapping homework as thoughtfully and as thoroughly as possible.

He really loved the come-from behind potential in that ninth race of the horse coming out of the 11th post position named Love Bite—a horse posted on the Tote Board at 20-1 odds. In his last race, Love Bite had finished a disappointing 5th, but the *Racing Form* blurb of commentary said: "Checked between horses in the stretch." That meant his jockey had gotten in trouble positioning Love Bite in his last outing. The race before that had been in the mud and while Love Bite had been advancing a bit from 12th at the three-quarters pole to 7th at the finish, the jockey appeared to have started his come-from-behind move too late for the track conditions. If you discounted those efforts, the races before suggested that he should be flying at the end of the one-mile inner dirt track affair that was listed that day as FAST—despite a few sprinkles of rain that had fallen.

Love Bite was also trained by Stanley Hough, a trainer who only had a few horses in his barn, but had achieved a very high 32% winning percentage at the Aqueduct meeting that fall. Hough was a trainer Thornton liked to follow. Hough was also changing jockeys on the horse to Jorge Velasquez who was a particularly experienced rider.

"Was this a betting coup set-up of some sort?" Thornton had wondered to himself.

The number 13 horse named Hot Milk—despite its outside poor post position—also appeared to be suited to the distance and class of the race. Thornton could imagine Hot Milk—a big white and gray horse with a long white tail that he had watched carefully in the saddling ring, try to grab the lead on the outside early on, and still have enough left in his tank to be hanging on for second or third place as they hit the finish line. Because Hot Milk had only raced twice—just having broken his maiden race with a win in his last outing—his odds were a ripe 10-1. This race was a step-up in class for him.

But other horses also had possibilities. The horse coming out of the number 1 slot, Angel's Fantasy was a filly dropping down into this claiming race from an allowance race eight weeks earlier—having taken a mini-layoff. One possibility was that there was something wrong with Angel's Fantasy. Another was that the trainer was trying to catch an easy score against a lesser field. The big brown mare had certainly looked frisky and active to Thornton's eye in the paddock. From a pure money winning historical perspective, Angel's Fantasy represented the most seasoned past stakes winner who—on her best day—should be able to handle this group with ease. A glance at the odds board showed Angel's Fantasy at a fairly plump 6-1 price for all her past accomplishments. Using the *Racing Form* information alone, she was an unknown entity, but the cynical side of Thornton felt attracted.

And then there were a few other tactical stalkers that Thornton could not dismiss. The favorite in the race, a horse named Tattoo, had run in-the-money in three out four prior races. But within the current large field of 13 horses, and assigned the third post position, Thornton somehow feared that Tattoo—with only a bit of tactical speed—could easily get squeezed and bumped enough at the start to be shuffled back behind horses. Some horses just don't like to have dirt kicked up in their face, and Thornton thought a smaller field with a post position further to the outside at the start would suit this horse better. He decided that he had to throw Tattoo out of his mix. At odds of just 2-1, it would ruin the payoff of any Trifecta that included it, so Thornton just decided to root for Tattoo's demise on that day—a favorite that he'd have to pray would disappoint for one reason or another.

Yet another horse named Syrian Devil, coming out of the 7 hole, was shipping into Aqueduct for this race from Laurel in Maryland. Under normal circumstances, Thornton might have put a big X across this name since Laurel generally had lesser quality horses than Aqueduct, and the trainer of Syrian Devil was a nobody. But after arriving on the Aqueduct backstretch, Syrian Devil had posted two "bullet workouts"—a black bullet dot next to each respective workout time in the *Racing Form*—meaning these morning workouts were among the most impressive of the day that they were achieved. Was this horse ready to fly? The odds on Syrian Devil weren't bad at 12-1.

In handicapping, if you ask too many questions, you can always rationalize a potential answer that leaves a horse as a possibility. Even when a horse showed nothing of great promise from past performances, workouts, or general pedigree—even when a horse technically looks like a piece of dead meat—the question could always still be asked, why is this trainer putting this horse in this race? What is he trying to achieve? What does he know that I don't?

Proper handicapping has a bigger element of psychology than most would realize. Someday, at an older age, Thornton would learn this about financial markets as well.

In the end, and in an effort to have a potentially big score by picking the top three finishers in a Trifecta wager, Thornton had decided to go with the #11 Love Bite "on top" to win the race, and then swing three different horses—1, 7, and 13—Angel's Fantasy, Syrian Devil, and Hot Milk—in all possible combinations below Love Bite to finish second or third. Such a combo bet only cost $12, but could pay off in the thousands of dollars if the right combination came in.

He'd also decided—for a second bet—to just ignore the #7 horse shipping up from Laurel and take another "Trifecta Box" that simply included 1-11-13 (Angel's Fantasy, Love Bite, and Hot Milk). With this bet, Thornton wouldn't care particularly what exact order these three horses finished, but as long as those were the top three finishers in any order, another $12 all-in wager would cover all bases.

The teller was a scruffy older man, bald with an odd and unattractive hair lip that curled above poorly cleaned yellow teeth. He had studied Thornton for a second before he turned to the keys of his Totalizer machine. For a moment, Thornton felt self-conscious about his age. Was this guy going to take his bet or send him packing? There was only three minutes at this point to the race, with the horses already approaching the starting gate. Thornton wanted to make sure that he got his bet made.

The teller looked into Thornton's eyes as if to say, "Kid, I know you are just a kid, and I shouldn't be doing this," and then finally hit his keys and handed Thornton his tickets.

"That's $24 total for the wheel and the box."

Thornton handed over a $20 and a $5 bill, and the teller handed him back $1 in change.

Thornton started to back away from the window, and another slow-moving old lady took his place at the teller's window. But then Thornton looked down at the two tickets in his hands. And he suddenly noticed a problem. Instead of the 11 on top in the wheel, this wheel ticket had the 12 horse on top, followed by 1, 7, and 13. Similarly, on the Trifecta box ticket, it read 1-12-13 instead of Thornton's requested 1-11-13.

"Hey mister, I think you keyed these wrong," Thornton quickly went back to the window complaining, trying to edge his way back in while the old lady was still betting. She scowled at him. He had to wait for her to finish wagering before getting the undivided attention of the teller.

"What the hell? I asked for 11 on top; you gave me the 12 on top. I asked for a 1-11-13 box, and you again gave me something different: 1-12-13. You've made a horrible mistake." Anger and dismay oozed from Thornton's voice as in the distance an announcer's voice came across the loud speaker saying "One Minute to Post."

"I'm so sorry, man. I must have hit the wrong key," the teller looked at Thornton sheepishly. "There's nothing I can really do about it now though my friend. I can't feed those back into the Totalizer machine and cancel them. The system just doesn't let us do that. Track policy is that once you walk away from the window, you own those tickets. If someone else happens to ask for that exact triple combo in the next minute, you can sell that ticket to him, but otherwise I'm afraid there is nothing that I can do. You own those combos, kid. I'm so sorry. I hope it works out for you."

"Well god dammit," Thornton bitched. "I'm not going to miss this triple because of your fat fingers. Can you sell me another two tickets with my 11 horse in there the way it was supposed to be? Please avoid hitting the 12 key this time."

"OK, putting the 11 on top, with 1, 7, 13 wheeled underneath, and boxing 1, 11, 13. I'm so sorry man for the initial mistake." Thornton forked over another $24, and shook his head in disgust. $48 in total was way more than he really wanted to risk—particularly at the end of a bad day, and when half of that commitment now involved this 12 horse that he didn't even know the name of.

The overhead announcer speakers crackled, "There all in line," followed by a bell sounding behind the betting counter just a second after Thornton's second flurry of Trifecta ticket buying had been completed.

"And they're off!" the overhead announcer boomed again.

Thornton gave a final glare at the teller, and stuffed all of his various tickets in his parka pocket and started to jog back toward his seat in the Clubhouse stands. As he did, he glanced up at one of the many television monitors and saw the most amazing thing.

"On the far outside, that's number 12, Pussy Cat away quickly and bolting to an early lead," the announcer offered.

"That's Pussy Cat now opening up an easy four length lead on Crimson Smoke second. Hot Milk is on his outside a close third." This Pussy Cat horse that Thornton had not even seriously considered had apparently come to run.

"Holy shit," thought Thornton, "that's the number 12 horse that I now accidentally have included in some of my Trifecta bets." His heart started to pound a bit faster, and he clutched the tickets in his pocket to make sure they were still there.

After the first half mile pole, the announcer soon was reporting "Pussy Cat is now taking a commanding eight length lead. Pussy Cat is leaving this field in the dust."

"Who is this horse? What did I miss?" Thornton thought. Glancing at the Tote Board, he was amazed to see Pussy Cat's odds at a huge 48-1. Glancing back down at his *Racing Form*, there was nothing in this horse that looked special—two lousy 10th place finishes—but then a long six-month layoff. No recent workouts at all to judge. How would have anyone picked this one? Very few apparently had.

Thornton was back to his seat by the time the horses started to round the far turn. Gordon was barely paying any attention to the race, his head down studying a newspaper clipping from the *New York Times* involving how best to play a certain bridge hand.

Thornton began to focus on the horses occupying second and third positions. There was no way any horse was going to catch Pussy Cat at this point. Pussy Cat had now extended his advantage to a 12 length lead. But were any of his other horses in contention for second and third?

Hot Milk had gone out reasonably well, and had slowly edged past Crimson Smoke on the far turn. Crimson Smoke, while still third, was starting to tire badly on the inside. Thornton could see Hot Milk's white-grey mane and tail now running nicely in the middle of the track. His heart took another beat higher. Hot Milk was hanging in there. But another group of horses was now stalking him. Where was his key horse Love Bite? Where was Angel's Fantasy and Syrian Devil?

Thornton strained to hear the announcer's words while glancing at the Tote Board across the infield of the racetrack. It showed #1 in third place just as Thornton heard the announcer say:

"And here comes Angel's Fantasy. But nobody is going to catch Pussy Cat today. This is just a race for second place."

In the end, Angel's Fantasy collared Hot Milk at the wire for second place, but overall for Thornton it didn't matter as long as no other horse interfered with these two. The favorite Tattoo was only a distant fourth—not even close to the second and third place finishers. Thornton's favorite horse, Love Bite, had done nothing, but now it didn't matter. The Tote Board flashed 12-1-13 as the tentative order of finish.

Thornton reached into his parka pocket and pulled out his variety of different tickets.

"You won't believe this, but...I think I hit the Trifecta, Dad," he said nervously, his hands visibly shaking.

Yes, there it was: a wheel ticket with 12 on top and 1, 7, 13 swung underneath. That ticket was a winner since the order of finish had been 12, 1, 13. But wait, he also had a second Trifecta box ticket 1-12-13 in his hands. That ticket was a winner too as each of those three horses were indeed among the first three finishers across the finish line.

"Oh my God..." Thornton said with a bit of incredulity, "I actually had this triple bet twice."

The Tote Board at that moment flashed OFFICIAL, and the payoff odds started to appear.

With Pussy Cat a 48-1 shot, Angel's Fantasy a 6-1 shot, and Hot Milk a 10-1 shot, this Trifecta payoff was going to be massive. The win-place-and show prices all came up first. Thornton held his breath. The Trifecta payoff would pop up in another few seconds. It could be anything. Then he saw the flash of lights in neon green: $7,235.00, and heard the announcer start to advertise the huge payoff—causing an extra "ooh" and "ah" in the now dwindling crowd.

Gordon looked at Thornton dumbstruck. "You had that twice? Geez Louise. Well, congratulations, Thorn. How the hell did you do that? "

Was this a moment to feign brilliance by Thornton in front of his father, or admit that it was all courtesy of a teller's mistake? While tempted to appear smarter than he actually had been, Thornton decided on the truth.

"The craziest thing happened, Dad. This teller keyed in the 12 horse twice on these bets when he was supposed to have keyed in the 11 horse. I actually thought Love Bite was going to be the winner, but he ended up doing nada. Middle of the pack. I won all because of this key-stroke mistake. And this guy, he made the mistake not once, but twice!"

The skies above Aqueduct were quickly darkening as the sun set over the distant silhouette of Manhattan office buildings. Most of the thin crowd who had remained in attendance were headed for the exits. Clutching his winning Trifecta tickets now carefully back inside his parka pocket, Thorn and Gordon headed instead toward the cashier windows.

And that is when Thorn saw the guy again. He looked more like a bum just standing there about fifteen feet in front of the five main cashier windows, but the same hair lip and scraggly bald head caught Thornton's eye. Then their eyes met, and Thornton knew immediately who he was. It took him another second to figure out why he was standing there.

"This guy must want a tip," Thorn thought to himself. "Had this teller keyed that 12 horse on purpose to help a kid who almost had it right, but was just missing the one key horse that was going to fly? Or did he honestly make a mistake, but now realized that the kid had won because of that mistake? Either way, it didn't really matter. He had the air to be looking for a cut of the good fortune."

Gordon became instinctually protective as the old guy took a step towards them. He started to shove Thornton to the side, away from the approaching figure.

"It's OK Dad, this is the guy who sold me the tickets," Thorn said softly to his father. "I recognize him, yea...it's him alright."

The old man with the hair lip leaned over and started to whisper to Thorn in a low voice: "If you go to the last cashier window on the left, I have a friend there. He'll take care of you. I'll just be hanging out here for a bit. Whatever you think is fair."

For the first time Thornton felt a bit of fear and confusion well up in him. What was going on? Why did it matter which cashier window that he went to? Weren't they all the same?

But Thornton dutifully decided to follow the advice that he was given, and approached the cashier window on the far left.

"Nice tickets, kid," the cashier told him as he looked them over. He held them between his fingers, not yet feeding them into the Totalizer machine. "Now I have just a bit of bad news for you. Under federal law, you have to fill in an IRS declaration W-2G Form for any income you make at the track greater than $600. I'm required to get this from you or else I have to automatically withhold 28% of your payout."

Thornton's heart sank, but then the teller lowered his voice a bit, as he pushed the W-2G form toward Thornton.

"Technically, I'm supposed to get I.D. from you. You have any I.D., kid?"

"No," Thornton answered truthfully.

"You're not even 18, are you kid?"

"Umm...well..."

"Listen, kid..." and now his voice dropped super low..."Just fill out the form any way you want. Put any name you want. Put any social security number you want. I don't care what you put. Be creative if you want. But then I think it would be pretty standard to take care of me to accept that form without any I.D."

It was yet another shakedown for a tip. Thornton was actually getting the double-shake down—one from the teller who had sold him the ticket who was now standing a few feet behind him, and yet another from the cashier paying him out his winnings to make any tax issues with the IRS go away—to leave Thorn and his new-found wealth as untraceable.

"Everything OK?" asked Thornton's dad leaning in beside him as Thornton started penning the W-2G Form."

"Yeah, I think I know what to do," Thornton replied, not entirely sure that he wanted to have his Dad see that he was turning into a tax cheat at age 13. Blocking his Dad's view of the form that he was working on, he slowly penned in the false name of James Frost to the tax form's top line (he didn't know where that name came from in his head, but it seemed better than John Doe). Then he wrote down a random series of numbers for his supposed Social Security number. He handed the form back to the cashier who by this time was feeding the two winning tickets into the Totalizer machine.

$14,470...that was 144 $100 bills that the cashier started counting, plus a $50 and a $20. Thornton had never seen so many $100 bills in one place...in one pile.

When the counting was done, the cashier pushed the bills across to Thornton, and then looked him in the eye anxiously. Thornton took the pile, and peeled off $400 and handed those four bills back to the cashier. He had no idea what the tax bill on his winnings would have been, but if it was anything close to the 28% withholdings that the cashier had threatened might be needed, $400 seemed like just enough to keep this guy happy, and still leave Thornton himself with a good deal.

Before he turned around to leave the cashier window, Thornton counted out another $500 for the original teller who sold him the tickets, stuffing the rest of the bills—folded awkwardly—into a now bulging parka pocket. Morally, somehow, he thought that the ticket seller guy should get more of a tip than the tax cheat guy. He had no idea whether he had come up with the right amount—whether it was too much or too little—but as he handed the $500 to the hair-lip old guy, the old fellow seemed genuinely thankful and happy.

Thornton's Dad was confused.

"What are you doing Thorn? Does he really deserve a tip?"

"Do you want to get out of here in one piece?" Thornton asked quietly. "I don't know what the right thing to do is, but I do know I have almost $14k in my parka pocket. Keeping these guys happy seemed like the right thing to do. Let's move, Dad."

"And oh by the way, instead of taking the subway home, maybe we can find a cab or car service. If we can, it's on me."

CHAPTER 3

A CURIOUS BRAIN
Newfoundland
April 1972

Marty Amwell looked out over the horizon of the Newfoundland tundra, and wondered what the fuck he had done with his career to achieve such a posting.

He was a computer scientist for god sake, not some bird-dog trained to sit in front of this bank of screens watching for an inadvertent "ping" that shouldn't be there. This was such a waste of his talent.

But alas, the Newfoundland posting was what he had achieved after computer school in southern New Jersey, and further training with the U.S. Defense Department. It was a job—and he had needed one. His Maplecrest, New Jersey home was a suburban wasteland. Nothing much of interest there...just convenience stores and gas stations...a father now passed away, and an aging mother to support.

Becoming a computer scientist had seemed like his way out.

Computers in the late 1960's had been the new-new thing. So he'd decided to give that profession a shot.

For the past two years Marty had toiled with estimating the trajectory of rockets at the Sarnoff Institute in Princeton, working under a defense department grant. Now he was supposed to apply his computer code in real-time—in defense of our nation—as a scientist attached to the Air Force, a first line of defense if any inbound provocations were to transpire.

"But the chance that anyone lobs an incoming guided missile my way is just too remote to be interesting." He thought. "How can I sit here day after day looking at this blank screen?"

"Wasn't this a job some other Air Force or Navy geek was supposed to be doing anyway?"

Books soon became Marty's salvation. At first, it had just been a small text about Julius Caesar's life that he had brought with him to pass the hours. Then it had been a text about the monetary system of Greece and Rome. Later it had been a tome about the 1869 Gold Panic.

Marty loved history—particularly monetary history. He particularly loved studying the period around 238 A.D. when Emperor Maximinus 1 doubled soldiers' pay and then went on a tax rampage to pay for everything, while also debasing the Roman currency by changing its precious metals content. Maximinus eventually faced a group of landowners who simply rebelled against the rising imperial taxation by killing the tax collectors. The velocity of money had collapsed as people tried to literally hide their wealth.

"Wasn't this all somewhat akin to what had happened when the Communists took over Russia?" thought Marty. "Could it be that economic history keeps repeating itself in similar ways—similar rhymes—repeated cycles of human foibles?"

So he studied early Athenian monetary history as well, and found that when Athens imposed tribute taxes on cities in its new empire, this led in part to a revolt known as the Peloponnesian War. Much of the tax tribute was spent on glorifying Athens rather than on building the empire, and brought to an end an otherwise golden period of cultural growth. After 27 years of struggle and great expenditure, Athens, bankrupt, had eventually submitted in 404 BC to Sparta.

It is during this period that the coinage of Athens, once renowned for its standard and international acceptance, became a mere fiat currency—debased of nearly any silver content. The once proud Athenian "owls," originally made of pure silver, were reduced to bronze with a thin layer of silver plating. With the Athenian treasury depleted, one of the first attempts at creating a single world currency soon collapsed. Thereafter, geo-political rival Sparta became famous for its military skills but not its administrative skills, and would prove even less than worthy in terms of any economic leadership.

"Where the hell did the concept of money itself actually start?" Marty asked himself. And soon he had been immersed reading about the first official coinage minted in Lydia (now Turkey) around 700 B.C. He learned how, in 546 B.C., the Lydian Kingdom fell to the invading army of King Cyrus of Persia. But interestingly enough, the Persians still found the Lydian monetary system quite useful, and had kept it even with the same old Lydian designs. They had only slowly migrated to the image of a Persian king towards the end of the 6th century B.C.

Later he had learned that the British "pound" as a monetary unit originated from the Roman monetary system where the "As" was a weight standard based upon twelve ounces equal to one pound. Throughout much of early Greek civilization, he learned that the first basic unit of money was the stater, meaning literally "balancer" or "weigher." A later unit of weight that emerged on mainland Greece was the "drachma" meaning "handful" of grain with varying standards from city to city.

Why the hell had he become a computer scientist? History was his real passion—particularly the history of coinage.

To Marty, coinage throughout the centuries provided great insight into the economic history of human kind. Coinage itself has left behind a detailed record of man's accomplishments as well as his trials and tribulations...and notably, the repeated seeming path by politicians to create rampant inflation.

"There is no better record of inflation than that provided by the monetary history of the world and its legacy continues into modern time," Marty wrote in his diary while sitting that day in Newfoundland. "The current penny as used in the United States and Great Britain is the direct descendant of the Roman denarius which became the denier, denaro, and English penny during the Middle Ages. It had been Charlemagne at the end of the Dark Ages who had promoted the denier—still then a silver coin—eventually to be referred to as a penny. Twelve of these silver pennies equaled one "sou" which later became known as a shilling in many parts of Europe. Twenty shillings equaled one pound."

Marty started to scribble notes to himself: "It would be the 18th century when the penny was finally reduced to copper and then reduced in size during the 1850s. During the 1980s, the American copper penny was further debased to mere zinc with copper plating. This debasement process seems repetitive and never-ending. I think history has shown time and time again, that with each currency debasement, every great speculative boom has been inevitably followed by the proverbial bust."

Marty loved the way it all tied together—with repetitive patterns. Amazing stuff.

But another period of monetary history that fascinated Marty was that around the Gold Panic of 1869. He'd grown up in an era when an ounce of gold was said to be worth exactly $35. Initially, as a kid, he'd just assumed that this was a given—the way that it had always been.

But then one day in high school history class, a teacher brought in an old black and white film entitled "Toast of the Town." This film was about Jim Fisk and Jay Gould and their attempt to corner the gold market in 1869 that created a major financial panic called "Black Friday." In the film, a very young support actor named Cary Grant stood by the ticker tape machine reading off the latest gold prices. Much to Marty's surprise, Grant exclaimed in the movie that gold had just reached $162 an ounce.

To Marty this seemed inconsistent. Marty already knew from all of his other historical readings that monetary debasement tended to transpire over time. How could gold have been $162 an ounce in 1869 when it was only $35 an ounce in the late 1960's?

"Surely, inflation was supposed to be linear or maybe exponentially log-normal?" Marty had contemplated. "If a dollar was a lot of money in 1869, this meant that adjusted for inflation, gold must have been trading in 1869 at a price equivalent of several thousand dollars in current-day terms. If value was not linear, then was anything linear?"

This is when the concept of cycles had started to creep into Marty's thoughts. As a first step, he took the very simple approach of adding up all the financial panics between 1683 and 1907 and dividing those 224 years by the 26 clear panics that he could find across that period. His result was 8.6 years.

That was interesting, but not initially earth-shattering. But the more time Marty spent back-testing this 8.6-year average, the more accurate it seemed to be to him. It soon became clear that there were periodic bouts of market intensity that led to sudden shifts in public confidence. Economics and politics were closely tied to each other during these transitions. During some periods, society seemed to distrust government—selling its bonds and embracing private investments. But then, after a good boom-bust cycle, sentiment would promptly shift as people ran into the arms of government for safety and perceived solutions. Politics seemed to ebb and flow together with some sort of business cycle. Destroy an economy—debase a currency—and someone like Hitler could very easily rise to power.

The concept of cycles related to the 1869 gold top had been an epiphany type moment for Marty, so by the time he reached Newfoundland, he had added cycle theoreticians to his reading list.

First he studied the writings from the 1300's by Richard Swinehead of Oxford University and Nicole Oresme at the University of Paris. He read as much as he could about the cycle thoughts of Leonardo Da Vinci, then devoured the work of Rene Descartes and Sir Isaac Newton. Newton at first had postulated that light was composed of particles. Theoretician Christian Huygens challenged this latter belief in the mid-17th century as the first to propose that light traveled in waves of cyclical energy.

Marty particularly loved Huygens—a man Marty considered somewhat lost to history. Light waves worked because they had a certain periodicity. Huygens had also begun to explore the exact measurement of time as well with the use of a sundial, and eventually had invented the pendulum as a regulator of time. It was the 1673 *Horologium Oscillatorium* and 1690 text *Treatise on Light* by Huygens which Marty considered the most interesting. These explained everything about how light behaved—from rainbows, to crystals, and other reflections of light. Without cyclical waves, light wouldn't be able to emanate and perpetuate. Christian Doppler would later expand this concept to sound. There are widening wavelengths of sound as an object making that sound moves away from one, and tightening more intense wavelengths of sound as an object moves closer.

Marty's training as a computer scientist had included some physics, yet he had had no formal college education. Indeed, he had gone straight from high school to computer school. But with a natural intellect and curiosity, he started to wonder if some of the rules of physics could be applied to economics. If music had natural harmonics, maybe economic history had harmonics as well. If his average cycle between crises was 8.6 years, maybe there were other cycles at 17.2 year, 34.4 years—a hidden economic rhythm so to speak.

It was then that Marty discovered William Stanley Jevons, a British economist who also became a metals assayer in Sydney, and was fascinated by the boom and bust cycle of commodity prices. Jevon's had written the *General Mathematical Theory of Political Economy* in 1862, and went on to try to correlate economic activity on Earth to sunspot cycles.

"Holy crap," said Marty to himself as he looked up from his desk at the empty tundra before him. "It's all one big cycle. Cycles are how energy travels—be it via alternating current from a light socket or the beating of one's heart pumping blood. It's how the brain works...we go through alternating states of being asleep and being awake. It's how we are born, grow, peak, and then start to decline. *It all has to apply to economics and markets as well!*"

It was with that revelation that Marty had decided that his career as a rocket scientist was going to end. Could he use his computer skills to program some sort of application of physical periodicity and other natural physical laws of entropy to financial markets?

Marty wanted to go to Wall Street and try.

CHAPTER 4

RAF
New York, NY
March 1973

Raf took a long puff from his vintage cigar, staring at the muni screen at the venerable Pierrepont Bank.

It was well before the days when smoking on trading room floors was deemed unacceptable.

"This new City of Chicago 40-year offering is going to go swimmingly," Raf said to his colleague Tom.

"Just watch."

Raf had just returned from the so-called syndicate meeting where a group of underwriters—including the Pierrepont Bank among six or seven other lead managers—had congregated to decide on pricing. The offering would have different tranches, different bells and whistles—some pieces subordinated, some secured by collateral, a few pieces that would eventually be pre-refunded—it was all a complex affair. But overall the syndicate meeting had gone well. There was tons of demand at different shops for this paper. Salomon Brothers clearly had a big customer order in hand.

There had been a wink and a nod on that one. Raf knew the game.

The muni-market of 1973 was an incestuous cesspool of dealer insider knowledge combined with naïve issuers who did what the investment banks told them to do. Issuers could easily be talked into deals that they didn't need, rich coupons that they really shouldn't pay, and bond placement concessions that made Raf's life at the Pierrepont pretty cushy and grand. You didn't have to be a great trader to make money in this market. You just had to rip the eyeballs out from the gullible hacks on the other end of the underwriting deal.

It was the end of the day. The Reuters terminal flashed the Chicago bond terms, and then a few seconds later, when-issued trading on the screens turned live on the actual bonds.

"Priced at 7% on the corpus, starting to trade at 101...buyers around," Tom informed Raf as he listened to a phone set to his ear linked into a bond voice broker several Wall Street blocks away. "Now up at 101 ½, wow, just lifted at 102." The Reuters screen was also now streaming the prices.

Pierrepont had bought the bonds at a two point concession to par in the underwriting. Easy money. The only question now was how long to hold them. Dump them for a quick four points? Or let the position ride? Take a bird in hand or roll the dice a bit? Either way, the bank was playing with house money already made. It was just a question of how to maximize the profits.

"Offer half our position at 102," suggested Raf. "I'm feelin' we'll get lifted on those. We can let the rest ride 'til tomorrow."

"Got it," Tom responded and quickly keyed in an electronic order.

With that, Raf dawned his herringbone suit jacket, and started to saunter to the door, the nub of his cigar still dangling from his mouth and his jowly cheeks shaking a bit with each step. He'd let Tom stay late to work that order. There was no reason to keep his wife Phoebe waiting. It was Spring Break time and his daughter was also scheduled home from boarding school. Raf had a vague sense that she might also be bringing a friend for the holiday. He hadn't listened closely to the plan—the schedule. But he knew that he had to be uptown soon for some reason.

A black car idled curbside outside the building's Broad Street entrance awaiting him. He never took the subway if he could avoid it. He was only a Vice President at the bank, but early on, he'd decided *"What the fuck? I'm making the bank a lot of money. So what's a few dollars for a goddamn car to and from work?"* His secretary Debbie had cleverly buried the expense within his entertainment account.

As Raf's car slowly edged onto the FDR Drive, he eyed the downtown skyline behind him.

This was exactly where he had dreamed that he would end up. He hadn't always started Raf de la Chouette. His real name had been Raf Blatz. That name just had to go. He'd decided on something French after he had graduated from high school and applied to Brown University using that new name. Yes, "de la Chouette" sounded much better. Screw it if his parents were pissed about the name change. He suspected that he was adopted anyway, although he'd never asked the question, and never been told. If they could deny the past, so could he. He felt just as entitled to a piece of the good life as those rich twats that were handed a position at Pierrepont just because of their family pedigree. Sure as shit, a "Blatz" would have been dead on arrival at the bank—at best, relegated to operations or something.

But wherever and from whomever he had actually be born into this world, Raf had inherited a most unfortunate mix of genes. Raf stood a Napoleonic five feet, one and a quarter inches tall, stubby and round at the edges, with an olive-like complexion to boot. And his kinky and curly hair made for quite the afro back in college. Now that hair was cut close and cleanly short—in banker fashion. Still, he did not exactly look like the Wall Street power-broker type. More like the guy who might sell you a sandwich at the local deli. But the name change helped, and he had worked to lose his Jersey accent. He'd learned to talk in a slow deep patrician way; he'd learned to play the game.

But perhaps the most masterful ruse in creating his new persona was landing his wife Phoebe. They'd met at Brown. What a catch she'd been: heiress to the Wellington Fund family fortune; gorgeous and lithe. More than anything else, it had been her pedigree that added legitimacy to his fabricated new life. Though as of late, dead tired most nights when he arrived home from the bank, he had not shown her much appreciation for it. When was the last time that they had had sex?

He pondered, daydreaming back in time.

The doorman of his Fifth Avenue building opened the car door. The trip uptown had been faster than he'd thought. A warm spring smell enveloped him as he stepped outside into the air...the smell of Central Park with its budding trees already hot for summer.

"Good evening Mr. de la Chouette" the doorman greeted him. He loved it when he heard that name. "You have a visitor waiting in the lobby."

"I do?"

"Yes, a young girl, sir."

Ah shit, what had he forgotten? What was going on?

"Hi, I'm Adelaide," a saucy tall seventeen year-old girl with an Australian accent greeted him as he walked through the lobby door. "I'm friends with your daughter Betsy up at Taft. Your wife had to get Betsy to a dentist appointment so she just dropped me off here. Didn't have time to let me in. Said they'd be back in an hour or two."

"Wow, I'm sorry, am I late or something?" Raf asked. "I had a vague sense I was supposed to be home for something."

"That would be to greet me, I think," Adelaide offered brightly. Then she made kind of mild grimace. "Your wife was kind of pissed when the doorman said you weren't home yet."

"She'll get over it," Raf said. He appraised Adelaide approvingly. Long, straight blonde hair. Winning, natural smile. Seemed like a nice girl. Beautiful thin frame. A real prep.

"Have you been waiting long?"

"I've only been here 15 minutes or so."

"Sorry about that," offered Raf half-heartedly. This girl's vivaciousness was downright distracting. "C'mon upstairs. We'll get you settled."

As the elevator climbed to the 10th Floor, Raf stared at Adelaide carefully. Jesus Christ was she beautiful with pert firm nipples clearly showing under a blue oxford shirt.

The elevator door opened directly to their apartment foyer. A leafy view of Central Park tree tops could be seen even from the elevator itself.

"Nice apartment, Mr. de la Chouette! Wow, look at this view!"

"Can I get you a drink?"

"Sure. A beer would be great."

"You old enough to drink?" Raf initially asked with some surprise. Hell if he cared either way really. "What's the drinking age in Australia?"

"Eighteen."

"So you're eighteen?" He smiled wryly.

She shrugged. "Close enough, I suppose."

Raf fetched two cold Heinekens from the kitchen fridge and opened them.

"Where you from in Australia?" He handed one of the beers to her.

"Sydney."

"So are you here for the whole holiday with us?"

"No, no. Just here for the night. "

Raf fixated on the way she put the bottle to her lips.

"I have a flight home in the morning from JFK," she said. "But they were closing the school for the holiday. We all had to leave. Betsy was nice enough to offer me a night here on my way."

"Are you good friends with Betsy?" He drained his Heineken to the halfway point.

"To be honest, we just share one class together. My advisor actually asked her if she could help me out tonight with a place to crash. We got to know each other a bit more on the car ride down. She seems lovely."

Adelaide was being polite, because like Raf, his daughter was slightly plump and short, but without Raf's dynamic personality. Those damn mystery genes had passed along to her with a vengeance.

"You ever been to New York City?" Raf offered small talk.

"Oh sure," said Adelaide. "I'm a singer and dancer. So I come down to audition for different stuff all the time. I actually took a year off last year because I had a minor role in the Broadway production of Bob Fosse's *Pippin*."

"Shit. No kidding. That's impressive. So you're an actress, too?"

"Well, really more a singer and dancer than an actress. But I try."

"That must be weird adjusting back from that life to being at Taft. What do you miss up there the most?"

Adelaide thought for a moment, and flashed a devilish smile. "To be honest, a lot of the boys up there are pretty immature. I miss the more sophisticated types."

Raf knew opportunity when he saw it. A door was potentially being opened.

"What does that mean?"

"Well, you know...I had this boyfriend in New York for a year. It was a blast."

With that Adelaide reached over and touched Raf's thigh. She smiled. Such a glorious smile, he thought.

"Maybe I shouldn't ask this," she said, "but you seem like a really cool guy. Do you have any pot? I've been stuck up at Taft for the last eight weeks, and I'm just dying to get stoned." She giggled.

He grinned, and eyed Adelaide a bit more knowingly. Though outwardly pretty and seemingly innocent, Adelaide was a bad girl at heart. And he wasn't one to resist a bad girl. A smile came to his lips.

"Don't have any pot, no. Sorry. But I could offer you something else."

With that, Raf reached down and moved Adelaide's hand from his thigh to on top of his member, which had already turned hard under his pants.

She didn't pull back her hand. She looked into his eyes. "Should we really be doing this?"

But already her hand was moving up and down, stroking his hardness—seemingly answering the question. Raf reached out and cupped her pert breast. He leaned in and kissed her. Hard. She groped for his zipper and he thrust his hand up under her shirt.

What an awesome school girlfriend to arrive at his door, this Adelaide was.

It was then that the elevator door re-opened, and Phoebe and Betsy walked in.

CHAPTER 5

BACKGAMMON & BLACK JACK
Paradise Island, Nassau, Bahamas
March 1973

The sound of dice rolled across the room. Dice everywhere. Shaking. Pounding back and forth in small cups. Dice being continuously dumped out on a cork playing board.

It was the 1973 World Championships of Backgammon in Nassau, Bahamas.

Thornton was there, and he was excited.

Playing in the World Championships at age 15 may sound kind of special, and to this day, Thornton still proudly posts this accomplishment on his resume, but in actuality to qualify, all that was really required was that you had to put up a $1000 entry fee. Anyone could effectively enter if they had the entrance fee to do so, and there was enough room to accommodate the entry.

As Thornton's birthday present—and after some pestering by Thorn—Gordon had agreed to bring Thorn along and allow him to enter the tournament. Thorn's sister Pam—just back from college for spring break—had come too.

It had been two years since Thornton had made that Aqueduct Trifecta score. Two long years. Thornton's older brother Dexter had died in 1972. It had happened out in Hawaii—something about Dexter having slept on the beach overnight, driving home a bit sleepy in the morning, drifting into the wrong lane. Who could be sure if he'd seen the oncoming tractor-trailer? No one had known exactly what had happened, but after a week in the hospital with no brain action, a decision had been made to pull the plug. It had been tough on the family.

Now there was just Thorn and Pam left as siblings, and this mini-vacation trip was the first time that they had all been together in a while. Pam didn't want to play in the tournament, but was mostly interested in the drinks, sun, casino, and men. She was six years older than Thornton—a hot 21-year old with long brown hair and a small dimple on her left cheek who attended the University of the Pacific. Thorn had the sense that she probably did a pretty good job of partying and getting regularly laid out in California. She definitely had a certain joie de vivre. But mostly, Thornton was ever so jealous that she could legally waltz into the Paradise Island casino, while still at age 15, he was nervous that he would more easily be thrown out.

But Thornton also had this badge around his neck showing that he was part of the backgammon tournament—entitled to be in this special side room adjacent to the casino where the backgammon tournament would be played. Maybe with this pass around his neck, Thorn could pass for 18.

So the first night there, Pam and Thorn made a plan to hit the Black Jack tables together.

Now Thornton knew the general rules of Black Jack, but he had never actually played it in a casino setting. He had read that pit bosses watched the dealers carefully, and that cameras might be checking for appropriate hand signals.

"You ready to give this a shot?" asked Thornton to Pam, as he gingerly walked down the few steps from the backgammon alcove into the casino floor. For some reason crossing the casino floor felt to Thorn like being in "No Man's land"—a place where they could too easily be stopped and ushered back to the entrance. If they made it to be seated at a table, he would feel safer. He headed to the nearest Black Jack table on the far left side of the room where a young black croupier was standing quietly alone shuffling cards.

"OK to sit here?"

"Why sure man, happy to have you man," a suddenly smiley croupier responded. "My name is Jimmy. Just call me Jimmy, man."

"Wow, I've done it. I'm actually here," thought Thornton. No pit bosses were arriving. Maybe they thought Pam was my date, or maybe the backgammon tags were enough. Thornton was just happy to be seated.

Jimmy started to crack various jokes in his Bahamian accent as Thornton and Pam played their first few hands, and while Thornton did not understand half of what Jimmy said, this friendly fellow seemed to be genuinely rooting for the young lad now sitting in the end chair playing Black Jack for the first time.

Pam meanwhile started to pay more attention to the hulk who had subsequently sat down beside her. Thornton wondered just how much sex she had on her mind.

Jimmy was dealing from a four-deck "shoe" of well-shuffled cards, and as was normal in Black Jack—at least during that era—he would always check his hole card at the outset of each hand when he had a face card or ace showing.

"Insurance, anyone?" he'd ask. At this prompt, any player at the table could optionally make a second bet to effectively hedge the first bet against the house having an automatic 21 blackjack. Few normally elected insurance, but in these instances, Jimmy absolutely knew what the house was already holding in terms of total points. Then he'd begin to sequentially canvas players for a "Hit" or "Stand" response.

With an initial stack of just ten $5 chips, or $50, Thornton somehow got off to a reasonable start at the table, and within a few hands, he felt quite smart to have amassed a larger pile of chips worth about $85.

The hulk guy down the table threw a chip across the board toward Jimmy after a winning hand.

"What was that?" thought Thorn, "Was that a tip or something? Was this common practice?"

Thorn had no idea. This was the first time that he had—after all—ever been in a casino, let alone seated at a Black Jack table.

Thorn didn't want to be rude and not tip as well, so soon, after successful hands, he found himself pushing a chip back towards Jimmy as well.

For the sake of pit bosses watching from cameras above or behind, Jimmy would then have to make an elaborate tapping of the donated chip on the side of the table, bow his head, and say "Thank You" while the chip itself would subsequently disappear into his coat pocket. No croupier would ever want to be accused of directly stealing from the pile of house chips in front of him. To clarify that such theft was not in fact transpiring, these substantive procedures were apparently required when tips were involved.

That's when Thorn thought back to his day at Aqueduct, and the last time he had been tipping someone.

Thornton had probably been dealing with pure corruption mixed with overt good fortune that day. It left him feeling elated, but also a bit dirty. The tax evasion part of that day still gnawed at him a bit. But what was a kid to do? Be a Puritanical dweeb when surrounded by such an opportunity?

Did that hair-lipped teller have inside knowledge about that Pussy Cat horse? Or had it all been just the most miraculous mistake of fortuitous fortune? Thornton had seen the moment of hesitation in the man's eyes when he had bought those tickets. While nothing would ever be known for sure, Thornton was pretty sure that he'd gotten that winning 12 horse in his parlays on purpose. It was just too coincidental given the way that horse subsequently ran. That teller must have known something—had some sort of tip-off from someone in the barns who knew Pussy Cat was ready and fit, and would destroy that field of other claimers.

That's when the twinkling of an idea came to Thorn about this friendly Jimmy croupier. Maybe he could be bribed as well. What a cheeky thought for a 15-year old, but that's what came to mind.

So the next time Jimmy had an ace showing, and thus had initially peaked to also know his hole card, Thorn decided to try an experiment.

With Thorn's first two cards adding up to a difficult 14 against the dealer's ace, Thorn quietly and somewhat despondently responded, "Whatever" when Jimmy swung down to his hit-or-stand turn at the end of the table. Thorn simultaneously made an oh-so tiny non-descript kind of flippant movement of his hands—more like a shrug of indifference rather than anything particularly clear.

Jimmy went whizzing by him, card undelivered. He turned over a five, took another hit for himself, and went bust.

On the next hand, Jimmy had a king showing, and peaked at his hole card again.

Once again, Thornton had a horrible 15, and when his turn came, took almost the same action as before.

"Whatever." Thorn followed with the same small shrugging non-descript hand gesture.

Bang, a card arrived on top of Thornton's 15. It happened to be a 5. 20 now in total.

"Stand," Thornton said more authoritatively at this point.

Jimmy turned to his own hand and had a 9 underneath. His total added up to 19. Thornton had navigated his way to a lucky win—but only courtesy of that fast and fortuitous "hit" from Jimmy that he had received.

Jimmy had just cheated on Thornton's behalf, Thornton was sure of it.

Having won three chips, he pushed a chip of compensation for Jimmy across the table.

Jimmy offered a big Bahamian smile while knocking the chip on the side of the table. Message delivered and received.

Effectively, for the next several hours, if Jimmy knew that he had 7,8,9, or 10 under his exposed face card or ace, and that Thornton was a loser anyway with his 12, 13, 14, 15, or 16 showing, Thornton's "Whatever" response and mild flippant hand movement would suddenly result in a card coming his way. Jimmy knew that Thornton had nothing to lose taking a card because he would otherwise lose anyway. Sometimes that low magic card would appear to leave Thornton with a win or at least a "push" (a.k.a. tie) at 20, or a magic winning 21.

Alternatively, if Jimmy knew that he had something lousy underneath that would likely see the house ultimately "go bust," Jimmy would just whiz past young Thorn.

It was a tremendous advantage, and a win-win situation for both Jimmy and Thornton. The more Thornton won, the more tips he kept shoveling Jimmy's way.

"Holy shit," thought Thornton as the night progressed, "Here I am playing Black Jack for the first time within a casino, and I'm already cheating the house thanks to a smiley but ultimately dishonest croupier."

Pam and Thornton stayed at that table until closing time at 4 am in the morning. At the end of that time, Thorn had accumulated $1,200 from his rather limited and modest $50 start. He didn't win every hand, but with Jimmy helping him on the tough ones, he had had just enough of an added edge to beat the house's huge natural advantage to always draw its cards last.

Was the entire world corrupt? Or did Thornton just somehow attract these fellows like Jimmy and the hair-lipped teller at Aqueduct? Thornton was certainly getting an early education on the slippery side of the gambling world.

Thornton was damned tired the next day, which was a Saturday, but he played his backgammon matches well, and remained alive into the quarterfinals that would take place on the third day of the tournament, Sunday.

At age 15 he had even started to accumulate a bit of attention across the room as the "wonder-kid" who in the last round of matches that day had been able to polish off Rocky Aoki, a well-renowned aggressive player and flamboyant owner of the Benihana restaurant chain. About a half-dozen people had actually congregated around their backgammon board to watch Rocky and Thornton's final few hard-fought games. Eventually, they ended up tied at 16 points apiece in a match to be the first to reach 17. In the end, Thornton had prevailed—only by the good fortune of rolling a set of double 4's just when needed—thus benefitting more from luck than great skill.

On their second night at Paradise Island, and after a light quick dinner, Thornton and Pam glanced back into the casino, but Jimmy was nowhere to be seen. Damn. Probably his night off. They sat down at another Black Jack table, but on this occasion, they both promptly lost $200 apiece within a scant half-hour of play. The dealer was also all deadly serious, and not much fun. Without Jimmy, it just wasn't clicking. They left the casino on that second night, and went upstairs to their room instead.

Gordon meanwhile was heavily involved in a side-game of backgammon downstairs, and had of course been drinking. Pam and Thorn had no idea whether he was winning or losing, but someone was going to have to go back down to look after him. That is when Pam decided to hatch a funny and crazy plot.

Pam had just been in a college play production. The role that she had played was that of a hot hooker, complete with a skimpy dress, a massive blonde wig, and heavy makeup. When Pam had decided to join Thornton and Gordon in Nassau, she somehow had brought all of her costume materials from the play in her suitcase—wig and all. She'd basically just transferred planes at JFK, and still had her college luggage with her.

So joking around, she suddenly popped out from behind the hotel room closet door and surprised Thornton with her steel blonde wig atop her head.

"So, whad'ya think?"

"Holy shit!" Thorn said. "Where'd you get that thing? I'd barely recognize you."

This reaction is what prompted Pam's next thoughts.

"How about if I get all dressed up in my costume, and we go back downstairs and see if Gordon recognizes me? Do you think that I could fool him for long if I put on some sort of deep Southern accent? Do you think he'd recognize me as his own daughter?"

"Of course he'd recognize you...but I guess that might depend upon the amount of booze in him," Thorn ventured.

And so Pam applied some heavy eye-liner, tucked her normally long brown hair under the platinum blonde wig, and dawned a tight fitting short dress together with some high-heeled shoes. As a final step, she tugged down at her dress and plumped up her breasts so that maximum cleavage was showing. Then she started practicing her accent.

"Well now, you all, what game do we have here? Is this what they call Backgammon?" she practiced in a faux slow Southern drawl, as she looked into the mirror. "I'd just love to learn Backgammon. Would anyone here like to teach me?"

Thornton convulsed in laughter. Pam was most convincing in her practice efforts, but even better when Thorn and she eventually descended downstairs. They approached what looked like a dead serious backgammon match with multiple people hovering over the table.

Pam, knowledgeable that it was rude to interrupt play, hovered over the table with the others for a few minutes, but finally started...

"Now why is this game so important that everybody is watching it?"

"Shh..." somebody in the crowd answered back. "They are playing for $1000 a point and the doubling cube is at 8."

"Holy crap, what?" Thornton found himself saying. Gordon usually might play for $10 a point and make or lose a few hundred bucks over the course of a series of games. What was this $1000 a point thing?"

"Dads, are you really playing for a $1,000 a point?" Thorn quietly bent down and asked into his ear.

"If that's what they say, I guess I am..." He responded, notably slurring his words, and clearly pretty sloshed.

This evil slimy guy that he was playing against just smiled. People mumbled around me that it had been a dare. I read it as an ass-hole huckster try to take advantage of a drunk.

The game was quickly ending though, and despite all of the slime-guy's best efforts, Gordon was actually winning. He wasn't particularly capable of moving the backgammon pieces swiftly or precisely, but Lady Luck was somehow smiling down on him—protecting him against himself. With a last flick of the wrist, he produced a set of doubles on the dice that saw him bear off the last of his pieces.

"Long live Gordo!" he bellowed, soon pounding his chest like King Kong.

"Try to collect, ass-hole," the slime-bag guy stood up—pushing his chair back abruptly, disgusted and slightly menacing. Then after a moment of thought, he continued: "That match wasn't for no $1,000 a point. Give me a break. What a joke. I'd never play a guy in your condition for that much. Here's $800 bucks. It was $100 a point." He flipped over eight hundred-dollar bills.

Slime-guy was clearly trying to get himself off the hook somehow—create enough grey zone of uncertainty and obfuscation—so that nobody would know what the truth was. The truth of what they had been playing for had been struck only between Gordo and him, and now Gordo couldn't remember. If Gordon had lost, it would have been $1,000 a point, and slime-bag would have claimed witnesses at the table. Now that Gordo had won, it was only $100 a point, and he could claim that he had paid this amount straight away.

The downside of drink.

This is when Pam made her presence felt once again to lighten the mood a bit.

"Well, I'm sooo impressed as to how you played that game. Would you teach a game of backgammon to this lil' ol' girl from Savannah? I would just love to play with a master."

Gordon looked up at the blonde bombshell of Pam, and squinted one eye as he often did to stabilize the image after a few too many Scotches, and asked: "And what's your name, miss? They call me Gordo."

"Well, I'm Armistead. Armistead Covington of Savannah, Georgia." She smiled and held out her hand for a dainty handshake. "It's so nice to meet a man who is as smart as you are."

It was all over-done soap opera, and Thornton could hardly keep back his giggles, but he did.

"Well, sure, I'll play a game of backgammon with you Armistead. Have you ever played before?"

"Just once or twice when I was a chi-ald. My daddy played backgammon and other games all the time, but he never taught me very well." Pam kept the Southern femme fatale farcical accent going. She was really quite good at it.

"OK, well this is how you set up the board, Armistead..." started Gordon, and they started to play. Gordon had no idea that it was actually Pam across from him, nor did anyone else watching except for Thornton. Pam daintily tapped her pieces on the board in counting fashion as she moved them—as an amateur player typically would—and she purposefully made several bad mistakes in her moves so that Gordon would have something to correct.

Gordon meanwhile—given this sudden female attention—seemed to be having something of a second wind from his earlier drunken stupor while playing the slime-guy. He now had a new mission to impress this attractive Southern girl.

"Now, now, Armistead, put those pieces back, and think about that move a bit more. You want to be as aggressive as possible in backgammon. Look around the board a bit and see where you can hurt me."

"I'd never want to hurt you, Gordo, but I might take care of you in other ways."

Pam—as Armistead—was now flirting like a hooker with her own father, dropping innuendos, and batting her eyelashes. Gordon reached across the board and took her hands.

"You know, I really like you Armistead," he said in an embarrassingly slushy way.

It was too much. Thornton burst out laughing.

"What so funny Thorn? Did I say something funny? I think you are being rude to our fine guest here, Armistead." More slurred words.

At that moment, Pam pulled back her wig, and Gordon stared at her for a bit.

"You're not a blonde, Armistead?"

He still didn't realize that it was Pam.

"Daddy, daddy. It's me, Pam. We pulled a trick on you."

"Ahhhhh...aghhh...Oh my God, Pam? What happened to Armistead? I was having such a nice game with Armistead. I thought she really liked me." He laughed. We all laughed. It was a family bonding moment.

Thornton and Pam wheeled Gordon off to his bed at that point. "You tricked me...how could you trick your own father?" he muttered happily as we went up the elevator. It had been a great prank.

But Thornton's backgammon skills failed to prevail in the quarter-finals the next morning. If Lady Luck had been looking down on Gordon the night before, it abandoned Thornton in his play. He got wiped, and was only thankful that once eliminated, he could actually step outside to see an hour of Nassau's afternoon sun after having spent the entire weekend inside.

Pam, Gordon, and Thornton had previously decided in their travel plans to head back to New York in a more leisurely fashion than by airplane. They would hitch a ride on the Norwegian cruise line Vistafjord currently docked at Prince George Wharf in the deep ocean channel between Paradise Island and the downtown area of Nassau. The cruise liner was on the tail leg of its maiden Caribbean voyage.

They boarded the boat on Monday morning. The boat just seemed massive to Thornton as they climbed the steps to the C-Deck entrance portal.

"How could this thing actually float?" he wondered.

Thornton had never been on a cruise-liner before. He also wondered whether the boat had a casino, and if so, whether another croupier like Jimmy could once again be found.

CHAPTER 6

HIGH SEAS
M.S. Vistafjord
March 1973

The slow rock of the seas had become mildly upsetting to Thornton's stomach.

A loud speaker bleeped and then crackled.

"We wish to apologize for the turbulence." a thickly Norwegian accented voice came across the air. "The captain is experiencing problems with the boat's stabilizers."

Great, just great.

Three-and-a-half days north of Nassau, on board the M.S. Vistafjord now somewhere off the coast of New Jersey, Thornton, Gordon, and Pam were anxious to get back home—off the damn boat.

It wasn't so much that the cruise itself had been bad. The sun had been hot, the sloshy small round pool refreshing, and the few activities that they had participated in—like Bingo and shuffleboard—perfectly quaint and enjoyable.

The boat had no casino—as things turned out.

"Tant pis," Thornton thought to himself in his eighth-grade French.

It was more meal time that had been difficult for the family—dinner specifically. Pam, Gordon, and Thornton had been assigned to a big round table of eight for each sit-down meal. Lunch was optional there, and mostly they stayed by the pool at lunch. But there was no other option than this assigned dining room table at dinner. One seating. One table.

The food was fine, but with Maiden-voyage kinks were still being worked out between the kitchen and the staff of waiters—few of whom actually seemed to be Norwegian. Different languages in the staff abounded. The service was slow, and the people at the table that Pam, Thornton, and Gordon were unavoidably stuck with could be described with just one word: tacky.

Myrtle and Fred were two New Jersey natives—both now in their mid-seventies—with thick North Jersey accents—the high-pitched singsong Bayonne variety—but who had only gotten married a few months earlier. Neither had ever left New Jersey except to step on an occasional cruise somewhere. For their age, Thornton supposed that they had some spunk. But they weren't particularly smart. Their ability to carry on a thoughtful or intelligent conversation was certainly sorely lacking. They both still worked—even at their advanced respective ages—at an American Can factory located in Jersey City.

With them was Marie, who before Myrtle's wedding to Fred had been Myrtle's occasional traveling companion, and wedding bells be damned, still remained so now. She too came from New Jersey and had a face that looked like a boxer had long ago punched it in, but with features that had never again quite popped back out. She was certainly an odd looking ugly little bulldog. She was also almost as dumb as Myrtle and Fred.

Lastly, besides the three of us, there was Ruth and one empty eighth seat. Ruth was reasonably sophisticated and well dressed, in her mid-fifties, but kind of a lost soul—all by herself on the cruise, never married. Maybe the boat's social director had planted her there with a man and his two kids in an effort to play cupid—make sparks fly between two unattached 55 year-olds. By far the most pleasant and reasonable of the crowd, Ruth was at the same time, not at all competitive or lively. She was instead just plain dull.

"Look Thorn," Gordon advised as they sat in the ship's bar before their finale dinner, "This is our last night at this damn table and it's Myrtle and Fred's seven-month wedding anniversary. They're all excited about that. I think they're planning a cake or something. So I don't care how long it takes to get through this, we're going to be polite for once."

He paused for a second to let that part of the message sink in, and then continued.

"And be nice to them for God's sake. Try to enter into the conversation a bit more! You too Pam!"

Pam rolled her eyes in mock dread of the evening to come.

Thornton nodded in forced agreement and told his dad that he thought he'd always been perfectly nice to everyone at the table—maybe not too enthusiastic and outgoing—but perfectly nice. Anyway, what did he expect from a 15 year-old at a table with a bunch of old bags?

Now standing at the entrance doorway to the dining room—perhaps mentally steeling himself for two hours of agony to follow—Gordon seemingly got cold feet.

"Thorn, Pam" Gordon said as if to prolong going in, "I'm going to go on back to the bar and get one more drink. I'll join you at the table in a second."

Gordon had already had two rum drinks that night—switching from his normal Scotch for some reason (perhaps as a waning honor to the Caribbean)—but still seemed alert and normal to Thornton, and after his semi-lecture to the two of them on how to behave at dinner, Thorn never thought Gordon might misbehave himself. He and Pam shrugged off the delay tactic by Gordon, and headed to the table by themselves.

The ship's orchestra was playing, a few people already dancing, and a generally festive mood in the air. How bad could this evening be?

Sure enough though, halfway through the meal when the band started to play some romantic song and they brought on a tall 7-month anniversary cake glistening in white icing for Fred and Myrtle, the fresh glass of straight rum and a little lemon juice that Gordon had gotten just before dinner lay empty on its side.

Gordon looked across the table at Thorn with an idiotic sleepy little smile on his face.

Some nights he would get loud and difficult to handle—beating his chest like an ape in heat as he had after winning that backgammon game a few nights earlier in Nassau. But at least in this instance he was sitting nicely and quietly, his head mostly down, occasionally mumbling a few words or mimicking to no one in particular the way Ruth ate her food. His mouth opened and closed in a slobbering fashion close to that of a horse.

Luckily, nobody at the table really noticed him at first, except for Pam and Thornton. But in an initial shuffling of seating, the two kids had been sprinkled around the table, and were not immediately next to him, but instead watching him from afar. They did so with increasing trepidation and fear.

Then Gordon began to snore...lightly at first, but eventually with increasing vigor and occasional snorts. Thornton went over to his chair and gave him a nudge to reawaken him.

"C'mon Dads, you need to wake up. You've been snoring." Thorn said with a gentle nudge.

Gordon mumbled to Thorn the words that he often did when he needed to go to the bathroom, when he felt sick, or when he was tired or bored. In this case, maybe it was all three. The boat was still rocking more than it should have been given the damn stabilizer problem.

"It's time to go home, Thorn..." He slurred softly.

But while the anniversary cake had arrived, Myrtle and Fred had yet to cut it. Some waiter had gone to fetch utensils—the service as always dragging on ever so slowly.

"Just a few minutes more, dads," Thorn responded. "They still haven't cut the cake yet, and you said that we needed to be polite. We can go as soon as they cut the cake."

Thorn returned to his chair and pretended as best a 15-year old could (with a drunk dad across the table) that everything was fine. Pam looked at Thorn and raised her eyebrows in dismay, and then shrugged her shoulders in helplessness at the general situation.

Myrtle was all full of laughter and toasts at this point, and things momentarily seemed to be holding together, when suddenly before Thornton's eyes—and soon the disbelieving eyes of everyone else nearby—Gordon's fingers plunged into a corner of the tall anniversary cake seated in the center of the table. Like a wild barbarian, he pulled off a corner of the cake, white icing dripping off of his hand, and attempted to shove the cake in his mouth.

Icing dripped from his chin. The table was silent. Thorn started giggling. Pam started crying. It was all just so typical. Soon Thorn was in hysterics.

Finally, just to break the silent stares of everyone except for Thornton's laughter, Myrtle spoke out in her usual chirping and light Bayonne-accented voice.

"Oh, Gordon, now where *did* you learn your manners?..."

Yet before she could really finish, his hand was reaching out for the cake again like a greedy child coming back for more. This time the dive bombing hit the middle of the cake and plunged deep within it, emerging with a large chunk as capture.

Pam screamed at him: "C'mon dads, pull yourself together. You are being a complete slob, and ruining the evening for others."

With that bit of advice, Gordon began flexing his fingers and flicking off pieces of cake and icing. Clumps of white icing started to land mostly in large splots on the dresses and coats of the others at the table—including Thornton.

There was nothing left to do except to quickly maneuver Gordon out of the dining room. So Pam and Thorn made quick apologies, and started lifting him out of his seat and then arm-in-arm across his shoulders pushed him toward the dining room exit. Their cabins were one flight down a nearby spiral set of lobby stairs, and they slowly navigated Gordon down those stairs one step at a time, holding him carefully.

But soon, he grew tired, and sat down wearily by the stairs' inner bannister.

"This is too hard..."

Then he started to snore again. He was now asleep on the main chandeliered stairwell of the ship.

"Oh my God, how are we going to move him?" Pam asked to no one. "He can't just go to sleep here on the stairs."

Drool started to emanate from Gordon's mouth.

But Thornton was a creative type and wasn't going to be defeated. He took off Gordon's shoes, and started to tickle the underside of his feet. Thornton knew that Gordon was extremely ticklish down there, and even in his drunken stupor, the tickling woke him up.

A last bit of reason got him to move again and finally down into his berth's bed. It had been quite the evening—an evening that long remained in Thornton's psyche and memory when he thought of his father.

Several hours later, as the early morning sunshine was just starting to lighten a gray-looking portal window, Thornton awoke to the toilet flushing. Gordon emerged from the bathroom and staggered back to his bed for an added dose of rest.

Thornton poked his head up from his bed, and asked: "Do you remember what happened last night, Dads?"

Gordon thought for a moment: "Well, um...Did I spill a glass of water, or something?"

The entire evening's events had completely disappeared from his memory.

They docked back in New York that morning and thankfully never had to see Myrtle or Fred again, although Pam and Thornton did make up a faux Christmas Card to Gordon from the couple several months later—expressing the couple's forgiveness for the final evening's events and suggesting a reunion.

Thornton and Pam were always full of creative tricks.

As usual, Gordon thought the card was real.

CHAPTER 7

THE ARBITRAGEUR
New York, NY
June 1974

Dr. Jacowski was a metals dealer. His New York-based firm Monroe Metals had always specialized in precious metals—in gold, in silver, in platinum, in palladium. He wasn't so much interested in the speculative positioning himself, as he was capturing a wide bid-offered spread, as well as the trading of metals across different locations and grades—in other words, he was focused on arbitrage.

And he thought he had built some of the best systems in the business.

Within an era where no exchange-traded options on precious metals or precious metals futures yet existed, he had been at the forefront offering speculative investors the very first over-the-counter option contracts on the metal. In fact he had built a computerized voice interface that retail investors could dial into, and trade options. It was one of the very first applications of an automated algorithm-centric trading system delivered by computer.

The investor would dial. Through a series of voice prompts, the computer would then verbally ask what metal, what maturity, what strike, and what size quote was demanded, and whether the investor wanted a put or a call. Once this information had been provided, the computer would then source the latest underlying spot price for the relevant metal from Telerate and apply the Black Scholes formula and a pre-coded volatility bid-offered spread entered by Monroe traders each morning to deliver an appropriate price.

"The November 5.50 call on silver is...[pause]...75 cents bid, at a dollar-twenty-five cents offered. Dial 1 to hit the bid, dial 2 to pay the offer."

It was a technology ahead of its time, but at first nobody had really cared. The metals market in the late 1960's and early 1970's had been sleepy and thin. It had also been constantly manipulated by steady U.S. Treasury selling of precious metals—particularly silver.

In 1959, government stockpiles of silver had been 2.1 billion ounces. Much of this was held in order to mint silver dimes that had long been 90% silver and 10% copper. But silver had slowly become increasingly scarce and quite a bit more expensive. Industrial demand for the metal was slowly outstripping supply. Officials at the Treasury feared future chronic shortages, and at $1.24 an ounce in 1964, the silver content alone of a dime was costing the government 8.9 cents per coin to source. This was before adding in the value of the copper within the coin, or any of the labor to mint it. This was an untenable situation.

And yet President Johnson—fearful that changing the silver content of America's coinage for the first time since 1792 might lead to the hoarding of old dimes—decided that in order to make a smooth transition, all that was needed was a little Government selling.

On July 23, 1965, President Johnson addressed the nation as follows:

"Our present silver coins won't disappear and they won't even become rarities. We estimate that there are now 12 billion—I repeat, more than 12 billion silver dimes and quarters and half dollars that are now outstanding. We will make another billion before we halt production. And they will be used side-by-side with our new coins. Since the life of a silver coin is about 25 years, we expect our traditional silver coins to be with us in large numbers for a long, long time.

If anybody has any idea of hoarding our silver coins, let me say this. Treasury has a lot of silver on hand, and it can be, and it will be used to keep the price of silver in line with its value."

In other words, your government was changing the rules of its coinage, but don't try to speculate against us. We will crush you, and will keep the supply of silver on the market such that it won't be worth your time to differentiate between old coins and new coins— at least not initially.

In 1965, with the formal passage of the Coinage Act of 1965, the dime's silver content was completely removed. Dimes from 1965 onward were to be composed of outer layers of 75 percent copper and 25 percent nickel, bonded to a pure copper core. But to keep the price of silver, and old silver coins, from shooting northward, the U.S Treasury would sell 400 million ounces of silver that year—54% of the total annual supply to make the transition seem trivial.

But to Dr. Jacowski that change had been anything but trivial. It had been an opportunity. Even as the government continued to sit on top of the market with continued silver sales in 1966, 1967, and 1968, the price of silver had still slowly risen to average closer to $2 an ounce. That meant that the silver content value of those old pre-1965 silver dimes was now worth more like 14.5 cents per dime.

Jacowski started buying as many pre-1965 bags of silver coins that he could find.

But then, there was of course, the risk that the price might go back down. Jacowski didn't like that risk. He liked things locked in—nice and tidy. That's where the retail option business came in. Most of the clientele were speculative types who wanted to buy calls on silver. This was perfect. He could be long these bags of silver coins and allow his retail option business to act as his natural hedge. The spreads in that business were just fabulous, and the continuous sale of calls on silver would nicely hedge the many silver coin bags that he was concomitantly accumulating.

"I'm buying cheap silver in bags and selling expensive silver in the form of derivatives," he used to brag to close business friends. "The fact that the market lets me get away with this again and again—year after year—doesn't lend itself to any efficient market hypothesis in my eyes. People are just plain stupid."

Jacowski had grown up in Heidelberg Germany, and initially studied to be a doctor—a psychiatrist—but the rise of Hitler and Nazi Germany had sent his family scurrying to London just as he had finished his studies. There, he had quickly found the metals business to be a more interesting application of his talents than medicine. He'd initially spent some time with a venerable old London dealing firm, Monroe & Goldsmid, a firm around from the 1600s, but soon decided that New York City was where the financial universe was fast migrating and opportunity lay. Jacowski could see in the 1960's that the $35 central bank peg for gold was likely to be abandoned with time. When it went, he expected a huge retail demand for precious metals to emerge—particularly in the United States.

And then it had slowly—or not so slowly—started to actually happen. The 1965 Coinage Act had been the first crack in the central bankers' facade. At first, government selling notwithstanding, silver had doubled in twelve months. After a brief consolidation, it surged another 33% in six weeks, and then without taking a breath, exploded another 70% higher in price. By 1974, silver—up to slightly above $5—had vaulted over 500% from where it had stood just ten years earlier.

Across this period, the Monroe Metals business plan was all working perfectly. Jacowski was getting rich—and he was doing so without even taking much risk. It was all arb. There was no need for speculation.

The fine doctor had his eye on a 37-room Victorian mansion on Gramercy Square built in 1887. He had also bought two islands in the British Virgin Islands—including one where 55 chests of pirate silver was supposedly buried from 1750. That seemed appropriate to him. If the treasure was really there, the cost of the island was a pittance— another arb of sorts in his mind.

But in 1974 something new was happening. Post the 1973 de-pegging of gold by Nixon, new exchange traded futures contracts on gold and silver were suddenly being established on an exchange called the COMEX. With all of the speculative interest in metals, these futures were also starting to trade on the rich side to their theoretical forward value.

Jacowski saw a way to scale his business to even greater extent by executing an even niftier arb.

"Let's assume we keep buying our silver bags of coins, and then take them to a bank as collateral for a loan," he had explained to his assistant Dani one day. "Since the coins not only serve as good collateral, but they also represent legal tender, if we pledge these coins to the bank, they will be able to use our coins as legal reserve collateral."

Dani nodded. He was catching on to where his boss was headed.

"They could make us a below-market-rate loan on that collateral given the reserve requirement benefit that they'd be getting," Jacowski continued. "Better yet, maybe we could effectively sell them the coins; then have them write us an in-the-money call so that we can guarantee getting the same bags back; and then use the difference in price between the coin bag sale and the in-the-money call purchases to buy more bags of silver coins. All of the silver content that we ultimately have the right to own will be hedged with short silver futures."

It was brilliant. A bank would be happy to follow Monroe Metals down this path. Indeed, the fine institution of Safri Bank eventually bought into the concept and became Monroe Metals biggest counterpart for this trade. Jacowski's bags of silver coins didn't have to just sit in a vault somewhere. Carefully structured with a bank, they could be used to generate added cash at an effective super-cheap rate because of their added value not just as standard collateral on a loan but as legal tender that could be applied to a bank's reserve requirement.

It was all an early use of derivatives to engage in so-called "regulatory arbitrage."

"How do you dream this stuff up, boss?" his assistant Dani had said as he looked at the blinking green Reuters screen in front of him.

Then Dani offered an additional thought: "Better yet, if we keep repeating this trade and the price of silver slowly heads higher—like it seems to be doing—we will keep taking realized short-term losses as well roll over our futures hedges, and if we make the tenor of the in-the-money options we buy more than six-months, we will be getting long-term gains on those positions. It could also be a great tax play."

It would not be until a later year that the tax rate on trading futures became one melded rate. As of the mid-1970's all futures sales were always taxed as short-term gains or losses, while any futures purchase held for more than six-months was treated as long-term gain or loss. "Where did the politicians dream this tax stuff up?" thought Jacowski. "They're just inviting tax arb activity."

"I think we should call this our Silver Vault Cash game," said Jacowski. "It really is an elegant and easy lay-up trade. C'mon Dani. Let's ramp this business to the next level."

CHAPTER 8

THE FLOOR OF THE NYSE AT AGE 16
New York, NY
June 1974

While Dr. Jacowski plotted six blocks away about how great his Vault Cash Game was going to be, Thorn uneasily stood by the guard booth at the Wall Street entrance to the New York Stock Exchange Trading Floor. As he stared at the brass-ornamental entrance door to the exchange floor itself, with the mild rush of bodies moving behind it, his heart pounded at all the activity—the scurrying, the noise.

It was his first day of work at a summer job.

Thornton's infatuation with markets had started, in part, because he heard about them all the time.

Despite all of his drinking issues, and a divorce to show for those problems, Gordon had actually not done too badly in business, landing on the floor of the New York Stock Exchange (NYSE) in the early 1950's. First it had been as a "$2 broker"—someone who charged $2 to handle an order on the floor when other normal brokers were busy. Then he'd had a stint as a standard floor broker for an upstairs firm. And finally he'd amassed enough capital to set himself up as a "Specialist" on the Floor.

Most brokers went from post to post with a variety of orders in hand. Specialists simply stood at one post and helped ensure an orderly market in an assigned list of stocks. It was deemed an enviable job.

"Hey, I'm John O'Dea," a rotund specialist clerk greeted Thorn with a warm smile and hand-shake. "We'll go downstairs first, and get you a floor badge."

Yes, Thornton's first real summer job—at the ripe age of 16—would be as a junior Specialist Clerk working behind Post 16 in the

NYSE "Garage Room" which was and remains one of the two smaller appendages to the stock exchange's main "Big Room."

John led him across the trading floor for the first time—ultimately headed for a basement office where he'd be photographed and have a Floor Pass issued in the bowels of the NYSE. The cavernous expanse filled with scurrying brokers reminded Thornton somewhat of Grand Central Station—except of course with more slips of paper all over the floor.

Nothing circa 1974 when Thornton arrived on the Floor of the NYSE was particularly automated, but instead Thorn found it all to be a wonderful cacophony of sounds and rhythms.

The horseshoe-shaped trading Posts themselves were wonderfully antique-looking semi-circular constructions of brass and varnished mahogany wood with small fold-down benches across the circular front where a foot-weary Specialist could catch an occasional moment of rest. Thorn would soon learn that in actuality, these benches were only used on the slowest of days when a Specialist might sit and read a newspaper. Otherwise, the Specialists stood on their feet all day—almost like doormen.

The Post itself contained a chest-high desk, and on each side of this desk stood thin loose-leaf order books within built-in metal bookshelves. These books looked from the outside a bit like wine menus—each one a different color for a different stock or share class of a stock. During market hours, these books could be easily accessed either by the Specialist standing outside the Post, or the Specialist Clerk standing inside the Post. After the market close, these books disappeared upstairs where they'd be cleaned up and prepared by the Specialist Clerks for the following session, each order in the book being re-checked against a "deck" of original actual orders. Days when a stock went ex-dividend, all of the orders would have to be manually adjusted lower throughout the entire book to reflect the dividend payout. Thorn would soon learn what a royal pain in the ass that was.

Towards the top of each Post, each stock had a manually maintained "Last Trade Price" Indicator that a NYSE Reporter standing nearby the Specialist on the outside of the Post would be responsible to dial up and down just after stock transactions transpired. There was a black "plus tick (+) indicator" and red "minus (-) tick indicator" as well that the NYSE Reporter was similarly obligated to maintain.

Thorn noticed up on one corner of the "Big Room" a large black board had moving panels, with different numbers on each panel, many of which were fluttering excitedly.

"What's that thing?" he asked John.

"If you are a floor broker and your badge number is flashing up there, you have to get back to your phone turret quickly to pick up a new round of orders, and then dash from post to post to execute what you have in hand." Thorn soon learned that you could literally judge how busy the market was by how furiously this board was clacking away. Like a Pavlovian dog, that clacking noise would automatically increase one's adrenalin.

But Thorn would also later learn that smaller orders could also be routed from upstairs firms directly to Specialist posts through pneumatic tubes that felt a bit like courier pigeons flying out of the pneumatic pipes, and eventually into a large metal bin.

With a "shhhuwpp" sound, a tube order would arrive to the base of its pipe from an upstairs firm's wire room. Then, a "Tube Man" standing by the magic machine would remove and open the circular container, pull out the coveted small script of paper, while dropping the tube itself into the vat of empty used tubes—each tube to eventually be reused for a return voyage.

"Who had invented all this shit?" thought Thorn. "It was all almost other-worldly."

The Tube Man would then hand the order outward from the middle of the Post to a Specialist Clerk who would look at the order for its size and importance, and then consult the physical spiral-bound order book where each page would represent a price level such as 46 on the first page, 46 1/8 on the next page, 46 ¼ on the following page, 46 3/8 on the next.

Thorn soon found himself standing between the Tube Man and the Specialist Clerk carefully observing this repeated process.

"1000 Cee-Wee to buy at the market," the Specialist Clerk barked. "Cee-Wee" was short for the symbol, CWE, which stood for the Chicago-utility Commonwealth Edison. Together, the Specialist Clerk and the Specialist examined the spiral book for existing resting orders, and determined that the best bid was 46 1/8 for 500 shares and the best offer was 46 ¼ for 700 shares.

"In this type of instance," John turned to instruct Thorn, "a Specialist has to make a decision. A few different routes are possible..."

And so Thorn got his first lesson in market-making.

The Specialist could announce to a NYSE Reporter standing next to him that 1000 shares of Cee-Wee trade 46 ¼, selling 700 shares to the market buy order off the book, and 300 shares from his own account (either out of inventory or going temporarily short) in order to accommodate the residual 300 shares to buy. He might then mentally join the bid at 46 1/8 for his own account if a sell order happened to trickle in a few minutes later. If so, he'd have to stand behind the other orders on the book in terms of execution priority.

Alternatively, if the Specialist didn't want to get involved, he'd simply announce: "700 shares Cee-Wee trade 46 1/4, and 300 shares trade 46 3/8; market going out is now 46 1/8 to 46 3/8."

Or if the orders stacked up at 46 3/8 were substantial, he might say: "700 shares trade 46 1/4," and then instruct the Specialist Clerk to report to the upstairs firm that the balance of 300 shares was being 'stopped' at a worst-case fill price of 46 3/8. If the balance of the resting sell orders at 46 3/8 started to get lifted, the Specialist would guarantee getting the 300 shares done for the buyer at that price, but first the Specialist would try to bid 46 1/4 for the remaining 300 shares.

In this instance, the Specialist had followed the latter route—trying to avoid a "split-fill" for the upstairs client, but not becoming directly involved himself by selling the shares from his own account. It seemed like a fair middle path.

Thorn watched the whole process and its fine almost orchestral integration. The NYSE reporter penciled in a few dots and dashes onto a computer punch card, and then fed the punch card into a card reader. A few seconds later, the CWE shares that had traded appeared on the electronic tape that whizzed by up near the Exchange ceiling, and was formally transmitted around the world.

It was all so new to Thorn, but also reasonably civilized. The system seemed to work well for the volumes at the time. Thorn loved all the action and the pulse of the exchange floor, which he soon learned would ebb and flow—almost like waves at the beach—always frantic around the opening, then typically busy for an hour or so, followed by a late-morning lull; then increased franticness again starting around 1:30 pm. At 2:30 pm everything would be done and finished with the ringing of the closing bell. It was only in a much later year that trading was extended to 4:00 pm. What a civilized existence for the brokers of that era.

Thornton had approached his dad sheepishly for some sort of job during the spring of 1974, and Gordon had initially tried to push Thornton off to work at the local newsstand on Broadway and Wall Street.

"It will be good for you to sweat a bit, learn what manual labor is all about sitting outside in the July and August heat" Gordon had said, "And I know this newspaper seller well. I think that I can get you a summer job helping him."

For months Gordon had come home each week, and Thornton had enquired whether this newspaper-selling job was real and confirmed. How much would it pay? What day was he starting? What time would he have to be downtown?

"Don't worry. You will have a job of some sort this summer," his dad had assured him. "I just haven't firmed up all the details yet."

This mild dis-organization was typical of Gordon. When Thornton had been about eleven years-old, they had once left for a vacation trip to upstate New York, and 70 miles north of the city whizzing up the New York State Thruway in a borrowed car and without a formal driver's license, Gordon had turned to Thornton to ask: "How much money did you bring?"

Thornton had responded: "About $60 to buy some souvenirs with."

Thornton could always remember his Dad's comeback: "Good. That will help get us through dinner tonight and our first night's motel. I didn't have time to get to the bank before we left, but I have my checkbook. Someone will cash a check for me along the way."

Thornton's heart had sunk at the time. Gordon also did not believe in credit cards and had none. How could an adult leave for a three week vacation on the road with an eleven-year old in tow, with no driver's license, no credit cards, and also without any cash in his pocket—but instead, dependent upon the souvenir money that his son might or might not have? After no one would accept cashing his check (even when he offered to make the check out for more than the cash delivered) Thornton and Gordon had ended up having to wait three days at a dumpy town called Keysville, New York for a local bank to allow his presented check to clear. Money for food during those three days had been pathetically limited. It had been a particularly inauspicious start to that year's summer travels.

Typical of this type of thing, and flashing forward to the summer of 1974, the newspaper seller had eventually expressed no need for Thornton, so Gordon was ultimately forced into a more nepotistic path. He had grudgingly told his partners that Thornton would be joining their Specialist firm for the summer, but would be paid out of Gordon's share of the partnership only. Gordon was loathe to force the unknown abilities of a 16-year old on the shoulders of anyone else. Thornton would just be an extra set of hands available behind the Post.

"So who's the new kid in the back of the booth?" one aggressive and slightly cocky broker named Roger Hochstein asked on Thornton's first day.

"Thornton," Gordon responded, "He's with us for the summer. He's my son."

"Thornton? What kind of name is that? That sounds fancy—almost royal. What's his middle name?"

When the answer "Emory" was proffered, Hochstein howled. "Thornton Emory...Wow. I think we should just rename him something British...like a butler...how about Mumford?"

Thornton's nickname for that summer was thus set as Mumford. Everyone started calling him that.

The first task assigned to Mumford for this job was to take a directory of floor broker names and clearing firms and memorize the association between the two. The floor broker Roger Hochstein might for example have badge HOCH, but Thornton would be responsible to know that HOCH actually lined up with clearing firm LRH—which stood for Loeb Rhodes Hornblower.

Thorn dutifully studied that directory every morning as he rode to Wall Street on the subway, and then again each evening when he went home on the subway, trying to pick off 10-15 broker/clearing firm associations per ride—all committed to memory. At times sweat would trickle down the small of his back as he stood in the non-air-conditioned subways of 1974, but he would continue to study that little directory no matter how hot and sweaty the subway became.

Then, when a given broker such as Hochstein would appear in a crowd around Post 16, and place a transaction in one of the firm's stocks, Thornton would immediately be able to announce without hesitation "Loeb Rhodes buys 500 MAI from a resting offer on the book by Merrill Lynch"—sending the broker happily away with his trade counterpart ML scribbled on his order slip, and LRH scratched into the order book next to a crossed off Merrill order. Thornton would then be responsible for writing up a commission slip showing the transaction so that the Specialist firm could correctly bill one or both sides of the order for helping in its execution. Any order held on the Specialist's books—even if being temporarily "stopped" by the Specialist at a guaranteed worst-case fill—would be eligible for Specialist billing.

This ability to share a portion of the upstairs' broker's commission was by itself a pretty sweet little business. It became substantially nicer at the time by the fact that the Specialist was the only person who saw the entire resting order book. Thus, if a Specialist saw tons of resting sell orders at 55, he would have a pretty good edge selling in front of this level at 54 7/8. At worst, he'd know that he was backstopped with the ability to get out of his short just an $1/8^{th}$ of a point higher at 55, and that the probability of blasting through such a level with so many sell orders stacked up there would be difficult to achieve. Thus, the Specialist could take a relatively low-risk trade to the downside, and in so doing, also facilitate someone else in the market getting a slightly better fill on a buy order than would otherwise have been the case. If the stock did indeed start to trade lower, then the Specialist—facing perhaps a relatively empty order book—would also have a general obligation to show some sort of fair bid when compared to the last traded price—maybe a bid at 54 5/8 or 54 ½. So some modicum of general stability was accomplished. And while helping to establish such stability—stepping in front of widely placed bids and offers—the Specialist in effect tended to sell high and buy low.

Some called this all a "license to steal" since only the Specialist was entitled to see the entire order book. This was in effect a substantive competitive advantage. There was also at the time something called NYSE Rule 390, which required that all orders by NYSE member firms effectively be exposed to the market on the NYSE floor. Thus even if a firm like Goldman Sachs had a client who wanted to buy 2000 shares of a given stock, and Goldman was willing to sell this stock to the client from their own account, they could not simply cuff a last price from the ticker to trade at. Instead, they actually had to send a broker to the floor with both the customer buy and house sell orders in hand. The broker would then appear at the Specialist post and query where the stock was bid and offered. If the Specialist announced 24 ¼ bid at 24 ½ offered, the broker might then announce to the Specialist and the NYSE Reporter standing nearby:

"Goldman bids 24 3/8 for 2000;" and then literally a second later, effectively trading with himself—"2000 offered at 24 3/8; 2000 shares cross—24 3/8." The Goldman broker would effectively have been involved in both sides of such a "cross." The Specialist would just stand there uninvolved (and unpaid) unless he blocked the cross so as to protect another order that he already had in hand.

Or if the upstairs order was a bigger more lopsided one to buy 10000 shares up to 24 ¾, with instructions to clean up the remaining shares of the client order out of the upstairs house account, the broker announcement might go something like this:

"24 ½ for 10000; how many did I get?"

"2000" the Specialist might reply. "Josephthal is your name."

"5/8 bid for another 8000."

"You bought another 1000 shares off the book, those are from Baker Weeks."

"How much is offered at ¾?"

"The book has 2000 to sell at ¾; I'd offer you another 1000 from my own account."

"3/4 bid for 7000," the broker would shout.

"3000 trade" the Specialist would respond.

"Goldman offers another 4000 at ¾ on a cross," the original broker would finally shout.

And a total 7000 shares would get posted on the tape trading at 24 3/4.

While this was all a time-intensive and very manual process, it was also reasonably fair to ensure that no buy order was executed at a higher price than a willing seller was simultaneously offering. All orders were "protected" from being violated or traded through without an associated "fill."

When Thornton first reached the NYSE Floor, it was still a market of innocence, with guaranteed best price execution, but admittedly high commission levels to ensure such execution.

As an aside, and to foreshadow the future a bit, all of this would eventually go out the window about six years later when the NYSE did away with Rule 390 (the rule previously requiring all orders to be exposed to the NYSE floor); when the order book was made electronic so that resting bids and offers could be seen by those willing to pay for "Level 2" market data access; and when orders could also be sent to upstairs electronic "dark pools" of hidden orders to pick up or dispose of stock without that stock actually printing on the public tape.

What previously had been an environment where the Specialist had a clear information edge suddenly morphed into one where the Specialist could get run over or just ignored. The Specialist appetite to step in front of resting orders on the order book thus diminished with time. There was suddenly too much risk that a big block of stock would trade away from the Specialist and leave whatever finessing of orders that the Specialist was trying to accomplish as moot and also unprofitable.

Moreover, once the order book became more transparent on a "Level 2" electronic quote screen, people started to become nervous about leaving *any* orders on the books at all. In other words, it's one thing to leave a 10000-share buy order under the market when only the Specialist could see it. But when everyone could see it, leaving a big visible order might lead to "pippers" bidding in front of the order. Many individual stocks thus became naturally thinner and flakier even as the general market also became busier.

And then eventually the exchanges decided to eliminate fractional increments in price quotations and replace them with decimalized quotes. The idea was a noble one to reduce transaction costs yet again. But now the opportunities for irritating "pippers" and "quant modelers" to jump ahead of resting bids or offers in the market became even greater. Risking a penny to "pip" a resting order was certainly less risky than risking $1/8^{th}$ of a point—a price spread of 12.5 cents.

In the end, it would in ways become harder to get a fair simple price, and many people would simply stop showing fully visible firm bids and offers. Instead, they'd use computer order algorithms to "participate" in a certain amount of the volume traded or to seek out hidden offers across different exchanges and "dark pools" of non-exchange traded internal liquidity.

Many of these algorithms today have developed names like "Stealth," or "Ninja," or "Ambush," or "Nocturnal." They are designed to grab volume quietly, but without showing hard bids or offers, and often without even printing the traded shares on the official "composite tape."

The cacophony of the NYSE in 1974 would slowly become ever-so-quiet computers trading with computers—orders getting moved and routed to different locations with the passage of a heartbeat. Screens would still flash and blink, but the noise of the Big Board broker board clapping or the pneumatic tubes popping would eventually be lost to a different era. And with that loss of noise, the guarantee would also be lost that any two market orders entered to buy and sell at the same time would always meet at the same price in the market.

Equity markets would become like a mad freeway of cars—with entry ramps and exit ramps abounding—but front-running brokers and squeeze artists extracting some pain along the way, and occasional pile-ups being all-too-common.

There was none of this of course back in 1974 as Thornton looked around the Floor. What there was instead—in the case of a particularly busy stock—was a huge group of men huddled around a Specialist holding an order book. There might be several minutes when nothing would trade, and then the Specialist would get all the orders organized to accommodate as many people at one price as possible in one big print; followed by more huddling, a bit of shouting, and a smaller round of ripple-on stock price prints.

Yes, tempers occasionally flared when one broker felt ignored or neglected to the Specialist's chosen path of transactions, but it was less random chaos in many ways than what we see in today's electronic markets. It was clunky and manually intensive, but eminently fair in terms of execution—albeit expensive in terms of commission level costs.

May 1, 1975 would eventually bring the end to fixed commission levels on Wall Street in what was referred to at the time as the "Big Bang" day. Commission levels would head south in a hurry. But anyone back in 1975 or even as late as 1980 would truly blanche at the sub-penny a share level for institutional business that commissions have reached today.

Thornton's summer on the Floor of the NYSE in 1974 was overall an eye-opening experience. He felt the pulse of capitalism as closely as any 16-year old kid possibly could—even if he would never have imagined all of the market-structure changes that would follow.

What struck him the most perhaps was the social ubiquity of the NYSE Floor. People who might not otherwise hang out together beyond the Floor were notwithstanding often the best of friends on the Floor. It was a true melting pot of American people trading American securities in a most American way.

And everyone on the Floor also loved a bet.

One of the lowest paid Floor employees of the NYSE at the time was indeed the lowly "Tube Man," and at Post 16 where Thornton stood, there was this Tube Man named Cliff, and he loved to gamble. A tall slightly debonair looking bald man, Cliff could have passed for a European butler, but there he stood unfolding tube orders to make a living. At most he made $15,000 a year in this profession during that era.

At first Cliff's bets were pretty standard. The Giants would be playing the Cowboys and were seven point underdogs. Cliff might like the Cowboys and would look for a bet against someone else who was a Giants fan. It was pretty harmless stuff. Discussions and negotiations as to point spreads filled the otherwise dull moments at the Post when the order flow was light.

But then Cliff started to muck with the point spreads and the odds given. He'd say that he wanted to bet on the Cowboys and receive an extra +10 points (instead of giving away the normal Las Vegas line of -7 points on the game), but for that less-than-generous point spread set-up that was very much in his favor, he would compensate by offering 10-1 odds to someone willing to accept the Giants at -10.

And despite being a Tube Man, Cliff would voice that he was willing to bet $1,000 versus a $10,000 potential risk if the Giants won big. Somewhere in the sea of brokers, news of the odd bet proposition would circulate, and a "syndicate" of ten Giants fans would be found willing to risk maybe $100 apiece at the chance to receive $1000 apiece if the Giants romped.

In the end, a sea of well-paid NYSE brokers would be betting versus Cliff, The Tube Man. Only in America!

Most of the time, Cliff won, of course. The Cowboys, already the favorite, would either win or keep the game reasonably close. Cliff might only have been making about $15,000 a year at his job, but he would typically pocket a nice chunk of gambling money on the side—maybe $1,000 on any given Monday morning after weekend football results were in. And sometimes his take was even more.

And as he won, so too did Cliff's willingness to bet in size. Suddenly, he was looking to risk losing maybe $200,000 should some 20-1 skewed odds proposition happen to come in, with the most that he'd ever gain standing at $10,000. Cliff undoubtedly saw this as his way to make ends meet at the behest of overly rich brokers who could afford to throw a bit of money away on unlikely betting propositions.

But then one day, well after Thornton had left the Floor in November 1974, there was a Knicks basketball game against a visiting underdog team. Cliff actually liked the underdog who by Las Vegas odds was a 10-point underdog on a standard betting basis. Cliff twisted the betting proposition odds around as follows: He would take the underdog +40 points, but lay 50-1 odds to anyone willing to accept the Knicks -40. The size of the betting had now grown to the point where Cliff was looking to make $20,000 on his bet against the risk of losing $1,000,000 should the Knicks somehow really romp and win by more than 40 points. Most of the brokers knew that they would probably almost always lose giving away so many points, but the odds being offered seemed so attractive that for $10 or $20 dollars or even $100, they were willing to give the wildcard outcome a shot.

Gordon called Thornton at school.

"Do you remember Cliff, the Tube Man, Thorn? Well, he's offering us 50-1 odds that the Knicks won't win by more than 40 points tonight. We're putting together a syndicate to take him on. You want in?"

So while still just a teenager, Thornton became part of the syndicate against Cliff, the Tube Man. He risked $10 for the chance to make $500. He hardly knew much about basketball and whether a 40 point winning spread in basketball was ever seen or not. But he supposed that anything was possible.

That night in November 1974, the Knicks did indeed romp. Thornton opened up the newspaper the next day to see the Knicks having scored 142 points versus 98 for the opposing team—an almost magical score that just covered the -40 point spread. It hadn't been the first time Cliff had been hit, but at a million-dollar payout, this was by far the largest gambling loss that anyone had ever seen experienced on the NYSE Floor for a sports bet at the time.

There was just one problem: Cliff didn't show up for work that next morning. He went AWOL. Some feared that maybe he'd committed suicide. Others suggested that he had fled the city.

With hindsight, one must wonder what an educated group of brokers really should have expected betting in such a manner with a Tube Man who made $15,000 a year in salary.

Thornton never got his $500, and remembered feeling cheated by someone. If Cliff didn't pay off, but Gordon had egged Thornton into participating in the syndicate, shouldn't Gordon perhaps be on the hook to pay Thornton the missing winnings?

"Sorry, but that's not the way credit risk works," Gordon had explained to Thornton. "None of us got paid. We're not even sure Cliff is still alive. This is just not a bet that we'll ever likely collect on."

And so Thornton learned an early lesson in "tail risk" events and counterparty exposure. Subconsciously, this bet story likely lingered longer than he realized.

Could a guy's life really be ruined by the outcome of a Knicks basketball game?

On the Floor of the NYSE, in the late fall of 1974, the answer apparently was yes.

CHAPTER 9

THE REGULATOR
Washington, D.C.
April 1977

"Geez, this soybean market just won't give it up," Olsen McDermott thought to himself, eyes fixated on the afternoon close that was fast approaching $10 a bushel. A small frown came to his face, and the weathered lines around his eyes became more pronounced.

Market surveillance was his beat; market manipulations his nemesis.

Olsen had now slipped into being an old-timer at the agency— actually a holdover from the prior Commodity Exchange Authority (CEA) that had originally been part of the Department of Agriculture. When Congress had authorized the Commodity Futures Trading Commission (CFTC) in 1974, the new Commissioners of that organization had asked for his continued presence.

It was his actions during the 1963 soybean oil scandal that had come to make him well known among his colleagues.

Just a naïve young economist fresh out of Georgetown, he'd nailed smelling a rat on that one—not that his economics degree had helped, really. Indeed, little that he'd learned in college seemed important to futures. He still didn't really understand why markets did what they did sometimes. But what a situation '63 beans had been on which to cut his teeth.

In 1963, the owner of a large soybean oil storage facility, Anthony "Tino" DeAngelis, had found that he could easily borrow money from brokers by issuing them warehouse receipts on soybean oil he controlled in his Bayonne plant. He further discovered that the guarantor of those warehouse receipts, a subsidiary of the American Express Company, was inexperienced and unprofessional in their inspections of his warehouses, so that it was not difficult to get them to issue receipts on more oil than was actually there. Tanks could literally be filled with salt water and false chambers of oil attached below sampling hatches, and oil could be jitneyed from tank to tank through pipelines as inspections took place. In addition, American Express had maintained no signature cards on its inspectors, so DeAngelis could eventually forge receipts himself as he decided to spend more money.

Olsen had met DeAngelis at an industry event—the National Futures Authority annual conference.

With his curved nose and slicked back white hair above a round pudgy face, DeAngelis looked slimy to Olsen's eyes. But alas the CEA had stayed on the sidelines. If financiers wanted to accept warehouse receipts as collateral for loans, and they were not prudent enough to inspect the warehouse themselves nor smart enough to see that they were accepting papers for a truly astounding quantity of soybean oil (more, in fact than the government counted in its monthly reports of all the salad oil stocks in the country), then so be it. This was a credit market problem, not a futures problem, and while the CEA might have sounded some sort of alarm, activities in the cash market were only on the edge of its responsibilities.

But Olsen had also seen early on, and reputedly in anticipation of a large order of soybean oil from Spain, DeAngelis had begun to use some of his borrowed funds to buy heavily in the futures market and continued to buy even when the Spanish order fell through.

Olsen thought that this latter fact was particularly odd and disturbing. Olsen also didn't like the pattern of trading that he'd watched. By 1963, several different accounts that Olsen suspected were all linked behind the scenes to DeAngelis were buying in the market each day. And these buy orders would always come in shortly before the close—thereby minimizing any chance that prices would ever drop below the previous day's level and that DeAngelis could ever be called for variation margin.

Olsen had done the math and was fearful that on some days DeAngelis might have been as much as 90% of the market volume in New York, and maybe 50% in Chicago.

Soon DeAngelis was spreading rumors of a Russian crop failure and of being in Moscow to negotiate a giant soybean oil deal, and he was increasing his purchase of futures contracts at a frenzied pace, pushing futures prices well above cash market prices in the process.

Yet as Olsen had watched these events transpire, and even called over to the Produce Exchange on several occasions to express his growing concern that oddly manipulative trading patterns seemed to be in motion, he was somewhat amazed that no sanctions, no rule changes, and no formal investigations had begun.

Instead, The Produce Exchange's Board of Governors' observation was that DeAngelis's buying spree was bringing boom times to the century old exchange the likes of which it had not seen for some time. "It's good business, and we are delighted," the President of the Exchange had formally stated, and no action was taken against DeAngelis whatsoever in New York. In Chicago, officials were similarly unconcerned with the build-up of DeAngelis's position. After all, DeAngelis had continually assured the exchanges, the CEA, as well as his creditors, that he was buying futures as a hedge against export orders. It was all just related to his booming business—as simple as that.

In his heart, Olsen hadn't bought it. Instead, he'd literally tossed in his sleep at night as he tried to fathom what the hell DeAngelis might be doing.

The major regulatory snag of that era was that if DeAngelis was indeed trying to corner the soybean oil market, CEA officials still felt that they had no power to move against him except on an after-the-fact basis. "It is only against the law to succeed in a manipulation," agency officials pointed out to Olsen, and again and again the team concluded that thus far there was not enough evidence that DeAngelis had broken any such law—"at worst, he was only attempting to break it." Until DeAngelis actually cornered the soybean oil market or "otherwise damaged traders by demonstrating manipulative prices," no legal action could be taken against him.

"Let's just do a surprise audit of his books," Olsen had finally pressed one of the CEA Commissioners. "See what we find. We're entitled to do that much."

That decision did the trick. With CEA officials quite literally sitting in his office, DeAngelis did not dare continue his buying ways. The market had plummeted, variation margin calls could not be met, and several of the brokers that DeAngelis was using soon took tremendous losses on DeAngelis's position. One major firm, Ira Haupt & Co. even went bankrupt when it was discovered that all the warehouse receipts it was holding were actually worthless as collateral. American Express eventually lost over half of its market value. Such corruption, deceit, and speculative pyramiding had seldom been seen before.

Olsen received kudos at the agency for having doggedly pursued DeAngelis and pushed for that audit. His next job at the agency was to help the CEA to lobby the Congress to amend the Commodity Exchange Act in 1968 to give them more powers. They'd actually waited way too long to move on DeAngelis. They'd only popped the bubble once that bubble was already fully hatched.

After Olsen's successful lobbying efforts in 1968, persons deemed to be "manipulating or *attempting* to manipulate" a market price could receive cease and desist orders, or become subject to revised position limits, or eventually face felony prosecution by the CEA— prosecution that was punishable potentially by imprisonment. These rules got even tougher when the CFTC replaced the CEA in 1974.

Olsen had been pleased. He was one regulator doing his job the right way, and had advanced several job notches within the Agency for all his efforts.

But the changes weren't enough to avert another futures market disaster in the spring of 1976.

The unthinkable of unthinkable in the futures industry—a delivery default—occurred on the New York Mercantile Exchange when the May 1976 Maine Potato contract ended with 1,911 contracts still outstanding that called for delivery of far more potatoes than actually existed.

What had happened? For a while no one was quite sure, but with time the following story had emerged.

Starting in August 1975 the U.S. Department of Agriculture estimated that the upcoming November harvest of Maine Potatoes would be 1.05 million acres, down 8% from the year before. Some traders interpreted this as bullish news, but others saw it as being bearish since 1974 had been a record year. Large positions were taken on both sides of the market, and the May 1976 contract soon became particularly volatile since May represented the end of the storage period when any overall shortage would be most acutely felt.

Then, on April 13, 1976, the U.S.D.A issued a second key report saying that stocks of potatoes in storage "totaled 67.3 million hundredweight on April 1, 11% under the 75.9 million hundredweight stocked on April 1, 1975" (a hundredweight is 100 pounds). Traders went scurrying to place buy orders and prices on the May contract shot up from $10.70 for a hundred pounds before the announcement, to $11.20 the next day, and to $11.95 on the day after that. "This was the most bullish report in recent years" one Idaho potato grower stated, and seemingly everyone—including farmers who normally would be short contracts—wanted to be on the long side of the market as the anticipated shortage developed.

Well almost everyone. Two large Idaho potato producers and processors, J.R. Simplot and Pete Taggares, decided instead that the government report notwithstanding, there were still plenty of potatoes around—particularly since Simplot himself (who usually used close to one-half of the entire Maine crop to fabricate frozen French fries) was not running his plants at the same processing rate of previous years. On the weekend after the U.S.D.A. report, Simplot and a group of others decided (perhaps together—telephone conferences were alleged) to sell the market at any price on the following Monday.

At the same time, it was reported that Simplot engaged in the unusual tactic of sending "one or more" "roller cars" of unsold potatoes east in order to depress prices by offering potatoes for immediate sale in local markets.

On Monday April 18, May potatoes dropped $1 to $10.95, on Tuesday to $10.45, and on Wednesday the contract fell as low as $9.70 before closing at $10.12. Then, throughout April and early May, Simplot and Taggares reputedly added more short sales.

As the futures market moved towards the last delivery day for the May contract, Simplot and Taggares remained convinced that there were still plenty of potatoes around.

But then strange things started to happen up in Aroostook, Maine. When representatives for J.R. Simplot tried to buy cash potatoes from farmers in anticipation of making delivery on his futures contracts, many farmers simply refused to sell. "If you are representing Simplot," one farmer said, "then I want you to know that I have a standing order for 25 cents a pound better than you can come up with."

While the actual prices that Simplot offered farmers is not known (some farmers claiming that Simplot was "looking for Cadillacs at Chevy prices"), it is known that Simplot did at least have representatives in Maine and that they were able to purchase some potatoes "at prices that were more than fair" according to one broker. But the large majority of farmers (encouraged in part by rumors of potato export ships coming in) simply were not willing to sell, and since only Maine potatoes were deliverable on the futures contract at that time, Simplot could not look elsewhere in the U.S. where similar grade potatoes were readily available.

What was happening, at least in Simplot's mind, seemed quite simple: "The longs were trying to squeeze me...They were thinking that I'd buy out my contracts and run the price up to $15," and yet Simplot and Taggares were unwilling to do just that. As expiration approached, the May futures price was a full $2 above the cash price and seemingly Simplot and Taggares were unwilling to pay any more of a premium. A showdown had developed and a giant game of "chicken" could only result—the longs hoping to squeeze out the shorts, and the shorts hoping that the longs would run first. But instead, as the last trading day unfolded, one long tried to exacerbate the situation by increasing his position from 2,500 contracts to 4,000 contracts, as did several smaller traders to a lesser degree.

So in the end, Simplot and Taggares simply refused to budge. Prices gyrated a wild 26% on the last day as people tried to determine whether a squeeze existed or not, and when all the dust cleared, 1911 contracts had been left outstanding. Together, Simplot and Taggares were officially obligated to deliver over 95 million pounds of potatoes at a time when there were at most 48 million pounds available (provided of course that farmers were now willing to sell, which they still were not).

Default was inevitable and shock waves swept the industry. The exchange had simply waited and waited in hopes that the situation would work itself out and that everyone would make good on their obligations.

The CFTC had also done nothing. The potato market had not been Olsen's responsibility—although he had watched the developments there with fascination from afar.

Although the New York Mercantile Exchange eventually tried to satisfy all sides of the dispute by arbitrarily setting a monetary settlement price of $10.66 per hundred pounds (the last sale had been $8.70), lawsuits soon went flying and the CFTC eventually launched administrative proceedings against both sides involved, as well as the Exchange. In the end, Simplot and Taggares were both suspended for several years and the Exchange accepted a fine of $50,000 for failure to enforce its own rules regarding emergency action and liquidations of positions on the last day of trading.

Now, the clock had rolled forward yet another year. It was 1977, and this time it was soybeans that were in motion to the upside. Olsen *was* responsible for that market, and he was damned if the CFTC would get caught flat-footed once again.

"Jesus, just look at these Hunt positions," Olsen had pointed out to then CFTC Commissioner Robert Martin, "If you add up all of these different accounts that we believe are all related to the Hunts, I think they've accumulated contracts calling for delivery of about 24 million bushels of soybeans! That means that they've laid claim to more than a third of the soybeans that the U.S. was expected to have on hand by the end of August—just before the fall U.S. harvest. We've got to do something!"

Martin had initially been less sure. A former exchange official from Chicago, he just hated to intervene in markets. Yes, he'd seen the news that exports of soybeans to the U.S.S.R. and Europe were higher than expected, and that crop yields were on the soft side. Yes, he'd heard the rumors of a potential 5% tax to be levied on soybean exports by Brazil in order to conserve beans for its own use. Maybe the Hunts were just astute investors helping the market reach an equilibrium clearing price faster than might otherwise have been the case.

He'd also talked to his contacts at Cook Industries—a major grain merchant at the time where he'd actually worked for a few years—and they were convinced that the Brazilian harvest was going to be exceptionally large. Martin knew that Cook had recently been doubling its short exposure to the bean market.

"Olsen, I think you have this one wrong. Just look at what Cook is doing. They're so sure beans are going down that they are selling more front month contracts—May and July 1977 contracts—while simultaneously buying more distant months—November 1977 contracts. The Hunts may soon get it between their eyeballs."

So even knowledgeable that the Hunts had a humongous long bet, Martin had sent Olsen packing.

"These things have a way to work themselves way out. Let's let these guys duke it out. Ned Cook and his gang are pretty smart campers. I know them damn well, and I'd rather believe they'll win this thing, and that these boys down in Texas are going to get shellacked."

But the harvest that Cook Industries was depending upon proved disappointing, and earlier rumors of a 5% Brazilian export tax actually proved true. Near term supplies of soybeans in the U.S. dwindled, and the near term futures price shot up to more than $10.50 a bushel while the more distant prices scarcely moved at all due to the expectation of a large U.S. harvest in November.

"Ah shit," Martin said to himself one morning as he looked through a fat sheaf of papers showing margin calls, "The wrong guys are winning this thing. Here we go again."

"Get Olsen in here," he had tapped on his intercom to his secretary.

Together they made a phone call to Martin's former colleagues at Cook. Just how bad was this thing? Could Cook come up with the margin required?

"You've gotta do something Bob," Ned Cook had pleaded. "OK, we got some of the fundamentals wrong, but this market is still being manipulated. These Hunt guys are nuts—they're running us over. A few more up days in the bean complex, and we may not make it. We've exhausted our lines of credit to keep meeting these damn margin calls."

At the end of the call, Martin and Olsen had stared at each other for a minute, both contemplating next steps.

"Leak it," Martin had said finally, flipping his sheaf toward Olsen, but reaching only the edge of his desk.

"Leak what?" Olsen asked naively.

"Leak that the CFTC is not happy with the size of these Hunt longs."

"But boss, wouldn't that be taking sides? I'm as worried as you are about these Hunt Brothers, but shouldn't we just privately land on them first?"

"Ah, we're going to land on them alright..." Martin replied. "But I don't think we have the time in the market for that now. I want the world to know that we're displeased. The market needs to know that fast. Just put out a press release that the CFTC believes that the Hunt brothers are trading in tandem, and on a combined account basis, have broken position limit rules. The market should take care of the rest."

Olsen was less sure that "regulation by news release" was the way to go, but he prepared the press release anyway, and showed it to Martin.

"Not tough enough," Martin shot back. "I want you to detail what we believe is their combined position sizes in there. Tell the market exactly what we know."

"Detail their position sizes? Isn't that really going too far?"

"Fuck em..." Martin retorted. "I'm tired of this type of shit. We're not going to have another Maine Potatoes default. I want to cut these assholes off at the knees."

The press release hit the wires shortly after the close of April 27, 1977. In thin post market over-the-counter trading the price of beans finally started to fall.

Herbert Hunt down in Dallas was furious. "Draft me up our own press release!" he had shouted at his secretary. He had made a few attempts at the exact words that he wanted to use before penning: "If upon investigation I find that the price of soybean futures have been, are now, or become artificial due to the action of the Commission, its members or personnel, I will charge the CFTC with manipulation."

But the Hunt retort was not enough. The price of beans went limit down the next morning, market participants assuming that the Hunts would be forced now to sell by regulatory authorities. If a squeeze had been in motion, it quickly fell further apart over the subsequent days. The Hunts sheepishly started selling.

Martin sat at his desk that morning with a small smile.

"Serves those Texas fuckwads just right..." he thought.

"If the Hunts had stood for delivery of their longs, it would have meant bringing almost all of the soybeans in the country to Chicago for delivery which would have been ridiculous," Martin said to Olsen over a celebratory cup of coffee. "Crushers would have had to pay God knows what for beans to run their soybean oil plants. It would have been crazy."

Had the Hunts been trading in concert? Was it fair to aggregate their accounts? Olsen wasn't so sure. But Martin didn't really care, and instructed Olsen to push forward to get a court-ordered injunction barring the Hunts from exceeding the speculative limit in soybean trading on an aggregate basis.

Round one had gone to the CFTC. The Hunt 1977 squeeze of soybeans had been broken.

But little did Olsen know that the Hunts would be back like a bad weed—bigger and tougher—two years hence.

CHAPTER 10

THE COIN DEALER
Princeton, NJ
Summer 1977

Marty had no idea how to get to Wall Street from Newfoundland. He was after all just a kid from South Jersey—a kid good at computers to be sure, and in love with history, but with no real connections in the world of finance. Shit, he didn't even have a college degree— just two years at the Sarnoff Institute for Computer Studies. How was he supposed to get to Wall Street with courses on his resume like Vacuum Tube Tech?

Upon quitting his job at the Department of Defense, the closest thing to finance that he could seemingly manage was to work in a coin store in downtown Princeton, New Jersey. It was his Uncle's shop. He'd worked there before during the summers while in high school.

It wasn't perfect—going back to this same old job behind the counter—but at least it was closer to his passion than incoming guided missile interception.

Coins had been in his life since boyhood. He'd had allergies as a child, seldom let outside. Stamps and coins had been something he found himself naturally attracted to. His dad had served in the military—under General Patton; it was a tight run ship at home in Maple Shade, New Jersey. Marty was always on a short leash about what he could and couldn't do. That's one of the reasons that he'd let himself get pushed towards the Defense Department.

He'd always wanted to be somebody, so initially he'd bragged to the kids in the neighborhood about his coins and stamps. Most just looked at him as an awkward little geek—a social twat.

"Go run home to your little coin collection, Marty-baby," they had taunted.

He had reverted to doing just that. The kids had laughed less when a local South Jersey paper ran a story in 1965 about Marty and his bags of rare Canadian pennies that turned out to be momentarily far rarer than even Marty had believed possible. A roll of 50 of these pennies vaulted to $1000 for a moment in one coin dealer reference guide. Marty literally had thousands of these coins in stuffed sacks. He had so many of these special Canadian pennies that he had made a beanbag chair, which he sat in like King Midas. Technically, he'd become a millionaire as a kid for a heartbeat. The price, though, had been a momentary blip—a customer mistake, or more likely a dealer-inspired rip-off of some neophyte collector. By the time he unloaded some of his collection, a roll of 50 pennies had fallen back to just $10. Still, it hadn't been a bad score.

The whole experience had taught him something about markets—and their fickle vulnerability. Worse yet, when he had cashed out some of his pennies, his father had encouraged him to invest in something reputedly far safer—an equity mutual fund. When he did so, Marty effectively caught the top tick in 1969 bull market. The following several years would only see his mutual fund investment dwindle in value. What was supposed to be "safe" turned into anything but safe. No, his coins were better—more reliable—something you could touch—something that exuded history which Marty could love and cherish.

As the hot June morning spread its warmth over Princeton's Nassau Street, Marty opened the street shop doors and prepared himself for another long day behind the counter. There really wasn't much demand for a coin dealer in downtown Princeton—just a few collectors, an old lady or two, and an occasional enigmatic bag-man who arrived and paid cash for his coins. Where this guy got the money, Marty had no idea.

"So, Marty, how's the spot price of gold today?" his balding uncle asked from the back room.

"Up a bit as usual," responded Marty. "Just a matter of days now until this thing takes out $150."

Gold had started the year down at $130, but had steadily moved higher throughout 1977. Marty was loving it. As measured from its August 15, 1971 de-pegging by Nixon, Marty expected some sort of crescendo in gold into the early 1980 first quarter. That was exactly 8.6-years.

He'd already concluded 8.6-year rhythms were everywhere, and after reading Russian economist Nikolai Dmytriyevich's Kondratieff's "Long Waves in Economic Life," Marty had also come to hypothesize that these cycles clustered in groups of six that added up to 51.6-year bigger cycles...booms in private free enterprise, followed by a reversion to more government-sponsored economic control. Kondratieff himself espoused 50-60 year cycles, and 51.6 years specifically seemed to Marty to fit history so nicely.

51.6 years separated such phenomena as 1869's Black Friday and the commodity panic of 1920, as well as the Second and Third Punic Wars. Nice! 51.6 years separated the first and second crusades. Nice again!

It was all like AC current. With direct current—as with that from a battery—electricity cannot travel very far due to the resistance of the wires that reduces the power of the current. But if you add cycles to electricity to create alternating current—bingo—the alternating cycle extends the life and the longevity of the power across both time and distance.

And Marty believed that cycles were not static or in equilibrium. They were dynamic and expanding—just like the pace of commerce and society—just like the world of physics.

When Marty considered the "phase transition" period where water moves from hot to suddenly boiling, or when a piece of paper moved from being just singed by a flame to suddenly burning, he was reminded of the way markets—at the end of moves—often entered a phase of exponential "chaos" until a sudden and swift moment of entropy would occur.

If Newton's Second Law of Thermodynamics held in the physical world, maybe he could apply it to the financial world as well? Could he identify not only key time periods where he might expect market reversals, but also key price levels where a market might turn entropic?

He mulled it over. His computer skills still might become handy. Could he program all this stuff?

"Marty, Marty…" It was his uncle calling at him again, with some urgency. "You day-dreaming or something, Marty?"

Marty looked down at his hands. He was supposed to be polishing up some small Johnson Matthey 10-ounce silver bars that they kept in the window for display. The bars had slowly tarnished in the sun. But the silver polish bottle had toppled as Marty had been pondering larger entropic thoughts, and liquid was now dripping all over the counter, slowly moving toward the display's edge.

"Shit," Marty offered. "Sorry Unc. I hate it when I have to clean this stuff up."

"Marty—you need to get your head out of the clouds, and your nose out of all those books. Forget all this 8.6-year stuff. We got a business to run here."

But while Marty cleaned up the counter, he didn't listen to his Uncle's larger advice. Instead, he drifted back off into thoughts about numbers and odd historical relationships.

While he believed that 51.6-year cycles were important and valid, 72-year cycles also seemed to have popped up in his work as well.

"Why 72?" he had wondered.

He knew that the numbers 72, 22, and 7 were all numbers held in great reverence by the Druids and other ancient cultures. 72 in particular appeared everywhere in Druid traditions. There are 72 letter-strokes required to write out the 22 characters of the ancient "Ogham" alphabet that Druid priests used for secret communications, and that alphabet contained 22 letters and 7 vowels—the ratio of which 22/7 =3.1428 is a pi approximation.

"Holy shit," thought Marty that morning. "8.6 years—my average period between economic financial panics—is actually 3,141 days—the mathematical constant pi!"

He continued his research. Author Graham Hancock was next. He kept Hancock's book in a drawer at the shop, and contemplated it periodically.

Within Hancock's writings, he found that many of the great pyramids of Mexico include designs using 72 pieces of jade, and 72 is also "hard wired" into the design of Egypt's Great Pyramid, since its original height of 5,813.23 pyramid inches (a pyramid inch being 1.0011 x a modern day inch per Sir Isaac Newton) * 72 * 12 (12 being the number of signs of the Zodiac) * 50 (72 minus 22) is extremely close to the Earth's polar radius as measured in pyramid inches.

And if in modern days we know that the circumference of any circle or sphere (in this case let's say the Earth) is 2 * pi * R, where in the Giza Pyramid had the ancient builders potentially shown us pi?

Peeking down at this favorite book as he mopped the counter-top, Marty considered this: The original height of the Pyramid's apex is 5,812.98 pyramid inches, and each side of the pyramid is 9,131 pyramid inches from corner to corner (in a straight line). If the circumference of the Pyramid (4 x 9,131 = 36,524) is divided by twice its height (5813.23 * 2 = 11,626.46), the result is 3.14159, which just happens to be pi. Incredibly, this calculation was accurate to six digits.

"So the Pyramid in many ways takes a square and turns it into a circle, showing mankind over the centuries an actual formula to calculate the circumference of the Earth," Marty thought to himself.

He grabbed a calculator at this point.

The final formula became the height of the pyramid (5,813.23 pyramid inches) * 72 *12* 50 (to bring it up to scale) * 2 * pi = 1,577,904,644 pyramid inches which when brought back to modern day measurements by dividing by 1.0011 PI/inch and turning inches into miles (by dividing by 12 in/ft and dividing again by 5280 ft/mi) = 24,876 miles.

Bingo. The earth's circumference, or at least very close—depending upon whether one measured from pole to pole or around the slightly fatter equator.

Per Hancock, other numbers existed within the Giza Pyramid as well related to the Sun and time. Each of the Pyramids four sides, when measured as a straight line, measures 9,131 pyramid inches, for a total of 36,524 pyramid inches. At first glance, this number was not that significant. But move the decimal point over by dividing by 100 and you get 365.24. Modern science has shown us that the exact length of the solar year is 365.24 days. The length of the antechamber (116.26471 pyramid inches) leading to the King's Chamber within the Great Pyramid multiplied by pi also happens to equal 365.25. Were the pyramid builders also showing us by the use of different scales that they knew of the base-10 mathematical system as well?

Marty thought the ancients' use of the base-10 system was even more probable when one considered that the height of the pyramid times 10 raised to the 9th power happens to equal the mean number of pyramid inches between the Earth and the Sun, while the length of the Jubilee passage within the pyramid times that magic number 7 times 10 raised to the 7th power equals the mean distance to the moon in pyramid inches.

Marty thought that there were too many coincidences here not to view the Pyramid of Giza as a mathematical treasure chest from history of some sort—a gift from the heavens perhaps—something left over from some ancient—potentially alien—civilization.

Marty also considered that the number 72 might stem from the cosmological concept of "precession"—alternatively known as the wobble of the earth on its axis. This wobble ever so slowly changes the point where the sun appears each day in relation to the 12 constellations of the Zodiac. The wobble specifically causes a minute one-degree shift every 72 years. In ancient times, there was of course much focus on where the sun was on the two annual equinoxes and two annual solstices that demarcate the shift in seasons. The ever so slow precessional slippage meant that each constellation on the horizon houses the sun at each solstice/equinox point for 2,160 years (360 degrees/12 zodiac signs = 30 x 72 years = 2,160 years), and all twelve of the constellations move past the four key solstices/equinoxes in a total of 25,920 years (360x 72)...yes, a number coincidentally ever so close to the circumference of the earth in miles.

Marty knew from his studies of history that the early Sumerian people believed in an "As Above, So Below"—type philosophy. This all fit.

Pi was everywhere—imbedded in our history, our monuments, and our markets.

Marty knew that it was time to do some computer modeling.

CHAPTER 11

HUNT SILVER—GETTING THE BUG
Princeton, NJ
September 1977

It had been a beautiful September day in 1977 when Thornton had been dropped off at 432 Joline Hall which formed the northwestern corner of Princeton's main residential Blair Courtyard quadrangle. His room was on the third and top floor, and had vertical wrought iron leaded Gothic windows poking out amidst wisteria bushes that climbed the side of the building.

The two-room triple looked more like it should have been a double, or maybe—in some bygone era—even a single with a living room. But clearly over time, the room had had extra beds squeezed into it in order to accommodate a burgeoning Princeton student population. The only bathroom and showers were all the way down in the basement. It was not exactly luxury living—more like the feeling of boot-camp.

Thornton had been the first of the eventual three roommates to arrive at the dumpy and very tight space, and surveyed the situation carefully. Could three beds be squeezed in the back room, and the front larger room be used as a living area, he wondered? No, the back room had at most enough space for one set of beds bunked on top of each other. It was going to have to be some combo of two beds in the back room and one-bed in the front room, or visa-versa.

He stared out the sun-filled windows at the courtyard below. Geekily walking along one sidewalk was a boy with his pants pulled up high, a calculator attached to his belt, and heavy glasses a bit askew on what appeared to be a zit-laden face. He lugged just one small suitcase by his side.

"Wow. I hope everyone isn't that nerdly at Princeton," Thornton thought to himself. "Pity the poor guy who has that guy as his roommate."

Seconds later—as things would turn out, of course—this same fellow entered the fourth entryway doorway of Joline, and Thornton had heard clumping steps coming up the stairs. "Oh shit..." his heart pounded, "This guy wasn't my roommate was he?"

In walked Jim. Jim was a 16-year old twig of a guy who hailed from Bayonne, NJ. He was awkward and spoke with that same heavy singsong Bayonne accent that Thornton had heard from that Vistafjord dining room table with Myrtle and Fred. It sounded as though Jim had lived with a bunch of old ladies for his entire life—his voice screeching up and down in a high-pitched undulation.

"Hello, my name is Jim. I have allergies," was his first greeting to Thornton. "Do you mind if I spray the entire room with Lysol? I need to kill the germs and get rid of the dust mites."

Thornton's early trading instincts hit him front and center. While it may not be entirely fair to judge someone so quickly, this guy certainly seemed like a loser. He could only hope that the second roommate would be better.

"Jim, I'm going to make an executive decision. I think you should take the back room all to yourself," Thornton offered.

"Oh really, wow, that's just wonderful," Jim beamed with a toothy awkward smile.

"You can spray Lysol to your heart's content back there. I'm sure that the other two of us will be just fine out here."

A few hours later, there was another clomping of footsteps to the top floor of Joline's fourth entryway.

"Hi, I'm Adam," a slightly crumpled but friendly looking guy greeted Thornton. He had a genuine smile, but certainly also appeared quietly intellectual. His brown hair was unbrushed. After a bit of small talk, the first major query he made of Thorn and Jim was: "So, do you mind if I hook up the phone to a modem once in a while?"

Now, this was 1977. Computers in general were still in their infancy—mostly big bulky machines located in formal computer centers—behemoth devices that could only be fed code on computer punch cards. Personal computers were certainly still the domain of hobbyists who read *Popular Mechanics*.

"Using the phone for a modem if fine with me," Thornton offered, trying to seem cool and non-plussed. "Are you a big computer gee...

techy guy, or something?" He'd almost used the word geek, but had avoided such at the last second.

"No, not really, I just do some work for a small company based down in Albuquerque. I need to dial in once in awhile."

"What's the name of the company?" Thornton asked.

"You would have never heard of it," Adam responded. "It's called Microsoft. We write software."

And so it was that during Thornton's freshman year at Princeton he shared a two-room triple with a sad little guy from Bayonne who called his mother every evening and recited that day's dinner menu to her, and one of the original founders of Microsoft. The Lakeside School in Seattle had been the seed institution for the Microsoft gang. Something about their program had spurred Bill Gates and others— like Thornton's roommate Adam, who was two-years younger than Gates—to be innovative and highly computer-literate.

As Adam explained it to Thornton, "Seattle had this growing traffic problem on the I-5. We thought that if you could measure traffic flow at different times of day, this might somehow help solve the problem. So for a school project, we invented those little rubber strips placed across highways that we hooked to an early computer box to count the number of times tires crossed. Once our invention actually worked, we thought we could make some money out of it. This was how we got started. But we moved on from there. Currently, I'm working on writing operating code for a new Canadian computer company called Commodore International."

"Commodore's new computer is well ahead of anyone else," said Adam. "I think you should buy the stock."

As Thornton later looked back on his discussions with Adam about Commodore, this was probably the closest that he would ever come to super-plugged-in quasi-insider information.

Thornton went to the Library and found a little S&P Stock Guide. He flipped to the "C" pages, and looked at this little computer company called Commodore. Across the summer of 1977, it had traded in single digits around $6-$7 a share, but over the month of September 1977, the stock had spiked almost exponentially to around $19 a share. It was then that the Toronto Stock Exchange had halted trading in the stock—"pending investigation for unusual trading patterns."

Thorn was intrigued. Commodore remained suspended on the TSE for multiple days. Adam and Thornton kept searching for the reason why in the financial pages of both U.S. and Canadian newspapers that they found in the library, but scant information was really available in that pre-Internet era. When Commodore eventually reopened, it started trading at around 13, down some -31.5%. There had been no formal news, but Thornton turned to Adam and said: "Something must be wrong; they've broken the back of this thing."

Adam mumbled something like "Maybe," but then dialed his own stockbroker and bought more shares.

Those shares he bought of Commodore went from 13 back to 19 pretty quickly, then to 29, 39, 49, 59, and then 99 within a few months. After that, Commodore split a few times, but even post-splits, ended up trading above 100 for several years. By 1982, the new Commodore 64 Personal Computer became wildly popular and acknowledged leader in the PC space. Commodore eventually fell from grace and went bankrupt in 1994, but not before Thornton's roommate Adam had made a killing on it. Adam later returned to Microsoft after graduating from Princeton, and became a billionaire. He bought a professional baseball team.

While Thornton had missed being involved in Commodore—and certainly kicked himself a bit as it vaulted higher—he did not feel like he had any particular "edge" in the tech world, other than a complete reliance on Adam for advice. He certainly wasn't as confident in tech investing as he had been in a Gil Peters "pattern match" horse set-up.

So what did attract Thorn as a first major investment?

Thornton's grandfather had passed away in 1971, and when Thornton turned 18 in 1976, Thorn discovered that an inheritance existed in his name. His grandfather had bequeathed $100,000 to each grandchild, or at least that is what had been there initially. Sadly, just as Marty had learned with his first unsuccessful foray into mutual funds, the stock market had gone down in the early 1970's. By the time Thornton was coming of age, he learned that his Uncle Bruce—as custodian of the account—had nursed the account down to a $68,000 marked-to-market ongoing value.

Crap!

To Thorn's eye, his account seemed to consist of a bunch of boring investments. Baldwin Piano was one holding. It would eventually go bankrupt. Defense contractor Fluor Corp was another. It would do better later on. But at that point in the late 1970's, these stocks had done nothing for years.

Thornton had just read Ira Cobleigh's book *Happiness is a Stock that Doubles in a Year*, and thought that he could easily do better than this mass of sludge that his uncle had created. So in the fall of 1977, he asked his uncle if he would please transfer the shares to Thornton's own brokerage account that Thorn had by that time set up to invest his past football, backgammon, and horse racing winnings. Once transferred, Thorn promptly started selling these inherited stocks one by one.

But where to invest the money?

Somehow, Thornton also was cognizant at the time that inflation was becoming an issue that was difficult to address and eradicate. Richard Nixon had taken the U.S. off the gold standard back on August 15, 1971, and while Thornton had not been particularly focused on this event, he had grown-up against a backdrop of angst and turmoil in the Watergate era where all politicians were to be distrusted. By 1977, Gerald Ford had been President for three years, and the best he could come up with to address an increasingly imbalanced economy with burgeoning signs of inflation was a campaign slogan "Whip Inflation Now" (or "WIN"). Thornton thought Ford's anti-inflation campaign was silly and destined to failure.

Silver—then at the ripe price of around $5.50—and continuing to tick higher, seemed like a better investment proposition to Thornton than equities. But since Thorn had no experience trading metals themselves, and already had an equity—not futures—account, he determined that investing in silver mining equities as a proxy for silver itself would likely be a good idea.

He started to do research. Thorn's roommate Adam informed him that there was this book called *Value Line* with one-page summary financial sheets on thousands of companies, and that you could review the latest copy of this book in the front lobby of most brokerage offices—even if you didn't have an account with the given firm.

So Thorn trekked across Nassau Street to a local Montgomery Securities office, and, sure enough, Adam was right. The discovery of *Value Line* sitting in that Montgomery Securities office lobby was like found wealth—a free new research tool at Thornton's fingertips.

And Thornton loved the fact that everything was scored: stocks with high prospects that appeared to be attractive investments were listed as 1's or 2's; ok companies with some issues came in typically as 3's; and stocks you probably wanted to avoid received marks of 4's or 5's.

"Why would one ever want to bother with one of those?" Thornton pondered with some naiveté.

Spreading out his papers and notepads on a long wooden bench in that brokerage office's modest lobby, Thornton started to pour over *Value Line* during much of his spare time. The brokers in the Montgomery Securities office came to know and also ignore the wiry kid sitting in their reception area. Courtesy of having previously looked up Commodore at Adam's recommendation, Thorn also started using another small *S&P Guide to Listed Stocks* within Princeton's Firestone Library. This latter book was a smaller horizontally laid-out soft-backed pamphlet that was updated monthly; with stocks listed alphabetically—without any commentary—simply with last traded price, average daily volume, price-earnings ratio, dividend, and historic and projected earnings out a few years. Thornton had no idea what he was exactly looking for, but he figured that historic and projected earnings growth was a good thing. He started filtering through his limited stock research resources looking specifically for smaller capitalization silver miners that fit such a pattern.

As opposed to tech investing, when it came to the world of precious metals, Thornton somehow felt different: more plugged in on a macro basis, and generally more sure of himself. He started buying a bunch of smallish silver and gold stocks—names like Pan American Silver, Silver Standard, Aurico Gold, TVX Gold, and Kinross Gold.

As 1977 slowly slipped into 1978 and on into early 1979, he didn't pay a tremendous amount of attention to his new precious-metals-oriented portfolio. Instead, he became busy with schoolwork, and became burdened with the constant pressures of his declared major: international affairs.

Periodically, he would check his brokerage statements, and the value of the portfolio seemed to be steadily crawling northward. Thornton was particularly excited when the portfolio value re-achieved the $100,000 original starting value that his grandfather had first bequeathed to him back in 1971.

But in late 1979, the portfolio seemed to take on a life of its own, as did the price of gold and silver.

Thornton had subscribed to the *New York Times*, and typically opened to the business section first over breakfast each morning.

Silver one day was up to $26, then $28, then $32, and then a few weeks later $37. In early 1980, there was something like 13 consecutive days when it traded limit up. By this point, Thornton had transferred his brokerage account to use Adam's Seattle-based broker, and one wintry day in January 1980 this fellow called Thornton to say, "Congratulations, you really nailed this thing. Your portfolio is now worth $250,000. Do you want to take any profits?"

Thornton might have done so had he any great idea for another place to put his money, but busy with school-work, he had no such ideas about a better area or general investment theme. He thanked his broker for the call, and went back to his heavy load of other work.

When the phone rang again in late March 1980, Thornton's broker had had a more frantic tone.

"Thorn, I just thought that you should know that silver just collapsed all the way back to $13; the Hunt Brothers are wiped out; some brokerage firms are in trouble; and your portfolio value has been cut...well, roughly in half."

"Cut in half?" Thornton exclaimed.

"Well, almost. You're still ahead from where I think you started, but as of today, your portfolio's liquidation value is back to around $125k, maybe $130k at most," he said.

Somewhat shaken, Thornton still decided to do nothing. If he had decided not to sell any of his stocks when silver had been up in the high $30's to low $40's per ounce, he certainly wasn't going to dump his portfolio with silver now down to $13 (although he did subsequently lighten his silver stock exposure when silver bounced to around $19 a few months later).

But on that initial March 1980 day, Thornton just thanked his broker, and hung up the phone. Intellectually, he was intrigued about what exactly had just transpired. How could silver have gone from $10 to $40 and then back to $13 in such a short period of time? What had happened to change market psychology so quickly and so dramatically?

60 miles away, a man named Dr. Jacowski held that answer.

CHAPTER 12

THE ARB, TAKE 2
Broad Street, New York, NY
January 1980

The phone rang.

"Jacowski here."

"Hey, it's Edmund over at the Safri Bank"

"Let me guess. You need more money; you want us to ship over more margin?"

"Seems that way Henry, I'm so sorry. You gotta get us another $13 mm by tomorrow's opening. Otherwise, I technically will be forced to start closing you out."

"But that's ridiculous," Jacowski protested. "You know I have the physical stuff on the other side. And I'm on the fuckin' Board of the COMEX. The COMEX knows we got all those shorts covered with physical metal."

"Can you deliver those bags of silver against the COMEX?" Safri retorted. "Nope. You can't," he said, answering his own question.

"You know the rules, Henry. Even if we consider you hedged, the exchange still needs to protect its integrity and collect margin on your short futures. I'm sorry about that. Is there any way you can collapse any portion of this trade?"

The vault cash game that Dr. Jacowski put together back in the early 1970's had hummed along so nicely for multiple years. It was now blowing up.

The infuriating thing was that business in general was so good. Precious metals had been climbing steadily higher across all of 1979, and Monroe's over-the-counter options business was on fire. Indeed, he was in a quasi-monopolistic position after the 1978 CFTC Reauthorization Act had grandfathered his OTC options business as one of the few around. All that he had to do was to demonstrate to the CFTC that Monroe was segregating customer funds and marking customer positions to market. It had been worth paying that government lawyer to work the grandfather clause into the legislation. A little payola never hurt.

And specs now abounded. He had recently introduced a $1000 strike on gold that was quoted $125 bid at $155 offered—what a glorious spread for any arb to salivate over!

But those long physical bags of silver coins and calls on these bags versus short futures—while conceptually all just long and short silver—net flat on a total silver content basis—was long and short *different* deliverable forms. Jacowski wasn't allowed to take his bags of coins and deliver them to offset his short futures. He needed to deliver 5000 ounce silver bars to settle each short COMEX contract. And fuck it, the Hunts owned most of the COMEX warehouse receipts for these type of bars already.

What were the Hunts doing in this market? He'd never seen anything like it. Each afternoon, the mere arrival of their Prudential broker on the floor—Norton Waltuch—would send the fuckin' metal limit bid. And then there were all these towel-head sheiks floating around in the market as well.

Jacowski cursed himself for not seeing how this would all pan out. The very size of the Hunts' initial position—some 10,000 contracts purchased in 1974 which called for delivery on over fifty million ounces of silver—indicated that the Hunts were not and could never have been your average investors, and their subsequent actions since then indicated that they really did not want to be.

For one thing, by even taking such a large position in 1974, the Hunts almost created a squeeze right then and there, and failed to do so only when the Bank of Mexico decided to sell all of its silver stocks shortly after the time that the Hunts were initially buying.

Then, instead of moving their positions into distant delivery months, the Hunts had continuously maintained their large futures position in near-month contracts over the next year-and-a-half, and by doing so continued to exert a certain amount of pressure on the market to come up with deliverable supplies if in fact delivery was ever demanded. Then, in the summer of 1976, the Hunts actually stood for delivery of substantial quantities of silver while at the same time re-establishing once again new positions in near- month contracts, and although no squeeze had transpired (since the Treasury was still selling the last of its $2 billion worth of silver), prices had jumped by over 18% from $4.40 an ounce to almost $5.20.

Yes, the Hunts were "investing," but they were doing so to such a degree and in such a manner that they could not help but have a visible market impact, and starting in 1975 and then again and again into early 1979, they had worked to increase this impact by recruiting certain foreign investors into the marketplace as well.

At first, this only had meant reprinting an extremely bullish report on silver in *"Myers' Finance and Energy Report,"* and having this report translated into Arabic and sent to over fifty wealthy investors—mostly in Saudi Arabia. But then there was that trip to the Middle East in 1975 to see the Shah of Iran's brother and the Iranian Finance Minister in an effort to talk them into buying silver. It had meant getting former Hunt lawyer John Connally to set up an interview in 1978 with Sheikh Khaled Bin Mahfouz to convince him to participate in silver; and then eventually it had meant forming a Bermuda-based holding company—International Minerals Investment Corporation (IMIC)—in 1979 with two wealthy Saudis as a joint venture designed to purchase of silver.

How had Jacowski missed seeing all these things until just recently? Had he been asleep at the wheel—perhaps sipping a rum punch on his private Virgin Island beach? He couldn't remember. These guys clearly wanted to squeeze this fuckin' thing, and now Jacowski himself was the unintended squeezee. The Hunts alone—not even counting the holdings of his Arab compatriots—already owned over 100 million ounces of spot silver, and had futures contracts to buy at least another 120 million ounces. The total available supply of silver was only around 600 million, and of that, less than 200 million ounces were in COMEX deliverable .999 pure 5000-ounce bar form.

The Hunts could actually get away with this squeeze in the short-term if they really stood for delivery come March 1980.

Could Jacowski send his bags to a refiner and get them all melted down and recast in 5000-ounce bars? He knew that it wasn't legal to melt U.S. tender officially, and even if he did so on the sly, there wasn't enough refining capacity to get it done in time. The all-important March 1980 futures delivery month was a scant seven weeks away. Engelhard in New Jersey had recently told him that with all the candelabras and jewelry getting dumped on the market, they were already working at capacity with a three-month backlog. Shiiit!

There had been one moment of hope when all of these problems seemed like they might be going away. Jacowski thought back to early July 1979 when the Hunts had broken their pattern and not rolled their August and September futures positions out to October and December as they normally had previously. They'd pushed them out instead to the CBOT February 1980 contracts and COMEX March 1980 contracts.

At the time, he couldn't figure out what they were doing. Why the change in pattern? They almost always kept their longs in the nearby contracts.

But then it had dawned on him, particularly after the Hunts had bought even more March 1980 silver contracts and sold the March 1981 contracts one-year forward. This was all the big kahuna concentration of positions into March 1980—and the trades were all being done for that maturity partly for tax reasons. If the Hunts had rolled to December and then rolled again, making a profit on those Dec futures, that would have been an extra tax bite in 1979. Who wanted to do that?

Alternatively, if starting in July through August 1979, they bought March 1980 futures, and could hold these contracts for longer than six months into late February 1980, that would generate a long-term gain under the then-current tax rules. Similarly, if they could buy the March 1980 silver contracts and sell the March 1981 silver contracts and hold that spread for six months across an anticipated time when silver price would rise, then the March 1980 longs would generate long-term gains after the six-month window, but the March 1981 short would always generate a short-term loss. Back in that era, all futures shorts always were deemed short-term no matter how long they were held.

On a cost of carry basis, "selling" this silver spread (buying nearby and selling distant futures) made no sense in a rising silver environment where normally that spread would increase with the underlying price of silver. But from a tax point of view and purposeful congestion point of view, the strategy made perfect sense.

"Fuck! I am so fucked!" Jacowski screamed inside his brain, while quietly trying to keep his outward composure with his colleagues.

"Get me that Olsen guy at the CFTC," Jacowski barked to his secretary.

The secretary dialed, a bit unnerved at the state of his normally calm and otherwise brilliant boss. "Was their firm in trouble?"

"On line 2, Henry" she chirped.

"Olsen—you're the only guy at the CFTC with a brain, so listen up. I'm going to call an emergency meeting of the COMEX Board for tomorrow morning. These Hunts are fuckin' too much with this market. It's got to stop."

"I certainly have my concerns Dr. Jacowski. I'm glad you're moving into action. But we're still seven weeks from delivery. What makes you feel that this situation is so much worse this week than it was last week?"

Dr. Jacowski thought for a second. The true answer was that his variation margin calls on his short futures were jeopardizing his firm's very survivability. This was not the politically correct answer however.

"Because the last $5 price pop has been on no volume. Everyone is scared shitless to touch this market. The market's depth is being destroyed. Legitimate hedgers are being hurt."

The last bit was as close to the truth as he could voice.

"I understand," said Olsen. "I've dealt with these Hunt guys before in beans back in '77. They certainly have some nasty investing habits."

"I'm going to propose that we establish tapered spec position limits into the March expiry. We need these guys to wind down their longs. There is no way that they should be allowed to stand for delivery."

"Would you apply those position limits to the short hedgers as well?"

"No, just the spec longs. If someone can demonstrate that they are using futures as a legitimate hedge to a physical position, they can stay in."

Jacowski was now talking his own book, feeling the waters with the CFTC as to their potential reaction.

"That feels a bit two-faced. Shouldn't both sides be put on the same footing?"

"Look, it is the Hunt Brothers creating this whole problem. I don't see any reason to screw up the activities of legitimate hedgers more than those guys have already gotten screwed."

"OK, I understand," said Olsen. "I'll bump your idea off of the Commissioners in our next market oversight meeting, and inform them of your proposed course. Let us know if the COMEX board approves your plan. If we have any issue with this, I'll call you back."

"Thanks Olsen. We'll fix this thing."

"Fix" was an unfortunate word. Jacowski immediately regretted using it. But it was perhaps the most appropriate verb usage.

Dr. Jacowski was not going to get fucked any further. Not if he could help it. If it served his purposes, Jacowski could regulate this problem away by changing the COMEX rulebook. He intended to take exactly that path.

CHAPTER 13

THE GEOPHYSICISTS
Dorset England
January 1980

The pattern was clear—the tiny ball bearings made a distinct pattern in the petri dish bottom as they had reached critical velocity. Chaos had turned into order.

Dr. John Buchanan—a quiet thoughtful British researcher who studied the vagaries of nature and weather patterns—stared at the results. Was nature supposed to do this? To be this ordered?

In the experiment he had just run, thousands of tiny ball bearings thinly coated in ink had been placed in a petri dish about 10 centimeters tall. Then a machine had regularly started to shake the petri dish up and down in steady constant motion. The ball bearings quite naturally started to bounce all over the place in initially chaotic fashion, but as the speed of the shaking reached a critical threshold, all of a sudden, the balls in aggregate started to make clear repetitive patterns. He'd seen these patterns under the microscope. There was no denying that somehow out of chaos, clear order had emerged.

Then, as the speed of the shaking was increased even further, the patterns had remained—just morphing a bit in the exact pattern that they created. Each degree of shaking had a different resulting pattern, but patterns were still there—ever so clear.

Buchanan had been studying fractal patterns for years. It had started with the weather, and then a leap in concept from the physical world to the financial world. If tornadoes were a natural phenomenon in nature—caused by the combination of various different factors from warm air flows to wind direction and intensity—could financial market storms also have a similar "natural" origin from different fractal factors? Could these factors all feed together in a positive feedback fashion to create sudden, but ultimately predictable financial crashes?

At the deepest level, Buchanan believed that physics was not just about things physical, but rather a science attuned to answering fundamental questions about order, organization, and change, about forms and their natural patterns of transformation—whether the order and form exists in a collection of molecules, galaxies, genes, bacteria, people, or investors interacting in a market.

For the better part of fifty years traditional economic theory was all built around notions of supply and demand equilibrium and efficient markets, and yet markets never really seemed that efficient at price discovery—grossly overshooting and then undershooting fair values as herd characteristics of human behavior alternated between emotions of greed and fear.

By looking at nature, could a better and more dynamic model for markets be made evident? If nature was dynamic and fractal, why should markets be any different? And if markets are fractal, does that mean that they have a memory—that with some log-periodicity, moving into unstable states of disequilibrium was natural, inevitable, and predictable? Isn't the history of finance really one mostly of so-called "surprises" that have actually emerged out of positive feedback loops from different concomitant effects?

Buchanan picked up the phone and called his fellow professor Didier Ornsette who was working on a book about the same topic.

"Hey Didier, how's the research going?"

"The book itself is still a long-time coming. But it's amazing John. I've been studying this silver market that's been going exponential for the last few months. It seems to me like a standard late cycle "phase transition" event—moving into the highly chaotic, but ultimately ordered entropic moment of exhaustion. Think water boiling."

"I just had a similar epiphany with my ball bearings experiment. It's all ordered, Didier. It's all ordered. Where conceptually most would expect to see random-walk chaos, I see patterns."

"The mainstream economists will eat us alive, you know that?" Didier mused about the future day that they would formally release their findings: their almost full debunking of traditional economic thought about naturally efficient markets.

"I suppose," answered John, "We need to go slow. Build up more evidence before we push the issue. How soon 'til the collapse in silver? Can you document your expectations there before it happens?"

"Should be days, at most a few weeks. I was thinking about calling the Pierrepont Bank and giving them the heads-up."

"You mean that dick Raf who never listens to us?"

Both Buchanan and Ornsette had been hired as consultants by the eminent Pierrepont Bank to find them an edge in markets—to make market calls. It was a way for the Pierrepont Bank to advertise its sophistication. If Goodman Sachs had hired options guru Myron Scholes, Pierrepont needed to have its own rocket scientists at work—if only for show to the clients.

With all the action in the metals in 1980, the bank had asked Buchanan and Ornsette to focus on the precious metals space first. Raf—having moved from muni bonds to precious metals in late 1979—was their senior bank contact.

"Yeah, Raf." Didier offered with a slight sigh. "I don't know why we bother with that guy. All he really wants to do is front-run clients to make his money. He wouldn't know a skewed distribution from a buxom blonde. I'll bet you a beer that if we tell him to sell silver, he'll give us three reasons that we've got it wrong."

"Give it a shot anyway. That's why we're on retainer. Do it in a formal fashion—a letter or something delivered by FedEx. Then at least you're on record formally that our methods of natural entropic fractal behavior lead us to believe silver is topping. "

"Will do," said Didier. "Talk next week."

And with that Didier started to type at his IBM Selectric typewriter.

"Dear Mr. de la Chouette…"

CHAPTER 14

OLSEN AND MARTY
February 1980
Princeton, NJ

"Mr. Amwell," the voice crackled over the receiver, "My name is Olsen McDermott. I'm with the markets surveillance team at the CFTC."

"Yes. How can I help you, Mr. McDermott?" answered Marty.

"You are the sole proprietor sir of the Economic Consulting Group of Princeton?"

"Yes, yes. That would be me."

Marty had been busy for the past six months. Not only had he done a tremendous amount of computer coding on his pi cycle models and his other models related to price amplitude and natural entropic reversals that he saw in nature and expected also existed in markets, but he'd also opened a newsletter business, and started his own active futures trading account.

He still effectively worked from his Uncle's coin shop, but nobody in the real world needed to know that.

He'd given a speech at a futures conference in New York offered by a friend of his, and the subscriptions had started to roll in after that. No Internet yet. Just great word of mouth.

Nailing the parabolic advance in gold that had transpired between the 3rd quarter of 1979 and the first quarter of 1980 had certainly helped. Now for the first time, he was recommending to sell the metals as his 8.6-year pi cycle from the Aug 15, 1971 de-pegging of gold by Nixon was due to reach an entropic reversal on or about March 21, 1980.

"It has come to our attention Mr. Amwell that you have started publishing active commentary and trade recommendations about the futures markets."

"I put out commentary about the markets, yes," answered Marty.

"And then you also trade the markets for your own account?"

"Yes."

"And you hold no CTA or CPO license from the National Futures Association?"

"A what license?"

"A Commodity Trading Advisor or a Commodity Pool Operator license."

"No, my commentary is simply personal opinion. I don't need any license to state my personal opinion."

"But you do, Mr. Amwell, if you are publishing them as investment advice—and also then trading for yourself in the market."

"Oh c'mon. Give me a break. That is almost un-American. I have every right to publish my newsletter and say whatever I want to say in it."

"There are provisions, Mr. Amwell. The public must be protected. Front-running your own published advice is a violation of the NFA Code of Ethics."

"This is bureaucratic bullshit!"

"No, Mr. Amwell, this is your first formal warning that we would like you to cease and desist your investment letter publication— unless of course, you choose to register with the NFA and CFTC. To do that, you'll also have to complete and pass a Series 3 test. We will be sending you a formal letter in the mail about this request."

"Go fuck yourself," Marty slammed down the receiver. He was not good dealing with government bureaucracy. He shouldn't have just said that, and regretted it almost immediately, but these obnoxious little government bureaucrats just pissed him off.

His business had just been starting to take off, and now they wanted to shut him down? No, he wouldn't allow that to happen. He knew his First Amendment rights to free speech. That's all his newsletter really was—free speech about the findings of his models—a discussion of his research.

In Washington, D.C., Olsen stared at the receiver. "What did that guy just say? Did I hear him right?"

Olsen quietly made a note to the file that Marty Amwell was likely going to be problematic and should be carefully watched.

CHAPTER 15

RAFFY AT PIERREPONT
February 1980
Broad Street offices of the Pierrepont Bank, New York

"It's your lawyer on the line," Tom turned to Raf.

"Speak to me," Raf picked up the phone turret. "Tell me some good news for a change."

"No good news, I'm afraid Raffy. You've really screwed the pooch on this one. You sitting down? She wants the apartment on Fifth Avenue and half of all your liquid assets, plus $10k a month in alimony payments, plus $5k a month in child support."

"But she's already independently wealthy. She doesn't really need any of my money. She's just trying to leave me destitute."

"You should have thought of all this a bit more before you hooked up with that kid...Adel was it?"

"Adelaide," Raf finished.

It had been a moment of ecstasy that had morphed into sudden disaster.

No sooner had Adelaide unbuckled his fly, and taken his dick in her mouth—riding it up and down in a more professional manner than he would have ever expected for a kid her age—but buzz, click, click... the front door of his apartment had swung open.

His wife Phoebe and daughter Betsy had simply frozen in their steps as they stared from the hallway into the living room.

"What the hell..." Phoebe had finally uttered.

If it had just been Phoebe herself, Raf might have just given a wry smile, and said something to the effect of "Honey, just how could I resist?" But with his daughter Betsy standing there, plump and squat, staring into his eyes, hurt reigned. It hurt him and it was hurting her.

He jumped up, tucked in his shirt, turning quickly toward the window to zip his fly, and then just put his head into his shamed hands. Adelaide quietly rebuttoned her Oxford shirt, avoiding eye contact with either Betsy or Phoebe, head looking downward.

"OK, I'm a dickwad," Raf offered, afraid to look up. "Shoot me. I come home to this beautiful thing after a long day at Pierrepont, and I succumbed to temptation. It was wrong. I'm so sorry."

"Pack, ass-hole," Phoebe growled, reaching into an upper hall closet shelf, and pulling down a medium- sized suitcase. She threw the suitcase in Raf's direction: "This is the last straw. Having fun and games with your daughter's prep school friend? Jesus Christ! What were you thinking?"

Then she turned to Adelaide.

"And I'm not sure exactly what type of girl you are Adelaide, but I'm sorry if Raf coerced you into anything you didn't really want to do. Maybe for the sake of your parents, we can just forget about all this. That said, how 'bout we move you to a hotel tonight. It suddenly feels a bit awkward in here."

"That's fine, Mrs. de la Chouette. I'm so sorry. I didn't mean to cause problems—I can get myself a cab. I know the city really well and have money."

And with that Adelaide had waltzed out of Raf's life after having waltzed into it a scant hour earlier. His world had been left ever so different from the brief encounter. Talk about a "Butterfly Effect."

Kicked out of the apartment, he had come back to the Pierrepont Bank that first night and taken one of the several small guest rooms that the bank maintained on premises for executives forced to work late at night. He'd moved on to the University Club thereafter.

He felt like a homeless vagabond. What a fuck-up he'd been to let this all happen. His daughter Betsy wouldn't even take his call of apology. He'd written a letter.

"You still on the line, Raffy boy?" It was his lawyer.

"Yeah, just thinking how to best handle this shit... Go back to her and say...um...she gets the apartment, the alimony, and the child support, but she can't also take half my liquid assets. That's just too much. And if that's not good enough, then tell her to go fuck herself too." Anger rose in his normally calm voice.

Raf put down the line, and stared instead at the screens.

If he couldn't fix his personal life, he could at least throw himself into his business life even more—and the days since starting Pierrepont's bullion trading business in late 1979 had certainly been a complete gas. He'd never seen a market on such a tear. $600 gold, then $650 within a scant few days, then $700, finally above $800.

He knew that a lot of arbs were hurting from cash and carry short futures positions that were generating variation margin funding issues. He'd been smarter than that. On the chance that gold would rip, and variation margin funding would become an issue on short futures, he'd gone extra long a modest amount of gold. He called it his "tail hedge." It had been saving his bacon over recent days. He was wondering whether he should make the long hedge even bigger.

"Hey, look what just arrived in today's mail," his ever-present colleague Tom piped up from across the trading desk. "I think it's from our professors."

"Throw it across," said Raf, and Tom pitched the floppy FedEx envelope into Raf's lap.

Raf was going to enjoy this—find out what these nutty professors were predicting.

He tore open the envelope, and read quickly.

"Hey, get this, Tom. Buchanan thinks that the silver market is about to reach its 'moment of entropy' and fall precipitously. He's proposing that we should short this thing."

"Too bad people who said that ten days ago, or even five days ago, are being carried out on stretchers," Tom answered. "Nobody can call tops and bottoms. You just need to go with the flow. Let the market tell you when it's ready to turn. Watch the customer orders. The market will do something that it's not supposed to do when it's ready to really turn, and then we'll have an "ah-ha" moment. I haven't had that 'ah-ha' moment yet."

"Me neither," said Raf. "Still, it's interesting stuff. That Buchanan has done a lot of work here." Raf was studying a set of charts labeled "super log-periodicity phase-transition extrapolated price expectations—Silver 1980." The chart showed a bar chart of silver with an overlaid sine-curve of some sort on it. If the curve was right, silver was about to take a precipitous fall back to $15.

"This guy must be smoking dope or something," said Raf. "He's got a chart here suggesting silver is headed back to into the 'teens by... let's see...like March. Isn't that when the Hunts will be standing for delivery? No fuckin' way this puppy is going to be all the way back to $15 by then. I sure wish the bank would stop wasting its money on this crap. You can't understand markets unless you're in markets. These quant guys are in left field."

"We really should show this report to the Treasurer, to Bob Embel, and get him to cut off the funding for this crap," suggested Tom.

"Good idea," said Raf. "Maybe that way, we can preserve a decent bonus pool of some sort. With this wife of mine, I'm going to need every penny."

Raf walked slowly to Bob Embel's office, shaking his head a bit and flipping through the three-page letter and associated charts as he walked. "What crap this all was."

The Hunts had the market by the balls. There was no fuckin' way this prof had it right.

As an afterthought, he turned back to the desk.

"Tom—buy me an extra million ounces of silver," he shouted back.

CHAPTER 16

COMEX BOARD MEETING
New York, NY
January 7, 1980

"From what I can tell, if the Hunts want to, they can call for delivery of more silver than exists in the COMEX warehouses. Do we want to let them destroy this exchange?"

Jacowski had been speaking for 20 minutes, and a dutiful group of COMEX Board members had carefully listened.

"What about these foreign groups?" asked one representative on the Board from a large brokerage firm. "You keep talking about the Hunts. But I hear it's more people like Naji Nahas, and someone trading through Banque Populaire Suisse—or maybe it's Volksbank—being the big kahuna buyers. Gillian Financial has been involved as well."

"Didn't some of these guys take delivery in December and then physically shipped their silver to London?" Another voice asked from the end of the table.

"Even more the urgency for us to move," Jacowski answered. "If the Hunts can squeeze this market all by their lonesome, think what they might be able to do together with all these colleagues. That shipping of COMEX bars to London was ridiculous—uneconomic. The same transaction could have been achieved with any dealer verbally for a 10-cent credit to swap bars loco New York for bars in London. Instead these Arabs take delivery, and then paid 7 cents per ounce to physically ship the stuff. If that doesn't smack of manipulation, I don't know what does. They want to squeeze silver, and they specifically want to squeeze New York silver."

"But if we change the rules on the longs—tell them that they have to liquidate by a certain date—won't we risk ruining this market for all-time? Won't all the future silver trading business just go to Chicago or London or something?"

"Just before this meeting started, I got a phone call from the CBOT. They've already approved the implementation of strict position-limit path as well. We need to at least match them."

There was noted rumbling across the table. The COMEX Board didn't like to play second fiddle to a CBOT move.

"The Hunts clearly have the wherewithal to pull this off. They've also been seen to do this before in soybeans. We really need to kick these spec longs out of the market before they destroy this market."

"With the language I've drafted, if anyone can be deemed a legitimate hedger on the short side, they can stay in," Jacowski offered. "It's the long specs that will have to pare their positions."

"How about all the candelabras and jewelry that I hear is being melted down? Won't that supply take care of this thing on its own?" It was the representative on the Board from Salomon Brothers. "March delivery is, after all, still more than six weeks away. Some of these guys may liquidate or roll their positions in that time. Between the supply coming on the market, and these natural position rolls, isn't it possible that this all takes care of itself?"

"Anything's possible, I suppose," answered Jacowski. "But I think that the refineries are too backed up. They won't make enough deliverable grade in time. There may indeed be plenty of silver floating around out there, but not enough 5000 ounce COMEX deliverable bars."

"You know what these rule changes are going to do to price, don't you?" The brokerage house guy again.

"I'd expect prices will go down."

"Does that bother you to be impacting price?"

"If these Hunts really love the stuff so much, they can go buy more in London at the cheaper price that may transpire. Maybe they will thank us in the end if this metal really is going to $100."

The room seemed to like that answer. There were mumbles of approval.

"Shall we put it to a vote?"

Jacowski had been the leader, but in the end, a tempered version of his proposal passed. The other Board members fell mostly into line. By a vote of 9-2, it was decided that the COMEX should move to impose the following new rules:

First, effective Monday, February 18, 1980 COMEX member firms were not permitted to allow any customer to establish or increase a silver position if that customer's net position at all COMEX member firms was in excess of a total of 2,000 contracts in all contract months.

Second, any customer who already had such a position of above 2,000 contracts, was required, effective February 18, 1980 once again, to reduce this position in excess of 2,000 lots by at least 10% of the excess each month and to own no more than 2,000 lots in aggregate with all COMEX member firms in all contract months by January 31, 1981.

Third, effective February 18 as well, COMEX member firms were not to permit any one customer to hold more than a total position of 500 silver futures contracts in the current delivery month nor a total gross position of 500 contracts in the next calendar month.

In addition, and effective immediately, no customer was allowed to establish or increase positions in January or February 1980 silver futures if the total gross position in either month were to exceed 500 contracts. (Later they amended this to just 50 contracts being allowed.)

Lastly, all COMEX member firms were required to report to the exchange identifying information such as name, address, and business affiliation for each account that held a total net position of 100 contracts or more of silver futures contracts.

So effectively, the big spec longs—many of whom held total contract sizes greater than 5,000 contracts—all conceptually had to bring their positions way down within a few weeks. Alternatively, if they wanted to be nefarious and evasive, they would somehow have to move and hide their positions into more accounts under different names to technically stay within the rules, but maintain their exposures.

The Hunts chose the latter path. More obfuscation transpired via account shuffling.

Something else then happened that was entirely unanticipated. When the press release about the new position limits went out at 10 a.m., instead of moving lower, silver prices jumped higher. The spec longs were selling COMEX futures, but they were buying even more physical silver in London under the theory that the COMEX actions smacked of supply-side desperation. Because the physical market was even thinner than the futures market, on an overall basis, prices net rose.

Jacowski scowled. Several blocks away at the Pierrepont Bank, Raf smiled.

CHAPTER 17

THE ARB SQUEEZED
World Trade Center, New York
January 16, 1980

The silver market rally that transpired over the next nine days almost killed Jacowski—both mentally and physically.

Sleep was hardly an option. The very survival of his firm was on the line.

He had pleaded with banker after banker to understand the absurdity of his dilemma—Monroe Metals was perfectly hedged in terms of silver content, but getting royally screwed in its ability to carry this arb position due to futures variation margin. And yet Jacowski was also unable to make the trade converge because of grade deliverability differences. What a fuckin' nightmare in the short-term. Jacowski had to adroitly navigate his way to the long-term.

"Get me Herbert Hunt," Jacowski barked to his secretary on a Thursday morning in late January.

She dialed a Dallas number.

"He's on the line now sir," the secretary came back a few moments later.

Jacowski closed the door to his private office, and turned on the speaker box.

"Herbert?"

"Hank-baby..." a Texas drawl came on his speaker box. "How's the life of my favorite big city arb?"

"You're certainly making my life interesting," answered Jacowski in a measured way, not wanting to sound at all desperate or defensive.

"Listen, Herbert," Jacowski continued, getting right to the point, "I know that you've taken delivery of a great deal of silver over the past few years, and may want more physical stuff as opposed to futures. Would that be a fair statement?"

"You bet," said Herbert, "We want as much physical stuff as we can get our hands on."

"Then I have a swap proposition for you," started Jacowski. "How 'bout I give you 5 million ounces of physical stuff—some will be in New York, some in London, it'll be in different sizes and shapes and grades, but we can match up the silver content—against you selling me the equivalent amount of your current futures positions?"

"Futures variation margin issues, eh, Henry?"

"Just trying to tidy up my books, bring down some footings," answered Jacowski, still not wanting to admit any duress.

"I think you're pretty screwed to the wall, Hank," said Herbert. "If you want out of your arb games, it's going to cost you. I'll take your physical against futures trade—but here are the conditions: the trade has to settle tomorrow. I don't want to be standing in line as just another creditor at the Monroe Metals bankruptcy proceedings on Monday. And to get this thing done, you are going to pay me a $2 premium per ounce to part with my COMEX futures."

Herbert might have been in Texas, but he wasn't dumb about the shit going on in the market. Others had already started to bid for COMEX silver at a premium to London silver. NYC was where the squeeze was in motion—both a futures variation margin squeeze and a deliverable supply squeeze—even while overall silver supply in the pawn shops and silver secondary scrap market was plentiful and growing.

Jacowski thought. He needed to do something, but he also had another COMEX Board meeting scheduled on Tuesday. If he could make it to that meeting, more actions regarding position limits and overall trading could be imposed. But could he even make it that far?

To pay a $2 premium for COMEX on five million ounces was effectively kissing away $10 million of past arb profits. It made him bristle, but it would also bring down his variation margin issues to a more manageable level. It was effectively like stopping out half his position, but allowing him far greater probability to see the day where the other half would survive and blossom.

"I don't really like those terms much Herbert, but I'm not going to haggle in this instance either. We're done on that. Have your team call our desk, and we'll give you the delivery specifics. We'll get the EFP [exchange-for-physical] posted on the exchange today for settlement tomorrow."

"OK Hank, happy to help. Now the next time you have one of them COMEX Board meetings, you remember this favor, Hank. I'm not trying to make anyone's life more difficult than it has to be. I'm just pursuing an investment."

"Can't make any promises, Herbert. The exchange will do what it does by majority vote of the Board. You certainly haven't made their life easy."

"I just can't stand all this rule change shit. Is this America or what? I feel like I'm running on a playing field that keeps getting tilted against me. You tell the Board that if they want a lawsuit, I'll give them a lawsuit. No more rule changes!"

"I'll tell them, Herbert."

But the line had already gone dead. Herbert Hunt had hung up.

CHAPTER 18

A NEWS FLASH
Broad Street, New York, NY
January 21, 1980

Raf took a puff from his Montecristo and stared at his Reuters terminal.

Silver was now $46.73, a full 10% higher than where he'd bought his extra million ounces just two weeks earlier. Thank God he hadn't followed the advice of that quack Buchanan, and tried shorting this thing. He would have gotten tire tracks up and down his back—run over.

As it was, what a great start his new career in bullion was off to. Screw those picayune penny and dime rip-off techniques of the muni world. The metals markets were a whole new animal.

The Reuters flashed a news release at the bottom of his quote monitor page:

"COMEX Board votes for LIQUIDATION ONLY trading in silver futures."

"What the hell does that mean, Tommy?...You see this headline? Tom?" Panic rose in Raf's voice.

Tom was already reading the text of the article itself.

"It says Raf...uh...um...'Because of a dearth of short sellers in the silver market a small number of buy orders are causing aberrational price increases in silver, and firms are unable to use the market as a dealer or a refiner for hedging purposes.'"

"Duh," said Raf. "What this liquidation only shit?"

At 44, at 43, at 41...the market was already plummeting.

"I'm reading, I'm reading...I haven't found that part yet."

"Well fuckin' find it, man. This stuff is tanking." At 39, at 38.

"'Although March open interest has declined some 20% and the large trader positions by over 27% since January 8, the COMEX has decided that effective the opening of business today, trading in all silver futures, in all maturities, shall be permitted for liquidation only—*except* for new sales made solely for the purpose of effecting delivery."

"Holy shit," said Tommy. "That feels like a game-changer. Can they do that? They also yanked margin requirements up to $60,000 per contract retroactive to all positions."

No new buying was to be allowed, and the cost to remain in the market was to be increased. Long positions of the largest traders had to be reduced to meet the still applicable February 18 position limit rules, and in the meantime, hedgers with any extra silver stocks sitting around with which they could make delivery, still were allowed to sell. Ker plunk.

"This sure ain't 'price neutral,'" Raf picked up the futures line to the COMEX floor. "Any bids around? Can you sell me 200 cars?"

"No bids, Raf. Just offers. We're at 34 now. No bids at all."

Raf was now out over $6 million on that million ounce spontaneous long foray into silver that he had made after receiving the Buchanan report. But he was damned if he was going to get fucked on this trade—particularly after having bad-mouthed Buchanan's bearish view to the Treasurer.

He hung up the line to the COMEX, and dialed another four-digit internal bank number. He was thinking quickly on his feet, but had always kept an emergency plan tucked away in the back of his head.

"Bill, it's Raf here." He was speaking to the manager of the bank's investment account. Bill was a friend. A buddy.

"Hey Bill, I got a brewing problem on my hands." Raf was talking in a slightly soft voice. He didn't necessarily want Tommy to hear what he was about to propose. "The COMEX just released some pretty arcane and heavy-handed rule changes that in the short-term that have knocked silver down about 20%. I own a million ounces up around $40. If I puke them out here, the bank is going to have to show a pretty nasty loss. It won't be good for the quarter's earnings. It won't be good for the bank. But also I have no justification now to own these things in the short-term as a trade. Do you want to maybe take this position from me for the bank's longer-term investment account?"

"At what price?" asked Bill.

"It would probably work best if I just gave them to you at my cost—where I traded them in the market. We can tell the accountants that I always bought them for you in the first place. They've only been on the books a few days really. I think we all agree longer-term that these metals are worth an investment. It would be a good diversifier for the bank's portfolio, and save us from printing the trading loss."

"So you want to just stick me with a $6 million up-front loss, Raf?" Bill said as he punched up a Reuters page showing the then current $34 offered price.

"No, I want to save the bank from printing it."

"That's the same thing."

Banks all run non-mark-to-market investment portfolios held at cost. What Raf was proposing would move a real trading loss into an unrealized and unrecognized investment loss still held at the $40 initial trade price.

"I'd owe you Bill, and you said the other day that you wanted some metals exposure for the bank anyway. It would be good for the bank as a whole."

"OK, Raf. You do owe me though. How about golf and lunch at Somerset Hills come the spring?"

"Done!" said Raf, and hung up the phone with a smile.

He was at least partially out of his hole. Off the hook.

"Buyers coming in now," the COMEX box squawked.

CHAPTER 19

ADVICE TO WOLFGANG
Princeton, NJ
January 21-22, 1980

Silver rallied all the way back to $43 later that afternoon.

Sitting alone late that day in the Pierrepont trading room, Raf felt like a real schmuck to have panicked out of his long.

But that same evening from his Princeton offices, Marty got on the phone to his buddy Wolfgang in Bermuda. Wolfgang was a subscriber of Marty's research. Of Austrian descent, he had inherited most of his wealth, but still fancied himself as a shrewd market savant. He lived in a posh house on a private island at the tip of Bermuda's Tucker's Town peninsula. Ross Perot and Prime Minister Silvio Berlusconi had neighboring vacation houses down the road.

"I don't think the real kahuna decline will come until March," Marty started.

"That will be the exact 8.6-year pi anniversary of Nixon taking us off the gold standard. But that date could be a low, not a high." Marty liked to hedge himself a bit. "In any case, I think you should start selling now. My reversal models kicked off a signal in silver yesterday. Unless we can get back above $44 promptly, this thing is toast. The general psychology of the market has been reversed."

Wolfgang had listened carefully. Wolfgang was the billionaire, and realized that Marty was just a newsletter writer, but everything Marty had forecast to date had been spot on since Wolfgang had started following the guy. It had been uncanny how good this Marty Amwell was.

And so, Wolfgang put in his orders that evening to start selling his cash silver longs when Europe opened in the morning.

And plummet it did—back down by $11 to $32 an ounce by the time the sun crept out over Bermuda's Frick Beach, and Wolfgang got ready for his habitual morning swim.

Wolfgang just sat there in his bathing trunks, towel looped around his bronzed neck—amazed as he stared at his Reuters screen. Marty had nailed this thing—yet again. The hair on the back of his neck literally elevated as he looked at the price of silver all the way down to $32. Maybe his own decision to sell had been part of it. Had his European brokers front run his order? He hoped not.

He dialed London. "Ya, Wolfgang here. Vat price did you get me?"

"You sold you out at an average of $41.23, Wolfgang. This thing just fell apart afterwards. We're down to trading $31 now. Nice trade, old chap!"

Wolfgang thanked his London broker and headed to the beach. His wife Marina was already in the clear aquamarine water waiting for him. She waved as he approached, her long black hair draped over her well-shaped shoulders. Marina was the grand-daughter to an American president, well placed in society, but still hot in bed.

Tossing his towel onto the pink sands, he plunged headwords into an oncoming breaking wave to reach her.

"Lose that bathing suit, Marina. The world is just vonderful!"

Marina complied, reaching up to untie the bow of her two-piece. She also reached out with her other hand to her hulking Austrian husband, and started to tug down his trunks.

On good days in the markets, this was their morning ritual. Wolfgang loved to fuck his wife underwater, and feel her clean warm wetness all around him. On bad days in the market, he just tended to swim.

But today had been a good day. That was for sure. Wolfgang exploded within her.

CHAPTER 20

A NIGHT AT A BAR AND A SUMMER AT THE BANK
New York, NY
June 1980

By having set up their Bullion Department in late 1979, the Pierrepont Bank was, with retrospect, buying into a bull market trend that was about to dissolve into a two-decade long bear market for precious metals. Those million ounces of silver thrown into the investment account would stay there unprofitable for all but that very first day's close.

Professor Buchanan had ended up being right—as was market guru Marty Amwell. By late March, silver had plunged all the way to $13 an ounce. The rules of the game had been changed in the heart of battle, and some entropic moment reached where speculative juices could go no further. The Hunts and their Arab colleagues had been screwed. Most believed that they deserved what they got.

But that did not mean that starting a presence in precious metals was a bad overall decision for Pierrepont. To the contrary, lots of different and odd alignments of spot and futures prices would exist across the 1980's. Efficient pricing of futures was still being perfected, and thus the more markets that one was involved in, the more potential arbitrage relationships existed.

Precious metals were no different. During those first few months of 1980—a period that would subsequently be referred to as the "Hunt Silver Crisis"—speculative buying had initially driven certain futures prices, like the March 1980 contract, to levels well above the expected cost-of-carry. Later, when markets turned more bearish, and mining houses became active forward sellers, both gold and silver futures would trade cheap to their theoretical forward values. The arbitrage opportunities were variable, but ever-present.

Jacowski at Monroe Metals would still be involved, but the episode of January 1980 had left his firm a shadow of its former presence, and

Jacowski's own appetite for arbitrage a bit less cock-sure. Jacowski had made back some good money in the end when the price had collapsed, but only after having reached the precipice of personal self-destruction. Whether he had acted as a truly "disinterested" COMEX Board member certainly was a bit farcical. He knew in his heart that he'd acted to save his own skin.

And now Thornton was going to become a part of all this.

Thorn had still been under the legal drinking age—a ripe 17—when he first met Raf, but he was hanging out anyway in a bar called Don Denton's on the Upper East Side. Denton's was notoriously lax in checking for any age-qualifying identification for liquor consumption. Backgammon boards lined one side of the room opposite a long Victorian mahogany bar. It was a natural place for Thorn to chill—knocking back a few beers and playing a few backgammon games against friends and, occasionally, even strangers.

Raf—self-assured and self-confident—had eyed Thorn carefully for a few minutes—a kid at a bar late at night who had been drinking, and from whom gambling money would soon easily be parted. In other words, Raf eyed a sucker. Raf had really come to Denton's that night to try to find himself a quick fuck with some chick at the bar. Life being single again was starting to get him down. But after thirty minutes standing there, the prospects for picking up any gal seemed dim. It was time for an alternate plan of action.

"You want to play a few games?" Raf had sauntered over to Thorn seated at the backgammon table already. "You good for maybe $5 or $10 a point?"

"$5" said Thorn conservatively, "Sure, you're on."

The dice subsequently rolled between Thorn and Raf until Denton's 3 a.m. closing time. Thorn's luck was on, and Raf became increasingly more frustrated the longer they played—trying to claw his way back from an initial deficit. In the end, a few hundred bucks changed hands from Raf's pocket to Thorn's. Raf had been pissed at the loss. No chick, and now beaten at backgammon by a kid. What a bust the night had been.

And then, as they drunkenly parted ways outside of Denton's, there had been the offer.

"Kid, if you can play backgammon this well at age 17, you need to come see me at the bank. You'd make a great trader someday." And with that, he had handed Thornton his Pierrepont business card, which Thornton had carefully guarded ever since.

So voilà. There it eventually was in June 1980 in front of Thorn's eyes: the entrance to the Pierrepont Bank's trading floor lined by a dark green carpet the color of a rainforest; the color of money. The carpet alone exuded wealth and excitement. But the room had other elements seemingly from the Land of Oz. In order to ease all of the early wiring of Reuters and Telerate machines, and facilitate visual contact between traders and sales people, the entire trading floor was elevated and tiered, with trading desks turreted to look like mini-castles. The room also had its own currency quote board with a scrolling news ticker whizzing past the price quotations of various currency pairs. It all felt pretty modern and nifty for the era.

Thornton had been hired as a summer intern, and compared to his earlier experiences on Wall Street, immediately thought to himself: "The New York Stock Exchange is a place where orders were *transacted*, but where the execution process quickly became somewhat repetitive. This Pierrepont trading floor was more the type place where orders were *decided* upon—which was intellectually more interesting." In Thornton's young mind, this was closer to where the real macro decision-makers were. Thank God his backgammon playing had been strong enough to allow him access to such a room.

The bullion trading area that Raf now was responsible for was located in a small cut-out alcove at one side of the main trading room, caddy-corner to the currency traders, but still somewhat private. Raf sat at a corner desk with five other desks around him, only one occupied by a secretary named Debbie, and two telex machines against the inside room wall. By the time Thorn was arriving, Raf's assistant Tom had left the bank for greener pastures.

"Take your choice of desks," Raf said as Thornton entered. Thorn looked around and chose the one with a bulky long gray chart machine on it called a "Tradecenter" terminal. He was not sure why, but the machine looked cool.

Playing with this machine over his first few days, Thornton quickly learned that you could divide the screen up into four different quadrants and watch multiple different markets trade across a single day on a tick-by-tick basis. What was amazing to his neophyte eyes was how correlated markets were. The chart of the Swiss franc and gold, for example, tended to move lock-step with each other. Silver meanwhile sported approximately the same chart as gold, but was just more violent and volatile in terms of its overall amplitude. Platinum was much like silver, just even thinner in terms of trading volumes—leaving the tick chart looking somewhat spastic and lonely. But the trading day definitely had a rhythm to it, and all of these markets reflected this rhythm in a very similar fashion.

This was of course still during the days when the personal computer had not yet reached bank trading rooms, before the first trade had cleared on any electronic dealing systems, and when the concept of the Internet and Internet day-trading were not yet even a twinkle in the eye of a Silicon Valley engineer.

It was a world of open outcry, of phone lines, and of telex machines. Foreign exchange salesmen and traders yelled at each other just beyond Thornton's corner cubbyhole, and taped phone lines were a new novelty in interbank currency dealing to help resolve any trade disputes.

Amidst the scores of traders and salespeople who sat in that Pierrepont trading room (and other rooms like it on Wall Street) few if any people had actually learned how to use the type of chart machine that now sat on Thornton's desk.

"Ping, ping, ping, ping…" You could almost sense the franticness of the trading floor as the noise of the machine beeped forth, changing its rhythm with the changing rapidity of the actual number of printed trades completed on the COMEX trading floor some eight blocks away. Thornton loved it. His boss Raf didn't.

"Can't you shut that damn thing off?" Raf would yell at Thornton, and it therefore became one of Thorn's first tasks to try to mute the machine that nobody wanted. He would quickly learn that the actual "pings" being generated by the machine could not be totally suppressed, although one could decrease the volume at which they emanated. He feared for the machine's very survival given its general annoyance to his employer.

But his fear was misplaced.

From that early Tradecenter terminal, an industry was born. Chartists and technicians had of course been around for centuries as a way to analyze price behavior and objectively look at trends. The earliest known technicians used Japanese "candlestick" charts in the 18th century to trade rice markets, but until the 1980's, most charting had always been done by hand. It was a time-intensive practice generally only updated at the end of each trading day.

Only after about 1980 would charts become on-line, real-time, and allow the intraday tic variety to be viewed with such ease of effort. Tradecenter would soon be followed by Teletrac and MarketVision, Ensign and MarketView, Future Source and Reuters Graphics, and then finally Bloomberg. Eventually one could not only monitor the technical behavior of markets on these systems but one could also back-test trading systems using systems such as Metastock and Tradestation. These systems in turn would lead to popular web pages such as BigCharts.com and Marketwatch.com. But in 1980 none of that existed yet.

There was just this one Tradecenter machine sitting on the desk that Thornton happened to choose.

Thornton quickly mastered the machine's commands and also thankfully stumbled across the classic text of Edwards and Magee's *Technical Analysis of Stock Trends*. He tore into it. "Edwards & Magee" was the early unofficial "Bible of technical analysis," and it was almost as if God had delivered it into Thornton's hands via the library of a beach house that Gordon had decided to rent that summer.

While others seemed fixated on breaking news, and what Salomon Brothers' economist Henry Kaufman was saying about the latest M2 figures, Thornton pre-programmed his library of technical pages and studies, and toyed with moving averages and envelopes, oscillators and RSI's, parabolics and stochastics. There was almost an endless plethora of different technical studies—some more intuitive than others to use and understand.

Thornton started collecting intraday chart patterns and took the time to categorize each daily pattern that he noticed with a different looking profile. There was the "no lookback blast-off day," "the choppy sideways day with a mild downward bias," "the tight range day with the 1 pm sharp break lower," and Thornton's favorite, "the noontime reversal day" where morning weakness would suddenly reverse into afternoon strength, or vice versa. There were obviously other day classifications as well. Thornton took a print-out of each and pinned them on a bulletin board full of other print-outs of earlier days' patterns. It was not a scientific approach. It was more the approach of a young inquisitive guy trying on different techniques to see how they felt and worked.

Thornton's job that summer was generally to "hold down the fort" in that corner cubby-hole while Raf went out on various lunches, meetings, and business trips to better understand and build the bullion business for Pierrepont. The Bank had not really advertised itself as a precious metals price-maker yet, but instead was generally a price-taker—a client—to the other New York bullion dealers, a firm taking baby steps to develop before it could fully compete on an equivalent basis as other more established shops.

Raf had given Thornton the following instructions: "I'm going to let you trade around by yourself a bit—mostly so we can just give a bit of business to these other dealer relationships—I need to keep them interested in us, and working with us. But here are the rules: under no circumstances should you ever have a bigger position than 8,000 ounces of gold; under no circumstances should you ever take an open position home at night—I want you flat by the end of each day; and under no circumstances are you to tell Bob Embel, the Treasurer of the bank, that I am letting you do this. He'd kill me if he knew that I was letting a summer intern trade the Bank's capital."

Thornton had been given a mission to be a nimble "day trader" before that term had even been coined—but to do so quietly, without fanfare, and on the sly even from the bank's own management. He turned on a squawk box of gold futures quotes being fed up to their offices from a clerk on the floor of the COMEX; he watched the pings on the Tradecenter machine; and he kept one ear attentive to any breaking news that the Forex guys might be shouting out next door to the bullion area alcove.

Now this was going to be a fun summer job!

And things actually went ok for a bit. Thornton would trade around, making a bit of money one day, giving a bit back the next—mentally thinking that he knew what he was doing, but in reality of course, hardly experienced at all.

Then one day, with Raf away on a business trip to visit the Central Bank of Mexico, Thorn got a bee in his bonnet to trade gold from the short side. The Swiss franc chart had broken lower, and Thorn saw no reason gold would not follow. He picked up the phone and called up dealer Johnson Matthey & Co. for a quote on 2000 ounces.

"623-625" came the two-way quote during the still volatile bounce-back period after the spring 1980 collapse.

"Yours," Thornton said with conviction.

Gold immediately dipped lower by a buck or so, and Thornton initially felt good about his trade, but then the voice box on the COMEX came back better bid.

"Four bid; four-and-a-half bid; five bid, six bid!"

This was silly. Thornton saw no reason why gold should be rallying. There was no news, and notably no confirming tics higher from other markets like the Swiss franc that he eyed carefully on the Tradecenter machine.

Thorn picked up the phone for a second time, and this time, hit the Phibro direct line.

"Gold please."

"Seven bid at eight"

"10 bars yours at seven," Thornton pounced quickly. Each bar of gold in the physical market being 400 ounces, Thornton had just sold another 4000 ounces. He was getting closer to his 8000-ounce position limit, and together with the earlier 2000 ounce sale at 623, now had an average short of 6000 ounces at 625.66...just a bit out of the money really.

A few minutes later, as the spot market touched 630, Thornton lifted the phone to sell yet another 2000 ounces.

He was now at his position limit, several dollars out-of-the-money on his average short price, and quickly getting a bit more panicked as the clock slowly ticked toward the end of the trading day. In that era, the COMEX would close at 2:30 pm New York time, and the spot market would dry up concomitant to that close. It was already 2:12 pm, and Thornton effectively only had another 18 minutes to get out of this now losing short exposure.

That was when Treasurer Bob Embel arrived at the office cubbyhole entrance.

"So Thornton, I see Raf has left you all by your lonesome," Embel stated in a deep patrician voice as he sauntered toward Thornton's desk, "How are things going this summer?"

"1 bid; 2 bid; 3 BID!" the broker box from the COMEX screamed. Gold was going vertical, and Thornton was getting completely screwed on his short, but he was also bound by Raf not to reveal that he was taking any exposures in front of Bob Embel.

"Well, just fine, Bob, err...just fine! Interesting world. Learning a lot. Wow, this gold market is pretty strong right now. Raf has me monitoring some cash-and-carry arb spreads for him. I better hop and make sure I don't miss something that he'd be interested in."

"4 bid; 6 bid; 6.5 BID, no offers!" the broker box boomed.

After Embel bantered a bit about how happy they were to have Thornton at the bank that summer, the clock was soon ticking 2:26pm.

"But sure Thornton, I understand you're watching spreads for Raf," said Embel, "I'm glad you're settling in ok. Don't ever hesitate to drop by my office if I can be of any help to you."

At 2:27 pm Embel finally left the cubbyhole, and Thornton quickly picked up the phone and hit the Macquarie Bank line.

"Gold on 20 bars please!"

"Sorry mate, we're done for the day, all square. Wish I could help."

"Shit!"

He quickly hit the phone line for yet another dealer—Citibank—and repeated his request.

Thankfully, it in the last few waning moments of the COMEX session, gold was finally correcting lower a bit. "At 5, at 4.5, 4s trade."

Thornton got himself covered just at the close, but had lost just over $60,000 on the day's trading. He was despondent. In 1980 dollars, and as a summer intern, this seemed like a lot of money to him—over ten times what he might earn from his entire summer's pay. He thought that his career at the bank might quickly be over when Raf got back from his business trip on the following Monday afternoon. Thornton spent a full weekend fretting about the fallout from Raf that he should expect. Raf liked Thornton a great deal, but

Thornton had also already learned that Raf could be a bad-tempered volcano of a man.

But then a second trading episode happened on Monday morning—even before Raf's return flight had touched down at JFK. It would set Thorn's heart racing even faster.

While Pierrepont was not officially in the market-making business yet, Raf had also told Thornton that occasionally a few big middle eastern banks or sovereign entities (like the Monetary Authority of Singapore) might come through on the telex asking for gold prices, and not wanting Pierrepont to seem wimpy in the eyes of these more distant clients, that Thornton should attempt to accommodate these quote requests, while immediately "back-to-backing" any deals that might occur by picking up the phone to other New York City dealers.

And so it was that Monday morning that the telex machine started buzzing, and the little blonde secretary Debbie called out to Thorn— in a thick somewhat shrill Brooklyn accent—while hovering over the telex machine, "I've got Credito Bandito looking for a price in gold."

Credito Bandito was Debbie's in-house nickname for Creditbank Bahrain—an entity that was quite active in the gold market at the time, and could often lift multiple dealers at the same time. Creditbank Bahrain was therefore also a dangerous counterpart—a bit of an action-crazed bandit, so to speak.

Thornton quickly got on the phone to Johnson Matthey and got a quote on gold 644-645.

Maybe still stung from his short experience of the prior Friday, Thornton was damned if he was going to lose on the short-side again, so he read Credito Bandito as a buyer, and shouted out to Debbie 644.75 at 645.75. It was a relatively aggressive skew in his quote—he wasn't sure why he had even made this price—and he held his breath half expecting to be hit on his bid.

"He buys—a TON!" Debbie shouted. A ton is 32,000 ounces.

"Debbie—I didn't make a price in a ton; wasn't that just for 10 bars?"

"Oh, oops. Sorry, I didn't see his size. He did ask for a ton; I just didn't see that. I didn't tell you."

"Jesus Christ," Thornton shouted, and immediately started fumbling for the phone to make outgoing calls to a series of different

New York City-based brokers. He would have to lift multiple dealers to cover that much gold.

"Gold in twenty bars." Monroe Metals.

"4 bid at 5."

"I buy."

"Gold in twenty bars..." Thorn asked across the Citi direct line.

"4.25 at 5.25."

"I buy."

Debbie was now waving her arms at Thornton. "Credito wants you to quote him again for another TON."

"Jeeez," Thornton thought. "Since I quoted this guy once for a ton—even if I did so by mistake—it would probably be bad form and inconsistent to not quote him again."

"Make him 5.75 bid at 6.75" Thorn shouted, not entirely sure what he was doing.

Debbie dutifully tapped out the quote, but was clearly flustered herself.

"He buys another TON" Debbie shouted back as the telex machine rattled in response.

Onwards Thornton plowed making calls as quickly as possible to as many phone lines as existed on his small phone turret.

"I buy; I buy; I buy..."

In the end, he paid four different brokers twice apiece on 20 bars each time for a total of 64000 ounces, but in the flailing, also lifted a fifth broker for an extra 10 bars. He did so effectively by mistake— maybe not being able to add up all of his own small trade blotter scribbles.

Just as Thornton got himself somewhat whole, and was trying to figure out his position, he heard the COMEX squawk box start to become more excited: "6 bid, trades 7, 7.5 bid, 8 bid, 0 BID, trades 2, lifting 3s!"

Someone from the foreign exchange room was shouting about a surprise comment from Salomon Brothers' economist Henry Kaufman that was on the dovish side in terms of his expectations for monetary policy.

In the end, gold rallied 17 dollars in about five minutes, and somewhere towards the tail end of the rally, Raf walked in the door.

He stared at Thornton who was now flustered, disheveled, and sweating profusely.

"What the fuck is going on?"

"Credito Bandito lifted me on two tons of gold," Thornton volunteered.

Raf quickly looking at the screens to see gold near "Limit up" on the day, and immediately assumed that Thornton had been run over.

"...But before you yell at me, I think I bought it all back ok...or at least I hope that I did" Thornton stammered. "I actually think I got 10 bars extra long before this thing took off."

The disaster of Friday was in the end more than fully offset by Monday's more successful—if somewhat frantic—trading.

Thornton would only receive a quiet reprimand from Raf.

"Maybe you should just cool this trading stuff a bit. I certainly don't think you need to be quoting Creditbank Bahrain for two tons of gold anymore—particularly when there was news breaking."

Thornton wholeheartedly agreed.

The Credito Bandito episode had left him shaken and less confident in his own technical trading abilities—at least in the short-term that summer. It had shown him what one crazy Middle Eastern bank combined with a minor piece of fundamental news could do to the gold market in the span of a few minutes. But whether that sharp rally was destined to hold or not was another story.

In the coming several years Thornton would teach himself a great deal about how to adroitly trade with a technical backdrop, and developed the following maxim: *although one can seldom anticipate the actual news, the value of a given news event is almost always a function of the preexisting technical position of the market.*

For example, when Anwar Sadat was assassinated on October 7, 1981 (arguably an important geo-political event), gold had already been in an overbought situation, and thus only rallied a few more dollars on the news, before dropping like a rock. Conversely, when in April 1982 the Falklands War erupted (arguably an event of less geopolitical importance than Sadat's death), gold was technically oversold at its outset, and the price of gold vaulted higher on each Exocet missile attack—far more than one would have ever expected for such a distant news event in the South Atlantic. Then, toward the end of the Falklands War, gold eventually became very overbought once again—with a Relative Strength Index (a measure of overbought momentum) above 80 and a Bullish Consensus number (a measure of market sentiment) equally as high. From such an extreme technical backdrop, the mere announcement of a Falklands cease-fire in early June 1982 sent the metal plunging almost limit down in thirty seconds.

In the real world, a given news event may or may not be that important, but when the market is off-sides or in a vulnerable position, even the most innocuous piece of news can have a huge impact.

Toward the end of his first Pierrepont summer, as Thornton was toying with his Tradecenter machine one afternoon, a middle-aged foreign exchange salesman with a thick Boston accent came into the bullion department cubby hole to offer Thornton some unsolicited advice: "I see you working with that chart machine all the time...um... err...I personally believe that the only reason technical analysis works is because everyone else looks at it. A trendline is violated and it becomes a self-fulfilling prophecy that the market breaks out."

Thornton argued vociferously with that salesman that this was not the case. He pointed out that since he was the only person on an entire Pierrepont trading floor even looking at charts, the salesman's point of view was likely already flawed. In the summer of 1980 at least, the world from a technical perspective was relatively crystal clear and pure: if you saw any of the patterns featured in that wonderful Edwards & Magee text—a "head and shoulders" pattern, a "continuation flag," or perhaps an "island reversal"—that pattern could generally be believed; if you saw a trendline break, it truly gave you an edge over others because you knew that the supply-demand balance was shifting—that one side of that balance had just overcome the other.

It was only in later years that Thornton eventually would become less sure of himself about this argument. By the first decade of the 21st century, everyone suddenly had a chart machine, and thousands—perhaps millions—of traders around the world came to look at the same chart pictures, and pounce on the same breakouts. The purity and usefulness of technical analysis thus became hostage to its very popularity in this latter era. In addition, large banks started gunning for chart points in order to elect the stops that had accumulated on the order books at a given critical level. Suddenly the term "fakeout breakout" occurred irritatingly often.

Overall, the Boston-accented salesman might have a better point today about technical analysis than he did back in 1980. The irony of such was not lost on Thorn's psyche in the years that followed.

CHAPTER 21

MARTY PROBLEMS
Princeton, NJ
August 1981

"Ah shit," Marty turned to his assistant Liz, "Not another one of those cease and desist notices from the CFTC?"

Liz was opening the morning mail in the new headquarters of the Economic Consultants of Princeton, and Marty spied a CFTC envelope on the top of the pile.

Marty had nailed the top of the metals markets and profited handsomely both for himself and his clients. His consulting business had grown such that he was now providing his forecasts by subscription over both Reuters and Bloomberg. Previously, he'd been using lengthy telexes. With the new technological changes, his subscription business had been brisk enough that he had moved from Unc's coin shop on Nassau Street to a second floor of a nearby office complex along Princeton's Route 1 corridor. Monetary memorabilia from Marty's burgeoning antique coin and note collection now lined the office walls. It made Marty smile every time he walked in.

"No, it's not a cease and desist order, Marty," said Liz. "It's actually a registered letter informing you of a formal lawsuit. The CFTC is suing you Marty!"

"Again?"

She continued to read: "Failure to register as a Commodity Trading Advisor, to deliver required disclosure documents to clients, and to maintain proper records; failure to disclose a commission-sharing agreement; misrepresented hypothetical performance results; and an omitted required disclaimer in advertisements..."

Liz read quietly to herself for a moment, and then said out loud, "Marty, it says here that they want full disgorgement of all of your trading profits for the past three years, plus fines."

"Those fuckers! They can't do this!"

Marty grabbed the letter out of Liz's hands and flipped to the second page of the cover letter to find Olsen McGreggor's signature, as well as his phone number.

"That little prick," Marty mumbled as he dialed Olsen.

"CFTC market surveillance," the phone answered.

"Olsen. God dammit, Olsen. This is Marty Amwell."

"Yes, Mr. Amwell, how can I help you?" Olsen's voice was calm.

"How can you help me? Get out of my face, that's how you can help me!" Marty responded, almost shouting.

"Mr. Amwell. The lawsuit that you are likely holding in your hand is nobody's fault more than it is yours. You're breaking the law in the way that you are running your firm Mr. Amwell. I've tried to warn you about this in the past. You've chosen to ignore all of those conversations. The CFTC has sent you cease and desist requests. You have ignored those as well. You are going to court, Mr. Amwell. If I have anything to say about it, we're going to shut you down."

"But my clients love me," Marty protested, "Have you gotten one complaint from any client of mine about anything?"

"No, we have not," admitted Olsen.

"Then why all the fuss?"

"Because you are breaking the law, Mr. Amwell. You are in violation of the CFTC Authorization Act of 1978."

"Doesn't the CFTC have anything better to do than to attack a guy with a nascent consulting business? I am protected by my First Amendment rights to free speech."

"You may see it that way, Mr. Amwell. We do not. You have held yourself out to be a trading advisor in the futures world. You collect fees for your advice. You also trade your own account. There is a potential conflict there. You could be deemed front-running your own publication release."

"This is all crap," said Marty, suddenly more despondent, spent from his prior ranting.

"Hire yourself a good lawyer, Mr. Amwell." Olsen ended.

Marty just stared at the receiver, and contemplated whom to call next.

CHAPTER 22

THE THEORETICIANS AND THE BANKER
Devon, England
December 1981

John Buchanan was flabbergasted. He stared at the letter in his hands from Pierrepont's Bob Embel, and could not believe the words: "While we appreciate the historic relationship between our bank and the research efforts of both yourself and Professor Ornsette, we have decided effective January 1982 not to renew our funding relationship with your research efforts. We wish you the very best in your ongoing research, and hope and trust that your research will prove fruitful."

"Will prove fruitful? It already has been fruitful," thought Buchanan. "OK, so we were about two weeks early on that silver bear call. But the spirit of our prediction had been pretty damn good. And what had Pierrepont done with that call? Nada. Absolutely nada. That dork Raf had sat on it."

Anger welled up in him. Explaining how the fractal behavior of markets worked to people like Raf was just so frustrating. Raf kept looking at the news for cause and effect. Buchanan was looking at natural repetitive patterns. Some minor piece of news was often just the trigger to unleash an entropic reversal that was ready to transpire anyway. Couldn't people see this?

There were still so many experiments to do, though—new behavioral experiments to fund. With Pierrepont pulling out, how were Ornsette and he to continue?

His office phone rang. It was Ornsette.

"John, I have great news," Ornsette's lilting French accent came across the line. "I'm in New York right now, and the Safri Bank were all over me to help them predict entropic reversals in markets. They want to become our sponsors. Do you think we can get out of our contract with Pierrepont?"

Buchanan was amazed at this providential turn of events.

"I don't think that will be a problem, Didier. That ass-hole Raf has never listened to our advice anyway."

There was no need to tell Didier that they had just been shit-canned by Pierrepont anyway. Why ruin his happy mood?

"There's only one small problem," said Didier, "These Safri guys are pretty aggressive. Sometimes it's actually them pushing a given market. They seem to get involved in some interesting pools of like-minded investors."

"What's that mean, Didier?" Buchanan was a bit lost.

"This isn't a taped line is it?" Ornsette asked softly.

"No, not unless someone else is taping it, and I don't know about it," answered Buchanan.

"It means that Safri and two or three other big hedge funds regularly consort to manipulate prices together. The Safri head, Edmund, didn't say this outright, but it was pretty clear. And he wants us to be his secret weapon to make sure that they get out in time... that he doesn't overstay an entropic turn."

"So we'd be aiding a bunch of market manipulators?"

"Maybe not in all markets. Not in all circumstances. But in some cases, yes," answered Ornsette.

"Is that something we should do?" asked Buchanan.

"They're offering us $500,000 in research money John! That buys us over a year more research in one fell swoop. It puts the current Pierrepont deal to shame."

There was of course no more Pierrepont deal. Gone. Finito. No other choice to fall back on.

"Let's go for it, Didier. Let's do this thing."

CHAPTER 23

INTERVIEW BLOWN AND THE BIRTH OF DERIVATIVES
Princeton, NJ
March 1981

After his summer at Pierrepont, Thornton returned to Princeton and began work on his senior thesis. The topic: the Hunt Silver Crisis. It had seemed appropriate as no one had yet told the "inside story" of what had really transpired.

But what was the inside story?

He spoke with the head of the COMEX; several directors for the COMEX; six people at the CFTC including two Commissioners; two U.S. Senators who had investigated the Crisis; the chief Counsel to the Senate Committee on Agriculture; the Chief Counsel to the House Subcommittee on Commerce, Consumer, and Monetary Affairs; two Office of Debt Management Treasury officials; three futures market academicians; the former head and a then-current Managing Director of the Chicago Mercantile Exchange; three private attorneys actively involved with futures market issues; a tax straddle specialist; five members of the press who had reported on the Hunt Silver Crisis for major publications; and dealers at Salomon Brothers, Rudolph Wolff & Co., and Phibro. He also had a brief chance to speak with a Director of Hunt Energy in Dallas and briefly with Herbert Hunt himself.

At first, Thornton groped for a unifying theme that would tie together the events of early 1980, and to determine how—if at all—these events were potentially related to the earlier futures markets problems that he was also soon studying. Even after talking to a whole host of people, he didn't necessarily understand the step-by-step mechanics of the 1979-1980 period. It felt like writing a book without a punch line, and he was frustrated.

Then one day, it happened: Thornton spoke with a trader at a small arbitrage shop called Easton & Co. The guy described the vault-cash game of Monroe Metals; he described the tax aspects of the

1979 trading patterns of the Hunts; he described the angst over variation margin by various arbs, and the lack of COMEX deliverable grade stocks even as silver poured into refiners; and he described a potentially conflicted COMEX Board that eventually implemented draconian rule changes that had driven prices lower first in late January 1980, and then with another whoosh in March 1980.

A light-bulb went off in Thornton's overall understanding of events; the pieces of the complex jigsaw puzzle all fell into place. It ended up being the trading community—more than any of his other interviews or research—that would bring clarity to his research mission. And while most people naively assumed that the Hunts had simply gotten what was coming to them, Thornton had more sympathy that markets had been monkeyed with by more than just the Hunt Brothers.

In Thorn's mind, the Hunt Silver Crisis truly represented the first time that financial regulators and exchange officials had changed the "rules of the game" to impact the outcome—more than just to protect a market's integrity. If you don't like the prices you see, then it became more acceptable to regulate those prices away.

To a certain extent, in years since then, the Federal Reserve would take a lesson from this playbook—suddenly changing the rules of the credit markets when the 1987 stock market crash transpired, when the 1990 S&L Housing Crisis hit, when the 1994 Mexican peso crisis emerged, as well as when the Long-Term Capital Management 1998 default loomed. It set the stage for government and regulatory changes where market rules could be adjusted in mid-stroke to achieve desired goals—where the "ends very much justify the means," but where the sanctity of fair market behavior is also somewhat abrogated.

Understanding this—and how markets were prone to behave—seemed important to Thorn.

It seemed less important when he interviewed for his first full-time job.

"So Thornton, tell me exactly what you'd like to do when you come to Goodman Sachs?" came an early probing question from a Goodman Sachs interviewer within Princeton's Whig Hall career services offices.

"Well, I am fascinated by the behavior of markets. I just wrote my thesis on the Hunt Silver crisis, and who screwed whom in that debacle. I think I'd like to be a trader."

"But if you want to be a trader, why'd you bother going to Princeton? We source most of our traders out of our back-office. This is a job interview for a corporate finance position, not a trading position."

"It is?" Thornton's heart had sunk.

"Don't you understand that Wall Street is bifurcated? People from places like Princeton put the deals together—arrange mergers and so forth—they are the bankers. People in the trading rooms are just executing the orders. You don't need a Princeton education for that."

"But what about options trading?" Thornton had asked, trying to regain his footing within an interview clearly off to a bad start. "Surely, the multi-dimensional aspects of options—second derivative risks like theta, gamma, and vega—line up more with the world of calculus than back-office operations? Don't you think you might need someone with a pretty strong mathematical background to be successful in that space?"

"Options aren't a big business," the gentleman from Goodman shot back. "Don't pin your hopes there."

Thornton was clearly ahead of his time; he did not get that job offer. As he sauntered back to his dorm room that early spring afternoon, Thorn also concluded that the Goodman interviewer was most definitely a prick. Imagine telling Thorn he shouldn't have bothered with Princeton if becoming a trader was all he aspired to do.

This was admittedly a 1981 world where the CBOE options volumes were still an anemic average of just 212,000 contracts a day (compared to almost 5 million contracts a day currently); the Black-Scholes formula was a scant five years old and too complicated and academically cumbersome for actual use in the trading pits or most Wall Street trading rooms, and an era when equity index options simply did not yet exist. Thinking that actual "rocket scientists" or "mathematical quants" would be needed to correctly value derivatives, to structure derivatives, and to hedge derivatives was just a stone's throw more remote than trying to fathom why any normal family might ever really need a personal computer.

A few trading job offers did trickle in after Thornton's thesis had been passed around by market participants, but in the end, Thorn decided to head back to the Pierrepont Bank.

The Pierrepont people had been kind to him that prior summer of 1980, and somewhat helpful as he had done his fall 1980 research into the silver crisis. The Treasurer there, Bob Embel, also sat Thornton down in his cozily furnished corner office and advised: "You can always go do the entrepreneurial thing later on. There is nothing wrong with coming to Pierrepont for six or seven years and getting a solid exposure to the capital markets. Then go become a Commodity Trading Advisor or something later if that's what you really want to do."

Embel's advice had seemed reasonable and Thornton swallowed it.

But within a few weeks of re-joining Pierrepont, Thornton was miserable.

The problem was that he saw mediocrity all around him.

One fat patrician metals salesman named Langdon Jones who sat next to Thornton really grated. He had no clue what the gold market was doing, or why it was doing it, but was plopped in his seat mostly as a favor to the Bank's Treasurer who had tried to find this aging banker a place at the bank to avoid letting him go. Langdon's job was to try to cultivate mining house clients, and he had this booming and irritatingly loud voice when he spoke to them.

"Gee, I don't think I've seen gold move all day," Thornton heard Langdon spiel to a Newmont Mining executive on the other end of the phone. My Reuters screen has been dead quiet."

"Langdon, Langdon...put your phone on mute for a second," Thornton said in a quasi-hushed tone. "Langdon, gold is limit down today...it's in free fall...the Russians are in the market selling...It's just that your Reuters terminal is frozen."

Frozen Reuters or Telerate terminals that just stopped updating for no real reason happened in that era upon occasion, so Thornton felt kind of sorry in a way for the slow-moving old guy. But telling a client that gold was dead quiet at unchanged while it actually was in a sharp decline seemed an almost inexcusable mistake no matter what the circumstances. There was only a whole host of people who had been shouting lower and lower prices right next to him. Nothing about that day had been quiet.

"Oh, err...I'm sorry Mark," Thornton heard Langdon regroup as he came upright from leaning way back in his chair. "Actually, I'm being told that gold has just started dropping—literally in the last few minutes—It's actually down quite a bit now. I seem to have had a technical delay on the screen that I was watching."

The whole episode irritated Thornton's sense of professionalism.

So too did an event a week later. Quite a number of people in the trading room had known that Thornton had become an adept user of the Tradecenter chart machine during his prior summer at the bank. One of these was the British pound trader—a slightly rotund schoolteacher type woman—who came over from the FX desk to the Bullion desk one day and asked if Thornton had time to give her a lesson on using the Tradecenter machine and interpreting a chart pattern on it. She had another Tradecenter machine sitting right next to her desk, but had never figured out what to do with it.

Thornton spent the better part of two hours talking to this young lady one afternoon, giving her both a minor course in basic Edwards & Magee technical chart reading, and also a minor lesson in the key stroke mechanics of getting the Tradecenter machine to do multiple different things. At the end of the conversation, the young lady seemed excited to give technical analysis a try.

A week later, she came back to Thornton awash with excitement.

"Wow, this technical analysis stuff really works. Just look at this chart I've been trading off of. It's been so easy and clear."

She then handed Thornton a chart of symbol LBZ1. The Z1 portion of the code stood for futures contract month Z=December and 1= 1981, but Thornton looked at the LB part of the code and scratched his head for a moment.

"Why are you looking at a chart of LBZ1?" Thornton asked. "I don't even know what futures contract this is."

"Isn't that the symbol for British pound futures?" she asked, "LB... like the symbol for a pound?"

"No, actually it is the symbol for December 1981 Lumber futures" Thornton had offered after quickly consulting an exchange symbol guide. "You've been trading the British pound while looking at Lumber futures?"

Sure enough, when he looked closer at the two charts, the approximate price levels were close enough that Thornton could see how a neophyte might have confused one for the other, but he doubted that the price charts overall had anything to do with each other. He laughed and handed the chart print-out back to this girl.

"Try watching BPZ1, and I think you'll be even more impressed," he suggested. "That is the correct symbol for British pound futures."

For over a week this gal had been watching Lumber thinking that it was British pounds. How pathetically moronic could one be?

Thornton thought about quitting Pierrepont, but tried to be patient.

Reprieve from his slow-moving peers only really came with the mid-1982 introduction of options trading on COMEX gold and silver futures. Beyond simply being involved with gold and silver, Thornton was sure that being involved with options trading on precious metals would be more intellectually challenging. He made a point to get himself educated enough on options trading such that he would be given that slot of responsibility.

There was effectively only one book on options trading at the time, Lawrence McMillan's *Options as a Strategic Investment,* which applied mostly to equity options. Thornton bought a copy and read it voraciously—taking notes about different directional strategies as well as things called "conversions," "reverse conversions" and "put-call-parity." Ideas of easy arbitrage pickings filled his imagination, and he soon petitioned his Pierrepont boss—still this fellow Raf—that the bank should be involved trading these options from day one.

"But isn't options trading kind of risky?" came Raf's initially conservative response.

"But mispricings will likely abound," Thornton argued in return. "How many people out there really know how to price options correctly, let alone options on a futures contract? We should be able to do profitable conversions and reverse conversions depending upon the market sentiment—just the way we currently do cash-and-carry and reverse cash-and-carry money rate arbitrage using gold futures."

Thorn had the jargon down by that point, and by using it adroitly, hooked Raf to sign off.

As a matter of background, for two years between 1980 and 1982, Pierrepont had been making nice money arbitraging the still buoyant speculative juices of the futures market whereby distant gold futures contracts were often priced above the cost of taking delivery of a nearby futures, financing the gold delivery with borrowed money, and then retendering the gold on the second later delivery date. That arbitrage should not have conceptually existed as it only required access to financing, a bit of storage expense, and a tad of savvy smarts about how also to hedge the risk of financing variation margin flows of the open short futures position.

Thornton knew, of course, that in 1980, lack of attention to the potential cost of variation margin issue had almost buried Monroe Metals during the Hunt Silver Crisis, but by 1982, arbitrageurs had invented the concept of "tailing" such cash and carry trades with a small extra long position. If gold went up, the extra tail position would help cover the cost of financing the extra variation margin flow of funds, and if gold went down, margin monies from the futures exchange would be received and lent out—generating extra revenue, but this extra gain would be offset by the loss on the extra long gold "tail." The size of the "tail" position was partly a function of both the gold price and interest rates, and got further adjusted mostly by the passage of time to match up to the remaining life of the arbitrage.

When these trades were done on a futures-futures basis further out in time, the newly listed Eurodollar futures could be used to lock in the interest rate hedge. In later more dour and bearish gold markets, the trade could also be done in reverse, shorting nearby gold futures, borrowing gold to deliver, investing the money, and buying back the gold with a more distant gold futures. Which way you did the arb all just depended upon relative sentiment levels in the gold and Eurodollar pits. Supply and demand sentiment in these two markets impacted the relative pricing of different futures maturities and created a relative arbitrage opportunity

In any case, by Thornton having used the buzzword "arbitrage," dollar signs danced in Raf's head. Maybe options would indeed hold similar types of mispricings to the arbitrage opportunities that already existed in simple futures pricing. Options were, after all, one degree more complicated than futures. It was natural to expect some anomalous amount of mispricing.

The trick of course was how quickly and easily Thorn would be able to analyze options prices. The first IBM PC had arrived on the Pierrepont trading desk in the fourth quarter of 1981, and by early 1982, there were a few PC-based options pricing systems starting to float around. Thornton made a mission to choose the best.

The first one that he looked at was called Devon Systems, which eventually merged into Sungard. It arguably had the best suite of option pricing models within it, where you could add in fancier pricing assumptions if you really knew what you were doing, but boy, was Devon clunky and slow. Written in a programming language called APL, it just crawled on the early IBM PC to price up a simple option, and at first, there was no ability at all to run a risk ladder of any sort showing a "synthetic delta equivalent" exposure of a portfolio of options and associated hedges. That ability only came several years later when Thorn took a look at the system for a second time. But even then, Devon was excruciatingly slow. It was a nice conceptual system, but written in the wrong coding language to handle the demands for speed of pricing in the burgeoning options business, and the PC firepower was simply lacking at the time to push it along. While the Devon salesman was ever so hopeful to land Thornton as a new account, and Thornton knew that most other banks across the street had adopted Devon as the accepted pricing tool of choice, he took a pass—at least for front office trading desk purposes.

Instead, he stumbled upon a small company called Software Options, which had a nice little stand-alone options pricing toolkit run out of Windows' early DOS operating system. This system had the innocuous name of Commodity Options Trading System (COTS). You entered the futures price of an asset such as gold, the maturity date of the option, the volatility assumption that you believed was fair, and the level of risk free interest rates, and Bingo - COTS could produce a theoretical options price in the blink of an eye. Circa 1982, it seemed almost like magic, and was ever so fast. The model could go "backwards" as well so-to-speak, and compute an "implied volatility" from the user inputting a given option price trading in the market. COTS still lacked a great deal in terms of risk analysis, and only offered a rudimentary ability to produce scenario analyses for different combinations of options, and a portfolio feature that could run a P&L report, but could not do much more. However, it was ergonomically friendly to use and maneuver around. Better yet, it was cheap. Thornton spent a total of just $5,000 for his first COTS license—and that was a one-time all-in licensing cost basically in perpetuity!

And with this simple PC-based COTS options pricing toolkit, he thus got himself prepped for the first day of COMEX gold options trading.

But what a disappointment that day was. Thornton's heart was pounding as trading started. Was he going to be nimble and fast enough to spot and then execute conversion and reverse-conversion opportunities? As things turned out, such pure arb situations were actually few and far between. The market was actually pretty efficient—at least on any given day.

What happened instead was that while options were relatively hard to arbitrage in terms of puts versus calls at any one moment in time, no one was quite sure what the right overall level of volatility should be from day to day. A "groping" process began where implied volatility levels could actually be quite variable—at-the-money options trading at 13% volatility one day and then 17% a few days later, before settling down somewhere in between, then plunging to 10% after a quiet few days, before shooting up to 20% on some sudden spike in the market. As long as one focused on buying options at cheap volatility levels (when offered), and selling options at expensive volatility levels (when bid), money could basically be minted.

Meanwhile, the COTS model also had no ability to price "a volatility smile" into different out-of-the-money options strike prices across a single maturity. So the price of out-of-the-money options trading in the market always looked theoretically expensive to any neophyte user's eyes. But Thornton also was not so naïve to go on a selling binge of 10 delta and 20 delta strike prices just because of this. He was aware that one of the major drawbacks of the Black-Scholes model was that it assumed that financial assets had constant volatility, but that in reality, markets generally exhibited something different: multiple days of compressed trading, followed by "jump moves" on a given economic release or other news. For those occasional "jump days," out-of-the-money options held special leverage appeal, and deserved an extra bit of premium. Thornton mostly mentally adjusted this away.

COMEX options trading carried on by itself for about six months before a soon-to-be larger OTC option market started to quickly develop alongside it. Dealers like Phibro, Swiss Bank, Johnson Matthey, and Credit Suisse bandied together and agreed to have standardized monthly expiry dates at 10 a.m. New York time two days prior to each month end. While COMEX traded options of 100-ounce futures contracts for delivery in New York, OTC options would mimic the spot market that traded larger 400-ounce bars for physical delivery "loco London." Standard inter-dealer option quotes were typically good for "10 bars" of gold—or 4000 ounces. Asking for an option on "20 bars" was deemed large size.

But Pierrepont was admittedly conservative jumping into this OTC derivatives dealing pool. Dealing over-the-counter options added an extra element of trading counterparty credit risk, and even as early as 1982, Pierrepont wanted to make sure that it had its i's dotted and t's crossed appropriately for any circumstance that might arise in such a negotiated derivatives contract. Pierrepont management certainly wanted to do so before getting involved with outside clients interested in bullion options—many of whom were mining companies.

So off Thornton went to a now-ancient Word Perfect program to start drafting what an over-the-counter options agreement should look like. This effort took multiple months and soon involved outside counsel at a major law firm. What Thornton initially conceived as a 2-page confirmation letter quickly morphed into a 30-page formal legal agreement filled with definitions, indemnifications, and other contract law verbiage. This all seemed to be a bit like overkill to Thorn—particularly when most other dealers also developed their own version of an OTC options agreement, but partly for pride reasons, no one would ever sign anyone else's agreement.

Then one day, it magically happened. A nascent group called ISDA put out an OTC derivatives contract that covered both metals and foreign exchange, and when Thornton looked at it, the formatting, the language, and indeed the entire contents of the document seemed more or less identical to Pierrepont Bank's verbiage. Yes, ISDA had poached his multiple months of work. Plagiarism is effectively the highest degree of flattery, so while Thornton giggled a bit with his colleagues, no one took any issue with this turn of events. At least ISDA had chosen the Pierrepont-styled document and not somebody else's.

After that event, over-the-counter options trading really started to flourish. Thorn made trips with Pierrepont sales-people to explain options trading to numerous mining firms in locales as far afield as Anchorage, Alaska to Johannesburg, South Africa. He also visited various central banks including the Monetary Authority of Singapore, the Abu Dhabi Monetary Authority, and the Bank of China.

Even for one who had grown up in a city as cosmopolitan as New York, It was all a cultural extravaganza.

On one trip, Thorn went down the mile-deep elevator shaft of the Durban Deep mine in South Africa.

Down, down, down the elevator had plunged into the ground, slowing in its descent only after a mile underground, and a 25-minute time span.

Thorn's guide that day had explained the mining business logistics in clear terms: "We have to mill over a ton of rock and haul all this rock to the surface just to extract one ounce of gold. As you will see, the miners also work pretty claustrophobic conditions. Sadly, about 20% of the workers have AIDS."

"This was a pretty shit business to actually mine the stuff," thought Thorn to himself. A few moral twangs about the gold business brewed in Thorn's heart after that day.

Pierrepont at the time actually had picketers on certain days outside its Wall Street doors condemning the bank for doing business in South Africa during an era when Apartheid policies still ruled.

"I don't like protestors outside our doors," a somewhat mousy bank president Rod Lewis had started off in one meeting Thorn had attended. "I think that we need to adjust our business policies to stop this."

"Rod, I will be god-damned if I will let any bunch of street protestors tell me how to run this bank," Chairman Mark Reston—who was a huge strapping man—had boomed back in a tone that reminded everyone that he was also an ex-Marine.

On that day, after much debate, and some screaming, the bank's head risk manager had struck the final compromise language in the end. The press statement released effectively said that "While the bank disapproved of Apartheid policies, it would conduct its international business in a manner it deemed appropriate for its shareholders." In other words, nothing was going to change.

On another trip, in Abu Dhabi, where Thorn made several options trading presentations, the Pierrepont team also got invited to attend the wedding feast of one of the country's royal family members.

"Why are they marching sheep around the dance floor?" Thornton naively asked.

"That is your dinner, my friend. They want to show you how fresh it is," the Middle Eastern sales specialist from Pierrepont had answered.

Sure enough, about ninety minutes later, the sheep all returned as cooked lamb on huge platters of rice.

Thornton had then settled himself on the ground and, following the example of those around him, had dug into this meal with his hands.

"Hela," his Pierrepont colleague had said with a grin. "Here is the sheep's head." A bony piece of meat was placed on Thornton's plate. "You get this as the guest of honor. The sheep's eyeball is considered a delicacy."

A slimy round ball imbedded in a crusty socket did indeed stare up at Thorn. For a moment, a wave of nausea swept over him.

But then, calming his nerves, and as the rest of the wedding party watched with rapt attention, Thornton did indeed eat the eyeball. He took it in one gulp, trying not to chew. He did so in similar fashion as he later ate a piece of fish in China that had had its head wrapped in a cold towel while the bottom half of the fish was dipped into boiling water. The fish had then arrived on his plate fully cooked except for the head portion where the eyeball moved around staring up at Thornton.

The things Thornton ate to generally support Pierrepont's new derivatives business!

His options spiel at these locales also generally went well except, perhaps, in one instance. Walking into the Beijing main branch of the

Bank of China in January 1983, Thornton was told by his Pierrepont sales colleague: "If you want to make your presentation in your overcoat, they won't be offended."

"Why would I ever want to leave my overcoat on during the presentation?" Thornton had asked.

"Because it's January, and damn cold, and the Bank of China generally has no heat in their building," was the response.

The slightly third-world nature of that chilly conference room, with an audience that was quiet enough that Thornton could not determine whether anyone really understood English, or not, had left him flustered.

Was he speaking too slowly or too quickly? Did they understand a word that he was saying? How could he appropriately translate put, call, and concepts like "time decay" and "vega risk" effectively into Chinese?

As things would turn out, the Bank of China never became a big option client for Pierrepont. Someone at Citibank seemed to impress them more.

But others seemed to appreciate Thornton's global jaunts. Pierrepont's options business generally flourished. And Thorn stood front and center within that growth.

CHAPTER 24

MARTY BANKRUPTED
Trenton, NJ
June 1982

"It is the opinion of this court that you have materially and brazenly violated the CFTC Authorization Act of 1978, and you are hereby instructed to surrender to the government $4.3 million of your past trading gains, and unless you register as a CTA and/or CPO, and duly pass all exams to achieve such, you must close your current research services at the Economics Consultants of Princeton, and all associated entities."

The judge looked up from the sheaf of papers that he was reading. The courtroom was hushed.

It was a death sentence to Marty. Everything that he had worked so hard to achieve—all of his study of history, of cycles, of physics, and all of his hard hours programming his models—puff, it was all being taken away from him.

Moreover, he had already spent much of his gains made from the 1980 collapse in the precious metals. He had invested a large portion of the money in more computers, in programmers, in advertising, and in office space. Yes, he'd also lavished a few hookers as well along the way, gotten himself the occasional chauffeur when he went out to dinner with a client in New York City, and also had splurged one day on the purchase of a BMW 720i for his own driving pleasure.

If the government wanted $4.3 million dollars, he simply didn't have that much. Barring a successful court appeal—which would use up even more money in legal fees—he was going to have to declare personal bankruptcy. Ugh.

Marty looked across at the judge delivering the verdict, the man's jowly lips speaking more words of boring crap and legalese. Marty hated the man. He hated the CFTC. He wasn't even sure that he didn't hate America.

This wasn't happening! No client had complained. It was all bureaucratic bullshit.

For three years, he'd built up his consulting business steadily. A 1981 *Wall Street Journal* story highlighting how he had nailed the 1980 top in silver had certainly helped. In it, he had been cited for charging $10,000 an hour in consulting time. The piece had given him added credibility. He'd had to hire a full-time sales guy to handle all of the incoming client enquiries. A few conservative congressmen had even become friendly towards Marty's espoused economic analysis and views. Margaret Thatcher had accepted his invitation to come speak at one of his conferences.

Now that was all kaput. Marty thought about his aging mother. Would they seize his family's residence too? No, the house was in his mother's name. That was good. A small break.

On the prosecutor's side of the hearing, Olsen smiled. He looked across at Marty's scruffy half-shaven beard and saw a charlatan, not a market genius.

"His success was surely all smoke and mirrors," thought Olsen. "This guy got lucky with a few calls, broke every CFTC rule in the book, and is fortunate not to actually be going to jail."

Marty lifted his head and stared across the room at Olsen.

"What a prick that Olsen dude is," thought Marty. "But I'll be back."

CHAPTER 25

EDMUND'S RHODIUM
Princeton, NJ
August 1982

"I understand that you've fallen on some hard times."

It was Edmund Safri from the Safri Bank on the phone to Marty.

Marty's office space was gone; the office phone line transferred to his home. Marty was seated on a crumpled living room couch still only dressed in his underwear, a cup of coffee balanced on his knee.

Despite his obvious fall from grace, over the phone, Marty maintained a veneer of quiet complacency.

"Yeah, these fuckers at the CFTC have landed on me pretty hard. It's all piddly-squat stuff, but they've made a big deal out of it. I've had to shut down Economics Consultants of Princeton, but I'm thinking of starting up a new research boutique. Maybe I'll call it Amwell Economics, or maybe I'll keep the name Economics Consultants of Princeton, and technically locate the new company in Switzerland or something so that I don't have to deal with this CFTC bullshit."

"Do you need funding Marty to get that off the ground? I know that you do awesome work, Marty...real cutting edge stuff with all your cycle analysis. The Safri Bank has always appreciated you as one of our best futures clients. We're happy to help in any way possible."

Marty's ego felt well stroked.

"Let me think about that Edmund," said Marty. "It's nice of you to offer. I actually spoke to a few of my Japanese clients over the past few days and they have an interest to work with me. I think that I will get some funding out there."

"OK, Marty. But just remember us at Safri when you get your new business model sorted out. We'd love to help in any way possible. By the way, have you seen the price of rhodium lately?"

"Rhodium? Why would I care about that market?"

"You should care, Marty. Trust me."

Marty punched up a few keys on his quote display terminal. He knew that rhodium was a rare, silvery-white, hard, and chemically inert alloy metal—a member of the platinum group. It was called a "noble metal" because of its resistance to corrosion. As such, it was typically mixed with platinum and palladium to create automobile catalytic converters that would last longer. It was also often used as a corrosion-resistant coating to white gold or sterling silver. There was another application to nuclear energy that Marty understood less well. Marty did know that rhodium was found in association with other metals mostly in South Africa and Russia.

The price Marty saw on his screen was a sleepy $273 an ounce, down from a 1980 high closer to $750.

"Looks pretty dormant on the screen, Edmund. What exactly are you telling me?"

"Look Marty, I can't go into all the details, but we've got this thing all set up. The Russians are going to pull back on their production; the South Africans are going to temporarily suspend exports to do an overdue country-wide 'inventory audit.' I've got my buddies over at GS on the bid and we're buying here at Safri as well. There are few select hedgies involved as well. We've all agreed to go slow until we get some inventory on board, but we're taking this thing higher Marty. You could get yourself healthy in a hurry if you want to join us."

Marty was struck by the overt brazenness of Edmund's plan. What a fucked-up bifurcated world it was. Here Marty was getting completely shafted by the CFTC for a bunch of picayune regulatory compliance issues—told that he had to disgorge his trading profits long since spent—and yet the real market manipulators like Edmund Safri and his friends were going untouched.

"I'll check what my cycle models indicate," said Marty. "I just trade my models."

"You do that Marty, but don't dally too long, or you'll miss the boat. Ta for now."

Edmund hung up. Marty sat there pondering for a moment. Then he pulled up his computerized cycle model screen, and tapped in M for metals, then RH for Rhodium, and finally Z2 for the December 1982 contract. Alt-C on his computer brought up his composite cycle map—his proprietary edge that analyzed a wide variety of both fixed and more flexible cycle approaches.

"I'll be damned," thought Marty as he studied the bars on his cycle map. "Rhodium is due for a panic cycle week next week. There is a composite low due this week. That could spell a breakout."

As long as he was going to get shafted by the CFTC, what the hell— he might as well get even a bit more scummy.

He looked at his clock. Still 9 am in Princeton. That meant more like 9 pm in Tokyo where Marty had a trustworthy trader Hiro Fukaido working for him on the ground. Yeah, his Japanese buddy Hiro would still be awake. Marty could get him moving into action on Rhodium using an offshore account. Fuck if he was technically bankrupt in the U.S. He did want to get healthy in a hurry. Edmund had touched on a soft spot with those words, and his cycle models were also pretty clear.

Marty dialed the international operator, and asked to be put through to Hiro's home number.

A slightly sleepy sounding, "Hi," answered but still with a short staccato Japanese accent.

"Hiro, it's Marty in Princeton. Sorry to bother you at home. But you know that offshore account we have in Sydney? I need you to start buying some December Rhodium nice and easy. Let's try to get 200 contracts in over the next day or two. I'll leave the specifics up to you. Maybe we can get some futures on EFP by trading in the London physical market and then swapping the stuff out. All I ask is that you leave Safri Bank out of the dealing. Don't want them to know we're involved. But let's also not dawdle. Let's get as much size on board as we can."

"Got it, Marty. I'll keep you abreast of how we do."

CHAPTER 26

CYCLES AND MOONS
New York, NY
July 1982

"So how are you going out for the long weekend?" Thornton asked his floor broker buddy Robbie Darman on the other end of the direct line to the COMEX trading floor.

It was a dull Friday afternoon in front of a 4th of July holiday weekend. The streets of New York were already emptying and markets across the board were generally stultified. Darman was a "local" trader—he stood on the floor and mostly traded his own account. He was a short thin little guy—but with a pistol personality. Thorn had always wondered how anyone in the pit actually even saw his thin little frame amidst all the arm flailing. But Robbie's hoarse and loud voice likely made up for his diminutive size.

"I'm actually long 300 contracts of silver," he responded. "A million-and-a-half ounces."

"Ooff, you really want to fret over that sized position all weekend? Why so big?" Thornton asked, already mentally ready to chill for the holiday in upstate New York.

"Well, if you have to know, I just always make a habit of buying metals into the 4th of July weekend, and when it's also a full moon—like it is this weekend—and the technicals look ripe, I have a rule to double my normal exposure."

"Let me hear that once more?" asked Thornton a bit incredulously.

"Don't ask me why it works. Seasonally, you're always supposed to be on the long side in the precious metals in late June-early July each year. Full moons on long weekends also tend to equate to trend reversals. Silver's been weak lately, but it fits the pattern for an upside trend reversal this weekend. The combo of those two things together tends to be pretty darn powerful."

"Have you been snorting too much of that white powder?" asked Thornton a bit facetiously, knowing that many COMEX locals were little more than drugged-out groupies eager for a next fix of action.

"No, not at all," answered Robbie. "It just feels right. It fits the typical pattern. I may be nuts, but I learned this from some of the old masters down here. The 4th of July long weekend is typically a great bull set-up in the metals."

Thornton laughed to himself a bit. Robbie reminded himself a bit of his own neophyte ways—his belief in certain repetitive patterns in intra-day market price behavior; his growing belief that markets had some sort of inherent imbedded rhythm.

That weekend there was no definitive news, but an inflection point did indeed transpire. From an otherwise quiet Friday afternoon, silver started to lift off as soon as London opened on the following Monday. By the time New York reopened on Tuesday morning— after Monday's 4th of July festivities—silver was bid limit up 50 cents. It traded limit bid up another 50 cents on Wednesday as well. It was a weird moment of downside entropy abating, and upside price appreciation suddenly harkening that there was a new trend.

"Why was this?" Thornton had wondered. "How could this COMEX broker—likely half drugged out, and certainly no expert market technician—have nailed this so perfectly?"

On Thursday morning Thornton picked up the direct line to the COMEX floor.

"Is Robbie around?"

"Nah, not in today. I think he's up in Nantucket."

"What's he doing up there?"

"Paying cash for a new vacation house."

Thornton did the easy math. A million-and-a-half ounces of silver with the market now a dollar higher from the prior Friday. Yup, Robbie had earned himself a cool $1.5 million—roughly equivalent to a super nice house—even a Nantucket beach house. Not bad for three days work.

And here Thornton was working his ass off for a $75,000 annual paycheck. No cocaine. No independence. No house in Nantucket. Just Pierrepont Bank politics made up of dolt salesemen like Langdon Jones and occasionally volcanic-minded bosses like Raf.

But there was a new presence now in the small bullion dealing room. A chief dealer had joined Raf named David Proude. Proude was a rotund and smiley Scotsman who had joined the bank by way of the Hong Kong dealing room of Darby Metals. Raf had drifted further up the bank's chain of command, and Thorn liked interacting with David more than Raf. David really knew the business. He was a good resource to a young kid—a wealth of metals knowledge.

"David—you know that local Robbie Darman? He just scored big on this pop in silver. Buying himself a house on the proceeds. Some crazy thing about the seasonals being right."

"It's not rocket science, Thorn. Gold always tends to be weak in June each year, and then in July it tends to firm up. It's just the natural seasonal."

Thorn felt surrounded by yet another crazy. Was he the only one in left field who didn't know about the "seasonals?"

"What do you mean by the natural seasonals? Why should gold be seasonal?"

"Well, I'll tell you one thing, Thorn. It's currently illegal to import gold into Taiwan. But all the customs agents are inevitably on the take. They get bought off, and gold comes into Taiwan like clockwork throughout the calendar...except for one month. You know when that month is, Thorn? June of each year. You see, the normal custom agents go on holiday in June. They're typically replaced by college interns for those four weeks. It's not worth bribing those college kids for their short stint, so gold imports into Taiwan just fall off to a trickle each June. The pent up demand makes July a particularly strong catch-up period."

"You've gotta be kidding."

"No, no...this is all true. Just part of the business. Almost everybody knows about this phenomenon—in the Far East at least."

"Are there any other seasonal influences, as well?" Thorn asked. "Why haven't I ever heard about this?"

"Fuckin 'a. Yes, there are other seasonals," said David in his Scotch brogue. "How long have you been trading precious metals, Thorn? You ever hear of the jewelry fabrication business? Guess what happens each year in front of Christmas? Each year, the fab guys need to buy their gold inventory before they actually craft their holiday-bound trinkets. But they don't need the metal as early as June. That would be excess inventory held for too long. They only start to need the stuff in July and August to have their jewelry ready for the Christmas shelves by October-November. It's just the rhythm of this business."

"Who'd you figure that out from?"

"Heraeus, the gold fabrication company in Germany laid it all out for me a few years ago," David explained.

Another thing that David subsequently taught Thorn was that come December each year, it was not only year-end, but also summertime in South Africa. The Pretoria-based bureaucrats at the Central Bank of South Africa (who in that era, and by law, did all the international gold selling of South African mine production) were mostly on vacation in December and had finished what gold selling they had to do for the year. There was simply a dearth of natural gold supply during this period. Gold thus naturally rose during each December and generally continued to rise into the early first quarter of the following year because of annual Indian demand for gold into that country's mid-February wedding season.

After Indian wedding season demand was over, gold typically trailed lower again each spring until reaching another June trough. It was very much a repeating circle—a natural seasonal cycle.

Learning all of this was like piecing together an odd global puzzle of idiosyncratic macro factors. It also helped Thorn think about his precious metals derivatives book positioning.

Later in 1983, Thorn would notice another Memorial Day long weekend with a full moon. In that instance, gold had been in a grinding rally period—a slow upwards-sloping wedge type of pattern—but without any clean momentum.

To Thorn's eye, it looked like a bear-market rally in front of another late June "seasonal" trough.

"So what do your charts tell you about the market?" Proude asked him on that sleepy pre-holiday Friday.

"In this case, it's all about sentiment and seasonals," Thorn thought to himself. He was learning.

"I think we'll get some short-covering into the weekend," he responded to Proude, "and then collapse on the other side of the holiday."

He'd left out mentioning the full moon part in between. There was no need to be accused of being a nutcase at a stodgy old institution as Pierrepont. But courtesy of Robbie Darman, Thorn had already come to respect the power of the moon on market sentiment. Ever since that eye-opening silver trade by Robbie, Thorn had penned full and new moons into his calendar. When these full moons happened on long weekends or particularly in conjunction with an eclipse, he'd learned to pay careful attention. Robbie's methodologies didn't always deliver, but they worked more often than they didn't.

During that 1983 Memorial Day weekend, gold did indeed collapse limit down on the Tuesday after the long weekend. There had been no news. Just a moment of natural entropy. A sudden swing of sentiment.

One-off special circumstances did of course occasionally intervene with normal seasonal patterns. A few years later, in the spring of 1986, the Bank of Japan gave Pierrepont a huge order to purchase something like 2,300,000 ounces of gold. The Japanese Ministry of Finance was minting a new 60th anniversary commemorative Emperor Hirohito gold coin. The coin would contain 20 grams of gold (about .705 of an ounce per coin) and was going to be issued as legal tender of 100,000 yen.

The Japanese central bankers were trusting that the average housewife would pay a premium over the legal tender value for the coins, and the Ministry of Finance could make a nice little profit selling them. The Japs had also figured out that if they bought the gold in New York and shipped it by a 747 cargo flight to Tokyo, that they could treat the "importation" of gold as part of their trade balance with the U.S. The gold purchase would effectively fudge the numbers to reduce Japan's constant trade surplus with the U.S. by well over half-a-trillion dollars, and therefore also be useful for political purposes.

Like any good red-blooded young front-running trader, once Thorn knew that this order was in the pike, he started loading up on some short-dated out-of-the-money gold calls. This was a levered way to get super long. In his mind, it wasn't really front-running; more like astute anticipatory positioning. Surely, with this Japanese buying in hand, the Pierrepont Bank had the order of all orders to determine gold's forthcoming price.

But who knows—maybe those weak seasonals did actually interfere a bit. Thorn was never sure. But when chief dealer David Proude started to buy the physical gold for Japan, it was like an oddly sideways food-fight in the market. While the volume of gold tonnage traded between Pierrepont and other dealers started to accelerate, the price frustratingly just didn't budge. Unknown to the Pierrepont dealing room at the time, the Bank of China had a huge gold order working concomitantly with Citibank—and it was an order to sell.

The clock was ticking in terms of time-decay premium bleed on Thorn's long options, and these options were still not in-the-money after multiple days of Pierrepont buying. While the Japanese order did eventually overpower the Chinese selling, it took far longer than one would have expected, and most of Thorn's options eventually expired worthless. This was an early lesson to Thorn never to assume that you are bigger than the market; never over-estimate the impact of a client order, no matter how big it was; and always be careful about the manner in which you express a view. Thorn would have had more success with a simple spot gold position than by getting tricky with short-dated out-of-the-money options. The Japanese buy order had simply not lined up with a market ready to pop.

One needed instead to respect the overall size and breadth of global flows. The supply-demand battle would always eventually become self-evident in the chart and volume pattern of an asset traded, and the winning side of that struggle would eventually be clear in that same chart. But it was always important not to over-anticipate an outcome, and the timing of an order's impact was always tricky. Delayed price reactions were more common than one would expect.

As one knock-on result of that Japanese Hirohito coin sale, the Japanese were initially able to sell the coins at a healthy premium, but the 100,000 yen legal tender value on each coin was so high, that it effectively was a useful imbedded put for the Japanese housewives doing the buying. They could own gold, but also be guaranteed that the coin they were buying was always going to be worth at least 100,000 yen no matter what the price of gold. When the price of gold later tumbled from around $400 an ounce to a low of $255 an ounce in late 1999, that imbedded put proved useful. The Japanese housewives eventually sold back their coins to the banks at the 100,000 yen legal tender value, and were able to buy their gold much cheaper from other sources. The Japanese MOF actually ended up regretting the issuance of those coins for the longest time.

It was a classic Japanese fucked-up financial transaction. Others would follow.

CHAPTER 27

THE GROWTH OF FX AND BULLION DERIVATIVES
New York,
September 1985

Bullion was a small business for Pierrepont. Foreign currency trading was a much bigger one.

"Would you like to try your hand at currency options, Thornton?" Bob Embel asked.

"Can I keep bullion options too?"

"As you know, the two areas report up to different group heads," Embel explained. "It would be tricky to keep everyone pleased, but if you want to give that a shot, I can see if both sides are amenable."

"Yes, please do so," Thorn responded.

Thorn's empire was burgeoning.

He was in the process of placing people in Tokyo, Hong Kong, and London to quote options on a global basis on behalf of Pierrepont Bank of New York. There were now salespeople in Paris specifically dedicated to developing options business. For some reason, French corporate clients found the concept of options to be particularly "chouette." Companies like Thompson and quasi-government entities like COFACE (which hedged French foreign trade receivables) were both early currency option-hedging adopters.

That one initial license to COTS software that Thorn had originally purchased soon grew to about ten licenses in multiple locations, and by mid-1985, there were about fifteen dedicated Pierrepont people across the globe all quoting options to other dealers, banks, and clients.

Thorn was also working diligently with the developers of COTS to create better risk management functionality. He felt like a temptress hanging out alluring pieces of bait: "How much would it cost to have you build a risk ladder report?" "How long will that take?" "If I pay you double that amount, can you get me something functional by the end of the month?"

Portfolio risk ladders were indeed developed across strike prices that could mush an entire portfolio of options, futures, and cash positions into a one-page snapshot of total risk exposure, inclusive of delta (price exposure), gamma (rate of change of that delta price exposure), and vega (volatility) exposures. Thorn didn't worry too much and rho (interest rate) exposure—even though interest rates and forward prices were indeed moving a great deal. Theta (time decay) risk and "pin-risk" (landing on top of a potentially difficult strike price) also eventually got reports dedicated to their management. Volatility "smile curves" arrived only belatedly so that all positions could be more properly marked-to-market. But for the longest time, Thorn's desks made do with simply one volatility mark by each option maturity cycle.

The justification for this one volatility by maturity was reasonably simple: interpolating volatility curves was a pretty complex task for any mid 1980's software package to tackle, and since most options only had a tenor out to three months, if mispricings on the bank's books existed in the short-term (as they most certainly did), these mis-marks would go away pretty quickly when an option either ended up in- or out-of-the-money—worth something or worth nothing. Conceptually as well, there would in the end mathematically be only one real "observed volatility" for any given period, so to start assigning different volatility marks to different strike prices risked creating relative option deltas that might in the end be theoretically incorrect to use for hedging purposes.

This was of course, most imperfect, but it was not so imperfect to prevent the business from moving forward. The bid-offered spreads and market inefficiencies were simply too attractive to stop the growth. Geographic differences quickly emerged whereby options were generally cheaper when sourced during Japanese trading hours, and sold during New York/Chicago trading hours. There was something cultural in the way the Japanese liked to sell options. Or maybe it was because of different accounting norms where premiums sold in Japan could simply be booked as a positive P&L.

Yeah, that was more likely the cause.

Intermediate brokers such as Cantor Fitzgerald and Tradition Financial Services started to act as go-betweens to facilitate inter-bank trading both domestically and with foreign banking counterparts, and as these brokers shouted over squawk boxes different volatility levels in different underlying assets, over-the-counter option volume literally began to explode.

The maturity tenor of options also started to lengthen, and with it sometimes the stupidity of market participants.

In 1985, one sleepy Canadian mining company that was a subsidiary of British Petroleum got sweet- talked by an equally sleepy Canadian investment banking firm to attach five-year warrants on gold to a bond issuance. With spot gold around $420, the Canadian banking firm priced the warrants with a strike of $500 and with an effective premium price of about $35. Where they came up with this pricing, Thorn had no idea, because at the time he calculated that the forward price for gold five-years hence was more like $560. In other words, these warrants were being offered *below* their intrinsic value when properly hedged with a forward gold sale. It was effectively free money as long as the mining house credit was ok for five years, and with BP's credit backing, the Pierrepont Bank was reasonably comfortable with such credit exposure.

Thorn had proposed to Raf and David that they should buy the entire warrant issue.

"Are you sure that you're not missing something? There's gotta be some sort of hitch," was Raf's comeback.

There really wasn't one. It was just a dumb investment banker up in Canada proposing a dumb arbitrary price. This was the type of deal emblematic of an entire era of options arbitrage opportunities across the early-to-mid 1980's.

In the end, the Pierrepont Bank bought about half the issue, and had a spectacularly profitable day when the COTS Black-Scholes software system marked that warrant's theoretical value up dramatically from the purchase price. Thorn threw a particularly low volatility mark on the trade, but the options were still worth considerably more than their issuance price. Thankfully, in thin subsequent post-issuance trading, the actual warrant price in the market also gravitated up to the same COTS-derived value. Otherwise, the accountants might have given Thorn a harder time.

Then one day the business in FX options also went to a new level.

"You good for some size?" the sweet but tough French voice of Silvie from French quasi-governmental client COFACE had asked of Thorn over a crackling international phone line.

Thorn had never met Silvie, but she sounded hot. Certainly smart.

"What are you trying to do?" Thorn responded.

"I need a 40 delta dollar put/French franc call in $100 million."

This was a huge deal for a time when dealers regularly quoted currency options for only $5-10 million at a pop. Thorn consulted his volatility indication pad that held scribbled updates of a range of volatility prices for different currencies and metals.

Thorn read Silvie as a seller of the dollar put, and showed her an 11.8% volatility bid while the broker market in one year French franc options was 12% bid at 13% offered.

"OK, I sell you those puts," Silvie said, and they had spent a few minutes booking out the actual option price details.

Thorn fortuitously then heard a voice broker at Cantor bidding 12.8% for one year French franc options. This bid had arrived out-of-the-blue, but was certainly most welcome.

Thorn had quickly clicked off of Silvie's line.

"I sell at 12.8!" he shouted into the direct broker phone line. "I can do size."

Thorn sold that bid at 12.8, then another at 12.7, then more at 12.6…he amazingly got his $100 million in size done. It had been a wonderful moment. The bank booked almost a $1 million profit in a scant few moments.

After the gold warrant deal and that large COFACE option deal, Pierrepont management started to notice the consistent and growing profitability of options trading.

Of course, not everything in the early days of options trading worked according to plan.

On an autumn Friday afternoon in 1985, dollar-yen started dropping in unusually rapid fashion. 281, 280, 279, 277, 276! The Pierrepont currency options team was short options on the yen, but even into its negative gamma position, Thorn still sold some more volatility late that Friday afternoon. The decline, while a bit odd, fierce, and persistent, also seemed overdone. Plus collecting a little extra time decay over a weekend didn't seem like such an unreasonable thing at the time.

Then that Sunday, Thorn was in his car, driving down from a weekend in upstate New York, when he heard on the radio, the third story deep on 1010 WINS Radio: "And in New York this weekend, a meeting of the G-5 finance ministers—held at the Plaza Hotel—unanimously agreed that the dollar should trade lower."

"What meeting?" Thorn asked out-loud to himself in the car. "I work at the Pierrepont Bank. If there was going to be a finance minister's meeting, wouldn't I have at least known about it?"

Someone obviously *had* known about this meeting with retrospect given Friday's precipitous dollar decline, but Pierrepont hadn't been one of these. The bank had been in the dark—not a clue; no inkling that any special meeting had been afoot.

Thorn stepped on the accelerator of his car a bit that Sunday, and made it home to the city in record time. After a quick call with his options team colleagues, he decided that the only action that was possible was to keep pace with the negative gamma situation in dollar-yen options by selling dollars in the spot market and maybe leaning a bit extra short.

But the yen gap-opened five yen lower in Australia and quickly slid to be eleven yen lower in almost a heartbeat. Even as Thorn sold dollars aggressively over the phone into the early Australian market, it wasn't enough to compensate for the explosion in currency volatility that would transpire the next morning.

On a mark-to-market basis, Thorn's group lost the better part of $800,000 by the end of that Monday. Within an era when a total *annual* P&L of $10 million would have been deemed mighty impressive, the poor positioning felt like a humbling experience.

The G-5 experience taught Thorn one thing fast: when an options book was working, everything tended to work. When it was not working, everything tended to hurt. One could potentially lose money so many different ways: from spot movement, from forward interest rates, from volatility shifts, from a changing shape of the volatility curve, and also from being long volatility on a currency pairing that wasn't moving versus short volatility on one that was. Time decay could also be an issue that occasionally caused issues. It was like playing a multi-dimensional game of chess, and this was what made the job of managing a derivatives book so challenging and yet exhilarating. Anyone could trade plain vanilla instruments. It took a special breed of intellect to master options.

But alas, it would not be the market that buried Thorn. It would be operations. After business had grown to be ever so busy, Thorn had gone to his FX boss Bruno Geissler and been flatly rejected about improving the processing speed of the back office's resources. That's where this story originally started. This decision by Bruno then promptly bit Thorn in the ass.

"What are you doing, Thorn?" Bob Embel asked one day, as he saw Thorn madly typing away at a telex machine.

"Sending out a provisional FX option confirmation, Bob."

"But aren't deal confirmations supposed to emanate from Operations?"

"Yes, err...They do, but just a tad slowly I'm afraid. Sometimes the options that we are trading have already expired by the time the confirmations get sent out. I implemented this extra front office procedure to just make sure we don't have any errors—particularly on short-dated option situations."

"Well, this we must fix!" Embel had boomed. And as things subsequently turned out, that was the beginning of Thorn's political fall from grace.

You see, somehow Thorn had made Bruno look bad; he had made FX Operations look bad; and he had made his own options group seem potentially out-of-control in the eyes of others.

Soon thereafter, the bullion operations team decided too that the days of running the bank's books and records from a PC-based software system COTS had to end. "PC-based systems are heresy; everything has to be on a main-frame," one operations consultant told Thorn. "You should never have been allowed to get as far as you did with this."

These same consultants conducted multiple surveys and interviews, and after six months of reconnaissance, reported that they could build Pierrepont a main-frame based system called GOPS

(Gold Options Pricing System) with a deliverable date one-and-a-half years hence, and a total price tag of $1.7 million. Given that Thorn had probably only spent a total of $100,000 over three years for all of his multiple COTS software licenses (inclusive of added licenses and the cost of improved risk modules), he was aghast at both the price and the long deliverable time of the newly proposed in-house system.

"Just go to the COTS people and they will build you a main-frame version of their system for half that price in half the time," he advised, but the bureaucratic wheels already had too much invested in their consultants and own internal plans.

It was a November evening in 1986 that Thorn's world came crashing down even further. Bruno Geissler came to Thorn late in the day with the news that the bank had decided to "split" his burgeoning option empire into at least three separate geographic books.

"We are split by competitive Treasuries—London, Milan, Paris, Zurich, Tokyo, New York—in every other product," explained Geissler. "We all effectively compete with each other. We don't see why derivatives should be any different. Each center should have its own options book. Or at a minimum, we should have a separate book in each time zone. It's just the way we do things. "

Thorn's heart was crest-fallen, and he went on a multi-pronged Blitzkrieg of attempted rebuttal.

"But options are a contingent liability asset," he babbled. "It doesn't make any sense to have different groups in different parts of the world all trading separate books. Each geographic center will have to leave separate sets of stop-loss orders and wake-up calls instead of having the overall book flow naturally from one center to another, with an able and awake set of eyes making hedging decisions for the global team.

"And you will lose access to so many arbitrage opportunities. You won't be able to buy cheap options anymore in Tokyo and then seamlessly hedge them against more expensive options on the Chicago IMM. Or at least it will be much more awkward and difficult to do this.

"And have you thought about what our clients may want? Do they really want to deal with multiple different Pierrepont branch entities, and end up long options from Pierrepont New York, only to sell these back to Pierrepont London if they are dealing in the early European morning? Or would they prefer to be able to deal and offset their option positions in any time zone in the name of one main New York City-based counterparty?

"And operationally, aren't we already struggling just to get things right just in one time zone? Do you really want to replicate these back office issues across multiple bank locales for multiple different options books?"

"This makes no sense!" Thorn may have been screaming by this point.

But alas, Thorn was a medium-sized stone hitting a brick wall. Just like the bullion operations people had decided to spend $1.7 million on an internal derivatives system that would likely be outdated by the time it was delivered, the decision of senior management with regard to the structure of Pierrepont's ongoing derivatives presence had been made, and nothing that Thorn could do or say was going to change that.

Thorn left Pierrepont a few weeks later. It would subsequently take the bank another five years to revert to a global derivatives book format that Thorn had originally built. The bank did so only when they saw others like Swiss Bank-O'Conner, UBS, and Goodman Sachs successfully executing global derivatives books, and poaching both client market share and overall profitability from Pierrepont as they did so.

The first six years of Thorn's derivatives education was over. It had been an exciting but, in the end, a frustrating road.

Another fourteen years of derivatives trading at other shops would follow. Thorn was only just beginning to learn about the difficulties of managing derivatives books within different bank bureaucratic cultures. And the derivatives markets themselves were only just getting set for a round of parabolic growth across the 1990's and 2000's.

CHAPTER 28

OLSEN AT TREASURY
Washington, D.C.
October 1987

The late 1985 manipulated dollar decline by global central bankers should have done the trick. It should have helped spur American competitiveness and decrease American imports. The trade deficit should have gone away.

Treasury secretary James Bacon knew this. He'd put the whole plan together, after all. It was such a nifty way out: no need for a harsh and politically unpopular U.S. recession.

Lowering the dollar's value was the finesse move—an easy solution.

Unfortunately, by mid-1987, the tactic hadn't worked.

The Japanese had basically eaten the impact of the dollar decline by improving efficiency and cutting their own profit margins. They didn't raise their U.S. prices. They were instead focused on maintaining U.S. market share at all costs. The trade deficit was ever-present. In fact, it was bigger.

"Shit, shit, shit! This should have worked," Bacon pounded his fist on top of his desk.

Olsen McFadden, previously of the CFTC, had now been promoted to Treasury and sat across from his new boss. Bacon's hardheaded Texas ways were a breath of fresh air from the bumbling bureaucracy at the CFTC. There was a suave self-confidence in Bacon—a master-of-the-universe attitude that was almost infectious.

"We could always go to the Japanese, and ask them to cut their interest rates," Olsen suggested. "That might proactively spur them into buying more U.S. goods. We could fix the trade deficit that way?"

"That sounds like a plan," said Bacon. "Get someone in Treasury to do some work on that...research it quantitatively...write up one of those white papers. Also get our Ambassador to plant that seed with a senior member of the MOF. When we have the white paper in hand, I'll then follow up by phone.

"Meanwhile, what are we going to do with these fuckin' Germans?"

German Bundesbank officials had recently done nothing but bitch about the declining value of the dollar. The harmony of the initial 1985 Plaza Accord was now turning into dis-harmony…something closer to outright acrimony between central banks. The precious metals had started to take off again in March 1987, and now the U.S. bond market was tanking, together with the dollar. Confidence in the U.S monetary system was on the wane.

"Do you want me to get the Bundesbank on the phone?" asked Olsen of his boss.

"Damn no. I was thinking more like just telling them to just go screw themselves. They seem to have forgotten what we are trying to accomplish here. They're trying to protect their fuckin' provincial interests. They're missing the big picture."

"So what do you propose, boss?" Olsen asked.

"Let's hit 'em hard and deliver our message. Tell them that we don't care what they think about the value of the dollar. Let's shut these little whiners up. Can you get a story planted in the *New York Times* to that effect?"

"You really want to do that boss? The markets have gotten a bit rocky already. A story like that might push things over the edge, and not be worth the ancillary damage."

"I'm sick of these little fuckers," said Bacon. "We need to put them back on message. Show them who's boss here. Get that gal Gretchen Morgenson at the *Times* to make our intent crystal clear: the dollar was overvalued in 1985, and we still want it lower today."

"OK boss. I'll get that message to her."

CHAPTER 29

BUCHANAN AND THE ENTROPIC MOMENT
Devon, England
October 15, 1987

For five years, Buchanan had closely followed the Rhodium market for Safri Bank, and not once received an entropic sell signal on it. The retainer research money had continued, but Buchanan only wished that he could show his methodology's value. Didier and he had continued their work on fractal market rhythms, but being focused on Rhodium seemed like a backwater—a waste of time.

Halfway around the world, Marty Amwell also continued to be focused on Rhodium. Up from its humble beginnings at $275 that September 1982 today, it was now trading at over $1000 an ounce. It had been a star metal compared to gold or silver, and even platinum and palladium. Edmund Safri had not misled Marty by telling him to get involved. The trade had certainly helped Marty get back into the game.

But metals had become overbought. Stocks were overbought. Bonds were sliding. Marty did not have another major pi cycle until the middle of December 1989, but all of his antennae were attuned to growing instability in financial markets. He had a minor pi cycle rhythm due to hit on October 19, 1987, and he wondered what it would be.

In terms of cycles, Marty had refined his theories both up and down the time continuum. If markets had bigger picture rhythms related to increments of pi stretching 3141 days (8.6 years) and 6282 days (17.2 years), there was also appeared to be more micro moments of entropy that he had discovered every 8.6 months. Yes, if you took 3141 days and divided that interval by the key number 12 (as in the number of signs in the Zodiac), 261.8 day sub-intervals resulted—or 8.6 months, with the golden ratio of 61.8 also making an appearance in that day count.

Marty was convinced that entropic rhythms completed on these key dates. It was almost as if the market got tired of one theme—one trend—and morphed to adopt a new one.

Oddly enough, Buchanan—sitting half a world away in Devon, England—was thinking the same thing: trends had a finite life, and the world was beginning to wobble. But he was less worried about rhodium than he was stocks.

He picked up the phone to dial his friend Edmund.

"I'm starting to get a signal," explained Buchanan.

"Rhodium's going to take a tumble? Time to exit stage left?" asked Safri with much anticipation. "You finally stepping up to the table John with some useful advice?"

"The precious metals are certainly getting a bit over-bought, Edmund, but I'm more concerned about the volatility signals that we're getting from bonds and the dollar. The moves in these other markets seem destabilizing in their magnitude and I just wonder if it won't spill over into stocks one day soon. We're also starting to see a loss of momentum in the equity world."

"So what am I supposed to do, John?"

"Be very careful. Volatility is like an over-sized balloon in an empty-sided box. Just imagine that each side of the box represents a different asset class—FX, fixed income, commodities, equities, credit. When you see that balloon pushing out too far on one side-of-the-box, the balloon has a tendency to go pop. Sometimes, if it is just sticking out one side of the box—one market misbehaving, so to speak—the central bankers can get together and push the balloon back in. But when that balloon is pushing out on multiple sides at the same time, it's like a bell going off. It's not stable. The central bankers may be losing control."

"So you think we're going to have a crash?"

"It feels that way. My models are certainly sending me warning signs to reduce risk; to watch carefully for entropic reversals. Maybe buy some equity put protection, pork in a bit of volatility."

"But nothing in Rhodium, yet?"

"Goddamn rhodium!" thought Buchanan to himself. "Here I'm telling this power banker to protect his entire goddamn business—

his entire bank—and all he cares about is his ongoing little squeeze in Rhodium."

"No, nothing in Rhodium, Edmund, no."

"You gotta get with the program, John. I want trading advice that I can act on, and for three years not a peep from you on Rhodium. All this other stuff is interesting, but less useful to me."

"I understand Edmund, but I can't relay signals that aren't there." Buchanan was crestfallen.

Safri wondered what his $500k per annum contribution to John Buchanan's research was actually worth.

It was like they were talking different languages—never connecting in terms of wants and needs.

CHAPTER 30

A FORTUITOUS KNIFE SLICE
Tannersville, New York
October 18, 1987

Thornton opened his eyes to the fall chill of a cold old house. Sun streamed in through the dust-covered blinds, placing ribbons of light across the bedroom floor, but it was still too early in the morning to be a warm sun.

The house had no heat. It was mostly a summer house in the northern Catskills—his grandmother's old house—complete with claw-footed bathtubs and musty old curtains. There was the occasional mouse scurrying across the floorboards at night and the smell of mouse droppings everywhere.

There was also that morning a scratching noise in the ceiling air vent above his head.

Claws on tin.

Thorn had become used to that noise. It was a raccoon, or maybe a family of raccoons—somewhere deep within the air vents of the house—a cozy burrow no doubt. The 'coons started to move around about six a.m. in the morning, like an alarm clock—scratching, gnawing, pause, then more shifting and scratching noise again.

If Thorn could only figure out how these critters were getting into the house, he'd love to plug up that hole; maybe fumigate the fuckers out. Try not to kill them though and have them die within the walls. That would be bad.

Thorn rolled over and gave his wife Kim a peck on the back of her neck. He'd married Kim three years before; no kids, both working, pretty good sex, and nice vacations. What was not to like about life?

And now they had a new project in motion—to build a new house up here in the mountains; to move on from this dumpy old familial homestead with mice and raccoons, and construct a proper home. They had brought up their architect Saturday morning to see the site of land that they'd purchased, and then packed him back off on a bus home. It had been a fun Saturday full of expectation and planning.

The end of 1986 had certainly been stressful—an entropic moment in Thorn's own career when overt success had suddenly morphed into the loss of a job. He'd decided to quit when Bruno had announced to him the new plan for competitive derivatives books from different geographic locales.

Fuck the Pierrepont Bank. They were myopic bureaucratic dweebs. How dumb could a bank be to have taken this path? Thankfully a former Pierrepont colleague had quickly recruited him to become a proprietary trader at a small investment bank. Life would go on.

More scratching from above. A grating sound like chalk on a blackboard. It was useless to try to go back to sleep.

"I'll make some coffee, and get breakfast," Thorn whispered to Kim who continued to seem more asleep than he was.

He rolled out of bed and hustled to get some pants and socks on. The floor was cold.

Within a house that had a total of eight bedrooms, and large Victorian mural paintings adorning the double-height wood-paneled living room, they were staying in the equivalent of the maid's quarters. It was the only part of the house that had any insulation within the walls. This area of the house had been used by his grandmother to spend a winter or two, while the main part of the house was shut down—left unheated as the price of heating oil had soared.

But then the forced hot air furnace had given out in total. Now there was simply no heat at all in any part of the house. Just fuckin' raccoons living in the vents.

It was sad to see former greatness slowly fade.

He walked to the old-fashioned linoleum-lined kitchen—a small rectangular-shaped kitchen perched oddly—almost like an appendage—above a lower-level terrace. The whole house sat on the side of a hill. You entered on what actually was the middle floor of the house, and an almost-hidden small circular stairwell off the dining room led to the main grouping of guest bedrooms on the lower level. There were more bedrooms upstairs. The maids' rooms were off to the side of the middle level, near to the kitchen.

A huge Victorian-styled water tower loomed just to the right of the house itself. To build this house where they had in the early 1800's—on the side of a mountain but with a glorious expansive southerly view—their drill bits to find water had not been able to penetrate the rocky mountainside. Instead, a well for water had been placed on a lower level of land, a pump house constructed to move the water uphill, and then a huge holding tank constructed in a tower above the house itself, so that the water could fall through pipes into the house by the eventual force of gravity.

It was the type of house you could almost get lost in, or hear floorboards creak where no one was supposed to be. Each bedroom—even the maid's rooms—still had a little button built into the moldings. In some yesteryear, a number would mechanically pop up in the kitchen, and Thorn presumed that the servants would come running with breakfast trays. How civilized the world once was. Now the button mechanisms were long broken—rusted numbers sitting ajar in the kitchen atop some ancient mechanical contraption.

He opened the refrigerator door, pulling a still gleaming lever on the rounded façade of the old-styled unit. Not much food.

The refrigerator contained exactly a carton of milk and two green apples. Why the apples were even in the refrigerator, Thornton wasn't entirely sure. Then he remembered. Their architect had brought them with him on Saturday as a house gift, and Kim had placed them in the fridge to ensure that the mice wouldn't get to them before they did. That had been a smart move.

After pouring some water into a coffee pot and filling the drip style filter with ground coffee he found in the freezer, Thorn looked down at the apples.

"I guess these will have to make do for breakfast," he thought and started to slice one with a knife.

The apple was rock hard from its chilly passage overnight. Thorn pushed down with his knife. The blade hesitated for a moment, and then Thorn pushed harder. As he did, the knife cut through the apple at a sideways angle and came out to slice the tip of Thorn's middle finger on his left hand.

"Shit! Goddamn it, Oh my God," Thorn screamed as blood spurted across the kitchen floor.

The tip of his finger was dangling, the nail mangled and effectively cut in half. Thorn grasped the tip with his right hand, and tried to use pressure to keep it back on.

Kim was now in the door, standing sleepily in her underwear, shivering but concerned.

"What the hell is going on?" she asked, as Thorn danced around the kitchen in pain.

He was groping to reach for paper towels while trying not to release the pressure on his middle finger. It hurt like all heaven. How stupid could he have been...cutting his finger while trying to slice a rock-hard apple. Fuck that architect for leaving those apples in the first place. Fuck Kim for putting them in the fridge. Fuck, Fuck, Fuck! His finger throbbed.

Trying not to look at his finger, Thorn turned the tap water on to give it a rinse, as Kim now grabbed paper towels and helped Thorn concomitantly wrap the finger while maintaining a modicum of pressure on the tip. It was all a soggy, bloody mess.

But slowly drier paper towels made their way around the now wet inner ones. Kim grabbed some scotch tape to wrap the improvised bandage.

Thorn looked up at Kim with tears in his eyes, and felt disheartened. Their weekend was over; they would be bound for the hospital in Kingston for stitches, maybe with a stop along the way at a pharmacy for some proper bandages if they could find a pharmacy open on a Sunday morning.

"Get packed," Thorn said. "This was so dumb, I'm sorry, but we gotta get some stitches into this thing. I don't want to lose my finger."

And so it was that instead of going off to hike, or play golf, or play tennis that glorious crisp fall Sunday weekend, Thorn and Kim headed south through the small town of Tannersville where at 8 a.m. the pharmacy was most amazingly and appreciably open—perhaps just to sell morning newspapers. The paper towels were replaced with a formal bandage and Band-Aids for added pressure, and the bleeding seemed to ease, even while the throbbing from the finger did not.

While in the pharmacy, Thorn stared down at the Sunday *New York Times* for sale, stacked thick on the floor in piles.

"Bacon tells Germany: Let the Dollar Fall."

Thorn stared just at the headline, in big bold black letters—big for *New York Times* standards—a full banner.

"That's it. Once I get this finger fixed. I'm going to work," Thorn said to Kim. "The markets felt amazingly fragile Friday. God only knows what this headline is going to do to them Monday. I think I need to buy some vol."

CHAPTER 31

WOLFGANG AND THE CRASH
Tucker's Town, Bermuda
October 19, 1987

Sitting on his back patio, Wolfgang dialed Marty.

It was still early in the morning, Monday, October 19, 1987.

The Bermuda sky was gray, the best of the weather season behind the island.

"Do you see what this idiot Bacon is saying? Does he want to cause a crash or something?" Wolfgang asked immediately after Marty had clicked on the line.

Marty stared at his tick charts. He always stared at his tick charts.

He had come to sell himself as a master of fundamental "global capital flows,"—people ate that stuff up—but what he was really was a pretty damn good market technician with a few extra tools in his toolbox—pi and phi cycles among them.

"It certainly holds the potential for a waterfall decline in equities. What they are doing to the dollar seems to be pushing the edge of the volatility envelope. As you know, I have a minor pi cycle date due today."

"So do I sell? Or do I buy?"

"Maybe both. I could see hard down today, but unless we break 215 on the S&P, we could get a ping of a bottom there."

"But Marty, we're going to open more like 280. 215 is miles away. That's not exactly useful advice."

"I know, I know. But that's where my weekly and monthly reversal points are. As long as we hold above there today, it's likely a buy Wolfgang. You just don't want to be too early catching this falling knife."

"Buying this market just above that reversal level—if ever offered— that is what my plan would be."

"But Marty, you are usually so bearish, and now this market is actually cracking, and you want me to think buy?"

"I can only tell you what I see Wolfgang. If we go down hard today, you can be sure that the central bankers will be there tomorrow to defend their global franchise with added liquidity."

Wolfgang pondered things for a moment, and then asked the key clarifying question.

"Marty, are you long or short?"

"I was short. Now I'm neither; I'm flat. I'm looking for an entropic moment to buy."

"OK, got it," said Wolfgang.

Marty was brilliant but obtuse at times. It was not always easy to get within his head. The world could be ending in one breath, but the market a buy in the next.

Wolfgang dialed his broker in London. The phone rang and rang with no response.

Then Wolfgang remembered: London was having some sort of freak hurricane-like weather today. He'd seen it on the morning news. A lot of people there hadn't even made it to work. Maybe his normal broker was one of them. The market was particularly thin because of that.

Wolfgang pondered what to do—if anything. No response from London complicated things. If he was going to trade something, where the fuck would he do it? His broker had a New York team, he supposed, but he didn't know or trust the people there as much as he did his guy back on Lombard Street. He was already short dollars and long gold. Maybe that was enough for now.

He decided to listen to Marty and just watch.

CHAPTER 32

EDMUND AND THE CRASH
New York,
October 19, 1987

Edmund Safri had seen the Bacon headlines like everyone else. He'd also paid careful attention to the geo-political developments overnight that had been lost amidst the other headlines.

President Ronald Reagan had called in air strikes on several Iranian oil platforms as retaliation for the Iranian Navy harassing various Kuwaiti tankers—some now re-flagged to be carrying the red-white-and-blue stripes.

"It's all such a mess," thought Edmund. "Maybe it's just enough to make Buchanan's forecast of huge market instability potentially right."

Edmund had been in the markets long enough to recognize a firestorm. Markets could often handle one crisis—maybe something geo-political would come and go. But when you hit the market concomitantly with something else financial—some poorly placed words by Jim Bacon, for example—and then if you threw in something geo-physical like an earthquake or a hurricane, well...markets could spin out of control. He'd seen it before. Not often, but it was a bit like hitting "a perfect storm."

He'd need to be a strong leader that day.

He flipped the squawk box to his secretary.

"Can you patch me through to the trading room loudspeakers?

"Sure Mr. Safri. There you go," she answered, flipping an intercom circuit switch. "You're on."

"This is Edmund Safri. I know many of you are busy already, but I just want one moment of your attention. I am of the opinion that markets may be extraordinary volatile today. They closed weak on Friday, and show every indication in the pre-market to become significantly weaker today.

"I don't want any heroes out there today. I want to keep our footings light. If any of you are carrying significant inventories of securities, think about getting rid of those if you can. Don't do anything crazy, but if a fair bid can be found, I'd suggest using it proactively.

"I have seldom seen a market hit from all sides as seems to be transpiring today. I honestly don't know what is going to happen, but I do know that we need to protect the honorability and survival of this institution. I ask you all just to use your very best common sense. Remember, no heroes. No drawing a line in the sand. These markets could literally do anything. I want you all to be flexible and smart. If anyone encounters a major issue following these instructions, they are invited to come see me in my office."

Edmund wasn't much for pep talks, but that morning had seemed like an important moment to give such a shot.

There was a mild rumble of voices from the trading floor. It was a concerned mumble—mostly from the unusualness of Safri coming across the intercom. But it was a healthy mumble as well. One or two team heads arrived in Safri's office within minutes to share their sector-specific perspectives. This was teamwork. The Safri Bank would survive whatever the markets threw its way—as long as people worked as a team.

CHAPTER 33

THORNTON AND THE CRASH
New York
October 18, 1987

It was no longer the hallowed halls of the Pierrepont Bank, but instead, the drab already dated trading rows of Eastman Webber & Co. that Thorn needed to reach that Sunday afternoon. The line at the emergency room of Kingston hospital had been interminable, and the six stitches that he achieved in his fingertip had been painful to watch—if not feel—once the finger had been all numbed with drugs.

Yes, the finger could be saved. Re-bandage it in two days. Get to a doctor if any pussing or further discoloration were to occur. Otherwise, the stitches would need to come out in a few weeks.

Kim and he had been on the New York State Thruway headed south by 1pm. Kim was at the wheel and had driven fast.

But by 3 p.m., their car was sitting atop the elevated West Side Highway around 62nd Street, and wasn't moving at all. Some sort of Sunday afternoon parade festival was blocking all traffic. Kim and Thorn were stuck going nowhere. Frustration ate away at Thorn.

His original plan had been to get the car and Kim back to their apartment in Brooklyn Heights, and then head back to midtown by the subway to reach the Eastman Webber offices no later than 4 p.m. That was about the time Australia would start trading a variety of different markets. If Thorn was to get a jump on whatever was going to transpire when New York opened Monday, the Australia open was likely not a moment that he wanted to miss.

"Kim, I'm out of here," Thorn said.

"What do you mean, you're out of here? You're on the middle of an elevated highway ramp for God's sake."

"Yeah, but I gotta get moving. I'm not going to make Brooklyn Heights. Sorry to ditch you Kim but I'm just going to walk on out of here. It's only another five blocks or so until I can get off this thing when the highway dips down to the ground at 57th. I can hoof it across to the office from there. It's my best shot to make Australia. Love you; hope you make it home soon."

And with that, Thorn—bandaged finger elevated over his head so as not to accidentally bump it while he jogged past idling cars—headed southward down the West Side Drive—by foot.

It had been a good decision made just in time. He arrived at Eastman Webber offices on Sixth Avenue just as the clock passed 3:47 pm. Thorn had a ripe 13 minutes to plop himself down, quickly study the screens for any early indications of market movement, re-check the incoming news headlines, and get ready to pounce.

His was now at a job where he traded less options, and more of everything—indeed, almost anything. He was running a small proprietary trading book at Eastman Webber, and would actively get involved in currencies, metals, equity indices, and fixed income. He still felt the least comfortable in fixed income. All this shit about relative durations still confused him. Delta and gamma on top of duration differences was even trickier.

His mission that afternoon was to get his book better prepared for what he anticipated might be financial Armageddon on Monday morning. Picking up the phone to Eastman Webber, Australia, he initially sold ten million dollars against the Deutsche mark. It was only down a big figure from Friday's close, and Thorn deemed that to be an under-reaction to the Bacon headlines that he had read.

The second order of action was to deal with a negative gamma position that he had developed in his group's bond options book. Because Thorn had spied strong Fibonacci fractal support in the T-Bond futures at a price of 74, he had assumed in the prior days that the market—which had been steadily falling—would bounce a bit from this level and eventually settle into a range. This was a nice typical set-up to sell well bid front-end volatility in the December 1987 T-Bond futures options, and Thorn had done exactly this. But because his view of the 74 level as simply short-term support, and he was less sure of the longer-term prospects for T-Bond futures, he had bought longer-date March 1988 and June 1988 options. It was a volatility calendar spread, and it left Thorn's group short of options with fast moving deltas, and longer of options with more sensitivity to levels of vega (volatility exposure), but less sensitivity to immediate price movement (i.e. long options with slower moving gammas).

In an instant, Thorn knew that he held an overly complex position that was inappropriate to the developing situation. If markets were going to be spastic in the short-term, there was no edge to be short near-dated options. Instead, potentially having to chase the rate of change of the delta in these near-dated options was a pure liability. Thorn knew that for risk management reasons alone, he needed to buy back some or all of the December options that he had shorted just a few days earlier.

As the late Sunday afternoon slipped into the early part of Sunday night, Thorn got on the phone to his floor clerk out on the Chicago Board of Trade.

"Kurt, I've got a mission for you tonight. I need to buy 1000 cars a side of the Dec 74 straddles and another 1000 of the Dec 76 straddles. I know vols are going to be up a bit on the opening, so just join the bid side of the market initially, and if any reasonable vol selling paper comes in, let's participate grabbing that. I likely have more size behind this."

It was a vague set of instructions, but Thorn had come to trust Kurt. Thorn knew that Kurt would use common sense. Night trading of CBOT Bond options was literally only a month old, but there was still reasonable volume going through, and Thorn knew that even if he had to pay up a bit, he'd get some size done to diffuse his short option exposure in the nearby December maturity.

And then there was this geo-political stuff going on...Reagan bombing the Iranian oil fields. Maybe that was the reason that the dollar hadn't gone down that much in early trading. The threat of war was generally always good for dollar strength. It was also good for gold. By about 8pm, Thorn reached for the phone yet again, dialing Macquarie in Sydney.

"Is it too early to trouble you for a price on 20 bars?"

"Are you a buyer or a seller, mate?—Still pretty thin out here," the Aussie dealer responded in a friendly singsong.

Thorn hated showing his side, but given the nature of the markets that evening—tense and tentative—he deferred.

"I'm looking at your offered side."

"Moment, mate." The phone clicked off. In a second it came back to life. "I could get you done at 628 if that suits."

Thorn stared at his Bloomberg for a brief instant and pondered. He was likely getting arbed for 25 cents or so against the inside offered price, but for the size, the offer wasn't a bad one.

"OK, I'll buy those."

"628, I sell you twenty bars. Where you want those bars delivered mate?"

"Settles UBS London, thanks."

At the same moment, the floor box to the CBOT options pit crackled.

"Got the 74 straddles done. 17% vol. You bought 1000 a side. Still working the 76 straddles."

Thornton was feeling better. The worst of his gamma risk was now diffused. He also had added torque on board with his added dollar short and gold long. While his finger still throbbed, his preparedness for a busy Monday had improved.

He sat there watching the screens until well past the 11pm CBOT night trading session ended. Along the way, he instructed Kurt to lift a 17.5% volatility offer on his 76 Dec T-bond straddles. Then, after entering his new trades into his portfolio system and generating a new T-Bond delta risk ladder, he was pleased at the result. Bonds could collapse, or they could explode. Thorn didn't really care anymore— as long as prices moved quickly and briskly one way or the other he would be fine. It was the way any able-bodied options trader would want to be positioned if a sudden onset of financial stress were to wash over the world.

And on Monday October 19, 1987 such a wave of overt angst did indeed overwhelm markets. Thorn was prepared.

CHAPTER 34

THE AUSTRIAN—SURE OF THE BEAR
Vienna
October 19, 1987

As Thorn snuck into bed back in Brooklyn Heights that Monday morning at about 2 a.m.—reasonably sure that he had a portfolio that could survive whatever the regular daytime trading session later Monday might deliver—the sun was just rising over the skies of Vienna, and a young value-oriented equity analyst Michael Statz poured himself a cup of coffee.

Statz was a tall patrician type, partial to bow ties and much formality. He had attended the University of Vienna, and studied the theories there of famed Austrian School economist Ludwig von Mises. He was a fan of hard money and deep value investing.

Michael's family roots were mercantile. A prominent curving nose dominated his face—consistent to his Austrian-Hungarian roots. In 1936, his father had had to flee the Kocise area of the Austrian-Hungarian empire (since remapped as part of Slovakia) where Michael had been born, and the family had eventually found temporary safe haven in Switzerland. Some fine art had been left on their ancestral walls in Kocise—a historical factoid that still particularly grated Michael—but thankfully their savings of gold coins had been enough to start a new life. After the war, Vienna had become home in lieu of the hinterlands of Eastern Europe.

And Vienna had suited Michael just fine. It was more urbane and worldly than Kocise. He loved everything about Vienna: its stoic architecture, its Opera, its food, its music. Yes, he had since traveled as an economic consultant for the UNDP and studied in London and Paris, adding the English and French languages to his abilities. Later, he had ventured for a period to New York, and then Peru—adding an ability to navigate Spanish linguistics as well. Eventually he had spent a year in Tokyo, and while the Japanese language had proved more difficult for him to conquer, he had nonetheless still found there his petite Japanese wife named Suchico. His tall strong Prussian frame and her small mousy demeanor were an interesting mix that some found incongruous. But there was a bit of complementary ying and yang to their marriage: intellect mixed with artfulness; Prussian authority mixed with Japanese obedience. Michael certainly liked the way that Japanese wives were generally so desirous to serve and to please.

But global travels eventually led back to Vienna as home. He had returned to Vienna after ten years of low pay and varied cultural experiences. It had been time to settle down and make some money; start a family. Enough of this globetrotting do-good stuff.

Their apartment on Vienna's Spittelbergstrasse was tiny: an alcove studio with just enough room for a queen size bed and a few tables and chairs. The bed was the focus. More than anything else, Michael loved to fuck. And Suchico was so subtle and elegant in bed, her gentle curves filling Michael with happiness and excitement.

But he also loved to think about markets, about macro themes, and about finance. On the morning of October 19, 1987 he was focused more on his newspaper than his young wife.

"These markets are going to end badly," Michael mumbled. He was sitting at their small kitchen table, perusing the *International Herald Tribune*, and had just noted the Bacon headlines of that weekend for the first time. Michael was never the first to see a piece of news. Sometimes he was closer to the last.

"You always think the markets are going to end badly," Suchico said, barely looking up from her own Japanese-language newspaper.

Suchico loved Michael and his eclectic individualistic thought process, his natural intellect, and his gentlemanly old-fashioned European charm. Michael certainly had such a lovely sense of humor. But she also knew her husband well enough that he was almost always bearish. It was too bad, as well, because the small private bank Vontobel et Cie. that he had joined after his UNDP years was starting to promote others instead of Michael. Michael's reputation had become that of a dour "worry-wart," and how could a dour "worry-wart" actually make an effective money manager and interact positively with clients? He had already been passed over on two different occasions for a promotion from his lowly equity analyst position.

"You will see, Suchico. I am not crazy. It is this world which is crazy. Stocks are of no value here. I only wish that I could get my colleagues at Vontobel to understand this. They should be getting their clients more short exposure, not looking for more longs. There is a business here somewhere. Maybe someday I will put that together, and get away from this long-only stuff. So ein Beschiß!"

With that, Michael gulped down his last swig of coffee, and headed out the door. He bent to give Suchico a kiss as he did so. His tall gangly frame and tough-minded demeanor was no match for the sight of her pert nipples under her tee shirt. He reached down to cup one breast as she stood to kiss him goodbye.

"Ich Liebe Dich," he said softly—I love you. "I'll see you tonight, and then you will see how smart a husband that you have married. The world might be oh-so different soon."

Suchico had heard it all before, and the financial world never quite cooperated with a meltdown. She was sure that Michael would be right someday, but wasn't timing just as important as longer-term vision? She wondered if Michael would ever make enough money for them to move from their tiny apartment; to have a baby; to really enjoy a life.

As Michael walked the five blocks from Spittelbergstrasse to Vontobel's Kartnerstraasse offices, he looked at the people around him on the streets. They all seemed so happy and oblivious to the wave of potential financial turmoil that Michael felt coming. Was he really that much smarter than all these people that he saw these unfixed macro problems in the global economy? Or did all these other people simply not care to take the time to understand? Or was there something just innate in human psychology for most people to be bullish and optimistic?

If so, Michael certainly had not received that bull gene.

The Crash of 1987 did indeed transpire that day. Michael watched his screens intently late into the Vienna evening. The Vontobel customers were all getting royally pasted. A few of Michael's colleagues stopped by his cubby-hole office and offered slightly snide and worried back-handed compliments:

"So this is what you were wishing for?"

But at least they acknowledged his prior vision—even as they detested the current Armageddon.

The whole move was almost surreal. The Dow Jones had opened -90 points, but then quickly was down -180...churning, high volume, small attempted and aborted rallies; then suddenly -250, then -300, the NYSE tape running extremely late. A mid-afternoon bounce was shallow and anemic. By the close it had been -508 points, on the lows, or a -22.61% single day plunge—a waterfall decline, the largest one-day percentage fall in the Dow's entire history.

With Michael still at the office, Suchico was tuned to the television news that evening, still struggling to understand the fast-spoken German. She could grasp just enough of the images and graphics with arrows pointed southward next to the words "Wall Street" to believe her young Austrian husband was indeed ever so brilliant. Just as he had predicted, the world had changed that day. Traditional financial thought had come unglued.

Traders at the Safri Bank in New York also praised their boss Edmund Safri. He had warned them that morning. He had felt the wave coming. Many presumed that's why he made the big bucks—a true market expert. Most of the traders had listened to his squawk box advice. Positions had been pared. Sure, there were some losses, but there were no disasters. Only Safri knew that Professor John Buchanan had set him on edge to be extra attentive.

Wolfgang in Bermuda had watched until just before the close when the S&P was printing 217. What was Marty's reversal support level, 215? He scrambled to find his morning telephone call notes. Yes, 215 was the number Marty had mentioned. Was it worth a shot to catch a falling knife against that support level? 215 had seemed like such a remote possibility to even be a meaningful price level just a few hours earlier that day. But now here it was close at hand. Surely this thing would bounce. Wouldn't it?

Wolfgang finally called the New York office of his London-based brokerage firm and bought some S&P futures with about 10 minutes to trade. The broker he placed the order with considered him crazy to take such a risk. Would the financial world still exist tomorrow? Or would the entire system fail?

Meanwhile, Thorn was back at his Eastman Webber perch wondering whether all of his trading activities of the prior night had done the trick. The one thing that he had *failed* to do was get short stock futures, and by 3:30 pm in New York, it was only stocks that were melting. Other markets seemed to be in momentary limbo— moving sideways, almost aghast in shock. All of his bond volatility purchased the prior night was more or less just sitting there not being of huge immediate value. Yes, gold was higher and the dollar was a bit lower, so Thorn's book overall was making some money, but he wondered if he had over-reacted on Sunday to buy all those bond option straddles. The thought crossed his mind that maybe he should sell them back out.

Then it happened. -508 on the DJIA into the close. Within seconds, the cash T-Bond market was taking off. It was a flight to quality mixed with rumors that the Fed would be cutting interest rates. It was all happening in the aftermarket, the futures markets already being long closed.

The cash bond market simply soared in a straight line.

A squawk box voice hollered prices for the then-current long bond: "101, 102, 103, 105, 108! No offers." The screens were electrified.

Thorn was amazed. He had bought all of his volatility the prior night more on the thought that the bond market might collapse on Bacon's comments, not explode. But gamma was gamma. It was part of the joy of the derivatives business to make a decision for one reason, and then still make a killing when the exact opposite transpired. As he looked down at his risk ladder, he realized that his 74 and 76 calls of December Bond futures were now well in the money conceptually even if the futures were only marked "limit up" two points in the post-market screens. The futures equivalent of the cash market was more like 83 or 84...up eight full points—a huge unheard of type move.

What was the right trade to do now? Sit on his hands? Sell cash bonds into his long gamma position?

Thorn decided to short a few on-the run cash bonds up those cool eight points. As a stand-alone trade, it might end up being a mild mistake, but who knew what the right price for anything was in this environment. He had to lock in some of this move. It would be inexcusable not to do so if this bond market rally subsequently faded.

"Sell me 20 million 7.5's of '07," Thorn told the cash dealer. The trade was done. Thorn smiled having just more or less booked over a million dollar gain—not even including the coming pop in volatility that was likely to transpire when the options trading night session began. And even with this new cash market hedge, he was still synthetically long bonds in a market still rising.

But what if the futures market failed tomorrow? What if all his gamma there wasn't allowed to pay off? Then he'd just be short cash T-Bonds probably still soaring higher, and his in-the-money calls might not be there to protect him. Anything was suddenly possible that day...a good position could turn into a disastrous one. Thorn quickly turned to the EFP (exchange-for-physical) dealer, and asked to get a price to swap his just shorted 7.5's of '07 back into an equivalent futures exposure. It was always good to keep your book as neat as possible, without unneeded or unwanted added "basis" exposures.

Thorn paid away a bit of spread in the EFP trade, but it was worth it. No reason to mix apples and oranges—even if cash T-Bonds and T-Bond futures were ever so similar.

Thorn pondered further. It was surely going to be a weird night session as well. Thorn expected futures would just sit locked limit up, but options on futures had no set limits to their trading. The second derivative options world would continue to trade even while the first derivative underlying futures product likely would not. It was going to be all screwed up.

Exhausted by his prior night's late session, Thorn decided to head for the elevators to make his way home on the subway. He wanted to be back to Brooklyn in time to see the treatment of "the Crash of '87" on the evening news, and also to see if the bond futures market would trade at all. He was standing at the elevator bank, when an added thought occurred to him.

"What if I happen to get stuck on the subway home, and futures don't open limit bid, like they should. Maybe I should leave a buy order just in case..."

So having just sold 20 million cash bonds, and having swapped them back into short 200 lots of short futures exposure, Thorn returned to his desk and dialed the direct line to Kurt on the CBOT once again.

"Hey Kurt, I'm leaving now, and I should be home in time for the night session opening, but just in case I'm not, and should the Dec bond futures not immediately go locked-limit bid, buy me 400 cars anywhere up to limit bid."

Cars, lots...it all meant the same thing: futures lingo for contracts. Chicago called 'em "cars" as in freight cars. New York called 'em lots as in feed lots.

"Got it, Thorn. I'll call you if we get anything done."

It had already been a glorious day for Thorn, but the subway trip home was indeed problematic and slow. When the subway doors eventually opened at Court Street, Thorn started home in a jog. Why were subways always so aggravating when you needed them to work best? As he eventually made it home, rushing into his Brooklyn Heights apartment, he saw the light of his message machine already blinking.

Thorn punched the playback button.

"Thorn, it's Kurt." The tape machine chortled. "You won't believe this, but futures did open limit bid, but then they actually came *off* limit for about five minutes. You bought your 400 cars at 77 and 24/32 average price. We're back to limit bid now."

This was almost too amazing to be true. How inefficient the markets had suddenly become. Thorn had effectively sold 200 contracts of futures before leaving the office up near 82, and now he was buying them back over four points lower, and getting even longer. When futures eventually would resume trading two days later, prices back in the 82 to 85 range were seen once again. Option volatility levels also exploded. It was a happy moment for Thorn.

It had also been a happy moment for Michael, for Edmund, for Buchanan, for Wolfgang, and Marty as well.

The power of fractals, as well as the positive gamma and convexity from options, were to be praised.

While The Crash of 1987 hurt some, it was only the best of times for our small cast of characters—Thornton in particular.

CHAPTER 35

POLITICOS IN MOTION
Varied Locales
October 20, 1987

The Fed "affirmed today its readiness to serve as a source of liquidity to support the economic and financial system."

So stated Fed Chairman Alan Greenspan on the morning of October 20, 1987. Having been in office a scant two months and a few days when the Crash transpired, Greenspan was still largely an unknown at the time. But with this one line, and the decisive opening up of credit facilities to all of Wall Street, Greenspan made it clear that his approach to the job wasn't going to be like that of his predecessor Paul Volcker.

Markets immediately rebounded. Wolfgang's purchase of S&P futures held nicely above his 217 price over the following days. There was still a great deal of churning and volatility, but Marty for one knew that the worst was over. The markets had made a waterfall decline directly on one of his pi cycle dates, but held above a key reversal level. Bullish set-ups didn't get any better than this. He went on the offensive telling others that this was a moment to buy, not to panic and sell.

Thorn worked feverishly to harvest his long volatility position in T-Bond options—book it all out. He'd captured some dramatic gamma trading opportunities, and the imbedded implied volatility pricing in options had gone from 18% to more like 23%. It had been a lovely premium expansion. But Thorn had also long since learned not to wait too long to take such profits. Implied volatility gains had a tendency to evaporate—particularly in a market that had stopped going down, and was rebounding back into a new trading range. There was a gentle balance between keeping some useful gamma for a few more days, and getting rid of options that would eventually melt in their time decay as the December futures options expiry date approached.

John Buchanan could hardly believe how timely his fractal models had been in his warning to Edmund Safri of impending market instability. He only hoped that his advice had proved useful to Edmund—even if there still had been no signal to sell that damn rhodium market. He did not however pick up the phone to call Edmund. He knew Edmund would be incredibly busy, and did not want to seem like the gloating type.

Michael Statz in Vienna grew convinced that this crash event was just a first footfall in much more market nastiness to follow. In his head, he made note that there should be more short-biased funds for this type of environment, and pondered how hard that it would be to set up such an entity himself someday. As he gave Suchico an aggressive session in bed later that October week, he felt all-powerful and ever so smart.

But at the Fed, Greenspan viewed his job as one to soothe Wall Street, not aggravate it. He wanted to paste over bigger macro problems that Congress or the U.S. Treasury were unable to solve, and to feed as much money as needed to keep markets buoyant and growing. If an occasional "rabbit in the hat" was required, he would provide it. The key was just to buy time and keep people from panicking. He'd studied the 1929 Crash, and was determined to move swiftly to avoid any similar outcome.

And so he cut rates. A bit like the Hunt Silver Crisis where regulators and exchange officials didn't like the prices that they were seeing, and thus they regulated these prices away, Greenspan regulated away the normal economic retrenchment mode that would have typically followed a Wall Street Crash of the magnitude that had just been witnessed.

Over a period of days, the angst just evaporated. To coin a term first used by George Soros, the Fed reacted with appropriate "reflexivity" to make the Crash look like little more than an accident—not a sustainable trend.

Meanwhile over at Treasury, Jim Bacon was pissed. Not only were some media pundits blaming the Crash on his inflammatory words about the dollar, but even after the crash, that damn trade deficit that he was trying to fix didn't seem to be going away.

"I'm going to take one more shot at this thing," Bacon said to his assistant Olsen. "Let's get a trip to Japan on the agenda pronto. We need those guys to jump start their demand for American goods and to do it fast—like yesterday."

Bacon had of course already negotiated the Plaza Accord to drive the dollar lower in 1985. At the same time he'd asked the Japanese to cut their interest rates, and they had done so fairly aggressively during 1986. The Bank of Japan (BOJ) had specifically taken the key discount rate from 5% to 3% across that year. The net result was that both Japanese property and stocks had been sent booming as global capital aggregated there amidst the attractive twin macro conditions of a strong currency and loose interest rates.

But Bacon needed some of that wealth to come back to the U.S. or at least make its way into emerging market economies—not pile up in Japan. He needed the Japanese to buy more American stuff and less Japanese stuff. The Japanese were doing the opposite. This was *not* what his economic mind had expected. The law of unintended consequences was already in motion.

The February 1987 Louvre Accord had then been a half-hearted attempt to slow down the dollar's decline. Within the Louvre Accord, Japan had slashed its rates yet one more notch lower to 2.5%, but just more of the same had occurred...more buying of Japanese property and of the Nikkei...not American cars or beef or other products. It was as if Bacon was now riding a runaway train that he'd set in motion, but couldn't stop.

James Bacon and Olsen McFadden eventually arrived in Tokyo to the chilly winds of January 1988.

In addition to wanting to speak with Kichi Miyazawa at the Ministry of Finance, Bacon knew that Yasushi Mieno, deputy governor of the BOJ, was the key person to coerce. The main BOJ governor Satoshi Sumita was a relative lightweight. Mieno and his banking lieutenant Toshihiko Fuqui were the two pulling all of the behind-the-scenes levers with different loan quota window guidance to the banks— more or less telling the banks how much that they needed to lend each month in a manner that only a centralized government authority could. Sumita was barely aware of what his deputy governor Mieno was up to. It had been Mieno that Bacon had relied on across 1986 to get rates lower in Japan—to pump and stimulate. Miyazawa had really only tossed in strong infrastructure building projects across Japan. Mieno and Fuqui were jokingly referred to within the BOJ as the "Kwantung Army"—a former 1930's military unit that acting somewhat autonomously had originally escalated Japan's march into Manchuria. In somewhat similar fashion, Mieno and Fukui had led the BOJ on a unique private-army type economic experiment during the boom-boom period of 1986 and 1987.

Their goal? Well, if the Plaza Accord was going to drive the yen higher and make life more difficult for Japanese corporates to export things, Mieno wanted super low rates to help support markets and thereby help spur domestic demand and thereby help Japanese businesses. He specifically wanted to create perceived wealth to help transform the Japanese economy to be less export-reliant and more domestically driven. If Japan bought more American goods in the process, and made Jim Bacon happy, fine. But the key thing was to help Japanese business thrive and flourish. If Japanese margins were going to get pressured on sales to the U.S., then corporates deserved some other offsetting benefit to help them absorb this margin pressure impact.

In other words, Bacon had wanted to drive the dollar lower so Japanese would be forced to raise their car prices in America and thus presumably sell less Japanese cars, while American companies would presumably sell more cars in Japan. It was supply-demand Economics 101. The Japanese reaction however was to not raise their dollar price for cars in America. Instead, they just left their prices the same, and ate the profit margin differential, making up for this loss in other ways. That had been Mieno's part to provide. The combo of effects had been "bubble-icious" in Japan, and ultimately frustrating to Bacon.

As rain drizzled across the windshield of their car from the airport, Bacon contemplated where the world stood. The Plaza Accord had worked; but now the Louvre Accord had not. As the dollar had failed to hold in early 1987, bonds had initially been hit until stocks in the U.S. had ultimately crashed. It had been a series of events that exhibited a clear loss of confidence in global central bankers. Maybe he deserved that slap in the face. Maybe he had exhibited too much hubris thinking that he could fix the global economy with his sweeping policy actions.

The failure of the Louvre Accord to stop the dollar fall had been Bacon's first moment of real angst. The next had been when Ronald Reagan had appointed Greenspan as Fed Chairman to replace Volcker. The dollar had taken another dive on the announcement. But then, as if to show that he was not a White House puppy dog, Greenspan had snugged rates in September 1987. Bacon had pled with the Germans and the Japanese not to follow suit, but fearful that inflation was starting to get out of control in their respective countries, both had done a round of tightening apiece.

"Damn them," he thought. "If they wanted me to firm up the dollar, they weren't helping that goal by taking their own rates higher. "He was determined not to destroy the American economy by forcing rates up in the U.S. That's when he'd thrown in the towel and planted the 'Let the Dollar Fall' headline. It had been a moment of exasperation more than anything else. He saw now that this last move of brinksmanship had been a mistake. Reaganomics and his entire grand experiment in global economic manipulation now lay very much in a shambles.

Bacon and Olsen were ushered into a drab 1950's-style conference room at the Bank of Japan. After several minutes sitting quietly staring at the non-descript walls, a corner door finally opened and Yasushi Mieno walked in followed by several assistants. He looked dour and serious.

"Mieno-san, so good to see you," Bacon stood and bowed his tall frame dutifully.

"Mr. Bacon, it is my honor."

There was initial small talk about his trip over; how long it had been since Mr. Bacon had visited Japan; and where he was staying. In the past, Bacon had seen entire Japanese meetings hardly get past such pleasantries. No one ever wanted to do the hard lifting—talk about the tough subjects. But it was a requisite initial ritual of politeness.

Then Bacon cut to the chase.

"Mieno-san, I know that you were most helpful cutting interest rates over the past two years, and I really appreciate all that you have done to support the G7's economic plan. But I need you to somehow get your domestic savings more productively in motion. I specifically need Japan to buy more American goods."

Mieno-san looked blankly and unemotionally back at Bacon. His subsequent words were practiced and precise.

"Mr. Bacon—we have allowed you to depreciate the dollar against the yen; we have hurt our own corporate competitiveness when we did so; but Japan has adjusted. We have become stronger for the experience. America has not. We did everything that you asked of us, and your Wall Street still crashed last October."

"Yes, but..." started Bacon.

Mieno was not going to allow Bacon a foothold. He leaned across the table and quickly continued.

"We need to be attentive to our own issues now. It may be time to start pulling back some of our past accommodation. Some believe that too much liquidity has gone into financial speculation as opposed to sustainable growth. Japan has rebounded smartly from the unfortunate events of October, but we view October as a warning sign that your policies for global economic growth have not worked, Mr. Bacon. We need to watch out for Japan now. There is only so much we can do for America."

"Could I simply ask that you go slow in removing your accommodation?" asked Bacon, knowingly making a retreat from his original goals for the meeting. "The world remains ever so fragile. I think that it would be better if you somehow encouraged more import consumption, not less."

"Mr. Bacon, I will try to be as helpful as possible, but you must know that there are political pressures afoot to slow things down. There has actually been increased talk of a new consumption tax forthcoming."

"Ah shit, Mieno-san, that's the last thing that the world needs—a Japanese consumption tax? You've got to be kidding." Bacon was losing his composure, and as he did so, became more Texan in both the level of his voice and his language.

"I knew that you would not be pleased Mr. Bacon, but yes, I think that there is enough political will that such a tax will eventually pass. I have heard rumblings already. Knowing that, and how such an action—if enacted—could indeed reign in the economy, the best that I can offer is that we will not tap on the breaks here at the BOJ as well. We will go slow. Feel our way."

Bacon had come hoping for more stimulus from Japan, and here he was hearing about a new proposed consumption tax. He would have to settle for the BOJ simply not tightening. What a disappointment—a bust of a trip.

As he left the Mieno meeting and returned to his waiting black car, January's cold rain splattered around his feet. Pulling his frame into the back seat, he immediately turned to Olsen.

"Remind me to pitch Ronnie about becoming Secretary of State before this economic morass gets any worse."

Bacon said this half in jest, but also in half-seriousness.

CHAPTER 36

BEATING THE JAPANESE AT DERIVATIVES
New York
March 1989

Thorn was never quite the same in his trading style after the Crash of 1987. The butterfly effect danced in his head.

What if he hadn't cut that finger? What if he hadn't made that last minute adjustment of exposures on that Sunday evening?

His world might have been an entirely different story. He surely would have survived the Crash, but chasing negative T-Bond gamma would have been a struggle. He likely would have lost money. He certainly would not have gotten paid as well when bonus time came that year at Eastman Webber. The vacation house in upstate New York might have been deferred or never built.

Thorn's phone also might not have rung in early 1989 with a job offer from Goodman Sachs.

Eastman Webber was OK, but at its heart, the firm was just a brokerage shop mostly looking to do client business. Trader limits were modest, and Thorn was very much the oddball position trader within a den of sharks eager to earn commission dollars on the back of their clients.

Thorn had a little spark-plug boss, Jim Stieber, at Eastman Webber. Jim had come from Salomon Brothers before Eastman Webber, and used to swing by Thorn's desk and say: "So, I just heard John Meriwether made $100 million for the quarter from his prop positioning back at Salomon. And how are we doing?"

This desk was never going to be a John Meriwether affair. Despite Stieber's joking encouragement, senior management just had no appetite for prop trading. The limits and risk appetite simply weren't there—even after Thorn's fine performance during the '87 crash. Thorn even heard one Eastman Webber bureaucrat espouse concern that if Thorn had been able to make $10 million across the Crash period, maybe that meant his limits were too big. Eastman Webber was in the B-Leagues, and Thorn set his mind to regain a slot in the A-Leagues where real money could be thrown around.

That's where the call from Goodman Sachs had fit perfectly. Goodman had lost a senior derivatives trader to Bankers Trust, and needed to hire someone solid and experienced as a replacement. Thorn had made his availability known, and then quickly landed the job.

As he left Eastman Webber for the last time, a senior colleague from his desk named Dieter turned to Thorn, and shook his hand: "You're going to be rich."

"What do you mean I'm going to be rich?"

"Everyone who goes to Goodman Sachs becomes rich. Congratulations. Just remember your friends back here someday if they ever come calling on you."

Oddly enough, Dieter would have been the one fellow from his group that Thorn would never have offered a job to. The guy's trading abilities were fine—particularly in fixed income relative value trading—but his attitude wasn't.

Amidst a row of traders—several of whom were women and none of whom smoked—complaints had risen up through the ranks that Dieter puffed on too many cigars. Everyone found that their clothes stank of cigar smoke at the end of just one day's wear. Even Thorn had noticed and detested the odor. A ban on smoking within trading rooms still rested somewhere in Wall Street's future, so how to handle this had been an awkward moment for Thorn.

Now Dieter technically reported to Thorn, but considered himself something of a big swinging dick. He had always been extremely difficult to manage. When Thorn had turned to him about the cigar smoke—mentioning all of the complaints, and making the gentle suggestion that Dieter enjoy his cigars somewhere away from the trading aisle—Dieter had turned back to Thorn and said, scowling: "Just buy a fuckin' fan."

It had been a singularly emblematic moment of the late 1980's. New York State restrictions about non-smoking on trading floors would only gain wider enforcement by firms in the early 1990's. In the meantime there was Dieter—what a self-centered jerk.

This was one prick Thorn was happy to be ditching. No, there would be no handouts to Dieter from Thorn's new Goodman Sachs perch.

Goodman was indeed amazing. Across the first few days at his new job, Thorn quickly surmised that the average person at Goodman was just a bit smarter than the average person at any other firm Thorn had seen to date. Goodman's systems were also a bit faster, a bit more robust, and a bit less clunky—the firm having previously made a key tactical decision to recruit some of Bell Labs' best quant programmers.

And Goodman's limits were just great.

Goodman was so different from Eastman Webber where auditors and compliance people had hovered over Thorn's every move. At Eastman Webber, if one little premium expense exposure, tail risk exposure, or theta decay number popped out of defined bounds, he could always expect a phone call or a compliance visit.

But at Goodman, Thorn never even saw any formal limits. Instead, there was just this quietly produced Monte Carlo simulation that ran in the background of their derivatives portfolio. If a tail risk exposure popped out of some sort, a question or two might be asked, but generally nobody threw a shit-fit or demanded immediate remediation.

At Goodman, traders were truly free to make money the old fashioned way: in any manner that seemed to make sense. This included running over other firms burdened with pesky limit issues.

And then there was this funny little new boss named Lloyd Blankstein that Thorn now reported to. The guy was always cracking a joke, and was very hard to pin down.

"Have you heard the new joke about the difference between a clown and a prostitute?" Lloyd might start a desk visit.

"The clown does cunning stunts, while the prostitute has a stunning cunt."

One joke after the next. It was like he wanted to manage the troops—those he recognized as being naturally smarter than he was—by being their best friend. Any needed seriousness could be eased into the conversation on the rebound after an initial joke-fest.

And what an era of options arbitrage opportunities Thorn was walking back into. Even though it was 1989, and derivatives had been around for almost a decade, the Japanese still had some ass-backward methodologies for doing derivatives accounting. Most Japanese corporate clients, insurance companies, and banks simply booked option premiums that had been sold as income, and premiums bought as an expense.

Guess what that led the average Japanese bank or corporate to do? They sold option premiums—again and again.

It was also an era where the Bank of Japan and Ministry of Finance had Tokyo traders eating out of their hands. If the BOJ said that dollar-yen wasn't going to trade above a 135 top limit or below 110, all the Japanese traders myopically believed them. If one called up the Bank of Tokyo, Tokyo and asked for a 135 dollar call against the yen, the first response that one would regularly hear was "That strike is worthless. The Bank of Japan won't let dollar-yen go above that level."

So Thorn and his colleagues would have to cajole their Tokyo-based counterparts to humor them, show them a price, go ahead and make it a low price if they wanted.

The price would come back something like a 4% volatility offered, and—boom—the Goodman traders would pounce. Thorn and his colleagues didn't even have to worry if 135 really was a market cap, because similar type options on the International Money Market (IMM) futures options exchange in Chicago were quoted 7% volatility bid at 8% volatility offered. Buying from the Japanese at 4% volatility and selling to Chicago at 7% volatility typically left one with a mild exercise-time cut-off difference (that might sporadically prove problematic if the market ended up on expiration day near the strike prices traded). But generally, this large volatility differential was worth that small risk. Indeed, it was like minting money.

The second thing that was happening in Japan was the invention of the "structured note" at the same time that New York-based quants had developed so-called exotic options. Structured notes were where the Japanese would buy a bond with a seemingly attractive variable payout by effectively shorting an imbedded option of some sort within the note's terms to increase the yield on the note under certain conditions. Bury a short exotic option inside a structured note, and the payoffs could get most interesting.

This all began with increased Japanese bond offerings in 1988 and 1989 that contained imbedded Nikkei puts. The average Mrs. Watanabe in Japan (Japanese housewives generally controlling the family finances) would readily accept earning a yield of 5% instead of a paltry 2.5% in exchange for giving up a "tail risk" potential loss of principal should the Japanese Nikkei decline. In Japan, everyone knew that the Nikkei was only going up. Per Japanese thinking at the time, the Bank of Japan would simply not allow the Nikkei to go down. So why not accept the higher yield while risking an outcome that just wasn't going to happen?

This grope for added yield had of course started in part because of Jim Bacon's prior plan to get the Japanese to cut their interest rates so that they would buy more American products. Instead, what was happening was that the Japanese just bought more complex and crappier paper with hidden derivatives risks that they should never have considered touching. The well-intentioned policy to fix "Problem A"—the U.S. trade deficit—was causing yet another unintended consequence "Problem B"—a massive spate of toxic mal-investment. And sadly enough for the average Mrs. Watanabe, most of these structured notes carried longer-dated expirations like ten years—just long enough in time to eventually prove problematic.

In the spring of 1990, so-called Japanese Samurai Bonds also came along in a similar vein. Here the Japanese investors might be offered an even sweeter 7% coupon, but if over a period of five years, the Australian-dollar versus yen relationship were ever to fall and just "touch" a given low Aussie-yen price level, then the note holder would only get back principal in the depreciated Australian dollar, not yen. The "touch" level seemed so far away that the Japanese still regularly gobbled up this paper.

Matching the neophyte Japanese against the sophistication of Wall Street derivatives traders and structured note experts was like giving candy to a baby. At least initially, everyone was happy. The Japanese simply gorged themselves on products that they thought that they understood and certainly fit their perceived market directional biases, but were concomitantly selling options way too cheaply. In the process, the Japanese note buyers were setting themselves up for a real fall, so to speak, should any of these "tail risk" outcomes actually transpire. And the derivative-trading arbs in New York and London just printed money from their Far Eastern counterparts' general naiveté.

Thorn by this time had a young son, Matthew—a cute little inquisitive kid. At age five Matthew looked up at Thorn, and asked "What do you do for a living, daddy? Where do you go every morning?"

Samurai Bonds on his mind, Thorn had answered: "Do you see that Toyota mini-van in the driveway, Matt?"

"Yes, that's mommy's car," Matt had answered—initially a bit confused where his daddy was leading him with this answer.

"Well, daddy paid for it. The Japanese build that car, and they build it pretty well. The engines last a long time. They don't tend to break down. We had to pay them $25,000 for that car. But then the Japanese don't really know what to do with the money that we give them for it. In fact, they often do really stupid things with the money. Sometimes they pay too much for investments like office buildings and golf courses. They also invest in other financial products where they don't really understand what they're buying, or in the risks that they are taking...

"So daddy's job is to trade against the Japanese in these other investments and see if I can't get the $25,000 back that we paid them for the car. If my colleagues and I are smart enough, we might get to have both the car and then also get the money back that we paid for it."

Matthew still hadn't entirely understood, but he liked the sound of the story. It sounded pretty nifty—like something Darth Vader might arrange. Thorn liked the story as well. Critics of Wall Street be damned! One of America's best effective "exports" was indeed its financial ingenuity, and Thorn had been front and center in the early days of this ingenuity within the derivatives trading world. He'd had this vision about the potential growing importance of derivatives back when he'd just been a kid at Princeton, and as things had turned out, he had been very much correct that derivatives had become a huge business.

Japan might be piling up the cash from selling cars and microwaves and televisions—getting richer and richer each year—but America was, in other ways, still eating Japan for breakfast. America was dancing on Japan's myopic financial investment proclivities and taking advantage of their inadequate accounting rules to eventually get back at least a modest chunk of money.

The Japanese bonds imbedded with short Nikkei put options were placed with Japanese investors all across the Nikkei's ascent in 1988 and 1989. By 1990-1992, these would eventually blow up those investors still holding them.

The Samurai Bonds tied to the price of Aussie-yen also did not end well. Many of the cheap effective "reverse knock-in" options that the Japanese were implicitly shorting ended up residing as stripped-out long options on Thorn's books. If Thorn had shown the salesman/structurer 11% volatility as a fair value bid for these options, he got given the options—courtesy of the fancy structuring—more like 9.5% volatility. There were lots of smiles and P&L to share all around as the "mark-to-model" machines would immediately mark the options up to at least 11% volatility. Then it was only the question of whether to arb out the profit, or wait for the Japanese to explode, or do a bit of both. Thorn initially locked in arb gains on about half the exposure, and kept the balance of the options as cheap out-of-the-money wildcard bets that the Japanese would indeed fall afoul of these exposures.

And then one day, Thorn saw what looked like a masterful and gigantic weekly triple top on Aussie-yen. The game was about to go to a new level—into real payoff mode.

Thorn turned to his colleagues at Goodman and pointed out the ominous chart formation. "We need to buy as much of this volatility as we can put our hands on. Get the guys in Tokyo to just lap the stuff up. Then I'd suggest we give this cross a little push to the downside—maybe try selling $50 million Aussie worth of the cross in the spot market, and see how it behaves. If this starts to crack, we give it another push by launching another $50 million Aussie out the door. We know that the Japanese will be vulnerable. It could set off a real cascade of panic."

So in the same way that Goodman would eventually smell the blood in the streets around the 1997 East Asian (Thai baht) currency crisis, when they egged hedge fund manager Tiger Management into aggressively pushing the baht lower, Thorn and his new Goodman colleagues smelled the Aussie-yen turmoil well before it started. They had allowed the Japanese to be neophytes. They had encouraged the Japanese to be neophytes. They sucked them in, and let the volumes build. It was all initially a happy symbiotic world. And then when the Japanese were loaded up with exposure, Goodman gave the market a little nudge to the downside.

The cross spiraled lower. First, it was driven by the Aussie, which fell against the dollar, and then later, it was driven by the yen which rose against the dollar. It was a glorious $30mm type of revenue generator over about a twelve week period of time—and another wonderful positive gamma type of experience for Thorn. Once that currency cross started going, it became another cascade "crash-like" move similar to the Crash of 1987 in equities—where both the positive gamma of long options and the positive vega attributes of being long volatility worked beautifully. Thorn loved that set-up so much that he eventually saved the chart of it. Market entropy and exhaustion had yielded yet another great trading year.

Yes, maybe Dieter back at Eastman Webber would be right. Thorn was going to be rich.

Goodman at the time had a payroll computer system that at bonus time could only produce checks that were denominated up to $99,999.99. If your bonus was more than this, you would get multiple envelopes each with a $99,999.99 check in it. How many "envelopes" you got quickly became a buzzword about one's overall success.

"Jesus Christ, did you hear that Frank got ten envelopes? He made a clean buck!" people would whisper.

Thorn never got ten envelopes, but courtesy of the Japanese constantly blowing themselves up on derivatives, he did eventually become a seven-envelope man in 1991.

Life was grand.

CHAPTER 37

THE GAIJIN INVESTMENT GOD
The Palace Hotel, Tokyo
May 1991

It was Marty's favorite venue to give a speech: the Palace Hotel in Tokyo with its sleek clean conference rooms and gorgeous view over the downtown Imperial Palace gardens. And each time he went back for a presentation, more Japanese pension fund managers seemed to line the walls.

First Marty had been able to accommodate the crowds in the Hotel's Yamabucki conference room, but after his successful and well-publicized pi cycle call made in early 1989 that the Nikkei would peak in mid-December 1989—missing the actual top by just a few scant days—the 1990 conference had been moved to the even bigger Aoki Ballroom facility. Marty also sometimes held special one-on-one consulting sessions with some clients in the Hotel's white-domed wedding chapel. He charged $10,000 for fifteen minutes of his time when he did so. It was like the Japanese money managers coming to see their *gaijin* investment God.

Yes, the kid from South Jersey had hit the big time, soon voted the number one "economist" in all of Japan by the Tokyo *Shinbun* daily newspaper—even though he wasn't really an economist—more just a market prognosticator. He had also started to regularly achieve invitations to meet with important figures from the Bank of Japan and Ministry of Finance.

These officials were grasping at straws behind the scenes, and needed all the help—no matter how eclectic—that they could find. As a result, Marty was in "the know" with all the latest scuttlebutt about governmental issues: problems with the ailing Postal system hurt by fixed interest obligations and yet diminishing JGB yields; what pension plans had hidden liabilities and mark-to-market issues within their portfolio; and what brokerage firms were on the verge of collapse.

Marty would mention some of these fundamental vignettes in passing during his conferences, and this only broadened his appeal and the power of his other technical perspectives.

Word had gotten out: "This *gaijin* has secret tools; secret sources. He is super smart. He called Nikkei top to the week! How could anyone have done that?"

Sadly, many people came back to listen to him more closely in 1991 partly because they had not actually followed his initial advice in 1989. Even while he had espoused selling everything Nikkei-related in December 1989, and the audience at his conference had nodded and made dutiful notes, few of the pension fund investment boards had allowed anyone in that room to pull the trigger. While the MOF found Marty interesting, they also had discouraged institutions from selling their massive portfolios of stocks. There was no need for panic. Everything was in control. The BOJ and the MOF would always keep everything in control.

But of course, everything was not in control. Because rates had been pushed too low and the currency was too strong, money had poured into Japan, and then been mal-invested all over the place. The Mrs. Watanabes were groping for yield. Pension funds, on the hook to pay guaranteed annuity products to their clients, were largely doing the same. Insurance companies had also made a wide variety of stupid investments. It was a financial world gone nuts.

It was in fact a bad mix of a traditional and conservative Japanese investment mind-set with Western-styled financial manipulation. The Japanese pot of money was James Bacon's ultimate perceived savior for the world—if he could only pry it loose of their domestic clutches. He wanted to get these funds more invested abroad and buying more American things. But trying to do so, he'd simply sent this money scurrying into the hands of Western bankers ready to suggest innovative structured products to get around the low rates that Mr. Bacon helped encourage. The Japanese were getting carved up both coming and going. Their traditional economy was being destabilized. True wealth had been destroyed.

On this day in May 1991, Marty stood at the Palace Hotel podium and looked across a sea of Japanese faces. They weren't going to like his message.

"The angst that began in December 1989 will likely persist for longer than you expect. Don't get me wrong, there will be some periods of global froth into July 1998 and late February 2007, but there will be deeper trough periods generally pointed to 1995 and 2002. Across this overall rhythm, don't be surprised to see your bear market extend for over a decade."

There had been audible gasps across the audience. From a high at 39,260, the Nikkei 225 Index had already declined to 28,000—or more than -28%. It was simply unfathomable to most that such a decline could persist—let alone get worse—for another decade to come.

"But Mr. Amwell, what do your friends at the MOF say about this prediction?" a brave voice from the audience asked.

"They don't believe it, but that's part of the problem. There is no recognition of what has been created here."

"What do you mean by that, Mr. Amwell?" came another voice from the other side of the room.

"Look, I've written many times that money is somewhat akin to a loose cannon on the deck of a tossing ship—flying back and forth. I got that quote from the memoirs of Herbert Hoover as he tried to deal with the difficult events of the early 1930's. Capital moves around the world following the path of least resistance—to where it feels that it is being treated the best.

"Between 1985 and 1989 the country where capital accumulated was Japan. You had a strengthening currency and a loose monetary policy. The combo was magical—maybe too magical. You see, December 1989 marked an entropic reversal in those global capital flows. Maybe there was some fundamental explanation for the turn. I'm sure people can point to something—a BOJ tightening, the change in some government tax or regulation. It doesn't really matter what the perceived catalyst was. More likely, it was just a natural cyclical time for the prior uptrend to end, and the downswing to begin.

"Sadly, at the peak of the bubble years, there was a lot of mal-investment in property, in stocks, and in bonds. Many of you in this room now realize this, and are currently dealing with the aftermath of this."

Marty paused, and looked around at the heads nodding. Then he continued.

"People forget that capital doesn't necessarily have to migrate. It can simply be destroyed. It gets poorly invested in stuff that no one really needs and then those projects drop in value. I'm afraid that Japan has suffered such a permanent destruction in wealth that it will take a great deal of time to heal. And the longer it takes to recognize this permanent loss of wealth, the longer it will take to recover from it. My friends at the MOF are in denial about this. Your accounting systems seem to be in denial of this. Maybe some of you are in denial about this. But I can't change the facts."

With that dour pronouncement, Marty suggested taking a break before he would step attendees through his very specific cycle maps for the balance of 1991.

Marty took a step back from the podium, and turned to a side table to get a sip of water.

Almost immediately there was a swarm of Japanese by his side, business cards extended.

"I am Mr. Kimo," the boldest of them started—a short little man, bald and plump. "I run the investment portfolio at Yakult. We make yoghurt. I understand very well exactly what you were just talking about. Could you pay me a visit at my office later this week? I have a potential business proposal for you."

Marty took Mr. Kimo's card and pondered where this conversation was headed.

"I generally charge for such a visit," Marty said, never to miss an opportunity to pull a fee out of someone. "And I'm not cheap."

"I will pay your fee, Mr. Amwell," offered another young Japanese standing by his side. Mr. Kimo, not to lose his starting advantage, also piped up: "I pay fee as well, Mr. Amwell. Please call." And with that he bowed and backed away.

Marty accumulated over twenty business cards during that break. Everything that he had just been discussing had struck a chord— assets under water, poor transparency in accounting treatment, internal angst as to how to get these assets off company books while saving face.

One young Japanese had effectively blurted out the issue right then and there: "If I sell assets, I lose my job because of the loss that I would take. If I don't sell assets, and assets don't rebound, my company is in big trouble."

Marty had arrived in the true den of pain.

CHAPTER 38

THORN: LONDON DAYS
London, England
January 1991

1990-1991 were fantastic years for Thorn. At the request of his boss, Blankstein, Thorn had moved to London on behalf of Goodman Sachs.

"When I send people to London, I feel like I'm sending them to Disney World," said Blankstein. "It's when I have to send people to Tokyo that it feels more like sending them to Siberia."

London seemed to Thorn like a city where people worked to live, as opposed to New York where people lived to work. That was an old expression often used with regards to the way French people conducted themselves, but it held for London life as well. There was always something fun going on—from horse racing at Royal Ascot, to some concert at Royal Albert Hall, to Wimbledon Tennis, to taking the Orient Express up to Aintree to see the Grand National.

Thorn's wife Kim kept bugging him to take her to Paris for the weekend, but there was enough going on in London that they never seemed to make it. Weekend jaunts to the countryside also fed Thorn's love of history and tradition...Blenheim Palace, the Cotswold countryside, Oxford, Cambridge, the towns of Battle and Rye, Corfu Castle, Bath, Exeter, Dartmouth...Thorn loved them all. He even sought out and found his own ancestral family home in Bideford, England on the north coast of Devon.

1991 was also a year where having a global derivatives book at Goodman really showed its stripes as a competitive advantage. While Thorn's old stomping ground Pierrepont Bank and places like First Chicago and Morgan Stanley stumbled along—typically quoting U.S. dollar pairings from New York or Chicago while their London groups focused more on other currency crosses—the real trade in 1991 was a changing correlation trade.

Previously, in the early to mid-1980's, the FX markets had mostly made moves somewhat akin to "student body left, and student body right" type behavior—all versus the dollar—the Deutsche mark, French franc, Spanish peseta, Italian lira, and even the Swiss franc all moving very much as a block against the dollar, with just mild degrees of varying magnitude. Suddenly, in 1991, that was no longer the case. The dollar was becoming less important as a focal currency. Crosses like Sterling-mark, Sterling-yen, Aussie-yen, Deutsche mark-yen, Lira-yen, Deutsche mark-lira and Deutsche mark-peseta were all starting to move much more dramatically, and yet their implied volatility levels were still quoted quite low.

The real trick was to combine the two tends together—shorting the overpriced U.S. dollar-based options and buying the other cheaply-priced cross-based options. Because most banks had their derivatives books set up on a regionalized basis or alternatively had portfolios with trader-by-trader sub-divisions of responsibility by the type of currency pairing, few banks could take advantage of these changing correlations.

Goodman saw the trade and had the "one global book" team structure to take advantage of it. This had very much been Thorn's vision back at the Pierrepont Bank when he had argued that global derivatives books were far more efficient and appropriate than regionalized derivatives books. Thankfully, he was now at a shop that was running their business the right way. Just that subtle difference in structure made all the difference.

Not only did Goodman have the structure and the vision, they also had the wherewithal to put these relative value trades on in huge size.

Thorn will always remember when mark-yen was starting to really bounce around. Thorn and his London-based partner Geoff—a good guy who hailed originally from South Africa—had huddled together in a strategy discussion for just a few moments. They both agreed that if there was one opportunity, mark-yen options—quoted 9.3 at 9.5 volatility—were just a steal.

Geoff then had gotten on the phone to his favorite interbank derivatives broker at Tullett's.

"Where do you think we could buy a billion in three-month mark-yen vol?"

Normally such a query might have elicited a query about hearing the size correctly, but the brokers had come to expect such a question from Goodman, if not others.

Instead, only excitement filled the broker's voice.

"Give me a sec mate, and I will fish around. I'll just line up some stuff up real quiet—won't spook anyone."

A few short minutes later, the Tullett's broker line flashed.

"OK, I know that there is 200 million mark-yen offered at 9.5. That's guaranteed. I'm pretty sure that I can source another 300 million at 9.6 behind that. To get the balance, I think you'll have to pay up to 9.8."

Geoff looked at Thorn, and smiled.

"All mine up to 9.8," he said back to the Tullett's broker. "Go get 'em."

So the Tullett's broker literally lined up every other bank on the street, and then lifted all of them concomitantly.

"I buy, mine, mine, I buy, I buy..."

Before many banks had received their counterpart name on the other end of these trades, Goodman's own phone turret was suddenly ablaze with incoming calls from many of the same banks that Goodman had just paid.

"Where's three-month mark-yen?" the counterpart would ask in a rushed voice.

"9.9 -10.3" Geoff had responded in a calm even voice—everything Goodman Sachs people did was in a calm even voice—even when moving the market bid well above all the prior offers just a few minutes earlier. A few counterparts—knowing that they had just been rolled by Goodman—would even panic and either immediately, or sometimes later in the day, buy the options back from Thorn and Geoff, to cut their loss—typically amidst a few uttered curses.

Thorn never quite understood why this would happen. If they had been comfortable selling these options in the broker market at 9.6 or 9.7, why the sudden change of heart to pay 10.3? Many years later, Thorn would learn from one Morgan Stanley trader in London that the trade "covers" often emanated from the wrath of their New York desk head—a hot-headed Greek gal named Zoe Cruz.

Zoe would apparently call up her London desk each morning and ask what they had done that day. When the response came, we sold 200 million 3-month mark-yen to Goodman at 9.7, she'd naturally ask, "and where is 3-month Mark-yen now?"

When the hesitating response came, "9.9-10.3," she would scream into the phone line: "Why didn't you just write Goodman a check? It would have been a lot fuckin' easier. Jesus, this is like déjà vu every day...Goodman just rolls over you. Cover the goddamn thing."

And since Goodman remained the market-maker quoting mark-yen options in the biggest size, the cover call would come back to Thorn and Geoff—even if MS-London trader egos might have preferred covering the options elsewhere.

Seldom did any of these Goodman aggressive forays go awry. It was like the Goodman traders had a better sense of the world, and of relative values of options than others. They also could buy all this Mark-yen volatility and finance it by selling dollar-mark volatility. Given that folks like Morgan Stanley—even while technically a global book—ran dollar-based books from New York, and cross-based books from London—this was not a trade that they could easily set up. Nobody could do this trade as well as Goodman could.

But Thorn's 1991 nirvana on top of the currency derivatives world soon encountered a new obstacle.

Geoff broke the news to Thorn first: "Blankstein just got a promotion back in New York. He runs commodities as well as FX now. I think that he wants to yank you back to New York to spearhead their effort in precious and base-metal options."

"But Kim is pregnant with our second child. We just made our reservation for a room at the Portland Hospital," Thorn had stammered. "We just signed a lease for a new apartment. What do you mean he wants to yank me back to New York?"

But alas, the phone rang the following day. Blankstein started off with a joke of course, and then slowly became more serious.

"Look, I sent you to London on a temporary basis, but now it's been almost two years. Unless you want to make London your home permanently, this is your ticket back to head office. You've traded commodity derivatives before; this job should be a lay-up for you. We're making a big push with the institutions to turn commodities into an accepted asset class. We just invented this thing called the Goodman Sachs Commodity Index. It's going to be a big business."

Grudgingly, Thorn said "OK." His London days would soon end. He was headed back to the New York home office.

CHAPTER 39

TOBASHI
Tokyo, Japan
April 1991

"What a drab little hole in the wall," thought Marty as he sat in the Yakult conference room awaiting his consulting meeting with Mr. Kimo. It was his second meeting with a new Japanese consulting client that day.

The first had been with another small Japanese corporation. It had been a hilarious meeting and yet, at the same time, so sad.

In a first round of discussions, senior management was present, and everyone praised the honorable and stable long history of the company. Marty wasn't even sure what he was accomplishing by being there. But he had an eye on his watch to still bill by the hour.

After about twenty minutes of this, senior management had left, and only the middle managers had remained. Marty quickly gathered that this latter group was somewhat less upbeat about the company's prospects—and particularly about the corporate pension plan. These middle-level managers said that they found the investment environment increasingly difficult and treacherous. They were looking for guidance to better navigate their way. When Marty offered his perspective that staying long high quality U.S. Treasury bonds was likely their best hope—actually embracing the foreign exchange risk of such since Marty was so bearish yen—this middle-management team had seemed disappointed with his solution, and left the room.

Only junior management had remained behind. The third round of discussions with this group was where the meat of the problem had been revealed.

"Our pension fund owns paper—both stocks and bonds, Mr. Amwell. Consistent with Japanese accounting norms, these are carried on the company books at our cost. But this paper has in reality declined by nearly -40%, Mr. Amwell. If these investments do not rebound soon, the company does not have sufficient resources to re-fund the pension plan. The company will be technically bankrupt. We'd like to sell our portfolio and start again, but we can't do so without all getting fired."

"It's too bad that you can't just get me a pool of money to trade," Marty had suggested. "I could get you healthy in a hurry." It was Marty's ego showing as usual.

"The only way that we can get you money is by selling what we have, but if we sell what we have, game over. We cannot admit to such a loss."

That is when Marty had first heard the term "Tobashi."

"There is one possible path. Would you ever consider doing a Tobashi transaction with us, Mr. Amwell?"

"A what transaction? I don't know what a 'Tobashi transaction' is," responded Marty.

"Mr. Tobashi is famous Japanese executive. He developed this trade that is now named after him. It would basically be an asset swap transaction, Mr. Amwell. We swap the assets on our books that we want to dispose of to you in return for a longer-term promissory note from your company. You take our assets and then sell them. You then invest the proceeds of that sale any way that you want, just so long as we get the par value of your promissory note at maturity—in like seven years."

"So you get rid of your assets, but don't have to technically have to sell them yourselves. You just swap them for something else denominated at par. This gets you back to even assuming that 'the something else at par' eventually pays off. And you think that I'm money good to be that 'something?'"

"Exactly Mr. Amwell. You are such a great trader. Even if we only gave you assets worth 60 cents on the dollar, I'm sure that in seven years you could take that amount of cash and make multiples on it. All we need to do is get back to par. Maybe we split any profits above that?"

"Would the MOF allow you to do this type of transaction?"

"They not only would allow us to do this, Mr. Amwell, but they are encouraging us to do it. Your company is specifically one that they have approved to act as a Tobashi facilitator."

Marty suddenly felt honored to have been selected by the MOF to help this Japanese corporate in such a manner. Admittedly, it sounded a bit sketchy, but then again, if the MOF was approving such transactions, how bad could it be?

"The one thing that we insist on Mr. Amwell is that the note we buy from you must pay back at par in yen, not dollars. We also would like some transparency along the way as to what you do with the assets that we swap to you. We need to be reassured that the account is indeed headed back towards par over time."

"I understand the transparency part, but why would you ever want yen back?" asked Marty. "The yen is going down."

"Our liabilities are in yen, Mr. Amwell. We don't really care where the yen is going. We need to match that yen liability to fund our pension plan."

It had been an eye-opening experience for Marty. The fact that this company wanted yen back not dollars was tricky from a hedging point of view—you had to pay away a lot of points if you bought yen forward as a hedge. But hell, Marty was bearish yen. Here was a company effectively offering him a chunk of money, and only insisting to be repaid in seven years in a currency that Marty hated anyway.

Marty was continuing to ponder this prior meeting when the door of the Yakult conference room opened. Would this second foray into Japanese corporate investment policy be similar?

Mr. Kimo entered, but unlike Marty's prior meeting, there was no trailing army of other attendees. Just Mr. Kimo himself.

He sat down opposite Marty, and in very un-Japanese fashion, came straight to the point.

"Mr. Amwell, since we are paying you to take this meeting as a consultant, I want to get directly to the issue at hand. Have you ever heard of a Tobashi transaction?"

"Not until today, but yes...yes, I have now." Oh my, here we go again, thought Marty.

"Good. The MOF speaks most highly of you Mr. Amwell. They also know that our situation here is not good. We would like to do an asset swap with you Mr. Amwell. I want you to effectively invest a great deal of money with you Mr. Amwell."

"What sizes are we talking?"

"I have pension assets currently worth about 300 billion yen. That's about $225 million dollars, Mr. Amwell. I want to swap those assets with you for a note maturing in seven years for 500 billion yen. You get to trade the proceeds you get from liquidating our assets anyway that you want Mr. Amwell so long as we get 500 billion yen in seven years. It will be an unsecured private placement of a bond—we can call them Princeton notes."

"And how about if I make more than the 500 billion par yen value trading across the seven years?"

"That is a point that we can negotiate Mr. Amwell. But I would propose that if you agree to pay me a small commission for arranging this transaction, that you could keep any excess profits."

"A commission?"

"Yes, a commission. It is quite standard in this country for a senior executive such as myself to be taken care of."

Oh just great, thought Marty. Now I have a Tobashi transaction *with a twist*—the guy wants a personal kickback. But Jesus Christ, this was a lot of money. And he could invest this money anyway he wanted... Keep the excess profits. It was a better deal than the last meeting. If he had to line this guy's palm with a few bucks, hell, he was finally in business as a proper—well almost proper—hedge fund manager. And the MOF was giving its blessing to such.

"Mr. Kimo—I'm honored that my friends at the MOF have suggested me for this. I understand what we are trying to do here. I will have my people contact you to draw up the docs. Everything will be taken care of—including a generous commission."

Mr. Kimo smiled.

CHAPTER 40

MISMARKED BOOKS
New York
August 1991

The Headline of *Grant's Interest Rate Observer* read, "Goodman Sachs massively short calls on gold."

It had a nice ring to it—certainly an eye-catching piece of text—but in this case, *Grant's* editor Jim Grant had gotten his story upside down.

During the 1990-1991 period Goodman was indeed making a push into the commodity derivatives arena, and was one of the largest market makers in OTC options on gold, silver, platinum, copper, aluminum, nickel, lead, and other metals.

Thorn—freshly back from his two years in London—was running the silver options book in a relatively even handed way, and also was involved in a variety of base metals options books. But every time his new partner Paul would pick up the phone line and quote a gold option—Shwack! He owned them.

It was depressing because at a price of around $340 on gold, the metal was arguably cheap, the world still unstable, and volatility was also not particularly expensive.

Despite a thoughtful and relatively conservative approach to the gold options market, Paul's position was simply not working. He was regularly eating time decay and facing gamma trading opportunities that were muted at best.

The only thing that Jim Grant had gotten whiff of was simply how many futures options Goodman was selling on the COMEX floor. This was of course only half of the equation. Thorn and Paul would try to lay off—let that read arb out—as much of the over-the-counter volatility that they were getting given, and that they could find reasonable futures options bids on, but often those COMEX bids would simply fade away and not be good for much size. Yes, they were short futures options, but they were about ten times longer over-the-counter options. Overall, Paul was massively long metals volatility up to his eyeballs.

One month after returning to New York for Goodman, Thorn had turned to Paul and queried the position.

"Paul, I know that you think gold options are cheap at 15% volatility. And as a general rule, when I was back at the Pierrepont Bank, I know that t was typically a good strategy to buy gold options around 14-15% volatility and sell them around 20-22% gold volatility—but in today's market, this position just doesn't have the right feel to it. There are simply too many vol sellers around. Would you ever think of just blowing out this position and starting again?"

It had taken a great deal of nerve for Thorn to even broach this topic.

A scowling expression had come over Paul's face.

"You've been trading FX options too long, Thorn. In the bullion market, it's not quite as easy to move a lot of size. For the amount of options that I already own, I would have to sell them down to 11% volatility or maybe even 10% volatility to flatten out my exposure. And since I'd certainly prefer to buy options at that level than sell them at that level, why bother even trying? I'm just going to hang on to what I have."

Paul had made over twenty million dollars trading for Goodman on his own the prior year across a period that included the first Gulf War, so Thorn was in no real position to question him. Paul was a naturally contrarian trader—opinionated and difficult, sometimes argumentative for the sake of arguing. So Thorn did not push the point. Instead, he simply crossed his fingers and decided to root for his partner.

It was not easy to do so because soon those levels of volatility where Paul had said that he wanted to be "long anyway" were actually being seen in the market...At 12 vol, at 11, at 10, at 9.5! Every day, option premiums would seemingly melt further. The market was turning into death warmed over, and meanwhile, Paul was singularly slow to mark his over-the-counter volatility marks lower.

Thorn's slight concern about Paul's gold option position turned into outright fear. Nobody around the firm was paying any attention to Paul's position, let along his volatility marks. Thorn knew that these marks were stale. It was not a disastrous mis-mark, but it probably represented a few million dollars of loss that was not yet being recognized. Plus Paul was now in a situation where if he had to pull the rip-chord on his position, he'd be selling his options down to 9 vol, 8 vol, or even 7 vol.

Then one day in the late summer of 1991, a magical moment occurred. Driving south of the FDR one Sunday afternoon, Thorn heard CBS radio interrupt their regular news commentary with a special bulletin: "In Moscow this evening, President Mikhail Gorbachev has gone missing, and may potentially have been kidnapped."

Now for any normal human being, surprise and concern might have been a natural reaction to such a news announcement. To Thorn, the emotion was more like glee. Paul was going to be OK. Vol would surely pop on this news; and there would be gamma to trade.

But it was still an era at the time before cell phones, and it was a Sunday afternoon, and Thorn suddenly had a thought: maybe Paul had not heard this news. Thorn should at least try to touch base with Paul as soon as possible to make sure that he had.

So instead of continuing across the Brooklyn Bridge to his Brooklyn Heights apartment, Thorn decided to continue south on the FDR and go directly to the Goodman offices. He could get to a phone there, check in with Paul, and get a read on the early trading of gold in Australia.

Nice plan—but as he pulled up to the Broad Street offices of Goodman, there was one logistical hitch: limited parking. Indeed there was just one illegal fire hydrant spot in front of Goodman's doors.

"To hell with it," thought Thorn, "I'm only going to be a few minutes." And he grabbed the fire hydrant space, jumped out of the car, and headed for the elevator banks to get upstairs.

There was always something mildly exciting about being in a huge trading room when no one else was there…small computer lights, Bloomberg terminals, and phone turrets still blinking within the darkened room.

Even without turning on the overhead lights (Thorn had no idea where the switch was to do so), he swung into his normal trading seat and tapped his way into the composite gold quote page on Bloomberg. Gold in Australia was opening up $20—cool. Perfect.

Thorn dialed Paul, and woke him up from an afternoon nap.

"You seen this Gorbachev news, buddy? Gold's up $20 bucks!"

Paul had *not* seen the news, and was appreciative of the call. He would get his screens turned on at home, and take over the gamma trading responsibilities from there. They both agreed that selling some gold up $20 was a good idea since the news was so vague and could easily reverse into a non-story. Up $20, their gamma made them synthetically long 100,000 ounces of gold. Selling a ton of gold—32,000 ounces—would lock in a nice gain, but still leave them nicely net long on the balance of their position.

Thorn felt like his relationship with Paul was a good bit of teamwork in action. It had been worth making the extra stop at work.

OK, time to run back down to the car. No need to get a ticket.

As Thorn came out of the darkened lobby, he squinted as he looked out through the building's frosted glass doors at his car parked outside. He wanted to make sure that there wasn't a cop issuing him a summons.

Was that someone sitting in his car? Thorn could vaguely make out the shape of a human figure where there shouldn't have been one.

Thorn pushed open the front doors of the Broad Street office building, and started running towards the curbside. "Hey, hey! What are you doing, man?"

As Thorn approached, he saw his front passenger side window shattered.

The big rotund black man was sitting in his front seat wearing a blue blazer that Thorn had left in the back seat. This fellow was bent over, madly trying to hot wire the car's ignition. But as this black dude saw Thorn fast approaching, he suddenly gave up that effort, and bolted down the street.

Thorn started madly chasing him. Panting. Huffing. Out of shape. Focused on his blue blazer flying away at lightning speed in front of him—up Broad Street. Then the thought suddenly occurred to Thorn—what if Thorn was actually able to catch this guy? What was he trying to accomplish? Get himself shot or killed?

He stopped. Hands dropped to his knees. Winded and pissed. He returned to his car to also see a fluttering parking ticket on the windshield glass, tucked nicely under the wipers.

What a crap exacta: first a parking ticket, followed by an attempted theft—likely having transpired just a few minutes apart. He'd only been upstairs on the trading floor a grand total of like twenty minutes. Thorn mentally cursed the city he lived in.

Crunchy window glass—some still partially attached to a thin layer of inner plastic—broke underfoot. Thorn grabbed the ticket off the windshield and then looked around for a cop to report the attempted robbery.

But when Thorn actually needed a policeman, the street was instead quiet and empty.

CHAPTER 41

METALS MARKET FUN AND GAMES
New York,
June 1982

Paul got sacked from Goodman Sachs in mid-1992 with gold vol piled up around his neck. The Gorbachev night had not been enough to save the ship. Gorbachev did eventually resurface a few days later, and gold languished in a sloppy low-priced range for far longer than anyone would have expected. Eventually, Paul had marked down his volatility exposure to 6%. It was a P&L blood bath.

Positive gamma and vega positions could be glorious when they worked (as in the 1987 Crash or the 1990 melt-down of Aussie-yen), but oh so painful when they did not and volatility melted on the vine. Drip, drip drip, the time decay would eat away at one's lifeblood, and then the implied volatility mark-to-market would simply accelerate the pain.

But being stubborn and wrong on gold volatility was oddly enough not Paul's ultimate undoing. It was a trade in zinc options that had done that. In the late spring of 1992, Marc Rich in Zurich was trying to squeeze the zinc market, and Paul had smelled this squeeze coming. Rich was buying slightly out-of-the-money zinc options for the same July 1992 prompt date that he was already long physical forwards on the metal. Paul expected Rich to surprisingly exercise these slightly out-of-the-money options (even if they remained slightly out-of-the-money) and then wreak havoc as people had to scramble to meet unexpected delivery requirements. It was classic London Metals Exchange (LME) fun and games.

Paul's answer was to sell these slightly-out-of-the-money options to Rich's broker at a ripe volatility, but then effectively join him in the squeeze by buy putting a 100% forward delta hedge long against the options—such that he ended up with a buy-write type exposure. It was a perfectly legitimate trading strategy.

The only bad thing that happened was that zinc actually started falling instead of rising. It was really just a slow slog lower—nothing dramatic. But it seemed that there was more zinc supply around than Marc Rich had bargained for.

Then Rich—apparently frustrated that his squeeze wasn't working as planned—started planting news stories in the financial press that there was a big U.S. investment bank caught short zinc. These stories were obviously intended to drive the price back up. The only big U.S. investment bank actually trading zinc and zinc options at that time was Goodman Sachs.

All eyes across the LME community stared Goodman's way. Sadly, the price still did not rise that much. Instead, zinc kept getting a tad weaker day by day. Paul—already an increasingly unpopular fellow in the trading room from his long gold volatility fiasco—was now losing money in another market, and in a new and different way.

Paul's second problem at Goodman was that senior management at the firm had also read the zinc press stories, and soon questions were buzzing around from those who normally would not have cared: what real involvement did Goodman actually have in the then-current zinc market? Paul's response was up-front, factually correct, and bold: he was in effect going with Marc Rich's attempted squeeze. Goodman was not being squeezed itself, but was actually helping create one (although that effort appeared to be failing).

This was however the wrong response at the wrong time. Goodman senior management was disdainful for being involved in this situation at all—effectively supporting the schlocky and potentially unethical behavior of a Swiss-based ex-patriot.

Paul got himself shit-canned.

Paul being shown the door came at the end of a long battle of ego between him and a Goodman partner named Jimmy. Now Jimmy was kind of a divide-and-conquer slime-ball of a guy. He'd hardly ever take an entire group of people into a conference room and tell them all the same thing at the same time. Instead, he'd talk to people individually—pretending to be their best friend, on their side, concerned about some other member of the team, talking up each individual's future at the firm, while quietly dissing the performance of others. It was overall an ineffective and irritating charade at management, but it was his style.

Similar to Raf over at Pierrepont, Jimmy also loved chances to front-run customer business. Once through personal connections, Paul had gotten a huge order to buy several hundred million ounces of silver for Kodak to fulfill their annual photographic paper needs. Paul had only received such a big order because the Kodak Treasurer trusted him implicitly. But Paul ran the options desk. Jimmy ran the spot metals desk, so technically, this order had to be handled by Jimmy—not Paul.

And with Jimmy controlling the levers, it quickly became an exercise in customer rape. Jimmy would get 40 to 50 million ounces of silver bought, and then ask Paul to tell Kodak that he'd only been able to get 15 million done up to the Kodak limit. Jimmy would suggest raising that limit a bit. Paul would sheepishly follow instructions—embarrassed a bit as he did so—and tell his Kodak friend that the market was thin and not that much size had been available. An amended higher price limit from the Kodak counterpart would typically be obtained. Then the process would repeat itself: one ounce of silver for Kodak compared to two ounces of silver for the Goodman house account. Of course, if silver ever started to back off a bit, that allocation mix could magically be adjusted and leave Kodak with a far bigger fill.

It was all a classic Jimmy-style of doing things. Thorn had to give him credit—he was almost a master at front-running. Kodak got their silver in the end, but the teeth-pulling way that they did so was embarrassingly slow and the all-in fill price certainly ended up higher than should have naturally been the case.

In another instance during that era, there was a large CTA named John Henry & Co. who would periodically come into the gold market and trade a mechanistic trend-following model. John Henry's sizes were generally too big for the gold market and caused significant skid every time that his traders had to make an adjustment or reversal in exposure. Correctly anticipating what day John Henry would be trading and at what price level could be a huge advantage to anyone with a front-running mentality.

So Jimmy was astute enough and cravenly enough to make that happen.

Calling two Russian-born quants into his office, Jimmy had said: "Here, take this diary into your back office, and study the dates where I noted John Henry came into the gold market for size. Then retrofit his model. I want at least 24-hours advance notice of when he might next pull the trigger, and at what price level."

So for several months the two Russian guys had toiled away trying to retrofit John Henry's past trading behavior to come up with a model that would predict his next action.

One day the quants emerged from their office.

"We think John Henry is currently long gold from around $328," the taller of the two quants offered.

"Yes, yes, that feels about right. He bought those several weeks ago. Gold's now $348; he's $20 bucks in the money. When's he going to be forced to flip?" Jimmy responded.

"If gold touches $344 today or tomorrow, we think his model will trigger."

"Good info. Thanks. I hope we get the chance to see whether you are right," Jimmy said, with a new glint of excitement in his eye.

The next action had been for Jimmy to call down to the COMEX gold futures floor broker.

"Stevey—I've got an assignment for you. Keep your eye on the Dean Witter broker—you know, the one who does all the big-sized orders for John Henry. If you see the price of gold touching around 344 and that Witter guy raises his hands to sell anything, I want you to start selling in front of him. You have a standing order to begin with 500 lots before you even tell us what is going on. But make sure that you let us know pronto. Got it?"

"Understood, boss."

And so a day slipped by and nothing had really happened. Gold sagged a buck to $347. The next day it sagged another buck to around $346. Quiet volumes. Sleepy summertime trading.

Jimmy went back to the Russian quants on the third day. "Where do you think he pulls the trigger today?"

"Could be a bit higher. Maybe $345 will do it."

Jimmy had eyed the COMEX screens: $346 to 346.20.

He decided to have a bit of fun—give the market a push. See if he couldn't get this thing into motion.

"Stevey—remember that order from the other day. I want you to keep working it, but raise the threshold a bit. If you see Dean Witter in motion trying to sell anything around $345, just don't let him out; sell in front of him..."

A moment later he continued.

"Now how hard do you think it would be to get this market to print $345?"

"If I offer out a few hundred lots in a sloppy fast fashion, that would likely do it."

Jimmy eyed the desk and the screen. He wanted everybody ready. "OK guys. You understand the drill. If we hear Witter selling, Stevey's going to keep the pressure on downstairs. I want everyone calling out to their assigned counterparts and selling at least 20 bars of gold apiece. This will be fast and furious. Everyone ready?"

There was nodding around the desk as people clutched their phones.

"OK, Stevey—give it that push. Sell 500 lots *and butcher it*. I want a 345 print. And if Witter comes, just keep going with that other standing sell order that we talked about."

The squawk box crackled back: "Going into motion...selling 500 in a rush...At 6, sold 50; at 5.80, sold 'nother 50. At five-and-a-half, making some noise now. Phibro takes a hundy from us. I just gave him another hundred. Looks like that shut him up. He's done. Still offering 5.5, now at 5.30, at 5.10. Printing 5's."

There was a moment of silence. Sweat was notably pouring off the forehead of one Russian quant standing behind the desk. Two months of work hung in the next few seconds—It might make a difference between whether the quant still had a career at Goodman or not.

"Witter trying to sell 500!" Stevey shouted at last. It was the moment of epiphany.

"Don't let him out. Go, go, go...everyone call out. Sell."

A cacophony of outgoing phone calls followed, while Stevey continued shouting over the COMEX box.

"At 4.5, 4's trade, at 3.5, at 3," "We sold another 500. Witter hasn't sold anything yet."

"Don't let him out. Sell another 1000. Go. Go. Go." Blood vessels emanated from Jimmy's forehead as he shouted into the phone. He was spitting into the phone, his face beet red.

"Selling another 1000." Stevey confirmed. "At 2, at 1, at 0! Jeezus. What a hole. At 438, at 7 now. Witter still has his hands up. I don't think he's sold anything yet."

"Do it again—another 1000."

It had been almost magical watching Jimmy in motion—he was like a professional orchestra leader leading a market fuck-fest.

After 434 was touched, Jimmy slowed down his pace of selling, and then let Witter get some lots out the door. By the time 428 and then 427 were reached, Jimmy was taking back gold from Witter's desperate belated attempt to complete his order. What a skid! John Henry had started with a winning trade $20 in the money, but courtesy of Goodman, they were not getting out much better than flat.

Nothing illegal done. Just street smarts and cunning applied to a bit of programming by some Russian dudes. Thorn thought the moment reminiscent of the final scene of the 1983 movie *Trading Places*—the only difference being that this was real, not Hollywood make-believe.

But Jimmy wasn't just known for front-running outside counterparts. Sometimes, he would front-run his own in-house traders. There had been another day when a tall slightly laid-back in-house prop trader named Bennett had sauntered over to the gold desk to ask Jimmy his opinion of the market. Bennett, like John Henry & Co., traded relatively systematically and was trying to apply models that he had successfully developed in the FX markets to gold. Bennett at the time was long gold.

"So what you think of the market?" Bennett asked Jimmy almost in a chit-chatty way.

"Gold's a bit heavy. Might be some Russian selling sitting on top of this. Hard to tell. Where do you flip to get out?"

Bennett had responded that a price level about $3 below the then-current spot price as his trigger point. Bennett then slowly started to saunter back to his own desk. No sooner than he had turned his back on Jimmy, but Jimmy had started to push gold lower. Yes, maybe there was some Russian selling around, but Jimmy saw red meat on the hook with his own in-house colleague.

By the time Bennett had returned to his own desk, Jimmy had caused a $4 skid in gold all by himself.

Bennett had come rushing back, a bit flushed. "Russian selling?"

"Looks that way, man. Jeez this thing is really weak."

"Sell me two tons of gold at the market."

"Look Bennett," Jimmy replied, "This thing is really fragile. It's down $4 on nothing in just a few moments. I'll do you a favor and take your two tons from you basis down another $2 from here. That's the best that I can offer you man. I think you'll do better accepting this internal trade than if I go start hitting bids. I'm doing you a big favor man."

Bennett agreed to Jimmy's proposed "basis trade" or internal transfer between their accounts.

Yeah, some favor. Bennett electing to sell out his gold to Jimmy just helped Jimmy cover the short that Jimmy had put on to trigger Bennett's stop. It was all just the same game as had transpired with John Henry, but applied in-house. As compared to the John Henry episode which had been somewhat beautiful, it made Thorn feel ill to watch this all transpire from his nearby options desk perch: one Goodman guy taking advantage of another Goodman guy. Any limited respect that Thorn had for Jimmy diminished after that. Jimmy was a cutthroat asshole looking to pad his own pocket at the behest of anyone—even another Goodman colleague. How could you deal with a guy like that?

Thorn's own time in the hot-seat with Jimmy soon followed in the fall of 1992.

"Hey Thorn, you're long copper vol, right?" Jimmy had asked one day in an excited fashion. "I think I have a customer who wants to buy some options. That suits, right? You've got the inventory to go?"

The entire group was still struggling to recover from a year of stultified markets and Paul having hung himself on that cross of gold volatility. But copper volatility was indeed cheap at around 7.5% vol levels—a historically low extreme. Thorn had bought a few at-the-money options. He was happy with the position, but his job was to be a market-maker, and he was always interested in someone willing to pay the offered side of the market.

"Sure, Jimmy, what you got?"

"Well, it's a forward-start one-year average rate put, but it don't start averaging until January 1 next year. I guess that makes this an exotic option. The guy says it's roughly a 10 delta put. He's got some pretty big size to buy."

"Who's the customer?"

"Big mining house—Freeport."

"What's the size?"

"I think he said a million tons."

"Holy shit. That's like the entire annual production of the U.S." Thorn was sitting up on the edge of his seat by this time.

"I told you I had a buyer."

Thorn got more specific details of the proposed deal from Jimmy and punched up the pricing in his computer.

"Jimmy—There is a price for everything, and I will put a price on this, but you have to understand something first—this 10 delta stuff for this size is like toxic waste. It could really bite us in the ass. Because of the forward start nature of this option, yeah, it's an exotic option, and won't be easy to hedge or back-to-back with anyone else on the street. Plus we'd be selling this just off historic lows in copper volatility. If copper happens to fall precipitously sooner rather than later, I can't guarantee Goodman won't be liable to lose like maybe, $30 million. We should think twice about putting this thing on our books."

"Hold on a sec," said Jimmy. "Let me understand this. You guys have been dying on the vine long metals volatility. That ass-hole Paul drops $20 bucks long gold vol. You're now long copper vol, and you don't want to accommodate a customer who wants to buy some volatility?"

"Jimmy—as I said, I will put a price on this thing. But we have to be super conservative given the nature of what Freeport is asking for. This is like apples and oranges. Sure, I'm small long some three-to-six month at-the-money copper options, but that has nothing to really do with selling a boatload of 10 delta 15-month options with bells and whistles attached. I'm just giving you my two cents on this. Not every piece of customer business is an opportunity. Some is more of a liability. Maybe this is something that we should take a pass on."

"No fuckin' way we're passing on this business." Shot back Jimmy. "I want to win this business."

This entire discussion was consistent with Jimmy's front-running mentality, but applied to a market and a circumstance that he did not really understand. "So what you thinking for a vol price?"

"Well, the normal at-the-money options are 7 vol bid at 8. But the COMEX vanilla back-end low delta puts are trading more like 9.5. For the size and the exotic features of this thing, I wouldn't sell it lower than 11 vol."

"Should I show the customer that? How much money would we make mark-to-market there?"

"Marked to the COMEX 9.5% vol level, you'd book up an up-front gain of like $3 million, but it would be all fake, not something that we could lock in. As I said, this option could then still bite us in the ass in a much bigger way. I'd rather let Pierrepont or some other bank win this biz Jimmy. I really would."

Jimmy bristled yet again. He just didn't understand how someone couldn't just love customer business. Wasn't it always an opportunity to rip someone's eyeballs out? Shit, if Thorn said they could book a $3 million gain marked-to-market, wasn't this worth doing every day of the week? Jimmy was mentally thinking that he'd even be happy with a $1 million mark-to-market gain. He didn't really understand the contingent liability nature of running an option's book.

"So you want me to show 11% vol offer—is that the fair offer? I want to win this thing. Don't embarrass me with this guy."

"I think 11% vol is something that I could live with. But I doubt if Freeport is going to like that price."

"Fuckin 'a. He better like the price. You better not be dicking me on this one."

And so Jimmy went on the phone to his counterpart at Freeport. Thorn heard the long drawl of a southern accent come on the line. Jimmy showed the 11% volatility offer.

"Shit man, you think I'm some hillbilly out here in the hinterlands who you can just take advantage of?" came the Freeport treasurer retort. "I know where volatility levels are. 11% vol is like a rip-off level, man. And I thought you guys said that you were players?"

266

Jimmy—face slowly turning beet-red—glared at Thorn as he clicked off the phone mic. "I thought I told you to win this thing, dickwad."

"I told you Jimmy that I doubted he'd like the price, but you really don't want to sell this thing. There is no liquidity in the market to cover it. I don't care how much money we book up-front. It's just not worth it."

"So you got no room to improve this price? You heard this guy—he thinks we're ripping him off."

"Look, if you sell this thing any cheaper than 11% vol, sure, you'll book some up-front gains. At 10 vol, you'll still book $1 million versus a 9.5% mark. But you won't be able to cover this option there. No way in hell. And I won't take any responsibility for it. You're flying solo on this Jimmy."

Jimmy thought for a second, and then clicked back on the phone line.

"Hey buddy, looks like there was a miscommunication on this end. My trader said this is doable at 10% vol, not 11%. I misheard him initially."

Thorn looked to the heavens. Fuckin' Jimmy was in over his head—didn't know what he was doing. Anger was slow to well up in Thorn normally, but he slammed down a sheaf of risk reports that he was holding, and marched out of the trading room.

When he came back, Jimmy stared at him, and then called him into his office.

"Thorn, you are a thoughtful guy. I know that you are also at heart a conservative guy trying to do your best to trade for Goodman. But I almost just made a complete ass of myself in front of that client. When I tell you to be competitive, that's what you're supposed to do. I also didn't get any sense of team support when you just left the room. I think your days at Goodman are over. You'll get a nice parting bonus. I think you'll be pleased. But I don't want you on my team any longer. Start packing up your things."

"Fuckin right, I'll pack up my things. Good luck with that option by the way."

Thorn left the room and went back to his desk where he quickly started filling his briefcase with odds and ends of things that he wanted to keep.

Thorn had been in the wrong seat at the wrong time. Putting up a stink, he'd gotten himself fired. If he'd put up less of a fuss, he would have gotten stuck with an unhedgeable tail risk exposure in his book. It was just one of those lose-lose type of propositions.

Jimmy rubbed salt in the wound the next day by marking all of Thorn's other option positions at excessively conservative valuations. If Thorn was long the 25 delta puts on something and short the 20 delta puts on the same asset for the same maturity, the 25 delta long puts got marked at 10 volatility, while the 20 deltas were pushed to 11 volatility. It seemed like Jimmy was trying to justify to management Thorn's dismissal with an allegation of another quasi-mismarked book situation. Then on the following day, Jimmy "basis traded" Thorn's proprietary trades into the books of other traders on the desk. He did so after Thorn had left early for the day because Thorn's daughter was having an asthma attack at home and being taken to the hospital. There had not been much risk or exposure in those prop book exposures—but again, using artificially wide presumed bids and offers that would hypothetically need to be crossed to close these position out in the real market, Ker plunk, another $1.5 million loss hit Thorn's P&L line.

Thorn's daughter ended up being fine, but not Thorn's ego.

It was all a complete joke—and Thorn was pissed. He went to Blankstein and then Blankstein's boss to explain that these losses were not real—but simply being manufactured by Jimmy—a way for him to turn the knife; set the bar ultra-low on a mark-to-market basis for Jimmy's other traders to make back the money once Thorn was pushed out the door.

Blankstein smiled, and said not to worry. He knew Jimmy was just playing games. He'd seen the drill before. That assertion made Thorn feel marginally better. Jimmy's trite games though crystalized in Thorn's mind how working with Jimmy was always destined to be a lose-lose proposition longer term. It was probably a good thing to be pushing on.

With regard to that 10-delta copper option, all Jimmy knew was that he had a $1 million up-front gain to show for the day's work, a happy client, and one less guy predisposed to long volatility on his payroll. He'd get someone else to figure out how to hedge that damn option. It couldn't be that hard to hedge, could it? After all, Goodman had plenty of smart guys around.

Copper dropped precipitously in April 1993. Volatility exploded. Somewhere halfway around the world, there was a trader long copper at Sumitomo Metals that was also quietly getting screwed. Consistent with Japanese non-mark-to-market norms, the world would only find out about these losses several years later.

The Freeport option booked out by Jimmy eventually cost Goodman over $13 million in losses. At that point, the story behind the loss got morphed further, of course.

"This was a legacy position left behind by Thorn," Jimmy told Blankstein. "We're doing our best to cope with it."

Yup, that Jimmy was quite the Wall Street shark—he never saw a patsy that he didn't hesitate to carve up. Thorn had been his sacrificial Thanksgiving turkey.

CHAPTER 42

TAKING ON A NEW SQUEEZE
New York
April 1995

Edmund Safri dialed his favorite eclectic hedge fund manager, Marty Amwell.

Marty had gotten big again—now managing close to a billion dollars. Marty mattered again, and Edmund was happy for him. It had really been a shame what the CFTC had done to him back in the 1980's.

"Economics Consultants of Princeton," a sprite receptionist voice answered. The name of the company had not been changed since the earlier CFTC-induced bankruptcy; just the legal domicile.

"I need Marty. This is Edmund Safri."

"Just a second Mr. Safri."

Marty came on the line.

"Edmund, Edmund, what evil tricks are you up to now?" Marty asked, as a smile enveloped his face.

"Never evil; just profitable. I wanted to check your read on the silver market."

"It's perked up a bit lately, but I still don't like it. None of my cycle work suggests that it's ready for a major move."

"We're starting a foray, Marty."

"Uh oh, another cartel?"

"One big guy behind it, Marty. You'd know his name. We're just going for the ride."

"Want to give me a clue as to how deep the pockets?"

"Hails from Omaha, hails from Omaha, Marty."

"You mean Buffett?"

"You said that, Marty, not I."

"But Buffett isn't a hard assets guy...he's a stock guy."

"The world changes Marty. Phibro has the order. Old Salomon connections there, but both Goodman and the Safri Bank are on board. This is going to be a fun one Marty."

"I wish I saw it in my cycles Edmund. I really do, but I doubt this foray of yours is going to work this time. My models just don't suggest that the time is ripe, Edmund. "

"I'm sorry to hear that Marty. I know that you do your own work, and march to your own drummer. I have no problem with that. Just don't fuck with us on this one Marty. I don't want to run you over."

Now Marty understood things a bit clearer. He had been doing a bit of silver selling over the prior few days, and this was Edmund telling him to take a step away—not to make the cartel's foray more difficult to succeed than needed.

"Edmund, I don't know what to say..." Marty ultimately volunteered. "I just don't think this is going to work for you."

"Just stay away Marty. You are a friend. I don't like to hurt friends."

CHAPTER 43

BUCHANAN PONDERS
Devon, England
April 1995

John Buchanan's book on fractal feedback loops within markets was making progress, but still was not nearly finished. When it did come to print, he was sure that the "efficient market hypothesis" community of traditional economists wasn't going to like it one bit.

As he looked down at his keyboard, trying to determine his next transitional paragraph, the phone rang.

"Buchanan, this is Edmund Safri."

"Wow, Edmund, it's been a long time."

Despite Buchanan's prescient work as to the expected market volatility into the 1987 Crash, Safri had ended his consulting research relationship with Buchanan in early 1991. The money had just not seemed worth it for the occasional moment of brilliance. Buchanan and his other academic associate Didier Ornsette had been working unsponsored since that time. Both taught university classes to make ends meet.

"Listen, John, I hope that there are no hard feelings about when we backed away from our relationship a few years ago. It was just a period of general bank cutbacks. Everything got slashed."

"That's alright Edmund. We have persevered without you."

Buchanan mentally cursed this big-swinging-dick Safri—someone he'd served up the Crash of '87 on a plate to; helped keep his bank out of trouble; only to be ditched as a consultant a few years later. But notwithstanding this animosity, John now acted passive and forgiving on the phone.

"In any case, John, I have a special project for you—assuming that you have the time and the where-with-all. I want you to keep a close eye on the silver market. It is starting to perk up a bit. We know that there are a few large buyers around. If, over the coming few months, silver ever starts to look top-heavy to you—ready for an 'entropic reversal' as you guys call it—you need to let me know right away. This is worth a consulting fee of $100,000 to me. Does that sound fair, John?"

"Sure. So this is just a one-off?"

"Just a one-off consulting gig for now. A bit like that Rhodium assignment—even though you never did give me a sell signal on that one." Safri knew how to give Buchanan a small dig. "Just a single market. But put all your analytical models behind it. This is important to us."

"Sounds fine, Edmund. I will start work on this later today, and let you know what I see. I can reach you at the same number as in the past?"

"Yes," responded Edmund.

With that, John Buchanan put down the phone receiver. He really hated these Wall Street guys. He could tell Safri was up to something, and mostly wanted validation of some market gamesmanship already afoot.

He punched up a chart of the silver futures market. The heady days of the Hunts squeeze were long over. The price of silver had slowly gravitated back to $4.60 in late February, but was now up to $5.60 in early April. It had been a steady and grinding ascent—a large percentage move, but nothing that was likely to be tripping any of his models yet. He went to work applying his computer models to the price stream, searching for positive feedback loops and log-periodicity patterns that might point towards future times of entropic reversal.

The models would need time to crunch. But the money would be worth it. Maybe John could parlay useful analysis of this situation back into a full sponsorship relationship.

Did Safri even deserve such?

CHAPTER 44

RAF AND SILVER
New York
April 1995

"So how high do you think his limit will ultimately be?" Raf asked quietly over the phone.

"I think Phibro has the go-ahead to take it all the way up to $6 without a lot of questions or problems," answered Edmund Safri. "I think $7 is a realistic target that they have in mind before you'd ever see them sell."

Raf had stayed involved in the metals business his entire career, plugging away at the Pierrepont Bank. He just loved situations where he knew about a piece of customer business that could be piggybacked. Riding the customer flow—front-running it if possible—was his favorite way to make money.

He was already long ten million ounces of the silver. It was a big bet for his typical style, but it was working, and he was thinking of making it even bigger.

"Where's he taking delivery of all this metal?"

"Most is going to vaults under Zurich airport in designated bar form, some will stay loco London non-designated," Edmund responded.

"No involvement with the COMEX?"

"Nah," said Safri. "This guy saw what happened to the Hunts with COMEX. He wants no part of that; wants to be real discrete; behind the scenes. No New York delivery."

"How long are you?"

"We have a sizeable position, Raf, but you know I can't answer that."

"Any central banks or miners going to stand in our way?"

"I don't see any around. There is this one spec—Amwell—who could be a pain in the ass. He seems to be bearish, and won't come on board with us."

Raf had heard of Amwell, but didn't know him personally; reputedly a smart guy; real mysterious with his models.

"We have enough fire power to run him over, right?"

"If he really insists on being run over, I certainly think so. But I'd expect that he'll just stand aside."

"Thanks for the update Edmund. Let's try to keep talking regularly about this."

"You got it, Raffy. Hey, make sure the Pierrepont remembers me at U.S. Open Tennis time. My wife really digs those center-court seats you get for us."

"No sweat, Edmund. Your seats will be the same as always—maybe even better."

CHAPTER 45

SILVER COMES UNDONE
Princeton, NJ
June 1995

Across the latter part of April 1995 and into the first few days of May 1995 silver moved steadily higher. Marty continued to hear rumblings of the cartel buying.

A floor broker friend called him one day and said that Phibro reputedly had an order to buy a million ounces of silver every penny lower under the market. But the order was being routed from Phibro through Safri Bank, and because Marty was a big trader who used Safri, some people believed that it was Marty was the one behind all the silver buying.

"Oh shit," thought Marty, "I can just see this now. The CFTC is going to land on me again, even though I'm not even involved."

He pondered what to do. He was not in fact involved at all in the silver market, and had a minor "panic cycle" date showing up on his cycle array for the first week of May. Marty knew the seasonals as well would be weak for the precious metals until late June to early July. This thing was ripe as a short trade, not as a long. Edmund Safri was going to get caught on this thing one way or another.

He picked up the phone and dialed his old regulatory nemesis down in D.C., Olsen McFadden. He'd kept tabs on this guy throughout the years—Olsen had moved up in the world—now some sort of senior assistant at the Department of Treasury.

The phone rang for several seconds, and then answered: "Treasury."

"Olsen? This is Marty Amwell."

"Marty Amwell?"

"You know, the guy up in Princeton that you dicked around about NFA filing requirements back in the early 1980's."

"Sure, now I got you. Wish you hadn't made me do that, Marty, but you were breaking every CFTC rule in the book."

"Well, Olsen. I want to give you a bit of a heads-up in real time. There is a big fish in the silver market right now playing more fun and games. Some people think that it's me. But it isn't. You should get your guys to look into this."

"Marty, I'm at Treasury now. Left the CFTC awhile back. That's no longer my beat."

"But you still have friends at the CFTC, right?"

"Sure, yeah...I suppose."

"Well just tell them that they should look into whatever orders Phibro is sending to the floor. Some of it is ending up being executed by Safri. This is manipulative stuff and there is a cartel of banks working around the core order. And oh, by the way, tell them Marty Amwell has nothing to do with it, but is just trying to be a good citizen to give you guys a heads-up."

"OK, Marty. Fair enough. I'll relay that message."

Marty replaced the receiver, and felt immediately guilty. If Edmund Safri ever found out what he had just done, a friendship would be severed. But in Marty's mind, this was for Edmund's own good. Better to head this trade off at the pass than to let it develop any sea legs.

Marty looked at his phone turret for a few more seconds. Then he dialed his friend Mark Stitts at Bloomberg. Stitts was a quality commodities reporter that Marty had been friendly with across the years.

"Mark, it's Marty Amwell here."

"Hey Marty! Good to hear from you. What you think of this silver price move higher? You involved there at all?"

"Some think I am, Mark, since its being fed through Safri pipes, but I'm actually not involved. I'm told it's all coming out of Omaha."

"Omaha? You mean like Buffett?" Stitts was fully attentive now—smelling a major story.

"You said that Mark, not I. Give it a day or two. Then get on the horn to your connections at the CFTC. See what they have to say about this."

"Marty, hold on a sec. You can't just call me up and tell me that Buffett is the big buyer in silver, and then not tell me what evidence you have of this. I can't run something like that."

"I'm not telling you anything, Stitts. Do your own homework. Check in with the CFTC. You'll figure it out. My models simply tell me that the time isn't ripe for this to work. Closer to a top than a bottom. I think the guys taking this market higher are going to get their hands caught in the cookie jar."

Marty bid Stitts goodbye, and returned to his chart machine. It was incredible how stupid and naïve some of these fundamental types were. How could they be buying this thing right into the wrong time of year? The wrong cycle set-up?

Three days later Mark Stitts posted a new Bloomberg story. It led with a simple first line:

"Market sources indicate that the CFTC is investigating unusual trading activity in silver emanating out of Phibro."

The alleged Buffett connection was not mentioned, but that headline was enough on May 9th to send silver spiraling back lower from just above $6 at the start of the day to closer to $5.25 by the day's end.

At Pierrepont, Raf turned apoplectic. This clearly wasn't in his game plan. How had the CFTC gotten involved? He raced to try to dump his ten-million ounces of silver in both the over-the-counter market and COMEX futures pit, but Phibro and Safri traders were selling as well—a bunch of caught mice all looking for the exit hole at the same time. It was not easy for any of the cartel participants to get any metal out the door.

In the end, Raf lost close to $5 million on the trade.

"Fuck those tennis tickets for Edmund," he thought. "That's the last time that I listen to that shyster."

Buffett—if actually involved, and disdainful of any possible public exposure—appeared to go quiet on silver until the dust settled, and the CFTC went away. He'd only gotten a toe-hold position to what he ultimately wanted to purchase. Leaving the rest for a future time was now the best path to follow. He wasn't a trader after all. He was an investor.

In Princeton, Marty—while uninvolved—smiled. The collapse had come in line with his panic cycle computer-generated array.

"It was just meant to be," he thought—even if he had, in reality, given that market a behind-the-scenes nudge.

CHAPTER 46

THORN GOES FRENCH
New York, NY
Summer 1995

Thorn kicked around for multiple months after leaving Goodman. He considered at one point going back to work for Raf at Pierrepont, but in the end, decided to leave that guy alone. Thorn had had enough of the front-running types given his recent experiences with Jimmy.

In the end, a cold call letter to a modest sized French bank—Societe Centrale—landed him a new job. Yes, cold-call letters occasionally worked. And the job was a good one—running their New York proprietary trading desk.

Societe Centrale had just come off of a horrible 1994 experience where fixed income exposures held by a small team of prop traders had lost the bank close to $100 million. It had all been a very carry-trade centric portfolio—not a good approach in 1994 when Greenspan had enacted a modest snug in rates. That team had been blown out.

But the Treasurer wasn't ready to give up on prop trading altogether. Thorn became part of his come-back plan.

A job offer over a handshake was proffered, but the Bank Treasurer made one hesitating remark as he did so.

"There is one thing I must tell you, Thorn, and this could be an issue for you," the heavy-set Luxembourg-accented Treasurer started to broach. "Paris right now has a set of limits on Proprietary Trading here in New York where you will have the right to spend up to $10 million in options premium expense, but you have no limits to be short any options. Is that a problem?"

Now Thorn admittedly had historically traded with more of a long option bias, but over his entire career he had never heard of a set of limits where you couldn't be net short any options. In reality, he was a relative-value type of trader: buy Option A cheaply and sell

Option B expensively. This limit issue was a huge problem. But he also needed a new job.

"I assume that we can petition to get that changed?" Thorn asked, dodging the question a bit.

"Oh surely, yes...but, err...ehm...you have to know that Paris isn't always the most responsive place to create change."

"You mean they can be bloody slow."

"Yes. I would expect that you can get things adjusted to your tastes, but it might take a number of memos and about six to nine months of time...Plus there's one other thing, Thorn."

"Oh yes, what is that?" Thorn didn't like these last minute changes to a job he was genuinely excited about.

The Treasurer stood and beckoned Thorn to follow him to a glass window in his office that overlooked the trading floor.

"Do you see that little guy standing by the FX options desk?"

"Yes."

"He does FX Options strategy and sales. Hasn't gotten much traction since he's been here. You know more about FX options than he does. You also already know a bunch of the folks at the big macro hedge funds—Odyssey, Omega, and Tiger. If I hire you for this prop trading position, I know it might sound a bit odd, but I'd like you to do that fellow's job as well. I want to shit-can him. Get a "two-fer" by hiring you."

For a guy from Luxembourg, this Treasurer certainly had American slang down—"Two-fer," of course, meaning a two-for-one deal.

"So you want me to be both a prop trader and an options strategist-salesperson? Isn't that kind of a weird and potentially conflicted combination?"

"At first glance, maybe, but I think you would be really good at this Thorn. You can make both sides blossom. Trade anyway you want—within those Paris limits—and with anyone you want—within normal credit limits. But help us beef up our market presence with hedge funds at the same time. You've got the experience to do both jobs very well."

Thorn stared at his new potential boss. This was not perfect. But then, nothing ever was. But it was better than dealing with that Jimmy fellow back at Goodman. It was better than remaining unemployed.

"Hell, I'll give it a shot."

CHAPTER 47

SAFRI BACKS OUT
Devon, England
Summer 1995

John Buchanan had only just started adapting his mathematical models to track the silver market when the price collapsed back from 6.00 to only 5.25.

Safri called back.

"Scuttle your work, John. Sorry, false alarm. We thought something big was going to happen, but now everything has been put on hold—wait-and-see mode."

"But I already spent about three days of work on this, Edmund."

"I'll make it up to you John, I really will."

"Edmund, I'm honestly kind of tired of being yanked around like a rag doll."

"OK, so bill me for your time, John, but that might be the end of the relationship if you do. You have to understand, John, the world changes. Situations change. What was happening last week isn't happening this week."

"I won't bill you Edmund, but you have to understand that all the work that you've effectively paid for in the past—it's going to end up benefiting some other bank; some other firm. That's really a shame Edmund. I just want to make sure that you understand that. Didier and I consider ourselves free agents to advise others."

"I understand, John. I really wish it were in my budget to go forward with you on a full time basis. But you also have to understand that it's been almost ten years since we started this research. That's forever on Wall Street. If things had clicked along a bit faster, then maybe it would be different."

Buchanan hung up the phone disappointed with Wall Street for the umpteenth time. He didn't know which was worse: the myopic efficient-market economists who didn't see the way that the fractal world really worked, or the Wall Street guys just dead set on creating the next mini-squeeze.

He looked out his window to the meandering River Mole going past his Devon property. The sun danced on the water. It really was such a lovely spot that he had chosen to live. But at the same time, he really needed to get out of England and over to New York—find a new partner, new backing.

CHAPTER 48

THORN AT SOCIETE CENTRALE
September 1995
New York

OK, Thorn finally had the seat that he really wanted: running a proprietary trading desk at a major bank.

Granted, his limits sucked, and Thorn's fifth memo to Paris about proposed limit changes had just gone into the interoffice mail. Sending anything to Paris really was like throwing a message in a bottle into a deep black hole.

But this job was going to be a blast overall. Thorn had never had so much freedom and opportunity to meander across different markets. Thorn hired others around him led by a fixed income arbitrage trader and a trend-following model trader. Thorn would be the discretionary macro part of the triumvirate.

Thorn's boss also had a natural willingness to spend a bit of money to do market research. Thorn initially tooled around a new system to which Societe Centrale already subscribed called the Logical Information Machine (LIM). You could input any number of different potential causal inputs that might be transpiring in the markets at the present time, and then query how many times this combination of events had occurred in the past, and learn what markets did afterwards.

Show every time that the S&P 500 has been up more than 10% in three-months when gold was down more than -10% over the same time, and what happened to both markets next?

Or...

Show what happened to gold for the next month after both copper and T-Bond futures decline by more than -5% in the same week.

Or...

Show every time that there was an outside-day-down formation on S&P futures on the day of a Fed Meeting, and what the market then did over the following 30-days?

Or...

Show every time the CPI release was higher than the expectations for CPI by more than .3, and how the T-Bond futures market reacted over a 10-day, 20-day, and 30-day time horizon.

The permutation of possible queries was endless. Fundamental data and technical price behavior could all be interwoven in the most creative way. The general thought was always that while history was unlikely to precisely repeat itself, there could easily be patterns in past market alignments that would relate to the present.

The LIM system was not cheap—something like $10k per month—and initially Thorn loved exploring it. But quickly Thorn concluded that most of the answers given by the LIM system were probably not that statistically robust—often perhaps, crap in, crap out: answers and relationships driven by happenstance rather than real causality.

That's when Thorn uncovered some writings by a fellow writing in *Nature* magazine of all places who seemed to understand something about the fractal repetitiveness—the importance of natural Fibonacci rhythms—that Thorn himself had so often witnessed in markets. In his articles, this writer was tying the behavior of the physical world to the behavior of the financial world in a way that resonated with Thorn's own experiences and beliefs.

The writer's name was Professor John Buchanan.

Thorn got on the phone one day and just called him.

"Dr. Buchanan, Thornton Lurie here at Societe Centrale in New York. I run our proprietary trading desk, and am looking for added research resources to our effort."

"I'm all ears," responded Buchanan, sitting up from his slouched desk chair in Devon. Here was his path back perhaps from the sidelines of unfunded fractal research.

Thorn started this conversation carefully—using as academic an approach as possible. "Dr. Buchanan, after some twenty years trading markets, I'm of the opinion that when Benoit Mandelbrot discusses the natural origin of 'fat tails' in market behavior, he stops short of the real punch line. While his 'fat tails' undoubtedly exist, they are not altogether random, but I believe may be driven by a certain natural market periodicity tied to mathematical constants such as pi and phi. What do you think of that statement?"

"I think you are the first person that I have spoken with on Wall Street who remotely gets it. Out of chaos—at a certain critical moment of entropy—comes natural order."

Thorn was impressed. It was the perfect response.

"What's your research showing you now?"

"There is something building in Asia that appears headed to an entropic resolution soon."

"You mean like a crash event?"

"Yes. Money has concentrated in Asia over the past few years, but it is an unstable situation. It is very much 'hot money' chasing returns—with much of the inflow going into illiquid assets. Meanwhile, Asian export growth is already starting to slow. This is not a sustainable mix. Greenspan's snugging of rates in 1995 is on the margin pulling capital back from Asia into the U.S. So a bit like a butterfly effect, this domestic tweaking of the U.S. economy is causing unintended knock-on effects in Asia. My models expect…"

Buchanan hesitated and stopped.

"Well, maybe I should save that part until we know each other better."

Shortly thereafter, Thorn engaged Buchanan as a consultant, and they soon became great friends. The focus of their work together started on the Thai economy, which Buchanan deemed was the most ripe for problems. Given Thailand's huge dependence on foreign debt, Buchanan believed that Thailand was perhaps structurally bankrupt even before a crisis began.

Since Thorn was also responsible for strategy work at Societe Centrale, he started to propose various put option strategies to Societe Centrale's hedge fund clients expressing the view that the Thai baht could devalue from its then-current official peg at 25 baht to the dollar. For some reason, he found a particularly welcoming audience with his trading counterparts over at Tiger Management.

Unbeknownst to Thorn at the time, there was also another currency derivatives salesman in the Far East at his old firm Goodman Sachs pumping Tiger with negative views on Thailand. Thorn and this other fellow apparently made a persuasive one-two punch. Tiger was soon fully on board the anti-Thai bandwagon.

But dealing with the Societe Centrale's currency options desk was like pulling teeth from a child—a painful experience. Manned by about twelve people—all French—the response time to get a firm options quote was typically slow and bureaucratic.

Thorn would turn to his colleagues there, and ask a price on $500 million of put options on the baht on behalf of Tiger, and from that point on, it became like watching an old Keystone Cops movie: scrambling, huddled discussions, much back and forth banter, and then at long last, the delivery of a most uncompetitive price.

Since Thorn also traded proprietarily for himself, and he generally knew what other counterparts were offering in terms of pricing, he often had to respond to Tiger (and other clients) that "Our guys are giving me a volatility level that I'm too embarrassed to show; just call Citibank, and you will get your trade done at a fair price."

This was not a good position to be in. Thorn might end up doing fine trading on a proprietary basis himself, but unless he could also land a few "big-swinging-dick" hedge fund clients and some associated business for the bank, the Treasurer who hired him was not going to be altogether happy.

And yet, Thorn was stuck between shitty pricing from a slow-moving band of French options traders and a credit department that was equally slow to approve new clients. Thorn quickly fell into the following routine: he'd find a new potential hedge fund willing to take his calls, entice them with interesting strategy work, and then wait nine months for the credit department in Paris to respond with a "yea or nay" response to actually setting up the new client account. On the surface, the bank said that it wanted to do more hedge fund business, but this desire was really moot given the slowness and conservative nature of its credit department.

Then one Friday afternoon, Thorn came to truly appreciate the problem that he had on his hands when the head of the currency options desk—a fellow named Francois—approached him.

"Hey Thorn, can we borrow your cell phone?" asked Francois with a smile and a gentle French accent.

It was still the early days of cell phone use, and Thorn happened to be one of the few people in the trading room who owned and used a cell phone.

"Sure, but why do you need it?" Thorn asked.

"Well, if you need an option price for yourself or a client, you call your cell phone."

"So where are you guys going?"

"That depends upon who's asking. If anyone from Paris calls, you tell them that we are in a very important meeting with New York management. If anyone from New York needs us, you tell them that we are up on the 23rd floor on a conference call with Paris."

"So where are you guys really going to be?" asked Thorn.

"We're going to the movies," Francois answered with a twinkle in his eye, and a slightly devilish look.

"You're going to the movies? All twelve of you? During business hours? Couldn't you just draw straws and leave one trader behind?"

"Yes, we thought about that, but we all really wanted to see this new James Bond movie. It's a quiet Friday afternoon. I don't think anyone will notice, and if something does happen—if you need a price—as I said, just call your cell phone."

So as Thailand was effectively beginning to melt, the French went to the movies. What classic stuff.

That was the moment that Thorn decided that he needed to extricate himself from his Societe Centrale seat. Interfacing with Buchanan was great, and being able to float between different market opportunities was fun, but dealing with the French around him was a bad dream—or maybe worse—it was a bureaucratic nightmare.

Thailand blew up in May 1997. Buchanan nailed it. No one at Societe Centrale really did. Yes, Thorn owned a few Thai baht puts, but he did not maximize his gains when he got spooked out of his exposure by the June 30, 1997 assertion by the Thai Prime Minister that the baht would *not* be devalued. That assertion was like the last attempted finger in the dyke before the dyke gave way in earnest. Thorn ended up hitting a single with Buchanan's help, but missed hitting the home run. Tant pis. Thorn seemed to be good at that, and was pissed.

CHAPTER 49

THE GURU
Palace Hotel, Tokyo Japan
June 1998

Marty stared out at the sea of Japanese faces once again in front of him. Each year, this conference got larger—the room hotter.

He looked down at his notes. The date of July 20, 1998 stared back at him for the umpteenth time.

The date was now only a scant few weeks away.

"Many of you in this room know that I highlighted mid-December 1989 to be the entropic high in the Japanese stock market. That prediction more or less nailed the actual high of the TOPIX on December 18, 1989.

"In that instance, the currency manipulation of 1985-1987 led directly to the Crash of 1987, and then the further machinations of government officials set off a period of repatriation of assets to Japanese shores. The Japanese bubble was created very much by politicians and the unintended consequences of their economic moves that caused capital to concentrate here.

"My truly important cycle dates only transpire once every 3141 days—or every 8.6 years—an interval of pi times 1000. July 20, 1998 is the next such pi cycle. It should mark an extreme in market sentiment. I'm expecting significant global highs in equities on that date, and my focus will be on the European markets this time."

The mathematical simplicity of the prediction was elegant. It was also—to Marty at least—crystal clear. Stocks were already ebullient and frothy in the spring of 1998, but patience in timing was required. There was no reason to attack early. The market would not be ready for reversal until the pi cycle was fully complete.

This suited the way he liked to trade as well. He'd typically hang at the Princeton office only around key cycle windows ready to pounce on an appropriate entropic set-up. If there was one larger 8.6-year pi cycle that he was attentive to, this cycle also sub-divided into twelve 8.6-month mini cycles. Why twelve? Hell, he didn't know. Maybe it had something to do with the signs of the Zodiac, but it worked. Of that much he was sure.

Then once a mini-pi cycle date passed, and he had attacked and then harvested a foray in the market—win or lose—he'd typically lose interest in the price action, and head to the Jersey Shore. He'd bought a beach house there. He had hired a limo driver as well to shuttle him up to New York when needed for a meeting or dinner. He'd also hired this really cute secretary named Tina. They had started an affair. He was thinking of proposing to her.

Life was good. But he also felt stressed. There were now so many different markets to follow. His research business had taken off, and yet his own ability to stay apace of his different model set-ups had waned.

A voice shouted from the audience.

"Mr. Amwell. If July 20, 1998 comes and goes, and nothing happens on it, what will you do then?"

"That's just not going to happen. Sure, I guess I could miss by a day or two, but I have come to respect this pi cycle so much that I know markets will be ripe on that date. Just look around at the most stretched situations, and be prepared for reversals. It's almost as if God's attention span will be used up."

Halfway around the world, Marty's spring 1998 speech at the Palace Hotel in Tokyo reverberated into the pages of *The New York Times*. Gretchen Morgenson wrote up his views. The Japanese postal system was fucked. The Japanese pension system was fucked. Now Europe was going to be fucked. It all made for good press.

Along the way, and in spite of all of his dour economic warnings, the MOF still favored Marty as a potential savior to Japan's failing institutions and had actually asked him to take over a Japanese brokerage firm named Crestar that had fallen from grace.

Once he had done so, Crestar had then stepped up the pace of Tobashi swap transactions and Princeton Note issuance on behalf of Economic Consultants of Princeton. Over time, Marty had in effect issued over $3 billion in unsecured debt to Japanese corporates all desperate to get out from under their wilting portfolios. Marty was going to be their savior with the MOF's blessing.

A few of those companies had executives with their palms out ready to be lined for agreeing to purchase a Princeton note. Marty had accommodated. Indeed, because he had seen so much of this type of activity, he had become even more knowledgeable about Japan—let that read, ever so cynical about the country. Everything in Japan was worse than he'd originally thought it was—worse than one could even imagine it being. The magic of non-mark-to-market accounting was simply hiding the pain. And Marty was just a small cog in the wheel that the MOF had sanctioned to try to grease the gears.

Hell, this all wasn't bad for a simple guy from south Jersey. Marty had been in the right place at the right time. Yes, he'd nailed the Nikkei top in 1989. That had really just been a prescient educated guess given the stretched nature of that market at the time and his pi cycle alignment. Everything since then had been more of a fundamental understanding of how myopic and desperate that the Japanese now were.

Across 1997, one smattering of research from other sources had also caught his eye. There was this guy named Thornton Lurie at Societe Centrale putting out technical research focused around Asia. Marty had no idea who this fellow was, but a friend had forwarded on one of Thornton's strategy pieces. Thornton had a nice flair for combining technical pattern recognition with option strategizing. Marty liked his style. As he looked down at his notes, a pattern match chart produced by Thornton caught his eye. Marty had brought it in his briefcase—contemplating a potential "idea poach" for his presentation.

But that could wait. First Marty needed to understand exactly what Thornton was doing.

On the chart, Thornton had somehow picked out July 20, 1998 as a key fractal date, and in the accompanying text he wrote about an entropic reversal around that time.

Marty needed to meet this guy.

How could someone else out there uniquely have identified his pi cycle date using a presumably different technique?

Or was this guy Thornton just poaching Marty's own work?

CHAPTER 50

THORN AT ECP
Princeton, NJ
June 1998

As Marty Amwell came bounding through the marble-clad foyer of Economics Consultants of Princeton to greet Thorn for the first time, he struck Thorn as something of a lookalike to Valdimir Ilyich Lenin.

Marty was a tall man, and he had a generally thin build that was interrupted only by a gravity-induced little potbelly. He was mostly bald, but with a scraggly beard, and Amwell's complexion included pock-marked cheeks presumably left over from some dermatologist's attempt to treat acne in Amwell's youth. If there was permanent scarring, the beard was clearly there to minimize this.

Amwell's eyes darted from side to side. He was naturally nervous, but his handshake was firm and his warmth genuine. He was happy to meet Thorn, and almost immediately complemented Thorn on his fine technical strategy work.

"I've really enjoyed a few of the pieces that I've seen from you. You do good pattern recognition work. I particularly liked your chart of gold denominated in yen. Too many people just think of prices in dollar terms."

The interview had been set up on the surface by Marty and Thorn as an exploratory session about Societe Centrale and Economic Consultants of Princeton doing some business with each other. In reality, Marty just wanted to meet this guy Thorn, and Thorn just wanted to meet Marty. Thorn knew, or at least strongly suspected, that Paris would be way too conservative to ever extend Economic Consultants of Princeton a proper trading line of credit.

As Thorn walked into Amwell's office, he could not help but be struck by the juxtaposition of old and new. There is a long row of Roman and Greek busts along one wall, a Japanese Samurai sword mounted on another, a small Renoir painting underneath it, but then a brightly colored Leroy Neiman painting depicting a crowd at a roulette wheel on yet another wall. This latter piece was original art, not a print—the paint heavy and thick to Thorn's eye.

Meanwhile, the busts clearly were ancient and authentic. Some sported long-since broken noses, while others showed a small circular tag on their bases saying "Sotheby's" followed by an auction number. Had Marty left these there because he was too lazy to remove them, or did he want to specifically leave the tags to highlight their auction house provenance?

The busts were staring out into the room almost as a constant reminder of history's depth and importance. The hallway leading into the office was also lined with Presidential decrees and signatures that caused similar emotive feelings towards the power of history.

"You have quite the collection of historical antiquities here," offered Thorn in a polite small-talk manner.

"At heart, I am a hard assets guy," explained Marty with a smile, "And each of these things represents not only a hard-asset, but also a piece of history that is important to me. Do you see that bust over there?"

Marty gestured to one black bust on the end of the row.

"That is the only bust done of Julius Caesar while he was still alive. Next to that one is the Empress Livia. That was Julius Augustus's wife, mother to Tiberius, and the great-great grandmother to Nero...the family matriarch so to speak. There is a twin bust to that one in the Louvre."

"And what's that rock?" Thorn asked glancing at the corner of Amwell's desk where he spied a small triangular piece of stone covered in some ancient writing.

"That's a Sumerian cornerstone," Marty responded. "The Sumerians would place one of these in each corner of a new house to bring it good luck. I keep it on my desk for the same reason, even though some visitors think it looks like a dildo."

Marty smiled again and gave a chuckle. It was clearly a line that he'd used before.

"So how did you get involved in markets?" Marty asked.

"Well, there was this little episode called the Hunt Silver Crisis," Thorn explained, and then went on to relate to Marty how he had invested as a neophyte college junior in a whole host of silver stocks and watched them vault higher and then subsequently collapse back down.

"Those were certainly crazy times," Marty responded, a mutual chord in history triggering his own memories. "I was in the coin and scrap metal business at the time. I would fill up four vaults a day with all the incoming scrap silver. I also would sell this metal forward to Engelhard after engaging them to refine it down. I got in the habit of over-selling my actual supply because I knew that there would just be more of the stuff coming in the next day. The forward sales were all for .999 pure silver. When the silver price finally collapsed, I had a strange but nice problem. The scrap supply stopped coming in, so I was going to have a hard time delivering against all of the forward sales that I had made, but these sales were all at very nice prices. Even if I had had the scrap, all the refining space had become fully booked up, so making delivery on the forward sales would have been tough. So one day I actually had to rush into the market and pay up for .999 pure silver to cover my forward sales and not let Engelhard walk away from those contracts. It all worked out in the end, but those were wild times."

Thorn volunteered that Marty's story sounded a bit like what he had learned of Henry Jacowski's "vault cash" games with silver coins hedged against futures, and Marty quickly piped up: "Oh yeah. Jacowski. I remember him. Changed the rules at the most opportune moment. Saved his own hide."

"Exactly," Thorn answered.

Marty shifted gears a bit. "So you worked at Goodman Sachs. What did you think of that fellow Jimmy in their metals trading?"

"The overall style of the metals department at Goodman is to figure out where the stops are from the big guys—the John Henry's of the world—and then push for them. That style of trading made me somewhat disgusted."

Marty smiled. Thorn had clearly answered appropriately. While Marty respected the tactical ability of Jimmy, he had also fallen prey upon occasion to Goodman's sharp tactics. He would not mind "burying" Jimmy in a trade. As he continued to talk, it becomes clear to Thorn that every dollar made at the behest of Goodman Sachs was worth more in Marty's mind than a normal dollar made in some other market from some other counterpart.

"The dealers on Wall Street always try to read me," Marty explained, "I understand that this is their job. But if they read me too much, or start to try to front run me, then I just go the other way on them. Fuck 'em over a bit with a misdirectional zag when then expect me to zig."

Trading gold and silver to Marty is like going into battle, and within the bullion dealing community, Marty has become well known, revered, and feared at the same time.

"So what do you think of the metals market right now?" Thorn asked. The price or both gold and silver had been firming that spring, and Warren Buffet had recently announced that he had returned to the market to accumulate over 300 million ounces of silver. What Buffett had started to acquire in 1995 he was finishing in 1998. Thorn himself was kind of excited by the recent price action.

But if Marty had ever previously been a precious metals bug, such was not now evident in his response.

"There is so much silver in London, the vaults are completely full," Marty explained. "Some of this silver is left over from the Hunt days—the Arabs never fully liquidated—and some of it is related to Buffett's 1995 buying spree that reemerged recently. Someone must have explained to Buffett that if he bought his silver in New York and then shipped it to London, that he'd create the illusion of demand, because that's what he's been doing this year. There's no real physical demand—just an elaborately executed plan to create that illusion."

Marty paused for a moment, and then continued, "Do you know Marwan Shakarchi?"

"Of course, I know *of* Marwan Shakarchi," Thorn answered "although I do not know him personally."

Shakarchi was a big Geneva-based metals trader at a firm called MKS that stood at the crossroads of Arab supply and demand for precious metals. His aggressive trading was somewhat legendary in both the metals and foreign exchange worlds.

"Well, Marwan and I are personal friends. He comes to my beach parties on Long Beach Island—all the way from Geneva. He tells me that there is so much silver in vaults under Zurich airport, that we will never have a shortage of this stuff for the longest time. Mr. Buffett is in way over his head, but he just doesn't know that yet. This bear market is nowhere near ending; maybe we need to go back to $3.50 support, or maybe even $1.80. But all this inventory has to get liquidated before we'll be able to really end this bear market...before silver can turn."

At least a portion of Marty's prophecy would indeed come true. He had recently been shorting silver at prices between $7 and $7.80, and soon harvested some of his shorts at under $5. Thorn was a bit flabbergasted by the extent of the potential decline that Marty still foresaw, but was respectful of a man who clearly had good contacts in the industry and a seemingly unshakeable vision of the future.

Marty got to the meat of the interview.

"So I saw on one of your strategy pieces, the mention of July 20, 1998 as an important date? Did you get that date from me?" Marty asked.

It was an awkward moment.

"Well, partly," Thorn admitted, "but I also am very close to this other quant consultant John Buchanan, and he is looking for a final moment of market entropy in mid-to-late July. Arch Crawford also has an astro alignment turn expected on July 20, 1998. That date comes from a variety of sources really."

"It's funny the way that happens...different people using different tools and methodologies. But bingo, the same window of time pops out," Marty offered.

Thorn had long since learned to look for such windows in time. When multiple different sources all pointed to the same period, it was usually good to pay close attention. No one was correct all of the time, but with a convergence of forecasts achieved in different ways, the probability of an entropic reversal markedly increased. Both Marty with his pi dates and Buchanan using his power laws and positive feedback loops both pointed towards something important happening in late July. Arch Crawford's astro work was just icing on that analytical cake.

Marty went on to discuss all of his activities at his brokerage company Crestar, and his hopes to build more automated global trading systems. To Thorn it all sounded like pretty nifty stuff. Then at last the session finally ended, and it did so on an upbeat note.

"I'm having a hard time keeping track of all the peripheral markets and what my models are forecasting in each instance. I could use a smart guy like you, Thorn. Let me know if you'd ever consider jumping to the buy side."

It was like music to Thorn's ears. He was going nowhere with the French. But he also did not want to seem too eager and too easy to land.

"Let's meet again and talk more about that," said Thorn. He looked down at his watch to check how long they had been talking.

Somewhat to Thorn's amazement, it was 9:30 pm. Marty and Thorn had been sharing stories for six-and-a-half hours. No food, no drinks—just talk of the markets, of institutions, of history, and of Marty's various visions of the future. Thorn walked out into the cool breeze of the parking lot and dialed his wife.

"I've just met a most interesting man—this Marty Amwell. It's hard to separate genius from egotistical bravado with this guy, but I was generally impressed."

A few weeks passed, and Thorn eventually met Marty again for drinks at the 21 Club in New York. Once again, they talked and the hours meandered by. Marty seemed keen to tell stories while Thorn was somewhat frustrated about Marty's inability to get to potential job specifics. Might there really be a role for Thorn within Marty's burgeoning empire or not?

Marty would never quite make it to that important subject, but at the end of all the stories, he did encouragingly offer Thorn a ride in his stretch limo to Penn Station. It was a friendly gesture as Marty walked northward to spend the night at the Peninsula Hotel.

Towards the end of the 20-block ride car ride, Thorn casually asked the driver, "How many years have you been chauffeuring Mr. Amwell around?"

"Ten," the chauffeur answered, "Mr. Amwell is the best."

Indeed, Thorn by now had the impression that Marty Amwell was a very likeable—kind of a cute simple guy with whom it was fun to be around. Marty might be worth millions, perhaps billions for all Thorn knew, but despite a sizeable bankroll and ego, Marty was actually quite unpretentious and enthusiastic. He had a vision for the future, but a deep respect for the past. During that evening, their conversation had ranged from the history of the Roman Empire and the coinage during those times, to trends in Internet banking and the ability that already existed to download funds to a smart card from your home PC. Thrown in the middle, they'd spent some time discussing clairvoyance and the writings of the Bible and Nostradamus. Marty was equally facile on all topics: a real Renaissance man.

Thorn and Marty met again a few days later at the Hyatt Hotel in Princeton—but not before Thorn decided to send Marty a presumptive business proposal for employment. Marty was like a cat too coy to make the first move, a trader who refused to give away the competitive advantage of making the first strike. Given this, Thorn decided to cut to the chase and lay his cards on the table. He did not want to have another meeting like the last where the stories were great, but the business discussion limited.

Thorn needed this job. He was tired of waiting. April had now slipped into early July.

But no. At this dinner, Marty was all abuzz about the upcoming July 20th turning point date. It was a date truly important to him—a major high in European equities, he suggested—probably; a potential high the U.S. stock market as well—perhaps, but he is more focused on Europe. He suggests that the forthcoming introduction of the euro is crazy—poorly thought out.

Marty's cell phone rang. "Yes, yeah...how much do they want to do? Oh, OK, I'll pay up to 4% on a billion dollars...Call me if that gets done, because I would want to do the currency conversion."

"What was that?" Thorn asked.

"Well, we have these good corporate relationships in Japan, and sometimes we sell them notes to help them out."

"But are you paying them 4% in dollars or in yen?"

"I'll pay them 4% in yen."

"But that's way above the going yen interbank rate of 50 basis points. Is that reflective of Economic Consultants of Princeton being a poor credit?"

"No, not at all. It's just a rate I feel comfortable paying them. I can still earn 6% on Ginnie Mae discount notes, and I take the currency risk. If I'm paying them more than a normal yen rate of return, it helps to cement a relationship. Few people really know how to do business in Japan. We have been there for ten years, building relationships. So what if I'm paying them quite a nice yen coupon? It helps build the relationship in the long term, and God only knows that the Japanese need some sort of higher interest rate than 50 basis points to survive."

This led to a general conversation about Japan and the overall deflationary trends that had been transpiring there.

"In the end, they will have no choice but to monetize," Marty stated, "just the way FDR did when he raised the price of gold in the Great Depression...that was a defacto devaluation of the dollar by 33%."

"So where do you think dollar-yen is going?"

"My minimum target longer term is 233."

"Wow, that would be amazing. But that seems pretty far away."

"Well, that is where my longer-dated cycle maps suggest that it is headed. The Japanese Big Bang is going to free up three trillion dollars that was previously captive to domestic deposits and postal receipts. The Japanese currently control almost 25% of the world's savings. The flow of money out of Japan should just be enormous, and I plan to tap those flows."

"By paying them 4% today when you should be paying them much less than that?"

"As I said, it's all about relationship management. We are launching yen-based fund products right now to help build a track record. We're considering a joint venture with someone in Japan to market our product. Merrill Lynch and Goodman Sachs are going nuts over there trying to tap into the Japanese market, but their gaijin managers come and go; many of the western brokerage offices actually shut down a few years ago when the cost of doing business in Japan became prohibitive. Now they want back in. We never left, and that gives us a head start on the others. The Japanese trust us."

Thorn did not fully swallow that explanation, but then again, he did not consider himself an expert on Japan. Marty's assertions were certainly possible, although Thorn seriously doubted that Crestar and the sale of Princeton Notes in Japan was truly any threat to Merrill Lunch or Goodman Sachs. Perhaps more bravado; more ego coming out. But he did just commit to borrow a billion dollars over the phone, over dinner, not even looking at the markets. This guy was cool and confident. But Thorn still couldn't get him to talk specifics about getting hired. Marty was seemingly quick at making some decisions, but slow and evasive on this one.

The job offer was finally proffered though oddly enough on Marty's key cycle date—July 20, 1998. Thorn came to Marty's office that morning to sign a contract. It was a wild moment to be there. Marty sat at his desk feeding orders on the New York opening into his brokers..."Sell 500 Sep S&P futures, sell another 500. Sell 250 DAX Sep futures. No make that 750. Sell 1000 CAC Sep futures. Sell 1000 Nasdaq futures."

Marty was like a kid in a candy store—hitting his sweet spot in time and price, putting his pi cycle theory into action.

The markets had started bid that Monday morning, but with no apparent news, and only Marty (and likely some of his followers) doing some selling, the market almost magically started to melt. It was a perfect entropic hit. Marty got his index futures shorts off, and was almost immediately in-the-money on them—never even experiencing a moment of angst or self-doubt. Prices simply fell away quickly.

No news accompanied the first day of market decline, or even the second or third day of decline. But within a week news did start to circulate that Russia was facing trouble in maintaining its currency band. Weak oil prices among other factors had hurt Russia's balance of payments, and not enough money was coming into government coffers to meet debt servicing, wages, and pension payments. Money had already started to first flee Russian GKO debt and then the currency itself was suddenly getting hit. This was all very much a leftover hangover to the 1997 Asia Crisis—but to Marty's credit, it was only after July 20, 1998 that this all started to come undone. It was almost as if some cyclical law of physics had somehow tripped in the markets. Markets went from ignoring the issue to suddenly being riveted by it.

At the time, Russia employed a "floating peg" policy toward the ruble, meaning that the Central Bank decided that at any given time the ruble-to-dollar exchange rate should stay within a particular range. If the ruble threatened to devalue outside of that range (or "band"), the Central Bank would intervene by spending foreign reserves to buy rubles. For instance, during the year prior before the crisis, the Central Bank aimed to maintain a band of 5.3 to 7.1 RUR/USD, meaning that it would buy rubles if the market exchange rate threatened to exceed 7.1 rubles per dollar. Similarly, it would sell rubles if the market exchange rate threatened to drop below 5.3.

The inability of the Russian government to implement a coherent set of economic reforms and to increase state revenues led to a severe erosion in investor confidence and a chain reaction that could only be likened to a run on the Central Bank. Investors fled the market by selling rubles and Russian assets, which also put further downward pressure on the ruble. This forced the Central Bank to spend its foreign reserves to defend Russia's currency, which in turn further eroded investor confidence and undermined the ruble. It is estimated that between October 1, 1997 and August 17, 1998, the Central Bank expended approximately $27 billion of its U.S. dollar reserves to maintain the floating peg. Much of this defense started only on July 20, 1998.

To Thorn, it was a seminal moment. Any prior thoughts that Marty was an ego-laden shyster evaporated into awe for his overall market prescience. Thorn was committed now anyway. He wanted to believe.

And Marty's call was just brilliant. While Marty traded around a bit on the edges of his core short position, he went home heavily short stock index futures day after day. And stock indices just kept falling. Soon the news headlines revolved around not only the Russian ruble, but Greenwich-based hedge fund Long-Term Capital Management which was experiencing huge problems with its convergence-oriented arbitrage trades. It was like the financial world was ending—a feeling Thorn had only felt once before during the Crash of 1987. And somehow magically, Thorn was now on the right side of this crash-like behavior for the second time—or at least working for a guy who was.

Then one day, in early October 1998 as Clinton testified under oath about his activities with Monica Lewinsky—a true moment of national societal angst—Marty walked into the trading room and said "OK, that's it. I'm flat."

"What do you mean you're flat?" Thorn asked, somewhat shocked. "Yesterday you said that you thought the S&P was going to collapse to 940. Today you're covering at 975? What made you change your mind?"

"Mainly my oscillators all turned," Marty stated a bit sheepishly, "and I had a minor turning point week on my cycle map. It's just time to stand aside. If this market bounces into November, I'll try re-shorting it then."

So off to his beach house Marty meandered. His immediate job was done—attack; harvest; then chill. Don't over-trade.

In July, Marty had just launched a new fund sponsored by a seeding group in Florida. He'd insisted on only one thing: they had to get the thing launched by July 20, 1998, and by the skin of their teeth, they had raised the capital. Seeded with $20 million on July 15, 1998, that fund was up some 63 percent by the end of August, and about 80% by the end of September. Then the fund just went to cash and sat there for several months. The sponsors had never seen anything quite like it. They named Marty their "Manager of the Year."

Deutsche Bank had also previously sponsored one fund that Marty managed down in Australia. The administrative people responsible for this fund called him one day to relay the following statistics: "Over the past five years, you have produced a +25.73% average annual return on your fund with us. But what you may not realize is that you have been actively invested in the market only 24% of the time. The other 76% of the time you have sat in cash—doing nothing. That is a most unusual type of record."

Marty concurred: "Most people feel that they have to be invested all of the time, and most think that it's right to be long-biased. I'm the opposite. I want to be invested in the market the least amount of time that I can, and because downdrafts tend to be faster and offer more instant gratification than slow grinding up moves, I love the times that I can attack from the short side."

In September 1998, the phone rang at Thorn's desk one day, and a voice on the other end asked with a steady tone: "Are these the offices of Martin Amwell?"

"Yes," answered Thorn. "I'm the assistant to the Chairman, how can I help you?"

"My name is Mark Lester. I work for the CIA. Is Martin Amwell available for a brief chat?"

Thorn was taken aback. The CIA calling? Marty always claimed strong Washington connections, but Thorn never quite knew where reality in this assertion stood. How much was bravado, and how much was real? But here was the CIA on the phone calling in for Marty.

And so it was that Thorn took a call from the CIA that eventually resulted in a late September 1998 meeting between Amwell and Lester. The CIA had heard of Amwell's success in predicting the Russian ruble crisis. They wanted to know exactly how he had done that.

"Could Amwell perhaps share his model with the government?"

"There is absolutely no way that I am sharing my model with the CIA," Marty eventually told Lester when they met face-to-face. "These models are proprietary to my business, my livelihood."

Lester left Amwell's offices with one last word of caution: "Mr. Amwell, you know that you are an American citizen. You have an obligation to this country. If you don't want to cooperate with us, that is fine. It is certainly your right to be protective of your research. That is understandable. But we do have our ways, you know."

With perfect foresight, Thorn probably should have worried about those words he overheard in the hallway. If the CIA is pissed at you, bad things can happen. Your life can become difficult.

Maybe this was the true beginning of troubles for Amwell.

Perhaps as an omen, and as stocks did start to rebound in mid-October 1998, Marty immediately faced a new problem: dollar-yen began to tumble; the Japanese currency was suddenly strengthening. It was as if the maestro had defeated one dragon, only to get bitten by another. Not counting Deutsche's Australian-based product and the Florida-based fund product, almost all of Marty's money was from the issuance of Princeton Notes in Japan—some zero coupon Tobashi swap related transactions, and other straight unsecured 4% coupon structures. Against these notes, Marty ultimately owed investors back yen.

Since Marty generally thought the yen was in trouble, he did not naturally mind this exposure, but he would periodically try to neutralize the risk if his yen oscillators or cycle maps suggested that doing so would be prudent in the short-term.

From 142 to 137, Marty seemed unconcerned—a normal pullback from resistance. From 137 to 133 he was buying yen futures—doing some hedging. And then the market just collapsed—131, 124, 111 in a matter of two trading days—the largest percentage fall in the dollar against the yen in such a short period of time that had ever been seen.

Marty certainly had some yen futures hedges on board, but was it enough? The move cost several options market makers a great deal of money, and at least one his job. Tiger Management had been long dollars against the yen, and puked out a sizeable amount of dollars. This selling by Tiger's Julian Robertson certainly was part of the reason for the dollar's waterfall decline. And Marty's old trading client Wolfgang in Bermuda had also been long dollars—largely following Marty's advice—and eventually was forced to sell in a panic. He cursed Marty Amwell as he did so.

Being long dollars against the yen had turned out to be a very crowded trade. The rush to the exit doors was swift and furious.

The big question though was: did Marty keep pace? Had he bought enough yen to be whole? Thorn never quite knew what Marty had up his sleeve—how much he was hedged or not. Marty was secretive about this type of thing—maybe in part to protect his own ego, or keep his ego at bay and not be influenced by it. The only thing that Thorn knew was that Marty was supposed to be getting on an airplane for Europe the prior night, but had talked to Thorn at about 9 p.m., and said that he'd decided to cancel his trip. Things were just too volatile. From his car on Long Beach Island he'd been selling some dollars.

Thorn dialed Marty's cell phone at 7 a.m.—having arrived at the office particularly early. 116 on dollar yen had suddenly turned into 111 in just a few minutes watching the screen that morning. Thorn had never seen anything quite like it.

"Do you see what is going on? Are we ok?"

"Yes, I'm actually net long the yen all-in. It's not a problem. I'm a little tired. I've been up all night, but we're fine. I just can't believe that Julian Robertson would precipitate such a move. It's like he just threw his entire position on the market. Very unprofessional."

Thorn inwardly worried how Marty's assertion of being whole could possibly be true. Was Marty's ego somehow preventing him from the admission of a loss?

But on the surface at least, Marty said he was O.K. Marty was a God.

CHAPTER 51

EDMUND AND THE IMF LOAN
New York, NY
August 1998

Edmond Safri stared at his screens. He'd survived the 1987 crash, but here it was starting all over again. Now it was Russia. Russia was so fucked.

It almost seemed to Edmond like the IMF monies being sent to Russia were being wasted. $4.8 billion was supposed to go out that night. He stared at the wire transfer authorization form on his desk. The funds were supposed to go directly to a Russian account at the Paris-based Eurobank. It was like sending money into a cesspool. Once it hit over there: gonzo—mushed into a Russian deficit that was uncontrollable.

Safri thought for a second, and then lifted the phone to call Finance Minister Dubinin in Moscow. It was best to check on the actual procedures being requested for this size of a transfer.

"The IMF funds are ready to go. I'm just confirming where they should be sent. Paris branch as always?" Safri asked.

There was a moment of hesitation on the other end of the line. Dubinin came back slowly.

"In actuality, given how fragile the world is, and how some creditors have started to attach our accounts in Switzerland and France, Yeltsin thinks that it would be better to use the FIMACO account in the Channel Islands. If you could use that account, we'd only expect in $4.3 billion there. You could send the balance to Bank of New York."

It was not usual procedure, but Safri knew Dubinin had the last word for the Central Bank of Russia. These Russian dudes were always playing fun and games. Now they wanted the wire split. Fuckin' hell. Safri would have to get the paperwork redone.

"I'm going to have to bounce that change off of the IMF folks. It's their money after all."

"Edmond...Edmond...err...the money that goes to Bank of New York...part of that is yours. Just keep it clean and simple. And don't worry—the balance of the funds will all make it to Russia—net of some fees."

Safri suddenly understood what was going on. Dubinin was going to carve up the IMF disbursement—maybe lose some of it along the way to some special accounts. Safri was being offered a bribe not to worry too much about the nitty-gritty wire instructions. Jesus Christ. Russia was in the middle of a financial crisis, and its own politicians were more concerned with lining their own pockets more than anything else.

"What do you mean some of the Bank of New York money is ours? How much?"

"We owe BONY $300 million for other fees. Is $200 million a fair split for Safri?"

Safri pondered for a second. This financial crisis was starting to ruin the Safri Bank's year. $200 million would certainly help smooth over some of that. Otherwise the money would go to a black hole anyway. All he had to do is switch a few wire instructions around the way Dubinin was suggesting—not make a big deal of it on this end.

After a small exhale, Safri finally answered.

"It will be taken care of," said Safri. "Does BONY know the amount that we eventually get back?"

"They should. I'll double-check that with them. Just push everything through the way we just discussed."

"Fuck the IMF," thought Safri. "Fuck the Russian people. This money is gonzo anyway. It might as well end up someplace more useful. It will be my swan song—my biggest score yet. I can retire next year. Move up and away from all this shit."

CHAPTER 52

WOLFGANG TROUBLES
Tuckers Town, Bermuda
October 1998

The waters of Frick Beach in Tuckers Town, Bermuda lapped at the sands as they always did. The heat of summer had now abated into the cloudy dampness of fall. The sky was gray overhead.

Wolfgang sat by himself in the sand. He looked down at the pink-speck laden sands around him, and drew a small tract in the sand by his side. How could this dollar-yen move have happened to him? He had taken a massive loss—more so than he could afford.

He was going to have to figure out some sort of bridge loan facility to stay in the game—make the money back.

As he continued to fiddle in the sand with his left hand, he picked up his cell with his right hand, and hit the speed dial button to his dad in Austria.

"Ja, Wolfgang here," he started. "Ja, I'm in Bermuda. How's the weather in Wien?...Ja...Ja...gut."

"Listen, I have an issue with one of my brokers in New York. It's Refco. Got myself into some illiquid positions. It's going to take some time to sort this out. I was wondering if you could help me. I need this broker to loan me $400 million, but they will look for a guarantee of some sort. Could your company guarantee my loan?"

There—it was out. He had dreaded this call, but was now relieved that the request had been delivered.

"Ja, I know that would be most unusual...but with your backing, I think that I can make this problem go away with time. You need to speak to Refco—Brian Brophy—on my behalf. I wouldn't ask if I didn't really need to...Ja...Ja...ok, much appreciated. I will wait to call Brophy until later today, and let you speak with him first."

Wolfgang was a great client to Refco. They would work with him. They didn't want to lose the commission revenue that he regularly helped them generate. If anything, they'd want to ingratiate themselves to Wolfgang and garner more of his future business. Maybe they could eventually hook his dad and get him to take a minority stake in the firm. Wolfgang had heard their pitch on this subject before. This hole was deep enough that it certainly needed dad's backing. Refco would play ball. They had to.

Wolfgang did secure an emergency $400 million loan indirectly from Refco later that day. For Refco's own purposes, they made it an off-balance sheet derivatives transaction. There was a separate entity that bought Wolfgang's debts from Refco, but then Refco lent funds to this off-balance sheet entity to make the purchase. It was better for their capital adequacy ratios that way. Wolfgang's father provided the ultimate verbal guarantee on the loan exposure.

It would take another seven years for that loan structure to come tumbling down and cause Refco to move into bankruptcy. But on that fall day in 1998, it provided Wolfgang with something that he desperately needed—time to survive and try to recoup.

Fuck that Marty Amwell. How could he have been so wrong on the yen?

CHAPTER 53

MARGIN PROBLEMS
Princeton, NJ
November 1998

Thorn tapped on Marty's office door, and then stepped into the office. He wanted to discuss a forthcoming mini-pi cycle window of time with Marty. These transpired every 8.6-months, but Thorn was confused about Marty's expectations and interpretation of the forthcoming event.

Marty was speaking to someone over the desk speaker box—clearly agitated—but waved Thorn to come further into the office in anyway.

"What do you mean that the Yakult account doesn't exist anymore?"

"That was one of the accounts we shut down Marty when you had those trading account margin issues," the speaker box offered back. It was the voice of Marty's Safri Bank broker, Bill.

"And these fuckers sent you an audit letter?"

"Looking at it in my hand. How do you want me to handle this Marty?"

"Screw it. You should never have closed that account. Open it back up, and transfer some money back into it. Then you can answer that audit letter in all good faith."

"OK, Marty, that's what I'll do, but Marty, you gotta realize that this is a real mess of managed accounts. You have 132 of them floating around, but you do most of your trading out of your one master trading account. How much any one account is owed by your master trading account isn't entirely clear to me."

"Let me worry about that," said Marty. "All the Japanese investors will get their guaranteed return back at the end of the day. Where exactly I'm making the money is less important. It's all offshore accounts anyway. There are no tax consequences that require us to perfectly track fund flows. All the Japs care is that I deliver them their principal and interest at maturity."

But on that day, at least one Japanese corporation seemed to want a bit more than their money back in seven years. They wanted to receive a verification of their account's current value.

"This sounds messy?" asked Thorn naively. "Is everything OK?"

"Just screwed up margin accounts," said Marty, exhaling with exasperation. "I truly don't know how the Safri Bank survives with all of their fucked-up systems. They closed an account I never told them to close. Now I need them to open that account back up again. Move the money back in. It's not going to look altogether pretty, but I think we can handle it."

"I hope so, Marty," said Thorn. "I hope so."

CHAPTER 54

WHERE'D THE MONEY GO?
Vancouver, Canada
Late November 1998

A group from the Princeton office travelled with Marty as he started a world lecture tour in Vancouver. Thorn was among them.

Marty was particularly popular in Canada—often carried on a daily radio business show in the Vancouver region. Over 150 people had signed up for a two-day seminar. His prescient July 20, 1998 market call had made him even more revered, and people wanted to hear his next big prognostication.

This is when Thorn first started to see a slightly different side of Marty, a slightly more debauched one—wanting to stay out late drinking, talking, flirting with girls half his age—while still rallying valiantly to give his morning lectures.

The lectures were not perfect, but they were good. Thorn never saw Marty impaired by any lack of sleep. It was as if after years of trading, with multiple wake-up calls on so many evenings, his body was immune from normal physical needs. He always sounded perfectly normal—even though Thorn knew that it would have been lucky if Marty had made it to bed before 3:30 or 4:00 a.m.

But what the hell was this tour anyway? Was Marty a money manager or still a market pundit? It seemed like he was trying to do both. After Vancouver, it would be Japan, Hong Kong, Australia, and then to London. He was scheduled to come back to Princeton for a week at Christmas, but then be gone again until March. Could he really constantly travel and still trade well at the same time?

In Vancouver, Thorn heard Marty talk about his "capital flow" models for the first time, and how his firm had tracked the capital flows coming out of Southeast Asia well before the beginning of the 1997-1998 crisis.

"Capital flow model?" Thorn asked him after one session. "What capital flow model?"

"The one we have downstairs in the computer room, Lido's area. You just haven't seen it yet."

Thorn wondered. Was this pure bravado and fluff, or was there really a model that he hadn't seen? Or maybe it was a bit of both—a model existed, but Marty just hadn't really finished it, but liked to pretend that he had. Thorn began to wonder: Marty was clearly brilliant, but he always seemed to push the envelope just a little too far—exaggerate his capabilities just a bit too much—some might say, stretch the truth. This certainly wasn't Thorn's style. When Marty would stand up in front of an audience, and claim that he had the single most extensive database in the world, Thorn would cringe. How could he say that? He didn't absolutely know that. He had a good database, but certainly not the best in the world. Saying such things only served to create a cheapened façade around someone who deserved better.

The U.S. equity market bottomed that year in mid-October shortly after Marty had covered all of his shorts. It did so on the willingness of Mr. Greenspan to cut rates in order to ease dislocations in the economy. Stocks vaulted significantly higher into November, stumbled slightly in early December, and then vaulted upwards once more with the New Year. Across this time Marty was mostly on the road, but by mid-March he had returned to Princeton and was sure that the market was about to make a definitive turn to the downside once again. But as the volatility of equity markets continued to build, several attempts to re-short the market ended up in aborted stop-losses.

To Marty's credit, he was far less stubborn about the market's unwillingness to go down than was Thorn. Thorn was trading a small sub-account for Marty, and had done extremely well initially, but had been struggling from November 1998 onwards—pissing away his earlier profits in small dribs and drabs. Marty in the meantime would occasionally wade into the market and buy a few thousand S&P futures puts, but these were tactical positions, and he did not wait long to either book his profits or exit to the sidelines. When a secondary turning point date that Marty was targeting on April 8,

1999 failed to stop the major indices, Marty took solace that there was a fair amount of sector rotation around that date—Internet stocks in particular taking a temporary breather.

Thorn was crawling the walls in over-anticipation of another leg down to equities, but Marty often seemed satisfied to watch and wait, trading only the yen from time to time, and increasingly not coming into the office at all. He was sure that another opportunity would come. It always did. In 1978-1980 it has been on the long side of metals; after that, it had been on the short side; in 1989 it had been in the Nikkei top, and he had stayed short Japanese equities for multiple years after that; in 1995 it had been a low in the U.S. dollar; by 1997 it had been on the short side of silver again; and in 1998 it had been the July 20, 1998 high upon which he had pounced like the true scorpion that he was.

"1999 will bring its opportunities, we just have to be patient," he kept saying.

But then Marty would retreat to his beach house, and Thorn would hardly hear from him for days on end.

In addition, across the months of May through August 1999, Marty was distracted by an audit of his broker-dealer Crestar by the FSA regulatory organization in Japan. He did not seem particularly concerned about it, just annoyed. Upon his occasional visits to the office he would bitch that the FSA had found some small back-office problems and a few commissions that had been shared (let that read "kicked back to") a Japanese client. But he told Thorn that this was "nothing serious"—simply normal business practices in Japan. In fact, because the FSA did not want to implicate any Japanese companies in any wrongdoing, Marty said that the FSA was unwilling to charge Crestar with wrongdoing related to the kickbacks. The FSA was searching for something else—something they could solely pin on the *gaijins.*

When the FSA apparently spotted that standard audit confirms for certain Japanese clients invested in Princeton Notes were all signed by the President of Safri Bank's futures subsidiary—a higher level person than they would have expected on the signature—the FSA contacted Safri to re-confirm the audit confirmation letters.

That is when the roof caved in on both Thorn's and Marty's world.

Thorn learned of the accusations sitting on the john at the Paradise Inn in Mount Rainier, Washington. It was his first vacation from Economic Consultants of Princeton, and after several days hiking, it was also the first *Wall Street Journal* that he had seen in days. "Safri Bank has NAV Accounting Issues with Hedge Fund Manager," read the mini-front-page headline under the financial news section—"See page A13."

Thorn had turned to page A-13 inquisitively, but initially still unconcerned that this likely involved Marty—It had to be some other Safri customer entwined in an accounting snafu.

But then Thorn read the text: "Upon an internal investigation at Safri Bank, over a billion dollars of Ginnie Mae discount notes held on behalf of Princeton Note holders— within accounts owned by the Economic Consultants of Princeton, a firm managed by Martin Amwell—have somehow shrunk to be only $50 million," the inner *Journal* page read.

Shit, this did involve Marty. Something was clearly very rotten and awry.

Thorn was shocked. How could this be? Marty had always been so vocal in his distrust of banking practices that he had often harped on the fact that he did not even allow Safri to repo his client's positions. "The only thing that Safri is allowed to do is to roll over maturing notes," he had said on numerous occasions. "Other than that, the clients' funds sit in segregated accounts that cannot be touched by anyone."

Remembering those words previously spoken by Marty with such conviction and even prudishness, Thorn still had some hope that Marty would be proven innocent. Maybe he was the victim of a disastrous back office and a potentially villainous broker who had been stealing clients' money from under his nose. Thorn certainly could vouch that Safri Bank back office statements were so difficult to read and interpret that he could not even prove his own sub-account P&L calculations to their statements. But then again—and Thorn's heart sank to think this—how could $950 million in funds go missing, and the guy charged with managing this money simply not notice?

Thorn tried to call the office that Friday. Oddly, there was no answer. He tried to call Marty's cell. Again, no answer. It was like the offices in Princeton had gone dead.

That Friday afternoon quickly slipped into Labor Day weekend, and Thorn agonized in incredulous but somewhat ominous ignorance about what had happened. Monday eventually brought a long flight back to Newark from Seattle, and across the miles, Thorn's mind ruminated with foreboding thoughts.

When he finally entered the office Tuesday morning, he saw a co-worker, and immediately asked what was going on.

"Well, if there was one day that it was probably good not to be here, it was last Thursday," this fellow stated. "The FBI arrived with their guns drawn telling everyone to stand back from their computers."

"You gotta be kidding?"

"Nope. They seized all of the firm's computers and took Marty away in handcuffs," the co-worker offered.

Another fellow in the office named Hal had also been led off in cuffs.

"Jesus Christ. What's Marty have to say about all of this?"

"Nobody has had a chance to speak with him. He hasn't been answering his cell phone. He may well be sitting in jail himself."

Thorn stared at the gutted research/trading room aghast. All the computers—his included—were indeed gone. Drawers were half open, clearly emptied of their primary contents, and scraps of paper lay everywhere on the desk and the floor. It was as though a hurricane had blown through.

But Marty wasn't in jail quite yet. Thorn finally reached him later that morning by phone.

"Marty—tell me something good. Tell me this isn't real."

"Well, it looks like my broker Bill has been stealing from me."

"Marty—how much money is reputedly missing?"

"Well, they say over $750 million."

"Marty—Let's start this conversation again. Bill is a nice Irish guy. Even if he was stealing from you—throwing every losing trade of his in your account, and you didn't notice because of your sloppy back-office procedures—how could you miss $750 million not being there?"

There was a momentary hesitation on the other end of the line, and then what followed was as much of an admission as Thorn had ever heard Marty utter.

"Well, some of the losses were mine. I did have some issues hedging the yen, but not what they say is missing."

"How much do you think you are responsible for?"

"Maybe $450 million. I had a bad trading year, but I did not commit fraud."

Thorn's heart sank yet again. Marty had not mentioned any yen trading losses to him or anyone else on the team. Indeed, Thorn had seen pro forma financial statements that Marty was preparing for a possible private placement of the company which indicated that 1999 was likely to be a good, if not banner year. And now Marty was saying something very different. It all smelled horrible.

After mumbling that he needed to think a bit about what was going on, Thorn hung up the phone. Then he suddenly wondered if perhaps the office phone lines were now tapped. If they were, Marty still had just claimed innocence, but had told a story surprising to Thorn's ears. Marty had either lied before to his team, or he was lying now with a new story of past trading losses exacerbated by an evil broker. Thorn knew nothing about what was really going on. He was lost and disappointed.

Suddenly feeling personally vulnerable, and yet trying to be as smart and as cautious as possible, Thorn decided to go find a public pay phone and call a lawyer friend that he knew at a well-respected New York law firm. The authorities would surely look at the company payroll and conclude that Thorn—as the highest paid employee under Marty Amwell—knew something. Thorn needed to be proactive about this—volunteer to be helpful and share what little information he knew.

By Wednesday morning, Thorn truly knew that he was in potential trouble. All he had to do was look at the front-page story on the *Wall Street Journal* that arrived on his doorstep. Holy shit—there it was: a major hedge fund scandal in an upper-right hand column with an artist engraving of Marty's visage staring back at him just above the newspaper fold. The Safri Bank's shares—recently sighted as a potential takeover target—had plummeted in Tuesday trading. The arb community in particular was pissed. "Marty the guru" was being accused of being "Marty the shyster."

And yet Thorn still could not discern what the truth of the situation really was.

Everything felt like smoke and mirrors. Nothing was what it was supposed to be.

CHAPTER 55

HANDCUFFS AVERTED
Princeton, NJ
September 1999

"Your timing was fortuitous." It was now Wednesday afternoon and Thorn was back in Princeton at the lobby pay phone nervously listening to his newly hired New York lawyer, Jim Donovan.

"What do you mean, my timing was fortuitous?" Thorn asked.

"The DA for the Southern District was all set to send a patrol car to your house tomorrow morning at 6 am, and take you away in handcuffs."

"But I haven't done anything. I don't know anything. How could they take me away in handcuffs?"

"It's kind of standard operating procedure to scare the shit out of you...they come early in the morning to catch you asleep, sometimes literally still in your underwear...embarrass you in front of your wife and children, your neighbors...put you on the defensive...and then hopefully you come in and spill your guts."

"They can legally do that? It seems almost Nazi-esque."

"Yes, it's all legal...just nasty scare tactics...but thankfully we headed them off at the pass. We will be meeting with them voluntarily tomorrow at their offices. Bring any and all documents that you might have that could be potentially useful to them. Let's meet at my offices before we go see the D.A. I can fill you in a bit better on what to expect."

"What's this all going to cost me?"

"$5,000 retainer up front. I bill at $700 an hour. If we ever go to court, it could add up. But hopefully we can talk to these guys for a few hours and this will all go away...In the meantime, I would think you should resign from Economic Consultants of Princeton today."

"Yup," answered Thorn, "I just did so. No reason to hang on to the sinking ship. Time to move on."

CHAPTER 56

SAFRI & THE RUSSIANS
Monaco
September 1999

It had all gone horribly wrong.

Edmund Safri read the September 15, 1999 *Wall Street Journal* lead article with both interest and alarm.

"Russians and Bank of New York Indicted for Tax Fraud."

It had all started in 1996—led by the wife of a Russian businessman who worked at the Bank of New York and set up special accounts mostly related to the avoidance of import/export duties—small time stuff at first. A Russian company importing construction materials might present an invoice to the Russian Central Bank for about a third of the real value of an import order. The tax would be paid on that value, and the importation of the materials allowed by Russian authorities. But another two-thirds of the actual payment would go through untaxed back channel accounts set up by BONY.

But about six paragraphs into the article was the particularly upsetting sentence to Safri:

"Authorities are also looking into whether any of the money that passed through the accounts stemmed from foreign aid to Russia, including loans from the International Monetary Fund."

"Shit, shit, shit," he thought to himself as he read the article. He read on…

"Indictments were expected for a Bank of New York Vice President, Lucy Edwards for transmitting as much as $7 billion in funds illegally. Some of the funds may possibly have been diverted from international aid."

This wasn't supposed to happen.

Safri had retired to Monaco. After years of hard work at the bank, life was supposed to be easy. Then had come Safri's first blow—the doctor's diagnosis that he had Parkinson's disease. The symptoms had progressed quickly—first only a familial tremor in his hand, then a balance problem, and then problems with walking—the development of an odd gate.

Now all this. He had just sold his bank to HSBC. He was supposed to be a happy rich old man. And yet he felt absolutely horrible.

Safri's phone rang.

"Ya?" he answered.

There was the mild hum of an international connection.

"Edmund, it's Marty. Have you seen the *Wall Street Journal* today?"

"I have Marty."

"What the hell is going on Edmund? Are you involved in this shit?"

"Marty—last I heard, you had your own issues to deal with: all those Japanese clients of yours looking for their money. Good luck with all that. Whatever shenanigans you got yourself involved with came close to screwing up my sale of the Safri Bank to HSBC. It's costing me a pretty penny to make this issue go away; to push the merger through. I'm not sure that I should even be talking to you, Marty. So why the sudden concern on my part?"

"Edmund, I think I know too much. I think you know too much."

"Ya, I do probably know a bit too much about how the world really works, but I'm retired Marty. Nobody is going to care about me anymore. I'm just an old guy with Parkinson's sitting in Monaco."

"But they will care about you, Edmund. Don't you see? When the Russian plutocrats discover that they have been cheated, they are going to look for the guys who had their hands in their pockets. I know that you were close the Russians, and close to the IMF. You always had the inside edge. I can only assume that you know something about what went down here. I think you should take some precautions, Edmund. I'm calling you as an old friend."

"Thanks Marty, but I think I will be OK," said Edmund—inwardly not entirely so sure of himself. "Your own shit with Japan sounds nasty Marty. Are you ok?"

"They appointed this fuckin' receiver for Consultants of Princeton—trying to grab all my assets. If you rub the government the wrong way, they certainly come down hard on you. I'm fighting for my rights though."

"Well, good luck with that, Marty. I appreciate your concern."

With that, Edmund Safri put down the phone and called his newly hired male nurse, Ted Maw.

"Let's double our security," Safri said. "Some ugly people out there may be pissed with me."

CHAPTER 57

THORNTON AT THE D.A.
New York
October 1999

The District Attorney for the Southern District of New York worked in a well-secured but dingy office building at 1 St. Andrew's Plaza on the edge of Chinatown.

Thornton had been prepped by his attorney: "Be forthcoming. Tell them what you know. But don't go beyond what you really know. If you don't know the answer to a question, just say so."

Thorn didn't know the answer to so many questions. This was all a bad dream. His mentor Marty was potentially headed to jail, and Thorn was now unemployed and a suspect in a criminal investigation. Could life get much worse?

"So how did you come to work at Consultants of Princeton, and what was your role there?" came the first question from the D.A., a tall, serious man with a slow manner of speech.

"I got to know Marty while I was a proprietary trader and strategist at Societe Centrale. He asked me to join him down in Princeton to help keep track of his models."

"Were his models real?"

"Yes, I thought so, albeit there was always an element of subjective interpretation when applying them. His models generally predicted important dates—potential turning points—but whether these dates would be highs or lows was trickier to always get right. Marty also had an ego. In my humble opinion, he sometimes cheapened his own research by claiming how perfect he was. Nobody is perfect. Marty was simply eclectic and different in his approach to markets."

"What do you know of his involvement with the Japanese?"

"Well, I overheard him negotiating a few different Princeton Note transactions. The first time was over dinner before he hired me. There were a few other times later, but I never saw any term sheets or documentation for these transactions. I just understood that Marty was trying to nurse gains from portfolios that had previously suffered 40-50% drawdowns. Marty would take these assets on swap for his notes, then sell these assets, and ultimately try to trade these accounts back to better health."

"Did you ever think these transactions were odd or potentially illegal?"

"I certainly queried Marty about how it was that he was guaranteeing back yen at maturity, and thus had yen overlay exposure. If he was issuing notes at 4% coupons in yen, but then hedging in the futures market where he effectively had to pay away points from the interest rate differential premium, I wasn't sure that made much economic sense. I did query him about this."

"And what did he say?"

"He said that it was just the way business was done in Japan."

"Did you ever see a Princeton note contract?"

"No."

"Were you aware of trading losses at the firm?"

"No—at least not until a few days ago. I actually did see brokerage statements come across the fax in August and September 1998 that showed Marty was making considerable profits. He was pretty massively short the market for the 1998 LTCM Crisis."

"And what happened after that?"

"More kind of a muddled outcome, I think."

"What happened when the dollar fell against the yen?"

"Well, during the dramatic part of that move, when the yen went from about 123 to 111 overnight, Marty was supposed to get on a plane to London, but he never went. I talked to him on his cell phone that morning. He said that he'd been trading all night, and thought that he was pretty whole. But if Marty had lost money, I don't think he'd have admitted it. Marty's ego sometimes prevented him from making a clean admission of losses."

"You think Marty has a big ego?"

"For sure. It is deserved at times. At others times, perhaps not. It can get him into trouble."

"Are there any other important points that you think we should know?"

"The dot.com bubble being what it was, Marty had spoken about taking Economic Consultants of Princeton public. He said that we had research—the content—that the media world really needed. He showed me a business plan that was filled with typos and errors. I was helping him try to edit it. I still have a copy, here—"

Thorn reached into his briefcase and produced a set of papers.

"The figures you'll find within this business plan certainly didn't show losses," Thorn continued. It didn't show a stellar year in progress for the firm, but still a profitable one. Do you think that these were all bogus?"

The D.A. stared back at Thorn. He liked the kid. He believed him. He found Thorn to be genuinely forthcoming.

"I don't know what to believe with this guy," the D.A. told Thorn. "But he certainly appears to have stuck it to a number of his clients. When $750 million, which is supposed to be there, only pans out at $53 million or so, something somewhere has gone wrong—I think we're done with you for today. Thanks for these papers and your insights."

Thorn had pulled it off. The deposition was over. He was going home.

CHAPTER 58

MARTY SURRENDERS BUSTS; EARLY DAYS IN THE TOMBS
New Jersey/New York
January 2000

A rented Chevy Malibu approached the Holland Tunnel for the third time that day. Poking out from the rear window was that singular bust of Julius Caesar that had been done while Caesar was still alive. Next to it was an ancient marble bust of Empress Livia, a 5000-year old Egyptian relief bought for $35,000, an ancient Chinese spear point, a bronze helmet and a gold wreath crown.

After having surrendered himself at a Trenton Courthouse, Marty was out on a $5 million bond, and was now scrambling to avoid a contempt of court prosecution. The authorities had taken his cars, attached his beach house, and asked him to deliver all of the other assets that he possessed. They had checked different auction records at Sotheby's and Christies. They knew that he had been one of their best customers in ancient Roman and Greek antiquities. They had other records showing Marty had bought a number of 100 oz. gold bars. Where were they?

"I gave those away as bonuses," Marty claimed, but the receiver and the prosecutor did not believe him. "Surrender all of your assets by February 1, 2000 or face a contempt of court citation," the prosecutor had told him.

"What does contempt of court mean, exactly?" Marty had asked his lawyer.

"It means we can hold you in jail indefinitely until you satisfy a judge's demand. If you are deemed to not be cooperating with the court, you could be in jail for multiple years."

"But what if I really don't have those gold bars they want?"

"Think one to two years in prison."

"Ah shit," thought Marty to himself, "This stuff ain't supposed to happen in America. What happened to due process?"

Marty was flabbergasted at how stacked the deck seemed against him. First the receiver for Economic Consultants of Princeton had forced his lawyers to disgorge the retainer fee that Marty had wired to them...not his money to even retain counsel they claimed. A court appointed attorney followed. This latter fellow was a useless dolt. Now he was being told that he was likely going to jail anyway if he could not produce every single item on a list of his reputed assets.

"Give them what you have..." came the attorney advice. "If you show that you are cooperating the best you can, maybe the judge will let the other assets slide."

But in the end, the missing gold bars were just too much.

On February 1, 2000 Marty was incarcerated at the New York Downtown Correctional Facility—"the Tombs." He was placed there not for any charge of financial fraud, but because he was held in contempt of court for not surrendering those damn gold bars.

Whose idea had it been anyway to pay the 1998 bonuses in gold? It had been his idea, of course.

CHAPTER 59

SAFRI KILLED
Monaco
December 3, 1999

It had seemed like a good idea at first to Ted Maw: loosen up the security around Safri so that if someone did come after him, Maw could be the hero, and take down a big bonus in thanks. Maw had been a Green Beret after all. And now he had this dick-wad senior nurse to whom he reported, and she likely wanted to send him packing back to the U.S. He was damned if he was going to let this plumb job paying $600 an hour slip through his fingers.

In any case, it would be a dark day in hell when he couldn't protect Safri.

Ambling outside the Monaco apartment building into the cool breeze of an early December night, he told the normal contingent of bodyguards that the boss was going to bed early, and to take the night off. He would be there. The boss would be covered.

"You sure this is cool, man?" the head bodyguard had asked. "I thought the old man was afraid the KGB or something was coming after him."

"The Parkinson's has gotten worse. He's a bit delusional these days. No one is coming after him. Enjoy the night. There is no reason for all of us to be cooped up in this place."

The bodyguards were not ones to shirk off without question, but Maw seemed like one of them—a military man, albeit one who had oddly assumed the role of a nurse. With some hesitancy, each of the bodyguards sauntered off into the Monaco dusk.

Now Maw had the boss to himself. He had a plan. If he could fake someone pounding at the door, and then rush to scoop Safri into the secure bathroom, then light a match to set off the fire alarm and scare away the supposed intruders and alert the authorities, he would be deemed the hero. His job would be secure.

The problem was that as the bodyguards had ambled away, their departure had not gone unnoticed.

Suddenly, Maw heard a skeleton key of some sort fiddling with the front door lock. In another instant, the door was swinging open and a hooded assailant was headed towards him. Maw drew his pocketknife, but in a flash the man was upon him. They wrestled.

Then there were more bodies pushing in through the front door.

"What the fuck was going on?" Maw was befuddled, confused, aghast.

Maw's knife swung out, but was deflected down. His arm was bent, and the knife suddenly lodged in his leg. Maw screamed in acute pain.

The arriving men lost interest in Maw as he rolled on the floor. They headed instead inward into the apartment, rushing to find Safri.

A bathroom door slammed shut. Safri had just made it within, having hobbled out of bed just as the commotion in the front hall had begun. Where were his normal bodyguards? The bathroom door was made of double-reinforced steel so as to purposefully create a safe room within his lush apartment. Safri was sweating profusely as he stood behind it. He could hear the ping of metal on metal outside in the hallway. Someone was shooting at the lock.

How the hell was he going to get out of there? How could he get some help?

He looked down at the bathroom sink where a small ashtray sat on the counter next to the toilet. There was a pack of matches in the ashtray. "Light a fire," he thought. "Set off the fire alarm, the sprinklers. The authorities would come."

Ironically, it was not dissimilar to the thought Maw had previously planned when he had purposefully placed those matches there.

As more pings hit the outer bathroom door, Safri grew nervous. How long would this door last from such an assault? He grabbed a hand towel and the matches. He sparked a flame and held it under the towel. The towel ignited faster than Safri had imagined it might. Heat started to sear up his arm, and he suddenly found himself dropping the towel. Now the bathroom carpet was ignited; then the shower curtain.

"Shit, shit, shit…"thought Safri, "this is not the way that it is supposed to end."

A few seconds later, as smoke billowed around him and he gasped for air, the billionaire trader closed his eyes for the last time.

CHAPTER 60

THE AUSTRIAN NOW A NEW YORKER
New York
December 4, 1999

"And in his Monaco apartment last night, financier Edmund Safri was found mysteriously dead, apparently from asphyxiation after a bathroom fire..." the television hummed within the upper West Side apartment of Michael and Suchico Statz.

Michael looked up at the television with curiosity, sipping his morning coffee as he did so.

That was odd news. Safri had been one of the most powerful Jewish New York bankers in his day. Michael had always admired his stature and wealth. How was it that he had come to die from asphyxiation in Monaco?

"Oh well," thought Michael, "just another part of this crazy world."

After the 1987 crash that he had so well predicted at Bank Vontobel in Vienna, Michael had packed up all of his worldly possessions, and moved Suchico and himself to New York. This is where the hedge fund world was based, and he had wanted ever so badly to express his bearish view of the world in a hedge fund format.

First, he'd had to toil a few more years as an analyst at Jefferies & Co.—a notoriously bullish brokerage shop—but where he had somewhat amazingly encountered a wonderfully prescient boss who saw the advantage of short selling in portfolio management. Michael had been tasked with finding good shorts, and with time, his boss had been impressed enough with Michael's selections that a plan was hatched: Michael would spin himself out into a hedge fund manager format, and his former Jefferies boss would seed him to do so, taking just a modest profit participation in his ongoing business.

Michael now considered himself on the cutting edge of portfolio management alpha creation. Short selling was admittedly a difficult— and at times painful—endeavor, but there was nothing better than catching a swift move lower in a given stock. Michael was generally good at his analysis, and despite no real expertise in market timing, he had posted adequate positive returns across the 1994-1998 period. His assets under management were slowly growing, and Michael generally loved the thrill of the game.

But this was late 1999—and boy, were markets bubblicious. Michael did not have much time to think about Safri that morning as he did about his own survival. He was shorting stocks like Netscape and AOL, and using an outsourced trading group to put the positions on.

But just the prior Friday he had given this trading group a sell short order on a basket of stocks with associated stop-loss orders, and then received back fills *both* on the shorts and the majority of the stops almost concomitantly. Everything was vaulting against him. After a successful early part of 1999, he had lost over 30 percent in the fourth quarter of 1999, and his entire business was in jeopardy.

"I just don't understand!" Michael would scream at his screens. "What are people thinking? How can they pay 120x earnings for this piece of crap?"

Searching for answers amidst the web, Michael stumbled on a website that offered some solace. It was called Sandy Spring Technicals, and amidst its pages—most of which were posted for free as a public service—there was a prognostication that Fibonacci fractals pointed to 11,785 on the DJIA and 5100 on the Nasdaq Composite as important potential tops when those levels were to be touched.

Moreover, Sandy Spring wrote about a chart formation called "Three Peaks and a Domed Top" that was currently transpiring in the Dow, and Michael found this work fascinating. It was so foreign to how his own mind worked in analyzing balance sheets, cash flow levels, and price-earnings levels. Maybe he was just grasping at straws to lean on, but it was reassuring somehow that others saw the silliness of current prices using different methodologies, and that technical levels not that far away existed that should not be crossed.

Michael particularly liked having that "line in the sand" offered to him. Value managers tended not to have such. It was a flaw in their general investment process that when cheap stocks get even cheaper, value managers just naturally want to buy more of them, and when expensive stocks become even more expensive, well, they could get carried out shorting the next growth darling.

Currently Michael felt so out of synch with modern times that he was wondering whether he should fold his cards and go home. Ever since Netscape had first exploded higher in 1995, the dot.com world had become ever so silly. Now four years of silliness later, with just one brief intervening bear move in the later summer of 1998, he honestly wondered whether this go-go environment would ever end. And if it did eventually end, would he make it that long? Would he still be sane? Or would his investors have pulled the plug on him first?

The Dow subsequently peaked at an intraday high of 11,750 on January 14, 2000, and the NASDAQ peaked at an intraday high of 5132 on March 7, 2000. The entropic reversals lower in stock prices from both levels was heart-warming to Michael. Sandy Spring had nailed it in their late 1999 call of important levels. Michael's bearish fundamental analysis would finally work better across 2000-2002, and at long last, he would become rich. All you really needed were three good years with reasonable assets under management, and that 20% incentive fee collected by hedge fund managers would do wonders. 2000-2002 would be those years for Michael.

"But who was this guy writing under the Sandy Spring label?" Michael wondered. "How could he be so precise?"

As the bear market of 2000 started to truly blossom, Michael studied the website more carefully and determined that one day, he would like to meet Sandy Spring's founder. This appeared to be a fellow named Thornton Lurie, formerly of the firm Economic Consultants of Princeton.

CHAPTER 61

THORN SCRAMBLES
Morristown, NJ
December 1999

Note to files: Don't be age 50 with no seat at the table, and with your former boss in prison. It is damn hard to find a new job. The age 50 part is probably the toughest. If you haven't found your leadership role by age 50—if you are not already running something of your own—then many will assume that something is wrong with you. For whatever reason, you are often deemed to be damaged goods. Others can likely be hired who are younger, smarter, and more nimble without the baggage of age that you carry.

Between October and December 1999, Thorn couldn't find a new job. And with three young kids to support and bills to pay, he had to scramble. He had to move fast to reinvent himself.

What Michael Statz saw as market craziness, Thorn saw as an opportunity. Thorn was naturally a bear, and was even more so than normal in the 1999 world. When he eventually picked up the phone to his old Princeton roommate Adam—now a Seattle-based billionaire heavily long Microsoft, Dell, and Oracle (all stocks then in the stratosphere)—Thorn's advice had been simple: "Take some money off the table—reduce your exposure to tech"—and it was advice proffered truly from his heart.

"As an alternative, why not try a market-neutral mix of hedge fund managers? And, oh by the way, I am perfectly positioned to help build such a mix for you," Thorn offered. "I just saw a hedge fund blow up from the inside due to operational sloppiness. This will make me particularly demanding. I know all the bad signs to look for."

What about Thorn's own back office? Would it reside in his basement?

"No, well, err..." Thorn would find an experienced partner to handle those types of things.

It was not an easy sell, but it did eventually succeed. Thorn partnered with a group in Westport, Connecticut for operational support, and Adam wired $20 million in funds—perhaps just to keep Thorn at bay more than anything else. Hedge funds weren't Adam's thing, but then it occurred to him that just maybe he should learn something about them—dip his toe in the water, and help an old Princeton colleague at the same time.

At the same moment that he was offering Thorn a $20 million commitment, Adam confided that he was making a 100 million pound investment into a British video-on-demand private equity deal. Over the next eight years, Thorn's mix of managers would generally chug higher. Adam's other large private equity deal would slowly flounder.

So it was that Thorn stumbled into the fund of funds/wealth management world, and over the years that followed, he often could be heard saying "Well, it's certainly easier just to 'eat the donuts' than to actually 'make the donuts.'

After all, what was not to like about a job that allowed you to travel and meet some of the smartest hedge fund managers in the world, interview them, get inside their head, and then decide whether there was a place for them in a portfolio mix or not? Part of the trick was to fit the manager to the perceived environment. If one could do this with any adroitness, attractive returns would naturally transpire. And conceptually, being a good technician, Thorn had an edge in evaluating trading environments—albeit with a natural bearishness in his heart.

But as the documents for his new endeavor were still wandering their way through Thorn's newly hired law firm, and before that fateful $20 million wire had arrived, Thorn had also gotten antsy. He needed to get as much revenue going as possible in as many ways as possible as quickly as possible to support his family. So he whipped out his pen. He started pitching magazine articles to publications like *Derivatives Strategy* magazine, *Plan Sponsor* magazine, *Treasury & Risk Management* magazine, *Financial Executive* magazine, Hedgeworld.com and Bloomberg.com. He also went to his local computer store and bought a book, "How to program HTML in a Week," and decided that he would launch his own website: Sandyspring.com.

That is how Michael Statz had come to find Thorn's article on fractal rhythms in the Dow Jones and NASDAQ.

Thornton had written a few articles for Bloomberg, but they considered them too technical, too sophisticated. So Thorn had posted them himself, and then planted a few links to them in other website chatrooms. Soon, eyeball flow to the website was a steady 50 viewers a day, then 100 per day, and soon 1000 viewers per day.

Thorn was producing solid work that was eclectic and differentiated in nature. Few others anywhere in the world were combining Fibonacci analysis as to market amplitude with longer-term pi cycles that helped pinpoint the timing of reversals. When the two tools fell into synch together, beautiful things tended to happen.

Together with his new Fund of Funds business, Thorn cobbled together a living writing about the financial world and allocating capital to it. This took some adapting. Thorn had directly touched markets for almost twenty years. Now it was as if he was riding above the markets looking down. He suddenly was more project-oriented, and less stressed than he had been previously.

Could Marty blowing up actually have been a good thing for Thorn? Out of initial disaster, opportunity now appeared to knock.

CHAPTER 62

PRISON TROUBLES AND A CASE GONE PUFF
New York
Summer 2003

The inside of the Downtown Correctional Facility stank of sweat, grime, and dirt. With a constant buildup of people placed within its cluttered cells, the prison was a fetid microcosm of the city that surrounded it.

Marty had now been there three years—and was still incredulous about his fall from grace.

"I was once voted the number one economist in Japan," he proudly told one guard who was sympathetic to his cause..."until the U.S. government shafted me."

Nowhere in Marty's ego was their room for the potential that he might have partially caused his own demise. Nowhere did he want to admit that the Tobashi transactions in which he had engaged (and the kick-backs that he had arranged for such transactions) had potentially abrogated the bands of appropriate business behavior. Nowhere in his psyche could he own up to having lost or stolen money that wasn't his.

"Look, the Japanese corporates were desperate. They needed me," he explained to his third court-appointed attorney. "I took deposits from them, and gave them back unsecured notes. There was nothing illegal about that. I was entitled to make those notes whole anyway that I wanted. If I wanted to put all my money into Roman antiquities, I would have been entitled to do that. If I had lost money, and not paid off the notes, companies default on unsecured obligations all the time. There would have been nothing criminal with that. The Japanese would have simply picked a bad unsecured investment. But the truth of the matter is that these transactions were all blessed at the outset by the MOF, and I never missed paying back a maturing note. I never had a client complain."

There was an element of truth to everything Marty said, of course. It was just the parts that he left out that needed more explaining—like where had the money indeed disappeared to. Yet he made friends in prison—particularly with the guards. They wanted to believe him—the ex-market guru in cell block 113.

As time went by, one guard arranged to get Marty a typewriter, and in one of the most bizarre moments in financial market journalism, Marty started to pen market letters from his prison cell. His son who visited regularly would spirit these letters out, get them published on a new Amwell Economics website as well as other web-based locales. And despite having no chart services, no data, no cycle models, some of what Marty wrote from prison was well-constructed and interesting work. Thorn continued reading him during this period, amazed by the man's resilience and perseverance.

One thing that did not go well for Marty was the disposition of his legal case with the government. Eventually acting pro se in his own defense, Marty filed petition after petition to the courts that the CFTC and FBI had no jurisdiction in this case. After all, the transactions in question all transpired in Japan, specifically under the auspices of the Japanese Ministry of Finance—indeed at their very request. No one Marty had hurt was a U.S. citizen. Indeed, the Safri Bank had eventually made all of the Japanese clients completely whole on their claimed losses. Safri had admitted that their broker Bill had made a few nefarious mistakes in his conduct. Safri had wanted the whole affair to fade away, and their merger with HSBC to be consummated.

But the judge Marty faced wanted to hear none of it. All he wanted to know was what had happened to those missing gold bars? Why wasn't Marty cooperating more fully with the U.S government in the disgorgement of his hidden assets?

Then the World Trade Center came tumbling down on September 11, 2001, and within those towers, all of the documents related to Marty's case were lost. If the government had previously been building any sort of fraud case against Marty, that case literally went up in smoke. There was no evidence anymore—if there ever had been.

So the government prosecutors just left Marty where he was—sitting in the Tombs—easily collecting the distinction of being a prisoner held for contempt of court longer than anyone else in U.S history. When the government wants to play hardball with your life, they could certainly play hardball. Marty was on the wrong side of every court judgment—even while many of his petitions academically made some sense.

Marty started to write about how the government was also trying to steal his models. Post incarceration, several hedge funds had expressed interest to buy them, but the receiver had dissuaded all comers. The receiver's wife was General Counsel to Goodman Sachs, and Marty began speculating that it was Goodman trying to steal his proprietary thought and analysis—or perhaps it was the CIA who had expressed interest in the models before Marty's entire fall from grace had transpired.

No one really knew the truth.

But then one day, a rough Hispanic inmate named Carlos that Marty hardly knew walked by Marty's open cell door and saw Marty sitting at his typewriter. In a flash, Carlos reached out and grabbed Amwell's typewriter and then cracked it across Marty's head. At the same moment, Carlos plunged a small, concealed pen-knife deep into Marty's gut. It had been a pre-meditated attack—a hit of some sort—that Marty soon wrote about from his hospital bed. Once again, he blamed Goodman Sachs. He knew too much. They wanted to shut him up and just take his models. He was sure of it.

Thankfully, Marty's skull was tough, and the pen-knife had missed hitting any vital organs. Marty recovered after two weeks at Bellevue Hospital, and then got shipped back to "the Tombs."

How the hell could they leave him in that facility? Didn't he at least deserve to be moved to some minimum-security country club for white-collar criminals? He petitioned the court for such, particularly in light of the recent attack on his life.

"Denied."

Finally, in 2005, after five years in prison, Marty's newest court-appointed counsel came by Marty's cell with a proposal.

"Marty—look, I don't know what you did or didn't do, but if you plead guilty to one count of fraud, the maximum penalty for that offense is five years. You've already been here for five years. There is at least a chance that the judge just lets you walk for time served."

Marty initially remained recalcitrant to accept any deal. "I didn't do anything wrong," he stammered. "This is all just one big fucked up set-up. I've been the fall guy."

But in the end, he decided to give the plea deal a shot. At least there would be movement in his case—some degree of finality as to what the government wanted to do with him.

That's when the judge handed down a sentence for another five-years in prison, no benefit for time served.

"Jesus Christ," muttered Marty to himself as the decision emanated from the judge's bench. "Our court system is so in the pocket of the District Attorney. If the D.A. wants to come down hard on me, that's what keeps happening. This shouldn't be happening in America, but it does. It is."

"If it pleases the court, defendant would like to make one special request," Marty found himself standing and facing the bench. "Can you at least move me out of the Tombs for the next five years? Make it a little bit easier for my family to come visit me? How about the Fort Dix Correctional Facility, your honor?"

"So ordered. The defendant is remanded to the Fort Dix Correctional Facility effective immediately."

CHAPTER 63

DUMB-DUMB MATT
Westport, CT
April 2007

Life for Thorn skated along in rebuilding fashion. At first it had just been some freelance journalistic work; then Sandyspring.com had started to generate some subscription revenue. Thorn was amazed how people from all around the world—Latvia, Poland, Singapore, Australia, even Columbia—would find his website and then subscribe. $275 per annual subscription wasn't going to solve all his problems, but multiplied by 100 subscribers, it did help send one kid to college.

Most importantly, and thankfully, his fund of funds business— seeded by Adam—did ok. Despite the steep decline in global equity markets that transpired across 2000 to 2002, the fund advanced each year. The gains weren't earth-shattering, kind of in the 6-7% per annum region, but it was certainly better than a poke in the eye, and those gains were net of Thorn stripping off a one-percent management fee and a 10% incentive fee. The Fund of Funds industry really was kind of a rip-off, but it was a fully legal rip-off—everything disclosed, no surprises.

Indeed, assets in Thorn's fund soon started to swell well beyond his initial seed investor. Thorn's chosen operational partner, Westpark Capital, poured in an additional $50 million of client capital, and at one point, Thorn was managing almost a $100 million in assets, and advising outside clients on another $1.1 billion. It was all pretty sweet. Thorn had gained a nice reputation within the industry as a straight shooter—an allocator who actually had traded and who knew what he was talking about. Both underlying managers and customers respected him.

But that's when the relationship with Westpark started to change. It was the retirement of Westpark's CIO that actually precipitated the downward spiral. Thorn was qualified for that job, but Westpark's

Chairman wanted to do an outside search—bring in some fresh blood—make a marketing splash. In the end, he hired an ex-Credit Suisse guy named Matt Haverman—a seemingly well-spoken, slightly academic-looking fellow that Thorn was initially eager to embrace and accept.

But that positive spirit of embracement lasted for exactly one week. As Matt and Thorn went on their first round of manager visits together, Thorn was struck by just one thing: most of the managers that Matt was excited to pursue traded ultra-complex credit-related strategies, many involving CDS and CLO structuring, some related to carbon trading, and yet others doing direct lending to illiquid real estate situations or PIPE transactions.

It took a bit of courage, but after two days of such meetings, Thorn found himself turning to Matt with a strongly worded query:

"Some of these managers that you like are quite unique, but they are mostly specialized credit-centric strategies, and credit spreads are already at historic tights. Doesn't that concern you a bit? You're not actually thinking of building an entire portfolio of these guys are you?"

Matt looked back at Thorn with an arrogant and slightly dumbfounded look on his face.

"Oh, I don't do macro, Thorn. I just invest in hedge fund managers."

"So you aren't concerned that you are embracing credit at the historic tights of credit spreads? Do you really think that a portfolio of all these guys would survive a period of credit widening?"

"Damn if I know," said Matt. "I just care about their track records."

"Oh, my God," thought Thorn, "I have a return-chasing idiot on my hands—and not a benign one, but one that could do some real damage."

A fiduciary feeling welled up in Thorn that he owed it to his investors to stay as far away from this guy as possible, but with Westpark having plunked $50 million of their client assets in Thorn's fund, extrication would be tricky.

The next morning, Thorn dialed Westpark's Chairman to chat.

"Albert," started Thorn, "I know you did a big search and all for our new CIO, but I'm afraid to report to you that Matt Haverman is bad news. He's going to blow you up. He has no appreciation for macro—

doesn't even try. He's a return-chasing guy who looks in the rear-view mirror, but can't differentiate a past favorable environment for a manager from actual manager skill. You've made a huge mistake."

"I'm sorry you feel that way Thorn, but it's too late now. I've hired the guy and there is no going back."

"I realize that Albert. That's why I have to leave. That's why I have to dismiss you as my co-general partner and force out all of the investors that you have placed in my fund."

Thorn was blowing up a business that he loved, but doing so because of a partner he no longer respected. He was trying to be as honorable as possible to his investors and his own asset allocation beliefs. After so many earlier twists and turns to his career, this was an extremely tough personal decision for Thorn to make, but it would ultimately prove prescient.

Westpark would grow larger over the following year after Thorn left. $2.3 billion under advisement was their high-water level of assets. Matt would have just enough time to get Westpark's remaining clients fully invested in a range of credit-centric and low-liquidity strategies—all just at the wrong time.

Then when the 2007-2008 crisis period hit, the firm would implode. 90% of Westpark's underlying hedge fund investments suspended redemptions or enacted protective "gate clauses." Meanwhile Westpark client redemptions rolled in. The liquidity mismatch eventually led to lawsuits. The SEC soon became involved.

Thorn had seen it coming—even while he wished in so many ways that he hadn't.

CHAPTER 64

ANOTHER PI CYCLE STRIKE
Morristown, NJ
February 2007

The date was February 24, 2007—exactly 3141 days from the July 20, 1998 pi cycle high that Marty had so adroitly predicted, and that had ushered in the Russian ruble crisis of August 1998 and the Long-Term Capital Management meltdown.

These dates only happened once every 8.6 years. Marty was in prison. Thorn felt like the lone protector of the secret cycle—one of the few people attentive into that date of a sudden entropic market reversal.

But what was going to reverse? What was the most stretched and unsustainable market this time around?

Thorn wasn't entirely sure.

Into the early winter of 2007, markets were buoyant again. Copper and other metals were particularly strong. But so too were global equities. And fixed income markets were also damn strong—wave after wave of mortgage issuance taking place into that period.

Thorn honestly did not know where the entropic turn would transpire—but he did feel the markets were ripe to shift gears. On Friday, February 23, 2007 he personally went 100% net short a variety of equity index futures in his modest trading account, and penned a Sandy Spring homage entitled "Marty's Date" whereby he told the story of July 20, 1998 and posed questions about what February 24, 2007 might bring.

That following Monday morning, Thorn turned on CNBC as he awoke at 5:30 a.m. and the hair stood up on the back of his neck. Even though he fully expected some sort of entropic reversal related to the pi cycle date, here it was in living color, in real time:

"...And in China today stocks took a drubbing, the Shanghai Composite down 5.5%; in Japan the Nikkei fell by 4%, and this negative price action has spilled over into Europe, now down 3.5%. The early trading in S&P futures points to a 2% U.S. market decline."

It was the first time that China had actually led global markets lower, and in Thorn's mind, an "ah-ha" moment was triggered: China was the lynchpin piece of market excess coming undone. It had been European markets falling from grace in May 1981, Japan falling from grace in December 1989, and now it was China's turn.

There was no news, no trigger; just a clean entropic momentum reversal.

Or was it?

Over the next few weeks, there was a wave of media denial that anything had shifted away from global market ebullience. *Barron's* featured a March 3, 2007 lead article "Still Betting on a Bull" with the picture of a Bear being diced by a Bull. *The New York Times* regularly buried coverage of soft equity prices on back pages of its business section, and Jim Cramer actually appeared on the NBC Nightly News encouraging people to "buy the short-term dip." On the air of XM radio, Thornton listened to a female CNBC commentator offer: "If you can't get excited about this bull market, well, you should just go see a doctor! What is there *not* to like about this market?"

Thorn knew better. But he was also careful to harvest some gains on his short index futures positions after the Dow Jones made a swift -8% retracement of its prior 2005-2007 advance. While upon occasion, Thorn had learned that "no lookback" trap door market moves could transpire, more often, enough residual bulls existed that the reversal of February 24, 2007 would likely just be a momentum turn, with yet another attempt to slowly regain the February 23, 2007 market highs still in the cards.

Thorn was also bothered almost immediately by yet another odd phenomenon. While China had led on that first morning down on Monday, February 25, 2007, it was the most resilient market over the following several weeks to rally back. So if it wasn't China topping out? What had the February 23, 2007 pi cycle represented?

The more Thorn studied his charts, the more confused he initially became. Then one day in March a news headline hit: Household Finance—a sub-prime mortgage lender—was in trouble and being taken over by HSBC.

It suddenly occurred to Thorn that credit was the thing that had been most stretched into February 23, 2007—sub-prime credit. Indeed, as he examined various charts, he determined that even as equity markets had rallied back from their late February losses, mortgage credit spreads had touched their historic tights to Government bond yields on February 23, 2007, and were now steadily moving away from those tights. Thorn started to write about the excess coming undone in the sub-prime mortgage space. On April 8, 2007, he wrote for his Sandy Spring website readers:

Similar to Countrywide, Washington Mutual—in its effort to continue to grow even as the housing market became overpriced for many of its potential customers, and traditional mortgage margins eroded as interest expenses increased—specifically embraced "option income ARMs." Option income ARMS are like subprime mortgages in drag. They may have been sold to a slightly higher clientele than sub-prime loans, but they typically are issued with low teaser rates for the first year or two that adjust upwards thereafter. The most popular feature is the "option" which allows the borrower to choose each month between paying the fully amortizing normal mortgage payment, the interest-only payment, or a below rate "cost of funds" payment that makes the loan negatively amortizing. Previously, home buyers were typically allowed to qualify for these loans based on the lowest payment options.

While Washington Mutual may claim only a 10% exposure of its portfolio to sub-prime lending, about 30% of Washington Mutual's originations and the same portion of loans on its balance sheet are option income ARMs. Back in 2005, 43% of first time buyers put no money down for their house, and 2005 was also the biggest year for option ARM loan issuance. This was not a problem initially when home prices went up, but it is now. Indeed, doing the simple math, it is easily possible that many homeowners now owe 10-15% more principal on their mortgages than their home is worth. In 2004 default rates were low and only 1% of Washington Mutual's option income ARMs were in negative amortization. In 2005 loans in negative amortization jumped to 55%, with some estimating that by 2006, 70-80% of these option income loans became negative *amortizing. This negative amortization effectively equated in 2006 to $1 billion of non-cash income on Washington Mutual's income statement, and represented approximately 20% of WM's reported pretax earnings. Do investors in WM understand that in lieu of earning real interest, that their bank is becoming a larger and larger property owner each and every day, and that some of the property that they own may no longer be worth the price on WM's books? Apparently not, as Washington Mutual as late as mid-2006 called option ARMS its "flagship product" which it was trying to increase, even as it also reduced provisions for mortgage defaults. Is WM the next Enron house of cards in the works?*

Bingo. It had taken Thorn almost six weeks post the turn to see what exactly had turned, but now he did see it. America's 2005-2007 fling with super cheap and increasingly exotically structured mortgage credit was the excess falling from grace.

Sixty miles away from Thorn's suburban New Jersey desk, Michael Statz—sitting atop the 33rd floor of 527 Fifth Ave—now poured over Thorn's writings with increasing attention.

"I need this Thornton Lurie on my team," thought Statz.

CHAPTER 65

UH OH, BACK TO THE TRADING DESK
New Jersey/New York
October 2007

Thorn was still deciding what to do with the remnants of his Fund of Funds business, and what if anything to do with his Sandyspring. com technical commentary business. Both were generating a bit of revenue for him, but in the wake of the split with Westpark Capital, Thorn was in need of a firmer revenue base.

Sandyspring.com was really more like a hobby business for Thorn, and it was hard to make it more than this. At a retail level, many people would subscribe to hear analytical thoughts for a $275 annual subscription fee, but push that fee any higher, and the airwaves would tend to go quiet. You'd be moving into institutional pricing. And Thorn wasn't quite institutional in nature.

Yes, he had subscribers who were hedge fund managers, and proprietary traders, and family offices, and some had remained subscribers for the better part of a decade, but it was still hard to scale this business much further. Thorn had advertised offering tailored single stock fractal trading advice to clients at $1,000 per month fee, and had gotten exactly zero enquiries.

But then the phone rang. It was Michael Statz.

"Is this Thornton Lurie? Ya? Of Sandy Spring Advisors?"

"Yes, it is."

"My name is Michael Statz. I have been a subscriber since 1999 when you wrote about *Three Peaks and a Domed House*, and nailed the January 2000 peak in the Dow. I'm not sure exactly how you piece together all of your different tools, but I know that you tend to be more right than wrong. I run a hedge fund and I need your help."

"You've got my attention, Michael. What do you have in mind?"

"Well, first I think we should meet for lunch. Break some bread; get to know each other a bit. But assuming you have interest, I run a $500 million fund, and I need to improve returns. My investors are getting bored with me. I need some better active trading advice, and I think you might be able to help me."

It was October 2007. Post the February 23, 2007 pi cycle momentum top, markets had clawed their way back northward for most of the spring and summer. For Thorn it had been somewhat infuriating—reminiscent of another summer 20-years earlier in 1987.

Statz had enjoyed it even less. First, he had been egged into being net long some European equities by his co-PM partner Mark Budis. That hadn't worked very well in July 2007 as Europe went down while the U.S. went up. Then Statz had pulled the ripcord to jettison his European longs at exactly the wrong moment in August 2007, and became even more net short U.S. markets, but U.S. markets had promptly rallied even more in September. Statz was getting all twisted up in his portfolio management—frustrated and grasping at straws to find a better path. He had to find someone that he could lean on for sound trading advice other than Mark.

Statz really didn't like Mark. That was a problem. He'd hired him in a rush to replace defecting staff in 2003. Statz had nailed the 2000-2002 dot com tech meltdown—an average 23% return each of those years. The money had come pouring in from investors, and yet Statz had been kind of cheap paying the staff around him—really just a few analysts and a secretary. And one day they had all quit—just walked out on him.

Not to spook his investors, Statz had rushed to find a senior replacement analyst. Mark had fit the bill—a former investigative journalist who'd picked up an MBA from Columbia, and floated between a few small hedge funds. He'd offered him a co-PM position to get him on board fast—gave him equity in the firm. It had all been a mistake.

While Statz was something of a patrician European with a love of the opera, and big picture macro themes and ideas, Mark was more of a New Yorker—the son of a police cop—who might regularly be found sitting at Shea Stadium watching the Mets. While Statz had style and savoir-faire, Mark was crass and loud. While Statz tended to be a meek simpering leader deferring to those around him; Mark was a bully at heart. He liked to even bully Michael. That is where the tension lay. It was after all, Michael's firm to start.

So began a five year stint for Thorn whereby he held the hand of an Austrian hedge fund manager who loved to short things, but really didn't know how to trade, and a co-PM who liked to boss people around in a nasty fashion.

Thornton was hired by Statz to offer added advice on single-stock positioning, to help with trade execution and portfolio strategizing, and to change the politics in the office away from Mark bullying Michael. Michael needed a new voice to be heard. The balance of power in the trading room needed to be shifted.

Tension palpably filled the air.

CHAPTER 66

THE ODD COUPLE OF MICHAEL AND MARK
New York
2007-2009

It had all started out as a grand experiment. Michael was a bottoms-up value-oriented fundamentalist, but he had an open intellect that wanted to believe in others. He'd been reading Thornton Lurie for the better part of a decade. He knew that there was a technical spark within Thornton that was unique and successful—if so very different from his own skills.

When Thornton had first walked in the door of Michael's firm, Glenn Water Asset Management, it was a scant few days from what would at that time be the all-time high in the S&P 500. Mark was aghast that the tilt of the portfolio was potentially too short.

"What do you think, Thornton?" Michael had asked in an initial grope for moral support.

"You need to be patient here Michael. You've done your homework on your short book. The markets are so very frothy that it can't last much longer. I'd maintain your position—if not get shorter."

Budis quietly fumed, and then fumed even more when that advice actually turned into a good market call. Even as the Glenn Water portfolio started to fare better, Budis started to make Thornton's life as miserable as possible. The words emanating from his mouth usually went something like:

"Hay Thornton, you see that news on XYZ stock? You asleep over there or something? We need you to be our eyes and ears, man. Look alive. Why am I seeing this news before hearing from you that it's on the tape?"

Thornton was admittedly not good at watching the news wires. As a trader, he'd seldom reacted to news—company-specific, macro, or otherwise. Instead, he'd be spending a great deal of time trolling through charts of different Glenn Water portfolio names. To Thorn, the charts should give him clues as to needed actions before news would actually hit. His was a desire to anticipate, not react. He'd be looking for the technically compelling trade of the day—buy more of this, and short more of that; or alternatively cover some of this short and sell some of that long.

He knew that Michael would not do everything he put forward, and Budis would fight him on almost every suggestion just to be difficult and delay the entire process. Thorn had to keep his proposals simple and clean—pick his spots.

As the early October 2007 equity market started to roll lower, one thing that concerned Thorn quite a bit was not the short side of the portfolio, but the long side. Here Michael's value instincts had caused Glenn Water to accumulate a significant position long a basket of Japanese small-cap value names. Some of these companies ran donut shops that traded at 3x earnings; others were car part manufacturers that traded for little more than the cash on their balance sheet; yet others ran breweries with land values that exceeded the value of the company's total capitalization; a few were in the pre-fab senior housing construction business.

When Michael looked at these stocks, he saw nothing but mispriced opportunity. When Thorn looked at these charts, he saw death warmed over—some of the most boring and sludgy chart patterns that he had ever analyzed. Most of the chart patterns seemed to suggest fractal patterns where the Fibonacci bands only would fit from significantly lower price levels. And this amalgamation of sludge represented nearly half the Glenn Water long portfolio. At best, these stocks might be a store of value place to hide, but there was no depending upon them to be dynamic to the upside. No, the Glenn Water portfolio was going to depend upon how the shorts performed more than anything else. The longs were dominated by a morass of Japanese goo.

And whenever Thorn tried to egg Michael into jettisoning a given Japanese long exposure, it was like ripping a baby from its mother's arms: pure agony and angst. Michael was always afraid that he'd be giving up on a given situation right on that stock's lows. This was also one of the few times that Budis would flip to generally support Thorn's suggestions—irritating Michael even further.

Thorn thought about the Japanese long exposure like a truly sick patient with multiple ailments, but one where Thorn only had the wherewithal to attack one disease at a time. If he told Michael just to blow out the entire Japanese portfolio—which would have been his real recommendation at the time—this simply was not going to happen. Michael would get too defensive and bristle. In Michael's mind, you had to be long something, and his basket of Japanese value sludginess was a portfolio that he could justify and live with—even though the short-term technicals of the portfolio looked poor.

And then Thorn would ask himself: "Why were these stocks all priced so cheaply? What was Michael potentially missing? Why did Thorn technically perceive so many missing lows still to be seen in these stocks, and how did this fit the fundamentals?"

Conversations in the trading room generally revolved around poor and un-dynamic Japanese managements who would have no idea how to maximize shareholder value—and often no real inclination to do so. The companies In Glenn Water's portfolio were admittedly cheap to asset values and cash availability, but they were cheap for a reason. Many of those assets and cash would simply never be unlocked. Japanese demographics were also an obvious headwind, and this topic was discussed as a longer-term issue. The strength in the yen was yet another factor that had hollowed out the return potential of many Japanese exporters. There was nothing quite like having high fixed costs in expensive yen and revenues in continually depreciating dollars.

Overall, Thorn came to believe that Michael was simply a myopic forgiver of all Japanese sins. He was after all, married to a Japanese woman. He valued her obedience and loyalty. He forgave Japanese managements for their hoarding of cash and their unwillingness to often act in the best interests of shareholders. If Japanese companies were cheap for a reason, he ignored the reason, falling into a classic value trap situation.

The good news is that the 2007 buoyancy in U.S. markets did abate, and some of Michael's financial sector shorts such as MBIA, Ambac, Wells Fargo, Washington Mutual, and Lehman Brothers really started to fall from grace. Home-builder shorts also started to perform admirably. Glenn Water was one firm that had seen the housing bubble for what it was, and was beneficially positioned for its demise.

Sadly, there would be no home-run positioning long Credit Default Swaps on sub-prime mortgage tranches though. As Thorn would soon hear across many highly-pitched arguments between Michael and Mark, Michael had come back from an investment conference in early 2007 all gung-ho to add some sort of long sub-prime mortgage CDS bet to his portfolio—but he had wanted it to be on specific credits, not an index.

"We are a stock-picking firm, and even if buying CDS is a bit beyond our usual sweet spot, I think it is important that we focus in on the most compelling names and situations—really do our homework," Michael had espoused.

Mark had done the actual work looking at the CDS market on sub-prime, and did not see a particular edge to get involved in narrowly defined CDS bets, and also questioned whether some of the single-name CDS markets offered sufficient liquidity in case Glenn Water wanted to get out. He had continually recommended just buying CDS against a sub-prime index. Michael meanwhile had resisted following this latter path.

In the end, they had done nothing, and missed the trade of a lifetime. Others such as Paulson Capital, Scion Capital, and Hayman Capital captured those asymmetrically positive trades and outcomes. But at Glenn Water the topic of sub-prime CDS would become just fodder for a repeated and ongoing fight between Michael and Mark.

There was also a real difference of risk management philosophy between the two team leaders. Mark, despite being a bully by nature, was actually more the weeny in terms of risk. If a stock started to misbehave on him, his natural inclination was to simply cut that name from the portfolio and move on. Michael's natural inclination would instead be to re-query the analyst who had done work on a given name, and if the thesis was intact, then add to a given exposure—using the temporarily adverse price action as an opportunity.

Thorn was literally stuck in the middle of these two different styles.

On one day when the market was ripping higher, Mark turned to Thorn and said: "We need to cut back these four short names quickly. Hop to it." Michael had conveniently been in the bathroom at the moment of that order. Budis had perhaps specifically chosen his timing of the directive to Thorn in order to avoid a long debate with Michael on the topic. But when Michael returned to the trading desk, his first reaction when examining the screens was quite the reverse.

"So Thorn, this market is very strong today. We should use this as an opportunity to build up some of our shorts in size. What names would you suggest?"

"Well...err...any except for these four," Thorn had responded, ticking off the four stocks that he was in the process of actually covering.

"And why not those four?"

"Because Mark just asked me to buy them back."

That is about when the fireworks in the trading room would begin. Shouting and screaming, stomping vein-popping curses at each other, personal epithets about relative work habits and portfolio contributions.

Thorn would initially giggle to himself at having set them off; then literally lean into his trading turret as a way to duck from the increasing level of vitriol filling the room; and eventually just leave the room altogether out of embarrassment to be a witness to the mutual enmity between these two gentlemen.

At the outset of Thorn's days at Glenn Water, Michael had said to him: "I think it is natural that there are disagreements between partners at hedge funds. It is part of the process to reach the right decision."

But there was nothing natural or positive about the fights between Michael and Mark. Their styles and philosophies were just so different that the resulting angst between them was destructive and counter-productive.

"Are Mommy and Daddy fighting again?" one oft-abused team analyst would ask quietly from a side conference room.

It soon became apparent to Thorn that how the portfolio was being managed was more a function of who was on vacation at any given time. When Michael was there alone, shorts would generally be increased. When Michael went on vacation, Mark would often cut several shorts back and add a few more longs. When the two were together, they would just fight about most decisions until Thorn would sometimes offer a middle-ground proposed path.

Amazingly enough, despite all of the hostility, 2008 actually ended up being an acceptable year at Glenn Water. While the Japanese long portfolio went down in value, the U.S.-centric short portfolio went down even faster. Financial shorts led the way until eventually Michael found himself nibbling at the long side of financials late in the year. Thorn made one huge contribution when he egged Michael into buying JP Morgan below $20 a share and ditching a long exposure to Bank of America and Merrill Lynch both still trading in the $30's—but destined in the final throws of the 2008 chaos to visit single digits. Overall, the dysfunctional team staggered to a 10% gross return. It was true that many others had not survived 2008 with such aplomb, so for a moment at that year's Holiday Party, everyone was relatively civil to each other.

As 2008 rolled into early 2009, Thorn did a little mental calculation in his head. If Glenn Water had made 10% gross on $500mm of assets, that was $50 mm gross gain to which would be applied the standard 20% hedge fund incentive fee—or a $10mm cut to Glenn Water. Michael and Mark as partners would keep the majority of that windfall, but Michael had specifically told Thorn when he joined the firm that firm policy was to take 20% of the incentive fee earned and reserved it for employee bonuses. So that meant a $2 million bonus pool should exist to be divided up by just ten employees beyond Michael and Mark. Since Thorn was easily the third most senior employee in a close footrace with the firm's CFO, Thorn mentally started to expect maybe a $300-$350,000 bonus; or maybe more.

But that lasted exactly a scant few weeks until a formal bonus discussion followed.

"So Thorn, last year I gave you $50,000 bonus, and this year I'm raising that to $150,000," Michael started, somehow expecting Thorn to be pleased.

"But in 2007, I was at Glenn Water for a total of three months and made $50,000 bonus for just that stub period. In 2008, I worked for the entire year and we made much more money than in 2007. Am I not right that there is a bonus pool around $2 million?"

"Yes, that is about right."

"And of ten people in the firm, I'm the most senior except for you and Mark—maybe at the same effective level as the CFO."

"Yes, that is right."

"And so you are giving me less than a pro-rata share of the bonus pool if it was simply divided up in equal shares between the ten of us? How does that work?"

"Well, I'm an employee here too; Mark is an employee." Said Michael.

An angry light bulb went off in Thorn's head. What a disingenuous cheap fuck. Michael had made this big deal when Thorn joined the firm about the existence of this well-defined 20% employee bonus pool, and the chance to be really well paid. And then he had just conveniently failed to mention that he included himself in this pool with the obvious potential that he could self-allocate to himself the lion share of the available revenue.

Smoke and mirrors yet again on Wall Street—a team leader playing games with his employees—seeing how much he could get away with.

"I think I should leave," Thorn found himself saying. "If that is how you run your firm, I want out."

CHAPTER 67

NAILING THE BOTTOM AND TRADING A FAUX WORLD
New York
March 2009

Thorn did not end up quitting, but he had been ready to do so. Instead, Michael came back to him the following morning with a mild act of contrition.

"OK, the bonus pool is the bonus pool. It has been allocated and I can't change that. Maybe I screwed that up. But I can offer you a significant $75 thousand dollar bump in your salary to make up for things."

In so far as the salary increase would perpetuate over coming years and if added to his actual bonus was just a tad light of his original bonus expectations, Thorn turned contrite. OK that would do. But Jesus, why do people have to make things so difficult? Why did Thorn have to fight for what should have just been rightfully given to him over a handshake?

The experience soured Thorn on Michael's overall honorability. Michael was treating his employees like playthings—tools to serve the master—but not much else. There was no real desire to be naturally generous or fair in Michael. Thorn saw that now.

In the meantime, markets in late 2008 had been extraordinary weak and generally remained that way across the first eight weeks of 2009. Now Michael was itching to get longer, and it was Budis who was all the nervous nelly about taking on too much net beta.

It was amazing how differently the minds of these two guys worked.

"So Thorn, you are going to tell me when I should get aggressively long, yes? The values are all there. I just need your help on the timing."

Thorn promised to be particularly attentive in this regard, and initially thought that markets would likely bottom on an early April

2009 mini-pi cycle date that would be 2.15-years (or a quarter of a full 8.6 year pi cycle) from the February 23, 2007 market high.

But on March 6, 2009 with the S&P 500 fast approaching a price of 666, Thorn had an epiphany moment. 3/06/09—the date—when the digits were added together—equaled 18. The S&P price level of 666 when added together also equaled 18. Thorn knew that in ancient Hebrew tradition, 18 represented a number of completion and finality. He thought of master technician W.D. Gann—long dead—but someone who would love the concept of time and price squaring each other so to speak. There was momentum divergence on a variety of moving average oscillators, and the Fibonacci bands all fit well when stretched to exactly 666. Market sentiment was also in the sewer.

Thorn waived the proverbial flag within the Glenn Water trading room loudly and vociferously.

"We should get longer today, right now—at 666 on the S&P. You've been egging me for the exact moment, Michael. Well this is it. Are you ready to step up to the plate?"

Thankfully Budis was out of the office that Friday, March 6th, and Michael was all ears. There would be no long debate—but instead organized and dutiful action. The first step of that day was to harvest shorts in order to get the portfolio net longer. In went orders in seven or eight short names to cover. The second step was to add a few new longs. Another batch of orders began. By the end of that trading session—on the dead market lows—Thorn busily worked to swing Glenn Water's portfolio from its prior beta flat positioning to 34% net long—a huge swing for a sleepy relatively low beta portfolio.

When markets vaulted higher that following Monday, and then continued to lift higher for the balance of March, this call felt to Thorn like his strongest contribution to Glenn Water since he had arrived at the firm eighteen months earlier. Thorn was a shitty natural bull, but he had nailed the bottom.

Budis of course never offered a peep of congratulations, while Michael just chastised Budis for having previously been too much of a namby-pamby chicken-shit to do what Michael had done.

Thornton was just the forgotten trader—a cog in the wheel—unimportant between these two dueling egos.

The only problem that would soon emerge was what the 34% net long was mostly composed of—which was of course a large slug of Japanese equity exposure. This part of the portfolio generally just sat there non-responsively as the rest of the world lifted. Glenn Water—despite Thorn's help at portfolio timing—was still going to be dominated by its remaining U.S. centric short book. Glenn Water was going to net remain kind of boring.

And when March's turn higher in the market soon brought a full 40% S&P 500 rally into April and May, Michael's natural instincts was soon to beef up the short side of the portfolio again.

"The Fed has gone crazy with this QE," Michael would pant. "While I recognize that changing the denominator in which stocks are traded can be viewed as uber-bullish in the short-term, this cannot end well in the longer-term."

With that type of thinking, the portfolio would go on to generally struggle for the next four years.

Another struggle also started within Thorn's stomach. He had long suffered from occasional bouts of diverticulitis, and the constant angst of Glenn Water's trading room soon exacerbated that condition.

He was having problems getting any shit out of his system—all constipated up—a stomach growling at him in protest most days.

Too much coffee; too much tension; too much commuting; and too many nights rushing home to trade Asian markets into the evening. There was hardly ever a down moment. This was no life for a guy now turning 52.

Thorn had been in front of screens for over thirty years, but now his body offered up a sudden revolt.

CHAPTER 68

HOSPITAL DAYS
New York
July 2010

It had started simply enough—a tight and irritated bowel—spastic and constricted. Then the slight twinge of pain on the lower left side of his stomach.

Thorn had dealt with these symptoms before and had a stash of antibiotics left over from past episodes—one 500 mg Cipro tablet twice a day, added to a 250 mg tablet of Flaglyl three times a day. The two drugs in combo almost invariably got things moving.

But in the summer of 2010, the antibiotics stopped working. Thorn's stomach issues weren't resolving.

A game plan was initially devised with Thorn's gastroenterologist to take intravenous antibiotics for a week to make the infection chill out, and then once stabilized, Thorn would have to get a resection surgery to remove the offending portion of the colon.

But even the intravenous path did not work. Thorn instead developed an abscess.

He sat one day trading in misery at Glenn Water, quietly hiding the tension in his stomach until after the 4 pm market close, and then immediately marched himself to the New York Presbyterian Emergency Room. An MRI followed, and then formal hospital admission. Thorn needed emergency surgery to make sure his colonic canal didn't burst and then dump toxic fecal waste into his body. Unresolved diverticulitis could be deadly.

The surgery itself took place promptly that evening, and at first, all seemed to be on the mend. By the following morning Thorn was seated in his hospital bed with his laptop open. He was once again being attentive to a data stream of market prices. No, he couldn't still fulfill his trading functions from the hospital, but he could still look at the chart action of the Glenn Water portfolio. After having been with Glenn Water for two years, he had recently been given direct responsibility for a small $10 million sub-allocation of the portfolio, and even while sick, he wanted to pay attention to this—not just leave things on auto-pilot. If he saw a chart set-up of major enough significance, he could always call in an order.

Thorn admittedly felt lousy—occasionally self-pumping a dose of morphine into his system via a magic button by his bedside—but he could still be dutiful.

But then things started to go wrong. At first, it's just the noise and clamor around him that precluded getting any rest.

"Veniaca, Veniaca, Yanina..." A Latin woman across the hall from his room was yelling at the top of her lungs. She had been doing so on and off ever since Thorn was wheeled into his recovery room.

"Yolinda!..."...long pause..."Yolinda!..." her voice reverberated down the hall as if in some sort of periodic tape loop. The woman apparently was suffering from Alzheimer's disease and calling for her two daughters. The daughters periodically showed up by her bedside, but not for long enough to allow Thorn much rest. The commotion only intensified when the Latin woman wrangled with the Irish nurse Pauline.

"Ah shuren, you can quiet down now Mammi," Pauline would lilt in a strong Irish brogue.

Thorn took a peak out his door across the hall.

The woman was responding by waving her arms up and down and shouting loudly "Whooa...whooa"—moving her arms as if at Giants Stadium doing some version of the wave. It was all a tad surreal.

Then, in the room next to Thorn, there was a rasped sound of a man unable to breathe...a nebulizer was running non-stop. More noise.

Thorn asked a nurse what this fellow's ailment is, and she initially declined to tell him.

When Thorn pressed that if he had to listen to that nebulizer all night, he should at least know what the fellow was dealing with, the nurse looked at him and whispered: "It's a very contagious chest disease. People like to hang out down there near the hallway window, in front of his door—but it makes me nervous. I'd stay away if I were you."

Only now was Thorn hearing this? Thorn had made that window his destination on several attempted 50-yard shuffles out of bed on that first day of recovery, dragging his catheter bag and IV drip rolling unit of liquid nourishment along with him each time that he went.

Thorn had a sudden bout of claustrophobia. The windows of the hospital did not open, and Thorn asked the nurse why.

"A man jumped out of an eighth floor window a few years ago," she said quietly, "Ever since then, we swelter in here all sealed off."

Her words reinforced his sense of tightness. Thorn hated the lack of fresh air, the noise, and all the sick people around him. The catheter still up his wee hurt and felt irritated. He wanted to rip it out. His testicles were swollen purple and almost the size of oranges.

Instead, he decided to test his walking ability a bit more—as per his doctor's instructions—but head towards the somewhat more distant "lounge" area instead of the nearby hallway window.

Along the way, Thorn made a friend with another gentleman patient wandering the hospital halls in Bermuda shorts.

"I dressed in civvie clothes today," this man winked at Thorn. "Been stuck in here too long...Tried to sneak down to the cafeteria; go outside...But they caught me—the white wristband gave me away, and the guards downstairs sent me back upstairs." The man smiled with a weary look.

"Great, just great" thought Thorn. Captive.

The lounge was really just a small waiting area with two sets of small banquets and a very sad looking palm plant. But the air conditioning seemed to work better here. The mild smell of excrement, vomit, and human sweat was less oppressive.

Thorn sat on one banquet and looked across at a granddaughter about 20-years old trying to play cards with her grandmother in a wheelchair on a small, attached tray.

"C'mon Mudge, do you want to play Mudgie?" this girl asked lovingly but with a very loud voice. Thorn supposed that Mudgie was a bit hard of hearing.

"Count the cards, Mudgie. One, two...what comes next Mudgie?"

Mudgie had however gone to sleep, and couldn't count the cards, let alone play them.

That is when Thorn suddenly felt a slightly odd feeling on the top of his left shoulder...kind of a trickle of pebbles going down across his shoulder towards his chest. It was not something Thorn had ever experienced before. Thorn sluffed it off initially as just an odd sensation—nothing to be concerned about—but within a minute or two, he found his breath shortening and his pulse racing. He tried to stand up, but was weak and winded.

He gasped at the granddaughter: "I think I need help. Can you find a nurse?"

Within minutes Thorn was back in his bed, fully re-attached to a bank of monitors, with an assistant doctor looking down at him.

"Your heart is racing; you're having a hard time breathing. Did anything odd happen to you?"

Thorn mentioned the feeling of pebbles, and the doctor instantly made his diagnosis.

"I think you've had a pulmonary embolism."

"What the hell is that?" asked Thorn.

"It's when a blood clot hits the lungs, and reduces your ability to breathe properly."

"That doesn't sound good," said Thorn, still not quite believing the doctor.

"It's not. I don't want to scare you, but it can be life threatening. We need to do a CAT scan of your entire body STAT to see for sure. If you have other blood clots floating around, this could get worse."

Thorn did feel wheezy, short of breath, but was this doctor over-reacting? Thorn wasn't sure.

"Go for it, doc. Do whatever you think makes sense."

Within minutes Thorn was being wheeled out of his room headed for the CAT scan machine. No bureaucratic waiting. No signing of forms. Instead, the technicians rushed to insert a needle into his arm. Dye was needed for the CAT scan machine to do its thing—identify any offending blood clots.

People were flying all around him—moving fast, with urgency.

"The dye is going in now; you should feel a warm feeling."

But alas the dye injection missed its mark. Thorn could feel his arm swelling oddly. It was the first of several mishaps.

"Ah shit," said the technician immediately. "I thought that needle was well placed. It missed your vein. I need you to hold your left arm up above your head. Your arm is about to balloon, but if you hold it above your head, it will drain back to normal size with time."

Thorn looked across at his arm, which was indeed already twice its normal size, skin stretched tightly over a bloated core.

Another different junior doctor approached him: "Thornton, I'm afraid that with that much dye now floating through your body, we can't inject you again. We can't do the CAT scan that we wanted. But all of your symptoms are of someone who just had a pulmonary embolism, and we would like to treat you for that."

"OK," said Thorn, "what's the treatment?"

"We need to put you on a blood thinner. It's called Heparin. If you had one blood clot already hit your lungs that's bad enough, but we need to make sure that you don't have other blood clots. Heparin will help thin your blood."

"Any risks?"

"Well, you just had surgery, and we generally don't like to use Heparin when those wounds are still healing internally. There is some risk it could cause complications, but if another blood clot hits your lungs, you could die. I think it is the right path."

And so it was that Thorn was wheeled into the Intensive Care Unit of New York Presbyterian Hospital that evening and set up with a new IV drip of Heparin. His breathing was fair; his pulse and heart beat just slightly elevated now.

Was this all a massive over-reaction?

Thorn looked up at his bloated left arm now propped up on three pillows above him, and internally shrugged. What would be would be, but this was all an unfortunate turn of events.

Thorn slept a bit—thankful at least that the screams of "Yolinda" were now no longer nearby, and there was no rasped nebulizer feeding an infected lung down the hall. His room was quiet, but there were no windows here at all. It felt like he was in the bowels of the hospital, hooked up to a variety of machines; cords and wires everywhere.

In the morning there was a mild moment of improvement for Thorn when yet another junior doctor came by and removed the catheter that had still been attached to Thorn's wee. It felt like a mild wave of freedom to be done with that device.

A plastic bottle was handed to Thorn with small lines on the side.

"You have to at least fill this bottle up to the second line over the next 9 hours," instructed the doctor. "Otherwise, we'll have to put that catheter back in."

Thorn now had a new mission. This bottle had to be filled. There was no way he wanted that catheter back. Thorn mentally cursed whoever had invented the catheter.

So now post his third night and full second day in the hospital, Thorn made a point at least once an hour to try to stand by his bedside and pee into this bottle. The only problem was that nothing came out on the first three attempts, and every time Thorn got up all of the alarm bells of his monitoring equipment would go off—pulse and heart rate too high; oxygen levels in the blood too low. And when the nurse came by for the periodic blood pressure cuff, Thorn's blood pressure was oddly low and dropping.

Doctors would poke their head in the room at the sounds of the alarm bells, but it was never the same doctor twice.

One would say: "You need to eat something. Has anyone ordered you any food?"

Another 45-minutes later, another doctor would say that the drugs that they had given Thorn were likely the culprit of his feeling sleepy and weak, but that he was to continue "not to eat anything"— as those were the instructions on the chart.

It was all most confusing—a disorganized set of analysis and instructions.

Meanwhile Thorn felt like he was fading. Something was wrong. Post-surgery, you are supposed to feel a little stronger each moment that time goes by. Thorn instead was feeling weaker by the hour. Every time he tried to stand for the effort to pee into the bottle, he felt a bit dizzier. Just a trickle of liquid had come out—nowhere near the line he needed to achieve—and he would then glance at the clock with the hours ticking by.

Thorn looked at the calendar on the wall as well. August 12, 2010—his grandmother's birthday. Would this be the day that God elected to take him away? He started to feel like it might.

At last, Thorn had some success with the pee bottle, but the effort to stand was too much. He fell back on the bed and the bottle spilled across the floor.

"You have to believe me—I just got to the line," he said as a cadre of med students and his primary surgeon came into the room. The surgeon looked with concern at Thorn's vitals and chart. He felt Thorn's stomach; listened to it intently with his stethoscope. He went back outside the room to confer with a nurse, and then asked the med students to leave. Then he came over to address Thorn.

"You sir are crashing. I've never seen someone go so far downhill in one day."

"What's that mean?"

"That means that I think you are bleeding internally. I can hear it when I listen to your stomach. You are losing blood into your gut. I've got to go back in there and fix that."

"You mean operate again?"

"I'm afraid so. I need to stabilize that blood loss, and then clean you out."

"When?"

"Like now. Or, at the latest, early tomorrow morning. What I would like to do is first get some blood platelets and plasma into you. Pump you up. We need to put a line into your curetted artery in your neck—get that blood into you. You'll feel a bit like a bloated balloon, but once your blood pressure has stabilized a bit, I can operate more safely. Another doctor will assist me is an expert in small filters that can be placed on the main vein coming up from your legs. The second CAT scan that we did today showed that you have some other thrombosis down there—small blood clots—they may have been there for awhile or they could be new. We need to make sure that they don't move up to your lungs like the other one did."

"And what about my high heart rate?"

"Not perfect, but we have to make choices—follow a path that is the lesser of two evils. I think you'll be alright but we have to move fast."

For the first time in this whole affair, Thorn felt scared. He became more so as the nurses and doctors around him started to fly around his room disconnecting and reconnecting monitor wires to new mobile units. Thorn had never seen a team of medical professionals moving as quickly. What exactly had the doctor said to them? How critical was he?

Suddenly, Thorn was getting moved again—wheeled through the bowels of the hospital—presumably headed to surgery. He didn't know. They didn't tell him. Then there were new doctors suddenly standing by his side, placing a towel over his head, asking him to stay extremely still while they tried to get a line into the key artery in his neck. They kept missing in their first few attempts.

This was turning into a real shit show.

By about 4 a.m. in the morning, the blood was pouring into Thorn through the line now placed into his neck, and he was indeed lying like a bloated balloon in what he presumed was the operating room. By 6 a.m. the doctor was with him again.

This was it. Thorn was gasping for breath—feeling asthmatic—heart racing. Sweating. He looked at the doctor beseechingly above him.

"Is this all going to work? Am I going to wake up?" And then he went black, the anesthesiologist already doing his work.

Thorn opened his eyes, no sense of the time elapsed. He was alive. There was sun coming in through a window. He was back in the room where the line had been placed into his neck. He supposed it had not been the operating room after all. Now he suddenly noticed that the room was on a low floor by the East River—with water flowing by his window just a few feet below the window-line. It was as if he was on a boat.

The sun was shining outside. A hot August New York City day in progress. He had lived.

But shit. Why couldn't he move his hands? They were tied down. What was down his throat, and up his nose? Tubes seemed to be everywhere going in and out of him. He couldn't speak, a tube filling his mouth. He kicked and writhed in his bed—trying to attract the feint attention of voices outside of his bedroom door. Claustrophobic waves shot over him. He was alive, but a seeming vegetable—connected to just too many machines. Pumps pumped and air hissed and liquid flowed out of his nose down a tube with a gurgle.

How trivial the markets all now seemed—his entire life's work. In three days he'd gone from caring about whether his execution skills in some stock ticker were strong enough to beat the VWAP (value-weighted average price) of the day—who really gave a shit in the big picture of things—to just wanting to live. Was this tube down his throat normal? Had something gone terribly wrong?"

At last a nurse heard his struggles, and came in with a cold-mannered all-business greeting.

"Ah, you're awake. OK let's get that intubation tube out of you, shall we?"

Thorn nodded his head rapidly, and after another ten days slowly recovering in the hospital, survived the entire ordeal.

CHAPTER 69

BACK IN TIME FOR THE TSUNAMI
New Jersey/New York
2011

The intubation tube had been left there as a precaution. The doctors weren't sure Thorn was breathing well enough on his own. That mouth tube had come out after Thorn woke up, but the nose tube stayed in for several more days, slowly draining gross green-colored bile from his stomach.

Overall, the recovery period lasted multiple weeks.

When he finally returned to Glenn Water, the summer months of 2010 were quickly waning into the winter months of early 2011. Portfolio monitoring systems that Thorn had originally designed had been replaced; upgraded by others. He felt as if he had fallen a step behind, a tad less needed than he had been previously.

But still welcomed back—at least superficially.

Thorn's problems were not primary to Glenn Water. This was because Mark and Michael were still fighting away as ever.

"This Japanese exposure just isn't working," Mark would say, jabbing at Michael's Achilles' heel of portfolio management. "These companies are all just shit boxes. They're cheap, but nobody cares about them. The Japanese managements are all undynamic. Cash on the balance sheet is only worth something if these companies actually unlock it, put it to work. But the Japanese never will. It's just not in their mindset. And the market recognizes that—is discounting for that."

"But Mark, where else in the world can you find companies trading at three times earnings? I don't care if others don't care. I'll earn my cost—get my money back—in earnings alone if I just stay invested for a few years."

"That assumes Michael that our own investors are patient enough to wait it out—to play the value game."

On the morning of March 11, 2011 those Glenn Water investors were sorely tested as the Great Tohoku Earthquake hit Japan's eastern shore and created a massive tsunami. Forty-foot waves drove ten kilometers inland, and thousands were dead.

Thorn had been sitting on his New Jersey toilet at 5:10 am when he first saw the news come across his cell phone. Taking a dump on first awakening and checking the early news was his routine, but holy shit, was he already late in his responsibilities?

Thorn had long been told that if a natural disaster ever struck Japan, his first standing order of action was to take off the portfolio's short yen currency hedge. Why? Because after a natural disaster, Japanese insurance companies should naturally need to repatriate money home, sell dollars to have yen to pay claims. While perhaps initially counter-intuitive, an unforeseen calamity to Japan would likely be bullish for its currency.

Thorn hopped off the toilet, and dialed Mark. Mark was awake, and had seen the news as well.

"Do you want me to go into motion and take off our short yen hedge?" Thorn asked breathlessly, ready to be berated that he should have done so already.

"Yeah, I guess we should do something like that," said Mark with relative calmness. Thorn was relieved that Mark did not expect Thorn to have already taken such action.

"Why don't you buy back half our yen hedge, and then we'll see how it feels before we do the other half."

As Thorn went into motion, quickly dialing his main interbank counterparties, he pondered Mark's overall calmness. Thorn thought Mark was amazingly put-together for a portfolio manager that was about to see half of Glenn Water's long book melt significantly lower.

But then Thorn realized that in a way Mark might perversely be experiencing a glimmer of happiness about the natural disaster. It would be Mark's way of telling Michael "You see, I warned you about this heavy Japanese long exposure. This was just an added risk sitting there all the time ready to bite us."

Mark might be unhappy to lose money, but at least he'd be able to rub Michael's nose in the dirt a bit. The competition and mutual dislike of these two partners for each other was palpable and showing yet again.

The Nikkei had immediately dropped 5% on the earthquake's arrival, and then markets had abruptly stopped trading. There was no getting out of Glenn Water's actual equity exposure in Japan, albeit U.S. Nikkei futures and ETFs would continue to trade later that morning when New York markets opened. There might be an opportunity to do some fast hedging—if Glenn Water could just be decisive.

But decisiveness was not a piece of lexicon in Michael's psyche.

While Thorn rushed to work to be ready for wild trading and potential hedging, Michael sauntered in only towards the normal 9:30 am, and his initial reaction was to do nothing. The team just watched the television screen of the tsunami wave that was played by CNBC again and again. Maps were examined as to how important the Fukishima region of Japan really was to industry; excuses were made by Michael that this might really just be a buying opportunity to add to their longs—pick up stocks during a fire sale.

Thorn sat there aghast. It was so obvious to him: their Japanese equity exposure was a clear liability that would at best now turn into dead money. They should be reacting. They should be hitting bids on the Nikkei or TOPIX futures that traded in New York. Take the -2% portfolio hit, neutralize the exposure, and move on.

But instead, Michael and Mark just started another fight. Visceral epithets crossed the trading desk most of the day. It took until 2:30 pm in the afternoon for Michael finally to give Thorn any instructions to sell Nikkei futures. The mild media buzz by that time about a potential nuclear accident in the making was the only reason that he finally capitulated to do so. Given where Nikkei futures had already fallen, another 75 basis points was lost for the portfolio across the intervening few hours.

Michael's inaction and Mark's mild happiness at Michael's pain led Thorn to just one conclusion that day: Glenn Water as a firm was not going to make it. These were two buffoons jabbing at each other as their portfolio was melting. That was not what crisp clean and dutiful portfolio management was all about.

Thorn needed to extricate himself, or risk getting extricated on an involuntary basis—should the firm face its own wave of redemptions.

CHAPTER 70

MARTY AND THORN RE-UNITE
Princeton, NJ
June 2011

It was with a mild thought of finding a better job that Thorn had reached out for lunch with his old friend and colleague Marty Amwell. After ten years in prison, Marty was finally out, and trying to launch something of a comeback under a new firm umbrella: Amwell Economics.

But Thorn had read a few of the recent web-posts made by Marty and was unimpressed. Well thought out in-depth articles soaked with history were no longer. Instead Marty seemed engrossed in constant Tweets and reactive blurbs of short and often conflicting commentary.

Instead of clear precise cycle date projections, Marty would bounce: markets could possibly trade down into xyz cycle date, but they would more likely go up into that date; what the politicians and central bankers were doing to our money supply was horrible, but the Dow Jones was still likely to trade higher in the short-term. It was all gobbledy-gook.

Why was Marty doing this? What had happened to the brilliant guy that Thorn had once known?

From the postings alone, it seemed as though Marty's ego had somehow eaten Marty's intellect.

"Jesus Chris, Marty was cheapening himself yet again," Thorn thought to himself. "This guy needs to be better managed."

But did Thorn have the energy to even try to do so?

Maybe the Economics Consultants of Princeton portion of his life was best left buried, but there was also a mild desire for closure within Thorn. What had really happened back in those waning days of the Economic Consultants of Princeton? Was Marty really a thief? The story had never been fully revealed to him.

There was also a natural curiosity in Thorn of how ten years in prison could have potentially changed Marty.

Thorn waited on a park bench within the grassy section of Princeton's Palmer Square. They had agreed to meet at the Nassau Inn, but a wedding was ongoing inside. It would be best to dine a few doors away at another old Princeton restaurant *The Alchemist and Barrister*.

Marty appeared wearing a tweed sports jacket and open-necked collared shirt. He was notably heavier than the last time Thorn had seen him—his potbelly of 1999 having grown in size despite ten years of prison food. The scraggly Lenin-like beard was still there with the bald head now just a tad balder. He could have passed for a slightly disheveled Princeton professor as much as he might also have resembled a guy making sandwiches behind the counter at a local South Jersey deli.

"Marty, Marty...so good to have you back," Thorn offered out his hand in genuine affection.

Marty demurred, mumbling that "Well, anything is better than where I've been."

For a decade Thorn's life had gone on—he'd built his little fund of funds business for eight years and then found his way to work for Michael Statz—all a bit of a scramble, but a reasonable existence. In comparison, across those years there had hardly been a week when Thorn had not thought of Marty sitting in some jail cell—his life completely on hold. At times, Marty had reputedly been put in solitary confinement—into the "hole." Just to be nice, Thorn had tried to send Marty a few books in prison from Amazon—one by Francois Mandelbrot entitled the *Mis(Behavior) of Markets* that was as close to mainstream academic acceptance of hidden fractal rhythms in markets as Thorn had read anywhere. But alas, an email notice flowed back from Amazon that the prison address had returned the books—mail and packages to the prisoner not being allowed. Was that legal in America to block the U.S. mail?

Now the man he saw in front of him was the same one he'd known 11-years earlier, but jowlier and certainly less mentally crisp.

Thorn had followed Marty's legal efforts from afar, but was certainly not privy to all the twists and turns. He knew that Marty's original attorneys had been dismissed by the court and forced to disgorge their original retainer fee. He knew that Marty had been called upon to surrender all of his assets to the court, and that the judge had found certain assets still to be missing. He knew that Marty had been left on Contempt of Court charges to pine away in the Tombs while the case against him—if one existed—went puff in the World Trade Center explosion. He knew that Marty had argued that the U.S courts lacked proper jurisdiction for this case since all the swap and note transactions that Marty had ever done were with Japanese corporations, executed in Japan, and sanctioned there by the Japanese Ministry of Finance. Marty had always been quick to point out that he had never defaulted on one maturing Princeton Note. And so what if he had put some of the money raised from those transactions into illiquid antiquities? He was allowed to do whatever he wanted with that money.

It was the Safri Bank that had taken the bulk of his funds, according to Marty. And even if he had eventually defaulted on some of the Princeton Notes as they matured, is it illegal to issue unsecured bonds and then default on them? Corporations do that all the time.

Where should Thorn begin this discussion?

Marty's bravado started it for him.

"Well, I think I'll finally get my passport back next week."

"They wouldn't allow you to have a passport until now?" Thorn asked. Marty had already been a free man for six months, but obviously not entirely free.

"No, they kept me in prison for ten years—the first five of those in the Tombs—and once I got out they told me I wasn't allowed to leave the country in case there were further civil charges that I had to answer to. There are no further charges. This is all finally over."

"What the hell caused all this Marty? What happened back there in 1999?" Thorn cut to the jugular.

"I think I just really pissed them off when I wouldn't share my models with the CIA. The government came after me. They set the whole thing up."

"C'mon Marty, you told me once that some of the losses were yours—that you'd had a hard time hedging the yen."

"I never said that," Marty backed up, seemingly affronted.

"But you told me that one day over the phone. I remember it distinctly. You said that your broker Bill had stolen some money from you, but some of the losses were yours as well."

"I don't know what you are talking about," Marty bristled. "I didn't lose any money trading the yen in 1999."

"So where'd the money go?"

"I don't know. I wish I did. That Safri Bank was all crooked. Edmund Safri had his hand in everyone's pocket—and the accounts were impossible to decipher. He took over $3 billion from the IMF and almost got away with it, for God's sake. OK, so his shenanigans ultimately caught up with him in Monaco. I think it is very probable that the Safri Bank took my money."

Thorn pondered whether it was appropriate to push. Marty was in clear denial of even his own words to Thorn eleven years earlier. The truth was continuing to bend. It was almost as if Marty had told his newest version of the story so often that he had come to believe his latest fictionalized embellishments, and forgotten the earlier versions of the same tale.

This lunch was going to be a bust in terms of obtaining clarity or closure. Marty was continuing to spin.

Thorn felt disgusted and disappointed. The fact that Marty's recent blog postings were so spurious and scattered irritated Thorn even further.

Jail had clearly made an impact.

Marty had been brilliant in 1999—albeit wrapped in a bit of unfortunate ego even back then. Now the ego had taken over, and the brilliance was less evident. Delusion had trumped substance, and there was no ability to undo the damage already done. Marty, as Thorn had originally known him, had been destroyed. What remained was a mess of a man who didn't realize how prison had changed him.

When the lunch was over, Thorn somewhat despondently walked Marty to his car. It had been an awkward and unfulfilling lunch for them both.

That's when Thorn saw something oh-so familiar: a certain Sumerian cornerstone—the dildo—flopped haphazardly on the back seat of Marty's car.

Marty had somehow saved it from the receiver's clutches.

Thorn wondered how many other antiquities Marty still might have stashed away somewhere.

CHAPTER 71

UNEMPLOYMENT AND A WORLD GONE AWRY
New York
October 2012

Glenn Water never quite recovered from the Japanese tsunami of March 2011. In the days immediately after the tsunami, Thorn had been instructed by Michael to buy more Japanese stocks—particularly in the housing sector where Michael believed the tsunami would only add to demand. But even as Thorn dutifully went on the bid to follow his master's instructions, stocks melted further. Over the subsequent months, Glenn Water's Japanese equity exposure traded lower.

Meanwhile however, other Western capital markets—particularly those in the United States—all lifted strongly, and within those other markets, Michael Statz remained mostly short. 1250 on the S&P 500 seemed high to Michael compared to the 666 low of 2009. After all, global governments hadn't really fixed any of the 2007-2008 debt problems, but instead just shifted those debt burdens from the commercial banks onto sovereign balance sheets. 1350 on the S&P seemed ridiculous, and 1450 even more so. Michael's was a portfolio that might have been conceptually correct from a pure value point of view, but it was clearly out of synch with the macro realities of the times. Money was starting to be attracted back to the United States, not away from it.

Overall, 2012 turned into a huge struggle for the firm. Most other long-short equity funds had a great year. Glenn Water limped to a soggy -8% net loss. One day, midway through the fourth quarter, Michael turned to Thorn with further bad news.

"Thorn, I can't afford you anymore. I'm temporarily going to outsource my trading again. I may just shut down as a hedge fund at year-end. I don't know exactly what will happen, but I'm afraid that I have to let you go."

It had been a shock. Thorn had been concerned that his days at Glenn Water might be numbered, but he'd expected maybe an eight-week transition period where he would be told to train up a young middle-office fellow to take over his responsibilities at a cheaper net cost to the firm. To suddenly be packing his desk and walking out the door for the last time after five years of dutiful service seemed like a surrealistic end.

And as Thorn soon started to peruse the job boards of the Internet, he found plenty of job postings related to compliance, risk management, and sales, but next to none for traders or portfolio managers. He found even fewer job offerings for funds-of-funds managers—his prior business that he had let fade away after joining Glen Water.

The funds-of-funds world—buffeted by a marked decline in hedge fund returns—had imploded in size by early 2013. Fees on top of fees just don't work so well when underlying hedge fund investment returns were hovering in the low- to mid-single digits.

What was the underlying story here? Just a few years earlier, America had had a vibrant hedge fund industry. Thorn used to refer to hedge funds as one of America's very best exports. Americans would buy stuff abroad; dollars would pile up in Tokyo, Shanghai or Beijing, and the money would then flow back to hedge fund managers in New York, California, or Connecticut.

Overall real wealth might still be accumulating faster in Asia rather than in the U.S., but hell, at least someone here could earn 2/20 percent on managing this wealth. And U.S.-based hedge fund managers were always among the most nimble and best-performing of the global hedge fund pack.

But quantitative easing—versions one, two, three, and then four—had changed all this. While hedge fund managers still wanted to be smart and nimble, they had increasingly faced an investing environment where most everything seemed a bit faux from a true economic perspective.

Thornton pored over the financial press and thought that the words of Leigh Skene of Lombard Street Research, a London-based economic research group, described this situation the most adroitly: "Government intervention is causing financial investor chaos by destroying the analytical value of any economic or financial variable it touches. The extremely wide ranging fiscal and monetary policies since the AIG/Lehman default have rendered financial variables such as interest rates, yield curves, credit spreads and various money supplies useless for either assessing asset values or forecasting."

In other words, in trying to artificially prop up the world, the Fed and other global central bankers had left savvy Wall Street investors relatively confused. A culture of general artificiality had evolved where you could either bet that governments would win in the short term (but risk losing your shirt over the longer-term) or bet against governments and be ever so frustrated in the short-term (and then see if your capital under management would survive long enough to potentially still win in the longer-term).

It was next to impossible to wager on both outcomes—or shift between the two views—with enough alacrity to also remain sane. Glenn Water had followed the latter path of betting against the central bankers and that decision had already ended badly. But Thorn could hardly bring himself to embrace the go-go path of betting with the global central bankers except that such firms were the only ones making any money and doing any hiring.

Mr. Bernanke had of course kept rates artificially low for a reason. Bernanke openly admitted to wanting to stimulate stock prices to create a wealth effect; this wealth effect would then hopefully make people feel better, so that maybe, just maybe, a few more people might eventually become employed. But as Yale-based economist Stephen Roach wrote at the time, "There's not one shred of evidence that links monetary policy accommodation to dealing with structural unemployment."

Thorn increasingly felt like a lab rat stuck in the middle of some grand experiment. His only solace was that the Fed's artificially low-rate policy had also hurt endowments and foundations, pension plans, and other retirees dependent upon earning a normal rate of return on their savings. Thorn met a with a few endowment managers and found them to resemble a deer-in-the-headlights—frozen within a horrific investment environment where making an acceptable rate of return while also maintaining some modicum of investment prudence did not necessarily overlap.

Money managers of all sorts had become resigned that the investment environment that they faced was just so lousy that little could be done to actually add value on the trading or research side of the business. Instead, it was better to focus on other things that could be fixed, or least improved upon, that would satisfy the investment box-checkers and help keep firms in business: compliance, risk management, and sales.

What once was a vibrant industry trading naturally moving prices had become a stultified morass of eyes watching artificial prices remain artificial. Everyone was running around trying to figure out what to buy in order to make money: stock, bonds, gold, real estate? But what they actually created instead was a game of trying to anticipate the greater fool who would buy after them.

Thorn contemplated. Within an overly indebted world, propped up only by central bankers, the better daily investment question to ask might be: "What asset (or assets) should one be short?" Thorn came to believe that Japanese government bonds, yen, copper, or deferred contracts of Eurodollar futures might easily be a few such short opportunities. But few people wanted to think this way. Thorn increasingly felt like the odd-man-out.

For every factory job that Mr. Bernanke was striving to create, was he losing another historically better-paying job in the financial sector?

Throw in the Volcker Rule, and Thorn literally felt like an endangered species.

CHAPTER 72

THOUGHT LEADERSHIP FOR A GO-GO EQUITY FIRM—
ALL PRIDE LOST.
Boston
September 2013

New employment did finally follow for Thorn at a modest-sized consulting firm that helped regional wealth managers make better informed decisions on their investment choices. It was an "Intel Inside" type business model, and Thorn got to run the Alternatives Research side of the business, with a few super-smart guys working under him. Now admittedly, Thorn was suddenly making half of his prior Glenn Water salary and working in an odd location in suburban Maryland, but it was a perch to start over again. All was not lost.

Or was it?

Within weeks of arriving at his new consulting home, Thorn paid a visit to its broker-dealer parent in Boston. The conversation with the CIO of the broker-dealer parent that day went as follows:

"So why are you here talking to my guys?"

"Because I was told by my boss in Maryland to pay you all a courtesy visit. Introduce myself."

"Well, that's fair enough, but I want you to understand one thing: I've been through eleven mergers. I don't lose. Don't even think of stepping on any of my turf. I will eat you for dinner."

"Geez, Louise," thought Thorn to himself. "Does this guy have an overly paranoid bully complex or what? Another Mark Budis type in ways—a real meanie."

The CIO was clearly scared of the somewhat more sophisticated and thoughtful high-net-worth team in Maryland, and absolutely adamant that he would not let anyone down there claw away at any portion of his business empire. Thorn subsequently heard that he had instructed all of his employees that they were subject to dismissal if they had any contact whatsoever with Thorn's firm.

Now there was teamwork.

Thorn decided in that moment that his new consulting gig was likely destined for failure with this guy at the ultimate top. He had been in his new role less than a month when this realization transpired.

Thorn had been hired by an honorable group of guys who would ultimately be dismantled by this ogre of a man—all for the sake of ego and turf. The Maryland guys would play nice. But this guy would play dirty.

"Jesus Christ," thought Thorn, "How do I keep stumbling into these dysfunctional situations?" First Marty, then dumb-dumb Matt, then Michael and Mark constantly at each other's throats, and now a full blown ass-hole at the top with a turf complex, with Thorn almost always on the wrong side of the political tracks.

Within six months, Thorn's fears came to pass. His original firm and the parent were being merged.

Thorn's Maryland colleagues were all pushed out one by one by the ass-hole, and within a general corporate re-org, Thorn suddenly found himself almost directly reporting up to the ass-hole himself. He was supposed to write thought leadership pieces for the ass-hole, but nothing Thorn produced—no matter how adroitly crafted—seemed to ever suit his new boss's tastes.

The ass-hole was slowly papering some sort of a formal trail to ditch Thorn one of these days. But for the moment, Thorn was hanging onto his job by a thread, albeit highly distasteful and distrustful of what the ass-hole ultimately had in mind for him.

The clock struck 9:45 a.m. on an early October 2014 morning, and Thorn dutifully started his daily dial-in to the morning "macro-alpha" conference call of the broker-dealer parent that he was now obligated to participate on. There was approximately $20 billion of client assets dedicated to rotational ETF and mutual fund model management awaiting the combined wisdom of their research committee. Thorn was one of about eight committee members, but just one of two from the Maryland side of the firm.

It was a morning obligation that Thorn dreaded.

How after 34-years on Wall Street—continually desirous of portfolios that exhibited strong risk-adjusted returns with as low a net beta as possible—had it come to participating on this call?

"Life is not progressive; it is mocking," thought Thorn.

The Boston-based technician of the group started off. The market was in the throes of its first 5% pullback in over three years.

"So, yesterday we had quite the sell-off. The 200-day moving average on the S&P gave way much faster than I would have expected. But I still think we should buy the dip."

"But what if this is the beginning of a real bear market?" Thorn found himself tentatively responding over the phone line. "What if the house view of a benign 10-15% 2014 market return is just plain wrong? Doesn't the 200-day moving average being blown away as easily as it was yesterday bother you at all?"

"It always pays to buy fear," the blustery CIO suddenly offered, joining the call a tad late. "We have to be brave; we have to be bold; we have to be smart."

"Agreed," someone else piped up.

"Yep, yeah. Buy the dip. It always pays to buy the dip," the senior economist offered.

"Make me barf," Thorn thought to himself.

This team was perpetually bullish. Hell could freeze over, and it would be "buy the dip." The myopia of both the technician on this call—ignoring what any good technician would deem a worrisome chart development—and the rah-rah attitude of the CIO were emblematic of a corporate culture built on some belief of a perpetually benevolent bull market God.

"Am I the nutty one?" thought Thorn. It had been a more or less constant 20-50 basis point daily advance in equities since late 2011—an almost unnaturally steady ascent day after day. If Michael Statz had been surprised when 1450 on the S&P was reached, prices had now marched up to 1550, 1750, and finally 2050. And now this gang of so-called market analysts were ever so confident that benign markets would simply continue to be benign.

But worse perhaps than anything else: in the short-term at least, their myopically bullish thinking actually worked! The stock market quickly regained its footings, and within seven days recouped its prior 5% swan dive. Both the S&P 500 and DJIA marched onwards to make new all-time highs.

Along the way, a day into the turn higher, a youngish-sounding guy on the call offered:

"We need to catch up on our benchmark. I think we should put the pedal to the metal. Take our betas way up. We're only 120 beta net long in our most aggressive best ideas portfolio. We can afford to push that to 130 beta. Maybe even 140. Let's also add to our long XIV exposure."

The XIV is the inverse volatility ETF. The lower that market volatility goes (particularly with an upward sloping volatility curve where volatility pricing generally slips lower down the curve over time), then the higher the XIV mark-to-market NAV will be.

But wait a second. These guys had just bought the XIV at a price of 35. And now just a week later it was at 25, a decline of almost 30% in a scant few days. And now they wanted to buy more of this toxic piece of derivatives engineering? Was there any modicum of risk management to this team?

If there was, it remained hidden. Thorn was the only one on the call inwardly worried about the thousands of truck drivers, school teachers, and normal Americans who had entrusted their money to some local broker in a rural town, with that broker in turn then outsourcing the management of their portfolio to this Boston-based group of idiots that promised active ETF model management. Embedded in the outsourcing and payable by the client was an added 75 basis point portfolio management fee. Yes, let's pay that wrap fee to the local broker, and then pay a second imbedded model management fee to the parent firm itself.

But fees never stopped this team. They thrived on fees. As long as that illiquid non-traded REIT or Business Development Company had a 7% up-front load payable to the salesman who placed these investments, what was not to love? Currently, the SEC even allowed these illiquid investments to be carried on a client's account at a nominal $10 par value without the 7% load being deducted from the client's portfolio statement—even though it had in fact already been paid. How convenient. How slimy.

The Business Development Company (BDC) due diligence manager mumbled to Thorn on a call one day: "I don't know why we bother with some of these things. The client litigation fees that we ultimately get hit with on some of these BDCs easily outstrips the money our firm makes on them, but the retail brokers just have an insatiable demand for the massive front-end loads."

The initial marketing shtick of this firm was, of course, so lily white—a supposedly "unconflicted" firm without any proprietary products of its own—excepting of course, those above-mentioned ETF models. Model management somehow fell short of being a "product" within this firm's lexicon. But overall, the espoused business set-up still sounded acceptable, right? Pure objectivity promised.

But wait a second.

While research analysts certainly engaged in independent work comparing different investment opportunities run by outside managers, ultimately no opportunity made it onto the "approved list" of this broker without a behind-the-scenes fee sharing retrocession being paid by each product sponsor to the broker-dealer firm. How un-conflicted was that really? Meanwhile, these same sponsors regularly funded regional broker-dealer conferences in an "I'll scratch your back, if you scratch my back" manner.

Overall, Thorn was struck by the vision of an evangelical preacher promising retail investors: "Follow me to the promised land of a perpetual bull market," while the preacher himself earned a kick-back on every dime that hit the collection basket.

Meanwhile, back at his desk, Thorn worried about global debt build-up that had merely been transferred from banks to sovereign holders over the prior five years. He worried about investors forced into equity investments simply because fixed income investment yield levels have become so paltry at the hands of our global central bankers. It seemed to Thorn yet again like a bad reason to be levered long stocks. Thorn worried about the high level of corporate stock buy-backs to massage earnings-per-share "beat" announcements just at the same time as there were peak margin-to-equity readings, and ultra-low mutual fund cash holdings. This all seemed to Thorn like the "perfect storm"—a set-up perhaps for the penultimate crash yet to come.

And then there was the next pi cycle date to think about: October 1, 2015...8.6-years from that February 2007 turn in mortgage rates...still a year off, but if markets made an initial stumble in late 2014, might that date perhaps represent an entropic turn of some sort leading to more significant macro problems on the other side? Might sovereign bond yields possibly be the next asset class ready to misbehave after October 1, 2015? And if global central bankers ever lost control of their own rate curves, what hope would the future hold for all the other assets that QE policies had induced?

But on these morning strategy calls in October 2014, beta was a good thing; not bad. The team would all get a better bonus if they beat the benchmarks. So what if they were rolling the dice with other peoples' money? Markets always go up. So why not go with the flow, and lever it all up?

Being the only bear in a den of bulls is always a dangerous position.

A day or two before October month-end, Thorn got the call.

"Today will be your last day with us. We are laying you off."

Oh no, not again, this can't be happening yet again?

Then Thorn experienced a second sensation: moral relief.

Somehow this news seemed fitting. There was no place for a conservative dinosaur in today's financial world—at least not at this broker-dealer. Thorn was going to be out of work yet again. What a shit-show, but in this case, the news was not entirely a surprise. Thorn's glimpse into retail brokerage practices had been eye-opening, and it was simply time to move on.

CHAPTER 73

BACK AT THE TRACK
Queens, New York
November 2014

The gentle cold November rain fell across Aqueduct. The inner dirt track wasn't quite muddy yet—the small ridges of groomed dirt still visible—but it seemed as if mud was in the day's future.

Thorn stood by the track railing and looked across the dull landscape—lost in thought.

The financial world had now thrice spat him out—first from a den of front-runners at Goodman Sachs back in 1992, then again from a den led by a perma-bear in 2012, and now a scant two years later in 2014 from a den of perma-bulls. Did Thorn fit in anywhere? Hadn't he always tried to do the right thing for each of his employers? Hadn't he made some strong trading decisions? How could he have ended up so badly sidelined?

If the financial world wasn't embracing, Thorn knew of no better place to lose himself than to head back to the racetrack.

It had now been over forty years since he'd hit that lucrative Trifecta as a kid. Times had been fun and exciting then. The world had held such promise—even if Thorn had gotten an early taste of corruption around him.

But there were no trifecta wheels in his betting style now; more just the odd $2 or $5 bet to pass the day. Thorn could ill afford to lose much money. Three kids sent to college—one still in. How could any mortal human being afford the $60,000 per annum tuition tab that each had cost him? At least the schools were good ones—Northwestern, Middlebury, and yes, one daughter who had gone to his old haunt: Princeton.

Thorn was proud of all his children, but worried about himself. He was supposed to be in the prime of his career—running something. But instead he had nothing but some memories of the way markets used to be, and stories of games that people had played in those markets along the way. He had an innate sense that markets had a natural fractal rhythm—and tons of anecdotal evidence collected across the years in support of that assertion—but he had failed to master that rhythm into a true science.

And what a cast of characters he had come across.

That guy Raf who had taken him under his wing after playing backgammon had lost a wife or two (or maybe three) along the way, but kept marrying well, and was now rich and retired.

So too was Bruno Geisler, Thorn's first FX boss at the Pierrepont Bank—even though Thorn had heard some whispers that Bruno had eventually been caught trading on behalf of an undisclosed personal account at Pierrepont and then asked to leave. Art collecting was his reputed passion now.

The arbitrageur Jacowski was naturally brilliant and continued to find creative ways to extract "vig" out of markets across the years. With time, he became a statistical quant active in high frequency trading—always looking for, and finding, an edge. Jacowski still had his private island in the Caribbean.

Buchanan went on to write multiple books on his fractal theories— not blockbusters, but texts that sold well for a financial subject. He raged against traditional equilibrium economic theory, and ever so slowly people started to listen to his more dynamic and evolutionary version of how markets actually behaved.

And although Marty barely said anything of substance anymore, based on his prior reputation in the 1980's and 1990's, he still could fill a conference hall with 100 people who believed that Marty was God and were willing to pay a $1,000 fee to hear his latest wisdom. Thorn supposed that made for an adequate living if Marty could pull such conferences off in different global venues two or three times a year. A film crew decided to put together a documentary on his life story. Maybe that would hold added insights when it came out. Maybe the next October 1, 2015 8.6-year pi cycle window would somehow make him famous once again. The regularity of those pi cycle extremes certainly remains of great interest to those with an open mind, and so many indicators of excessive financial asset valuations have already reemerged into global markets yet again.

Only Safri was dead—surely the worst outcome of the bunch—albeit dead only after having achieved billionaire status.

And Thorn was now effectively unemployed without a proper seat at the table.

Was that maiden in the fourth race in there for any particular reason? Thorn stared down at his *Racing Form,* and tried to concentrate on the here and now, rather than the distant past. Thorn didn't know; he really didn't care much any longer. The spark of gambling instinct originally so prevalent in his 13-year old blood had slowly trickled out of him.

All that he did know was that on Wall Street, the line between huge success and just stumbling along was a very narrow one. Did people understand that? It was important to also understand that the good guys didn't necessarily always win. Nassim Taleb of *Fooled by Randomness* fame might have academically understood the true nature of "fat tailed" markets, but it was generally the dumber carry traders that got richer than Taleb in the trading seat. The smarter guys like Taleb only got their share of fame on the rebound. Maybe Thorn would too.

One friend of Thorn advised: "Thorn, you just weren't enough of a dick to succeed wildly on Wall Street. That's not such a bad thing." But at the same time, Thorn had touched and brushed against so many wild and interesting situations. He had witnessed the birth of over-the-counter derivatives trading, and gone on to trade so many different markets—and he had traded most of them generally well.

Would people care about the Wall Street world that he had experienced?

If stretched markets experience another entropic reversal on October 1, 2015, or gold bottomed that day or interest rates troughed, maybe concomitant with the sudden outbreak of war, maybe they would indeed care.

As the rain at Aqueduct started to come down in heavier droplets, Thorn decided that it was time to go home and find out. It was time to put added pen to paper and finally finish those notes that he had started on the 6:08 pm commuter train a few years before.

In your hand, you hold his story.

Life -- like the markets -- was so very fractal. Of that, Thorn was sure.